IN THE MIDST OF THE SEA

"Dark, emotional, and incredibly creepy . . . *In the Midst of the Sea* is a haunting debut from a talented new voice."
—*Foreword Reviews*

"Strong characterizations and startling imagery give powerful dimensions to this riveting novel. A very compelling read."
—**James Hanna**, author of *Call Me Pomeroy*, *The Siege*, and *A Second, Less Capable Head: and Other Rogue Stories*

"A pitch-perfect blend of psychological realism and horror that will appease fans of literary fiction and horror alike. Trust me, this novel will haunt you long after you put it down."
—**duncan b. barlow**, author of *Of Flesh and Fur*, *The City*, *Awake*, and *A Dog Between Us*

"Sean Padraic McCarthy's lyrical gift contributes substantially to this literally haunting tale. Long after the reader has turned the final page, McCarthy's portrayals of both heart and spirit will continue to make their presence felt."
—**Toni Graham**, author of *The Suicide Club*

"A beautifully written and multifaceted novel . . . a detailed exploration of the impact of isolation on the human psyche, reminiscent of Stephen King's novel *The Shining*, but with lively twists and unique notions that make McCarthy's characters and story stand on their own. It really is a book that you won't want to close until the story is over."
—**Michael Hathaway,** publisher, Chiron Review

"Dysfunctional families, creepy dolls, dangerous ghosts, *In the Midst of the Sea* creates compelling characters whose tragic lives will haunt you."
—**Alisha Costanzo**, author and editor, Transmundane Press

IN THE MIDST OF THE SEA

Sean Padraic McCarthy

Pace Press
Fresno, California

Published by Pace Press
An imprint of Linden Publishing
2006 South Mary Street, Fresno, California 93721
(559) 233-6633 / (800) 345-4447
PacePress.com

Pace Press and Colophon are trademarks of
Linden Publishing, Inc.

ISBN 978-1-61035-334-2

135798642

Printed in the United States of America
on acid-free paper.

Library of Congress Cataloging-in-Publication Data

Names: McCarthy, Sean Padraic, author.
Title: In the midst of the sea / Sean Padraic McCarthy.
Description: Fresno, California : Pace Press, 2019.
Identifiers: LCCN 2019009350 | ISBN 9781610353342 (pbk. : alk. paper)
Subjects: | GSAFD: Ghost stories. | Horror fiction.
Classification: LCC PS3613.C34586 I58 2019 | DDC 813/.6--dc23
LC record available at https://lccn.loc.gov/2019009350

I used to think that after we are gone
there's nothing, simply nothing at all.
Then who's that wandering by the porch
again and calling us by name?
Whose face is pressed against the frosted pane?
What hand out there is waving like a branch?
By way of reply, in that cobwebbed corner
a sunstruck tatter dances in the mirror.

—Anna Akhmatova, "March Elegy"

The trouble with our times is that
the future is not what it used to be.

—Paul Valery

This book is for my mother and father, Mary and Richard McCarthy, who introduced me to books, and told me my first stories.

1

Oak Bluffs, Massachusetts

1994

Diana tucked her chin to her chest and cut down the alleyway that opened into Cottage City. She could hear music coming from the kitchen in the restaurant to her left, but it was still early morning, and the restaurant didn't open until noon. And sometimes, this time of year, it didn't open at all. If the owner wanted to take a day off there weren't many people banging at the door, looking to get in. There was an enormous steel pot lying on its side in the alleyway, steaming in the cold November air, and it looked as though it had just been dropped, left there to drain. Soup or broth of some sort. The door to the kitchen was open as Diana passed, just the wooden screen still in place, and Diana could see a squat, dark man cutting onions inside, the flat of his hand pressing down on the backside of the blade. A small transistor radio beside him. An old song from the seventies. Melissa Manchester, "Midnight Blue."

The man didn't look her way, and Diana kept moving. A faded summer tourist map of Oak Bluffs blew by her in the breeze. She turned and watched as it caught on the steps to the kitchen, hung there for a moment tittering, and then moved on. Most of Circuit Avenue was closed for the winter and there were few people about. Even less in Cottage City. Trinity Park. You couldn't see Trinity Park from the street. Hidden behind the buildings and

stores of Circuit Avenue and the hotels and homes across from
the waterfront, it was its own enclosed little village with the open-
air tabernacle at its center. The tabernacle was empty now, too,
row upon row of benches vacant and cold, and the pulpit and
lights long gone from the stage, the Revival at rest, merely the
echoes of the voices and testimonies of summer's preachers and
singers hanging in the wind. If Diana listened closely she sometimes felt as if she could still hear them, or glimmers of them.
Even in the dead of winter. Nothing ever disappeared completely,
not sights, sounds.

People?

There was an old man watching her from the veranda of one of
the gingerbread houses. A white house with red-and-green jigsaw
trim. The sight of him startled her; it was rare you saw anybody
in these houses this time of year. The gingerbread houses formed
a circle, lining the road that curved around the tabernacle, and
they spread off into the distance, forming their own separate
village. All small, looking like dollhouses, with carved wood
doilies, and cantilevered balconies, pulpit porches, surmounting
the front and side verandas. Double doors in front, matching
windows to either side. It was a fairyland of sorts, and in the
good weather there would be flowers in the window boxes of all
the houses, and flowers smothering the gardens of the lawns,
everything alive with color, the porches cluttered with furniture.
Rockers and tables, and an occasional kerosene lamp, or paper
lantern, for decoration. But not now. Now all the flowers were
dead, the earth brown and gray, and all the porches were empty
except for the house with the old man, and he wasn't supposed to
be here. He looked angry, and he was speaking to her, pointing.
Shouting. But Diana couldn't hear a word he was saying.

She stopped on the street, not twenty feet away. The man had a
white beard and was bald on top. A high collar and bow tie, and
long dated suit. A costume. It had to be a costume. He slapped his
open palm against the rail. And then, before she had the chance to
look away, he faded. Gone. The veranda empty, the rocking chair

vanished, and only a rusted steel cowbell remaining. Clanging slowly in the early winter breeze.

Diana's heart stuttered. She looked at the porch a moment longer, half expecting him to reappear, wanting him to—so at least she would know she wasn't seeing things—and not wanting him to, all in the same breath. But there was nothing, the village silent, and then the cowbell came to a stop. But he had been there—she was sure of it. Diana turned and picked up her pace, now just wanting to get home and not wanting to look back. If she looked back and he was there again, she wasn't sure if she would be able to take this route from town anymore. And she might find herself one step closer to affirming the belief that had been hovering about her for most of the past year, ever since they had moved to the island. The belief that she was losing her mind.

It was better once she left the park, and she stopped to catch her breath. Now back in the open, beyond the oaks, and the wind moving in off the harbor and across Sunset Pond, a car roared past her as she reached the street, and blared its horn. She hadn't realized she was in the middle of the road.

Diana lived on the hill up beyond Trinity Park, above Sunset Pond, the road and sidewalk traversing the hill crumbling from salt and time. Her own home was on a dirt road, hidden by dense growth and trees in the summer, but now just appearing set back in the stark winter landscape. There were small communities like this all over the island, communities that would disappear once everything turned green and began to grow, and then reappear again in winter.

Ford was on the front porch, doing something with his telescope. He had a drink on the table beside him, whiskey and ice. Diana had thought he would be sleeping still, but if he was up now, it meant he would be up for the day. At least until eight o'clock or so when he would lie down to get a couple hours' sleep before going in for his shift at eleven. Ford worked at the post office, sorting mail throughout the night. He always drank before going in, and sometimes he drank during his shift, and sometimes he would bring some of his co-workers back to the house to drink and play darts if things were slow. Sometimes they would smoke a joint, and once in a while he would coax Diana out of bed to have her fix them something to eat. "This is my supper," he would say. "I've got to eat some time."

Now he barely looked up as she started across the lawn. Ford was good at that—seeing you without acknowledging you. They had been married a little over a year and a half, and Diana was twenty-four.

She stopped, put her bag down on the porch. Ford's eyes looked tired. Heavy, hooded, and red. Tired eyes weren't good with Ford. She thought about telling him what had happened, what she had seen, but then decided to keep it quiet. He would either laugh at her and call her crazy, or if he was in a bad mood, he might get angry; Ford usually didn't like to talk about anything like that, calling it all a "load of crap."

"Is there some type of celestial thing scheduled?" she asked him now. He was adjusting the lens. Ford had been watching the stars for years, and Diana had saved up the money to buy him this telescope two Christmases earlier, their first Christmas. Diana was still working then—had just earned her RN—and the telescope cost her two weeks' pay. He had bought her a fourteen-karat gold ring, set with an amethyst. A dozen long-stemmed red roses. Now he picked his cigarette up from the small table beside him, still not looking at her. Took a drag and blew the smoke through his nose.

"Maybe," he said.

"Where's Sam?" she asked.

"No idea," he said. He blew some imaginary dust off the lens, held it up to his eye. "Upstairs, I guess."

Diana opened the door and put one foot on the threshold.

Ford still hadn't looked up. "Diana," he said, "I told her if she messes with those dolls again, I'm going to smack her."

Diana was silent. Still unnerved from Trinity Park, and not wanting a battle.

"I found the one with red velvet dress in the back alcove earlier," he said. "Her face was sticky."

The dolls. The dolls had come with the house, relics, antiques, from the nineteenth century. China dolls with real hair and fancy Victorian garb. Ford obsessed over the dolls because he was convinced they were worth a great deal—and he blew a gasket every time Samantha went near one of them. He had never hit Sam, and Diana didn't think he would, and yet, she wasn't completely sure. She was no longer sure about a lot of things. She had told him several times that he should lock them up if her was going to make such a big deal out of it, she would buy him a glass hutch. But he insisted that he wanted to keep them out on display. "They're part of the house," he said. "They belong out in the open."

"I'll talk to her," she said now.

Ford dragged on his cigarette again. "You better."

Diana shut the door behind her, sealing off the island and Ford. A fire was going in the fireplace in the den off to the right. Gas. Modern. They had it put it in just a few months back, replacing the original, Ford complaining there was nowhere to cut wood on the island. It was one of the few modern things in the house. They had kept the original fireplace in the dining room. Everything else was old and everything was quiet once the door was shut in the winter. The house was always quiet, and always clean, and that was how he liked it. Both qualities that were broken only if and when Ford decided to break them. And one could always lead to the other. Coloring papers left on the floor by Samantha, a bottle of ketchup left on the counter, and of course, the dolls. Anything out of order could lead to a tirade, and a tirade almost always ended up in a mess. Broken dishes, broken doors. Diana stood in the foyer. She could hear the voice of the little girl upstairs talking to someone, talking to her dolls. And then for a moment she could hear someone else, a voice distant and pretty, and quietly singing.

2

The house was a larger version of the gingerbread cottages in Trinity Park—the campground—and it had been in Ford's family since the mid-nineteenth century, his father's side. According to family lore, a cousin of Ford's great-great-grandfather who had built it. It was a light gray, with dark blue trim. A wraparound porch, a wolf with a rose in his mouth carved into the center of the latticework, with more roses carved high in the corners. There was a cantilevered balcony above the front porch, and another off Diana and Ford's bedroom overlooking the cemetery. Double doors, reminiscent of the entrance to a church, opened onto the front porch, and the downstairs windows, too, were shaped like those of a church, running from ceiling to floor. One on the side of the house faced the rising sun. There was even a stained glass window. The steps needed to be fixed; one of the boards, rotten from time, shifted every time you stepped on it, and Diana had yet to take in the flower boxes for the year. Wilted vines and dried, fragile petals.

Diana and Ford had moved in nearly a year ago, just months after they were married. The house had been passed along to Ford's great-aunt, Dorothy, and she had no direct descendants. A woman over ninety, small and crooked, with wispy white hair and opaque glasses. Ford still kept one framed picture of her in the kitchen, and another in the dining room, this one black-and-white. A younger version of the woman, taken on her wedding day. Her husband was a fisherman, Diana had heard, and she had lost him during the hurricane of '38, and never remarried. Both Diana and Ford had grown up on the South Shore of Massachusetts, and Ford had come down to the Vineyard sometimes in the good weather to help the old aunt out around the yard, trimming hedges and mowing the lawn, once even building a shed, and that was why the house had been left to him. He had seven siblings, but he no longer spoke to all but one of them, nor did he speak to his parents. "That old bat thought I was the cat's meow," he had said to Diana after the aunt had passed. "I liked her, too, though. She was pretty witty, and she made me laugh. And now we have a piece of property we could flip and sell for a million dollars if we want to, and we don't have to worry about your mother knocking on our door every five minutes."

Now, in bed, Diana still couldn't clear her head of the image of the man in Cottage City, his silent shouts. She replayed the image of him fading into nothing over and over in her head, and it still made no sense. Perhaps if she had been in bed then, she could pin it all a dream—she had read about "lucid dreams" during a neuropsych course she took during nursing school, about waking to apparitions in your bedroom, apparitions that were nothing more than projected dreams, the awake portion of the brain a few steps ahead of the portion still asleep—but she hadn't been in bed, and she hadn't been dreaming.

She peeked at the clock. It was ten thirty. Almost time for Ford to go to work. He put his feet on the floor, and reached over to light a cigarette. He reeked of booze, and Diana wondered how much he had drunk. She had talked to him enough times about drinking before work, but it never got anywhere. Sometimes he would laugh, and sometimes he would snap, but it was always the same thing. "There's nothing wrong with it," he would say, "I drink. I sleep. Then I work. Then I pay the bills." And then sometimes he might wink. "If you want to start paying the bills, sweetie, just let me know." But tonight she hadn't confronted him. She had gone shopping over in Vineyard Haven with Samantha after dinner, and Ford was asleep when they got home. That much had been good. That way there had been no questions. Who was she

buying for? How much had she spent? And it gave her the oppor-
tunity to hide things. Most of it in the cellar. Anything she ever
wanted kept hidden, she kept in the cellar because Ford would
never find it there. Ford didn't like the cellar.

Something had happened to him down there—he had seen or
heard something—but he refused to talk about it. "Rats," he said
when Diana pushed him. "I don't like rats." But that was all. Up
until that point he had been going down there quite a bit. He had
been building a workbench, and a telescope stand, and now the
bench still sat against the stones of the far wall, as did the stand,
half-finished, tools left out atop of it. That had been a couple
months back. Diana herself had never seen anything down
there—certainly not rats—but at times she could feel something.
Another presence, a quiet one, unobtrusive but alert, watching,
and Diana was never sure if it was a legitimate feeling or just her
imagination.

The cellar was dark, dirt floor and wooden beams and two
yellow light bulbs dangling from the ceiling, and Diana, too, for
a time, had refused to go down there by herself, always keeping
Samantha close behind her. But now she didn't mind as much.
Most everything down here had come before they did, left behind
from Ford's ancient aunt, and some of the things—the books,
some furniture, the kerosene lamp on the shelf above the workbench, covered in cobwebs—maybe from even before. There was
a rocking chair, the blue paint peeling, that had a strange design
up near the headrest—a multicolored bird, looking something
like a rooster, in the middle of a circle of flowers—and Diana
thought she had seen the design before. Pennsylvania Dutch. It
looked something like the hex signs you sometimes saw on the
outside of old barns, used to ward off evil spirits. And there were
also numerous old fishing rods, boxes of old books. Magazines.
She had opened one box and found and issue of *TIME* from
1967. December 15th. Then farther below, one from 1942, still
saddle stapled but the cover coming loose. She imagined that if
she kept digging through the boxes, the issues would keep going
back even further. There was a pair of antique ice skates, the

leather cracked and blades rusty, and on the far wall, above the workbench, hung a picture.

The picture was black-and-white, sepia tinged, and set in an ornate gilded frame. A wedding photo. At least she assumed it was a wedding photo, but the woman was wearing a dark-colored dress, held flowers in her hands, and had her lips slightly parted as if she were startled. Or possibly even frightened. She was a beautiful woman with wide eyes and her hair pulled back tight, and the man beside her looked to be considerably older. Muttonchops and his hair slicked over the pate of his head. Tight suit and bow tie. And his eyes . . . Dark and severe, and empty. As if still watching, or seeing something beyond; the eyes in the picture seemed to follow you as you moved about the room, and Diana wondered if it was something about the picture that had unnerved Ford.

If Ford was sleeping the morning after a shift, and Samantha was as at school, Diana, not wanting to make noise upstairs, would sometimes spend time down there doing the laundry and reading while she waited, sometimes reading romance mysteries and other times reviewing her nursing texts to keep her mind fresh for if and when she went back to work. *When*, she kept telling herself, when. She would quiz herself the way her friend, Ford's sister, Cybil, used to quiz her while she was studying for her nursing boards, and she would listen to the quiet hum of the machines, once in a while taking a toke or two from the occasional joint she kept hidden behind the empty mason jars lined on the horizontal studs at the bottom of the stairs. Her cousin Freddie sometimes brought her a little bit of pot when he visited from the mainland—Freddie worked for Pepsi Cola and made regular deliveries to the A&P over in Edgartown—and Diana would sometimes make him something to eat if Ford wasn't home.

Freddie was small and happy with a bald head and a goatee, and he kept her attuned of the family gossip. He was always involved with any functions going on with the family, but always, somehow, managed to stay on the fringes whenever the dysfunction began to arise. He had been adopted, so Diana sometimes humored herself, telling herself that was probably the reason why he wasn't crazy. He had never been married but he had a couple children, and he worked two jobs to keep up with the child support. He was a few years younger, but had grown up less than a mile away, and Diana remembered threatening—and if came to it, beating the hell out of—any of the older kids who gave him a hard time.

"Your mother is getting into it with my mother again," he had told her last time he had visited. Sitting on the washing machine, dressed in blue-and-white-striped Pepsi shirt, and a knit blue hat on his head. They had just smoked half a joint, Samantha at school.

"About what now?" Diana had asked.

"She said she needs money to bury Grandma," Freddie said. "Money for the tomb."

"Grandma is sitting on about fifty thousand dollars," Diana had said. "Grandpa left it to her."

"I know."

"And she is probably going to live another twenty-five years."

"I know."

"My mother is crazy."

And Freddie had nodded, smiling. "I know."

There was a well in the cellar, made of stone. If you had a flashlight, you could see the black water some twenty feet below, and if you dropped a coin, made a wish, and listened carefully, you could always hear the quiet splash, little more than a ping. And echoing up like a watery voice. Diana and Samantha liked to make wishes.

Samantha had just turned five. Wide brown eyes and sandy brown hair, streaked with blonde in the summer. She couldn't see over the edge of the well unless Diana hoisted her, but she liked to look down before dropping the coin. Samantha didn't like to keep her wishes private and she was always wishing for something different. Tickets to Disney on Ice, Malibu Barbie, a trip to Disney World, the inflatable killer whale they had seen in the toy store down on Circuit Avenue. It changed every week, but Diana's was always the same. She would win the lottery, enough for Ford to retire and then he could dedicate all his time to astronomy, travel about the country if he wanted to, and then he would be happy. And if he was happy, they would all be happy. Even if it meant they were living apart. She was sure of that.

Now when Ford went to sleep after his shift, it was always Diana's favorite time of the day. In the good weather, she and Samantha could play about the yard when the little girl got home from school—sometimes hide-and-seek in the big graveyard—or take a walk into town to get an ice cream. They always needed to be quiet, but it was the only time of day when they really had the house to themselves. They could make cookies or try on new nail polish, or sometimes they could just lie on the couch and watch TV. Repeats of *Matlock* and *Murder, She Wrote. Jeopardy.* Diana would carry Samantha to bed, and sometimes, depending on Ford's mood, she would feign sleep on the couch, her eyes shut tight, waiting for him to leave for work.

Tonight hadn't been bad after the talk of the dolls though. The Pisces constellation was scheduled to be more visible in the sky the next few nights, and he was excited. In a good mood while drinking during dinner, looking at his charts. And then he had been out on the balcony with his scope for a few hours before coming in to take a nap before his shift, sleep off the booze, so Diana had figured it was safe to come up to bed.

Now with his back to her, he coughed twice, cleared his throat. The lights were out, but the moon shone through the bedroom window, bathing everything silver and blue. Ford stood and turned on the light. Diana shut her eyes as he did. It didn't matter if he turned the lights on while she was sleeping, he had told her, because she didn't work, and didn't have to get up, and could always go right back to sleep. She *did* have to get up—always to vacate the room once he got home in the morning, and to get Samantha ready for preschool—but she didn't argue this point with him. Pick your battles wisely. How many times had she heard that? From friends, her cousin, and a therapist she had seen a little while back in the aftermath of yet another falling-out with her mother. She did want to work though, wanted her own money. She had worked at the South Shore Hospital in Weymouth for over a year before they were married, and she was a good nurse, a handpicked personal scrub for the best surgeon in the OR, but now, despite her RN and the fact that there was a hospital on the island, Ford didn't want her to work. There was too much to do with the house, he said, and besides, with Samantha still in half days, they would need babysitting in the afternoon. It was true they would need babysitting—but only if she worked the night shift, too—but she secretly believed that Ford was afraid that she would make as much, if not more, money than he did. Again. But next year, she had been telling herself, next year, Samantha in kindergarten, then she could do it.

Ford left the light on, and went into the bathroom. His cigarette still smoldered in the ashtray. Diana listened to the sounds inside, him urinating, the toilet flushing, him brushing his teeth, gargling, the shower running. All on schedule, and then in a few minutes he would be gone, and it would be quiet again. He opened the door, and the steam sent a rush of warmth into the room. Diana lay on her side, watching him carefully through eyes she hoped appeared shut. He was still naked, and he had half an erection. He went to the mirror and rubbed some gel into his hair, then brushed it back. She shut her eyes tight again, listening to him putter about, and then a moment later she felt his weight on the bed, his knees sinking in, and then he was peeling back the blankets. Diana wore a T-shirt and panties, and the T-shirt had rode up over her hips. Ford began to run a finger along the small of her back, and then with the other hand, he cupped her ass. Held his hand there a moment.

"Can you get up for a minute?" he said at last.

Diana still didn't move, hoping he'd go—she was tired—but then he spanked her lightly. "Come on," he said, "let me do you doggy style. It will only take two minutes, I promise. I'm horny as hell."

Diana groaned a little, feigning just coming out of sleep, and then she got up on her hands and knees. Better to do it quick, than to get into a fight before he left for work; all that would do is set the mood for when he got home.

"Quick," she said. "I was sound asleep."

"No, you weren't," he said. "And besides, you have all night to sleep. I have to work."

He ran his hand over her buttocks again. "I like these bikini panties." He put his hand underneath the band, and snapped them back. "You don't even have to take them off this way, I can just push them aside like this," he said, and then he did, pushing his fingers inside her, just for a moment, and then pushing himself in, both hands on her hips. He swung her around, so her head was at the foot of the bed, and they were facing the mirror on the dresser. He started moving quicker. "Open your eyes," he gasped.

"What for?" she asked.

"Because," he said. "I like to see your facial expressions."

"But I'm not going to be making any."

"Why not?"

"Because. I'm tired, Ford. And I'm not in the mood."

Ford was still moving. She watched him in the mirror. He still did a lot of pull-ups and push-ups, and his muscles were still well-defined. Chest and biceps. Jet-black hair combed back from his forehead and blue eyes with dilated pupils, bottomless pits. He must have been excited. He pulled out for a second, spanked her a little, and then pushed back in. Diana winced, and he giggled. "I knew I could get ya," he said.

"Tell me what you want me to do," he said.

"Ford, I'm tired," she said.

He spanked her again. "Tell me."

"I want you to fuck me," she said quietly, laying the side of her face flat against the mattress. It was all routine, the same repertoire, whenever he wanted, needed, to be quick. Or sometimes when he was too drunk, and couldn't get it up.

His whole body was tense. He was on the verge, she could feel it. "How hard?" he gasped.

She turned and looked at him, lips barely parted and eyes at half-mast, trying to look sexy, sleepy, and just wanting it to end. "As hard as you can," she whispered.

"What?"

"As hard as you can. I like, need, to be fucked hard."

He spanked her again. "What?!"

"Please, please fuck me," she said. "I just want you to fuck me. Fuck me as hard as you can. Please. Ram it inside me. Please. I'm a little slut. Oh, please."

Ford thrust once more, and then he pulled out, and then it was over.

He got up from the bed and went to the bathroom again, urinated, and then came out and pulled on his briefs. Tighty-whities. And then his postal pants. He looked into the mirror again, and widened his eyes. Dropped in some Visine. And then he looked toward the chair by the window.

"Where's my shirt?" he asked.

Diana was already back under the covers.

"On the chair," she said, her eyes once again shut. It was the same routine every night. She ironed his shirt—short-sleeved blue with the eagle emblem on the pocket—put it on the chair, his shoes beneath. Ford was a stickler about the shoes, making sure they were polished at least once a week. Diana would polish them, sometimes at the kitchen table, listening to quiet classical music on the radio, hoping for Bach, Bach was her favorite.

"What chair?" he asked now.

"The chair is where it always is, Ford," she said, trying to close down his voice. "You know where I put it. It's there every night." She felt raw and sore between her legs. Her period was coming. Everything more sensitive.

"It's not there."

Diana sat up in bed, the sheet falling down about her waist, and pointed. "Yes. It. Is," she said, but even before the word had cleared her lips, she realized she was wrong. She swung her feet around and put them on the floor, looked at the chair, and quickly scanned the room. The shirt wasn't there. But it had been there. She was sure of it—she had ironed it and folded it and put it there, right before climbing into bed. Not an hour before.

"I know it was there," she said, "I just put it there."

"Maybe you forgot," he said, stepping over and picking up his shoes. He didn't look angry yet, just a little irritated, and that much was good.

"I didn't forget," she said. "I just did it." She got up out of the bed, scanned the room again. The room was small and spare— Ford didn't like much clutter. All the clothes put away, the closet doors shut. Just his cologne, deodorant, and hairbrush on his dresser—she had to keep all her toiletries, jewelry, and beauty products in her top bureau drawer—his guitar in the corner, and a biography of James Taylor beside it. Ford couldn't play the guitar, not much anyway, and he had yet to read the biography of Taylor; he had bought it last winter when they moved to the island, saying he could relate to him—his sadistic father and chaotic upbringing—and he felt as if they were soul mates.

She had almost laughed when he said that—envisioning Ford driving about the island, searching for James Taylor, or better yet, the two of them running toward each other in an open field, arms spread wide, but she didn't say that to him. There were many things she would never say to him. Couldn't, not even in jest. Now the bookmark was still lodged at the very beginning of the book. He hadn't made it out of the prologue. Diana began to move about the room quickly. It was better to move quickly, and she took things in quicker than he did. If it were here, she would see it. And she didn't. But it had to be here. She was sure of it.

She opened the closet door, second-guessing herself for show but knowing it wouldn't be in there. Not unless he had got up and hung it up himself. But Ford wouldn't do that.

It wasn't in the closet. Diana dropped to the floor and checked under the bed. A long, shallow Tupperware full of summer clothes, pieces to an old telescope, and Ford's box of old porn. Movies and magazines.

"Diana, what the fuck?" he said now. "I have to be at work. I thought you said you ironed it?"

Diana didn't want to look at him, didn't want to meet with his eyes. "I did. I ironed it, and folded it. I'm sure of it. Let me check downstairs."

She ran down the stairs, glancing into Samantha's room as she passed. She was still asleep. That was good. She wanted to keep her asleep, and if that were to happen, she had to keep Ford from screaming. She moved through the kitchen, the breakfast area, and into the dining room—she had set the ironing board up in the dining room, but now it was put away, the iron, too. Both in the closet. But the shirt wasn't in the dining room, nor was it in the closet. Ford was downstairs now, too. She could hear him in the kitchen, slamming the refrigerator door, cursing. Diana checked the back parlor at the rear of the house, the room with the alcove and window that looked out over the backyard, the graveyard, and then she checked the den. Nowhere. She hesitated for a second, and then moved toward the cellar. More laundry in the cellar. He had more than one shirt. Another one must be clean. She could iron it quick—Ford was a stickler about his shirts being ironed. Always pressed, always neat.

Diana flicked on the light and hurried down the stairs, the quiet almost feeling to carry a hum. Dusty and old, and . . . watching? Why did it always feel as if someone was watching? Eyes behind her, and eyes in the shadows. It was almost enough to make her retreat, but she couldn't retreat now, that would just make it worse. She was almost to the dryer when she glanced over at the workbench, half in the shadows, half in dim light. And the postal shirt laid out on top. Ironed and folded. Diana stopped in her tracks. She hadn't been down here tonight. Hadn't been down here since the morning. And she never went near the workbench; she didn't have any reason to.

But the shirt was there.

Diana could hear him stomping around upstairs, his footsteps getting louder, and then she could hear something else. A dripping noise, coming from the well. And that just then made her hair stand on end, too; unless they were dropping coins, the well was always silent..

Ford met her at the top of the stairs. Locked with her eyes and yanked away the shirt. "I thought you said you put it on the chair."

Diana stopped. "I thought I did," she said quietly.

Ford just nodded. "You think a lot of things. And you know what? When you're done thinking? You're just as stupid as you were before you started."

3

It was all a matter of meeting him when she did. She loved him. She wanted to love him—she believed that—but if she hadn't met him when she did, she would not have ended up with him. The wrong place, the wrong time. Her brother Phillip lived on the second floor of a three-family with his roommate Barry Fortunato on Chestnut Street in Brockton, and Ford lived downstairs.

Ford was pretty, if not handsome. Blue eyes, and long thin red lips. A ski slope nose and a pockmark on his cheek. He would come upstairs to drink and play cards with Phillip and Barry, and from time to time, Diana, with Samantha still a baby and sleeping at her mother's, would be there, too. Diana had gotten pregnant with Samantha a month out of high school, two months before she was scheduled to leave for college, three years earlier, and she had been single since she had broken up with Sam's biological father. Billy. A twenty-one-year-old ex-high school baseball star turned Nintendo-playing stoner. Jobless. Billy had made it quite clear in the first weeks after Sam was born that while he was interested in maintaining a relationship with Diana he wasn't particularly interested in one with Samantha, and that had been that; Diana had made it quite clear she wasn't particularly interested in hearing from him again.

But Ford seemed different.

Ford both worked and was going to school, part-time—night classes at Harvard Extension—and he lived independently.

Organized and neat, he seemed to have a grasp on the world much beyond that of someone his age—he was four years older than Diana—and he never made excuses for anything. And that was something that attracted her to him. All most of her family did was make excuses, knitting delusional veils to cover faults and failures and lies—and to see the absence of it in someone else, even someone with problems of his own, made everything seem somehow more real. Diana was looking for real.

And Ford had problems of his own, and she had known that from the start. She remembered their first time talking. Their first *real* time talking. Three a.m. Post-party of some twenty or thirty people. Her brother, and Barry, asleep, and the apartment littered with overflowing ashtrays and empty bottles of beer. Vodka and gin. Cheap rock 'n' roll mirrors—the Led Zeppelin blimp and Aerosmith logo in loud colors painted on the glass—were scattered about the room, rolled-up dollar bills on the side, and scratches from razors. Ford had done a little coke himself, and was coming down. Dark circles below his eyes. They sat in the kitchen, the lights hard and bright above. Tears in the oil cloth covering the table. Spilled cereal, and more cans.

Diana had told him about what had happened after the pregnancy. About Billy. And about her mother, Charlotte. First placing Diana in quarantine so the neighbors wouldn't see her, then being forced to forgo her undergrad plans at St. Elizabeth's and exiled to her uncle's house in Connecticut until she came to term. She had returned in shame after Sam was born, and Charlotte forced her to send a letter of apology out to everyone they knew, including the local priest.

Diana had told Ford everything, and Ford had shook his head. "That sucks they treated you that way," he said. "But you're lucky."

"Lucky?" she asked. "How is that lucky?"

"Well, it's not like they're criminal or anything. Just a bunch of crazy Catholics. It sounds like they love you, they just have their priorities a little messed up. Things could be worse."

"You think?"

"Sure. I don't even talk to my parents. I have seven siblings, and I talk to *one* of them—my sister Cybil. One. That's it. And she's kind of a fruitcake." He laughed a little. "Worse."

"But why?"

Ford shook his head and snubbed his cigarette out in the ashtray. "It's just my old man," he said at last.

"What? What about him?"

"How old did you say you were?"

"Twenty-one."

"Twenty-one." Ford took a breath. "Well, you seem like a nice kid, and you know what? It's probably better you don't know. No one needs to hear that stuff. He's my father and everything, but let's just say the world would be better off without him and leave it at that. He's a piece of garbage. Your mother sounds like she can be a pain in the ass, but at least it sounds like she loves you, in her own messed-up way. That's important, having two parents that love you. You need to think of that when it comes to Samantha." He lit another cigarette. "Any chance that you'll get back together with her father?"

Diana shook her head. "No."

"Really?"

"I haven't talked to him in over two years. My decision."

"Well, your decision, his loss. Your daughter is a cute kid, she cracks me up, and she seems smart as hell. My daughter, with Tara, would have been about her age. A little older, I guess."

"What happened?"

Ford lit another cigarette. Blew the smoke at the ceiling. "She was a stillborn. Got tangled up in the umbilical cord and she got stuck coming through the birth canal. Couldn't get enough oxygen."

"You're kidding me?"

Ford shook his head, cracked another Bud Light. "No. It was terrible. I didn't even know what was happening at first, and then I saw the doctor looking at the nurse and shaking his head. And then everyone was panicking. Tara almost coded. The baby stuck like that. She was beautiful, too. So small and so precious. And she just looked like she was sleeping, so I just held her. I held her for like an hour, just hoping she would open her eyes. I could see our whole future together, her whole future, but none of it was ever going to happen. None of it. Ever. I didn't want to let her go, didn't think I could. And then when they came to take her away, I just started sobbing like a little kid."

Diana reached out and put her hand over his. "You poor thing. I'm so sorry. I can't imagine how that must have been for you."

"The whole thing was a nightmare. I wanted to end it all right there. To go with her, the baby, be there—wherever there is—to protect her, but I couldn't. I had to be strong for Tara—they had her sedated, and she still wasn't really clear about what was happening. So I just held her hand and kept whispering in her ear, telling her I loved her, telling her she was going to be fine."

Diana had thought back to her own delivery with Sam. Billy nowhere to be found. No one from her family was there. Not even Charlotte. It was after three in the morning when she went into labor, and her friend Allison from high school had driven her to the hospital, stayed until six a.m. when she had to leave to get ready for work, and then she was on her own, Samantha coming just after eight. Charlotte arrived later that afternoon, and she leaned over and kissed Diana's forehead, but she wouldn't touch or hold the baby. Not yet. Not until they saw the priest, she said. The baby was soul-less, she said, until they saw the priest.

"So what happened with Tara?" Diana asked Ford.

"We broke up, broke off our engagement, a few months later. It was like we couldn't go on together anymore, couldn't look at each other, without thinking of her, thinking of the baby. You know something though, I would go through it all again if it meant I could see her precious little face again. She was just so beautiful." Diana had wrapped her arms about him, and then Ford was pulling her tight. First just sobbing, and then brushing his lips across her cheek.

She had wanted him that night, she remembered wanting him—it had been a long time; she had been on dates since Billy but hadn't slept with any of them, had never slept with anyone but Billy, despite their pushing, telling herself she wouldn't, not unless it was serious—but after a moment, he had kissed the top of her head and whispered good night.

It was the next day he had asked Phillip if he would give him her phone number. If he could call her.

Their first date was the following weekend, and when he called, Diana figured he would suggest they go out to dinner. Or maybe to a movie. But he didn't. Instead, he suggested they go out in the afternoon, and take Samantha with them, take her someplace she would want to go, so they drove into Boston and took her to the aquarium. Diana remembered Ford holding the little girl up at the top of the enormous tank to peer down into the water. Squealing over the sharks, the fish, the enormous turtles. He seemed a natural, the way he acted with her. Nothing forced, nothing phony. And then he carried her all the way down Atlantic Avenue, heading toward Faneuil Hall, and the food court for lunch.

They stopped at Rowe's Wharf, watching a cruise ship coming in to dock, and Ford pointed out several of the harbor islands, spotted with crumbling buildings and green foliage in the distance. He told the little girl a story about a giant sea turtle named Melville, and an old hermit named Jackson that lived out on Bumpkin Island, hiding in the remains of an old military fort.

"Every day, every morning, old Jackson goes down to the beach with a new plan to catch Melville, but every day he comes back empty-handed."

The little girl's eyes were wide. "But why does he want to catch him?"

Ford chuckled. "To make turtle soup, and to make a house out of his shell so he can stay nice and warm for the winter, and not have to worry so much about his raggedy clothing. He'll just grow his beard even longer, and that will help keep him warm, too."

"But how does the turtle get away?" Samantha had asked.

"How does he get away? Well, the seals help him, of course. There are seals all over Bumpkin Island, and when they see old

Jackson coming down the beach with his net, they flop into the water to let Melville know."

It was a nice day, and the wharf was alive with activity. Sidewalk musicians with upturned hats on the ground before them, people lining up for the whale watches and harbor tours, diners at the outdoor tables, and a man with a megaphone shouting about Clinton. The cruise ship had sounded then, and Ford picked Samantha up again to give her a better view of people climbing aboard.

"I want to see the turtle," she said.

"Well, you can't see him from here. You have to be out in the harbor, out in a boat, or on one of the islands." He was quiet a moment. "My family has a house out there on one of the islands, so maybe we can visit some time. That one is on the other side of Cape Cod though."

Diana looked at him, not sure if he was still joking. "Which island?"

Ford wasn't looking at her, he was still holding Sam, watching the look of wonder in her eyes. "Martha's Vineyard," he said quietly.

"You have a house on the Vineyard?" Diana asked.

"My aunt does. Great-aunt. More like a grandmother to me, though. She's like ninety-something years old. I go out there a lot to help her out though. Or at least I used to, been tough with work. I'll have to bring you guys sometime. Would you like that, Sam? Would you like to go to Martha's Vineyard?"

Samantha had smiled at him. "Do I get to see the turtle?"

On their next date, they went to the movies, *The Little Mermaid*, back in the theatres, and then to the Science Museum, a few trips to the park. And he and Diana had gone out to eat twice, but other than kissing her goodbye, he tried nothing. Just held her hand once while driving in the car. Two months had passed before she began to wonder if he ever would. It had never been like this before with the few guys she had dated after Billy. She was very young, a single mother, and if not by the first date, at least by the second, they all assumed she would have sex with them. Of course she would, she had gotten pregnant at eighteen, she *had* to be easy, right? Easy. The word stuck with her. Most of the guys she had dated were at least a little discreet, willing at least to pretend they were interested until she said not yet for the second or third time and then they were gone. And the only one who had been different was Ford.

And then when it finally happened, it was just before Halloween. They had taken Sam to Salem for the afternoon, Ford holding her close when she became afraid of an old woman, dressed as a witch, hobbling out of one the haunted houses, and that night, after they had put her to sleep in Ford's spare bedroom, and Diana had made him a dinner of chicken parmigiana, they lay down on the couch. Ford held her for what seemed forever, and then he moved his lips down over her neck.

"It's been so long," he whispered. "So long."

Diana felt her entire body reacting. Stiffening, tingling. And then she moved her hand between them and began to tug at his jeans.

They ended up on the floor, rolling off the couch and landing with a thump. Ford whispered something about her brother waking up upstairs, and she said she didn't care. And she didn't. It had been too long for her, too, since the months after she conceived Samantha, and Diana had almost forgotten how it felt. She didn't want to forget again. Ever. He cried out as he came, and then she came with him, and then they wrapped themselves in each other's arms on the linoleum floor, and he was saying he was sorry. He respected her, he said. He wanted her to know that. He had wanted to wait a little longer. Really.

"So did I," she whispered, holding him tight. "But you know something? I'm glad that we did. I'm so glad that we did. Keep a secret?" she said, nibbling on his ear. "A dirty secret?"

"What's that?" he asked.

She leaned in to whisper. "I could fuck you all day long."

Ford laughed a little, and then he was back inside her. It went on like that, every day for the next few weeks, and they were perfect for each other. Young and hardworking and happy. Strong survivors of scarred pasts, and quickly falling desperately in love. Perfect for each other.

⤝

"We are," she told her mother when she finally approached her about him. "Perfect for each other. I've never met anyone like him."

Charlotte had just looked at her a moment, and then started across the room, walking with a limp. Diana wasn't sure where the limp came from—she hadn't noticed it before. Charlotte's eyes, a beautiful blue, looked both empty and heavy today, overly medicated. Painkillers and little helpers. Charlotte was in her late forties, narrow shoulders and round about the middle. She had high dark hair, and colorless lips. But a perfect smile. One that often seemed too perfect to be real. Diana and Samantha had been living with her parents since Samantha was born, and the house was full. Diana had worked as a waitress while going to nursing school, and her mother had watched Samantha while she did. Still watched her now that Diana had her job at the hospital, and Diana paid her two hundred dollars a week, which included room and board.

"Where's he from?' Charlotte asked, picking up a wet rag and pretending to work on a spot on the counter.

"He's originally from Willington," Diana now said in response to Charlotte's question.

"Willington," Charlotte repeated. She looked up suddenly, her eyes on the wall, feigning thought. "I wonder if the Romanowskis know him. They know just about everybody in Willington. They've lived there a long time."

"He comes from a big family," Diana added, her fingers pulling at the edge of the tablecloth. She had been putting off this moment, dreading the conversation, and her entire body felt tense, belonging to someone else. As if she were just visiting inside. You could never tell how her mother would react; it all depended on her mood but the problem was her mood could change from one minute to the next, and Diana knew how Charlotte could be when it came to someone breaching the family's inner circle. But Thanksgiving was coming, and she wanted to have Ford over for Thanksgiving dinner. One thing her family did every year, as crazy as half of them were, was spend the holidays together. It was important to them.

"Seven brothers and sisters," Charlotte said. "Eight kids. Hmpfff. I thought we had a lot. The Lord must have really seen fit to bless his mother."

"He's very family oriented," Diana added. She had a photo mug of tea in front of her—a picture of Charlotte emblazoned across the front—and she wrapped both hands around it to take a sip. She could see Ford's face in her head. She wanted to see it, to give her strength as she approached Charlotte. He was already saying he wanted to adopt Samantha, as soon as they were married; Diana laughed when he said that. Married? They had only known each other a couple short months. It didn't matter, he said. When it was right, it was right. You could just tell.

"Well, with that many brothers and sisters you don't have a choice," Charlotte said. "You have to be family oriented, don't you? Same as us." The spot was apparently gone, and now she had set to unloading the dishes from the strainer by the sink. A dishwasher was just a pipe dream, she told her friends. She stopped and looked Diana head-on, her eyes just a shade more distant. "You know, I'm glad he has such a big, close family. It's important around the holidays. Important to be near them."

So that was it, Diana thought. Charlotte was more clever than she ever gave her credit for. Had seen this coming. Probably looked at the calendar, the date, noticed the way Diana was sitting nervously at the table. She wasn't going to allow anyone to breach the circle. The holidays, and immediate family. Never had, and she wasn't going to change now. Not yet. Diana took a deep breath; she had already come this far.

"Well, that's what I wanted to talk to you about," she said. "I was wondering if he could come to Thanksgiving."

Charlotte didn't immediately respond. Instead she stood staring at Diana a moment—eyes now completely blank, no one home, no one inside.

"I'd really like for you and Dad to meet him," Diana said.

"Well," said Charlotte, taking a long breath. "I think that's a great idea."

"Really?" Diana asked, a guarded hope suddenly rising.

"Yes. Of course I do. If he's important to you, he should be important to us, too." She picked up the broom and started in the floor. "Why don't we have him over for lunch the Saturday after Thanksgiving? That way it gives everything a chance to wind down a bit." She turned and smiled, false and wide. "I wouldn't want to overwhelm him with all the chaos over here on Thanksgiving Day."

"But, Ma, I told you," she said, her heart already sinking, knowing she had lost. "He comes from a big family. He'd be fine with it."

Charlotte nodded. "Well, I'm sure he would be. But, I think it's important that you spend it with your family, and he spend it with his. Families need to stay together." she said. And then she started in talking about gravy.

The Saturday after Thanksgiving Charlotte had cooked spaghetti. Gave Ford a big welcome at the door. No one else was there except for Diana's father, Paul; her little sister Lucy, big dark eyes and hair in a ponytail; and her brother Stephen. Charlotte was subtly insulting throughout the meal, regularly reminding them she had to go to the four o'clock mass at Saint Rocco's, and Ford was polite but quiet, and spent most of the dinner sizing up Diana's younger brother Stephen. Stephen was nineteen. Stephen wasn't confrontational, but he was always high, or looking to be high, and because of this he could never be trusted. His hair was blond, and his eyes were wild and blue. He was skinny as a rail. Too much heroin. Speedballs. He rarely ate, and that's how you could tell if he was actively using. If he was using he wouldn't eat, and he wasn't eating today; he kept complaining that his stomach was hurting.

"I had too much for breakfast, Mummy," he said. "Those sausages were delicious." His hands were shaking, and his skin looked waxen, clammy. He had told Ford he was an artist, and when Ford mentioned astronomy, Stephen had lit a cigarette and kicked back.

"I like to paint a lot of pictures of the night sky," he said. "Sometimes I don't even have to paint them. I just compose them in my head, and there they are, stuck with me for eternity. It's kind of hard to explain. But I think art is art whether it is an idea, words, or paint spread across a canvas. Once it exists, it exists, whether it be for ourselves or for everyone to share. Because we all share everything anyway, right? I mean we're all connected. We just don't understand how to use the connections. Our brains haven't evolved enough. But someday we'll all just be able to share ideas without even speaking. I know it. It's going to be incredible."

"Well," Ford said, "I think that's what separates art from science. There is nothing subjective about science. Science is concrete. Measurable."

"I like astrology," Stephen said, blowing the smoke from the corners of his lips. "That and astronomy go like hand in hand, but astrology is subjective, right?"

"It is," said Ford. "That's why it can't be considered science."

"I hear ya," Stephen said. "I still think it's all connected though. It's wild. It's beautiful. Makes me kind of teary-eyed sometimes. Makes me start to cry."

Ford looked at him a second, frowned. "Astrology?"

"Stephen is an incredible artist," Charlotte chimed in. "Just last month a man who runs one of the galleries on Newbury Street called asking if he had any paintings available for a showing."

Stephen snubbed his cigarette out. "Really? You didn't tell me that. That's amazing."

"I meant to tell you," Charlotte said. "I even wrote myself a note, but I must have forgot. I left the note by the phone, and I think your sister must have thrown it out."

"Wow," said Stephen.

"I've never seen any of his paintings," Diana said.

"He practically has his own gallery upstairs," Charlotte said.

"I have a couple things," Stephen added. "I did some nice stuff back in high school. A couple miniatures. And I did a clay sculpture of Charles Bukowski. Bukowski is madness. He writes some serious shit. Crazy shit, though. Crazy."

"Stephen, watch your mouth," said Charlotte.

"Sorry, Mummy. Stuff. I meant he writes some serious stuff. I don't know what happened to the sculpture though. I think Roger broke it. He might have sat on it or something."

"I keep telling him to stay out of your studio," Charlotte said.

Diana's father had been watching CNN on the little TV on the shelf above the counter. "What studio is this?"

Charlotte patted his hand. "Upstairs, dear. I keep telling you about it."

"Well," said Ford, "I'd love to see some of your work."

Stephen lit another cigarette. "I'll make something to show you. I've got a lot of ideas."

He stood up then and asked Charlotte if he could have five dollars to run to the store and get a pack of cigarettes. "I'm almost out of cigarettes," he said.

"You still haven't eaten anything," Charlotte said.

Stephen put his hand on his stomach. "I told you, I'm not really that hungry. I don't know what it is. I think I should probably see the doctor or some shit like that. Can I have five dollars though? Cigarettes make me feel better."

Charlotte stared at him a moment, and then went for her wallet.

"He must have that stomach bug," she said as he headed out the door. "I heard it's going around."

Samantha had climbed up on Ford's lap, and Charlotte just stared, watching and measuring. After a moment, she got up to fix dessert. Samantha was wearing a long plaid dress with a matching bow in her hair. Long hair with streaks of blonde, and wide brown eyes. Diana never talked to her much about her father, and Samantha was too little to ask. And now it seemed she was taking to Ford. But how could she not? He doted on her whenever they were together.

"So what do you do for work?" Diana's father asked after Stephen had left.

Ford cleared his throat, sipped his beer. "I work as a retail consultant at Benjamin's Paint Store, but I'm scheduled to take the postal exam next month. It's a lot of studying though. It's pretty hard. I'm also going to Harvard."

"Harvard?" said Diana's father. Diana had hoped her father would just stay focused on the television. "What the hell are you taking the postal exam for if you're going to Harvard?"

"Harvard is more for my own personal growth," he said.

"Harvard is pretty expensive for personal growth."

"Well, I'm just taking a course or two. I want to keep my options open."

"That is why I asked Stephen to have lunch with us," said Charlotte. "Diana told me about your interests and I thought you two might have something in common. Stephen is very focused on school."

Ford cleared his throat. "Well, he seems like a nice guy, I enjoyed talking to him, but if he wants to put any of his ideas to good use, I hope he can find someone to talk to about his problem."

Charlotte just looked at him. "What problem?"

"Well, Diana tells me he has a substance abuse problem."

Charlotte turned her stare on Diana, and Diana felt herself go hollow.

"Everyone has problems," Charlotte said.

"They do," said Ford. "But heroin is serious."

"I know it is serious." Charlotte stood then, started to gather the dishes. "And Diana tends to remember things that never happened. I don't know what she's talking about. If someone in my house, had a problem like that, I would think I would know about it. Now, it's been very nice meeting you, but I promised Father Turkowsky I would get some new flowers for the altar before the four thirty Mass, and I need to get going. So I'm afraid you do, too."

Ford was silent all the way back to his apartment, cranking Supertramp on the tape player. "Goodbye Stranger." They had left Samantha back at the house with Diana's father.

When they reached the apartment Ford popped open a bottle of champagne from the refrigerator, the cork bouncing off the ceiling. He took a swig, then offered the bottle to Diana. "Want some?"

"I thought we were saving that for our anniversary," she said.

Ford stared at her, but looked more to be looking past her. "We can get another one. What did it cost? Ten bucks?"

"It was forty dollars."

He shrugged, took another belt. Lit a cigarette.

"I'm sorry about my mother," Diana said.

Ford snickered. "Yeah, she kind of didn't like me, huh?"

"She pisses me off," Diana said. She's in denial about Stephen, in denial about everything, and she's got this thing about anyone coming into the family. She's always been like that. I don't get it. It's like she wants to contain her immediate family just like it is, for good. Like we're still all little kids."

"That's okay," he said, "because I don't think I'll be going over there anymore anyway. I don't need to put up with that." He walked into the living room and took a seat on the couch. Old and beige and sunken in the middle. He put his feet up on the coffee table and flicked on the television. Swigged from the bottle, and nestled it into his lap. Diana hesitantly followed him into the room.

"Well, she was being rude, but it's not like I want you staying away from my home. I mean, I want you there. I want you to feel comfortable coming by. I live there."

Ford focused on the television. A *Sanford and Son* repeat. Fred was chasing Lamont around with a frying pan, one hand holding tight to his suspenders as he did. The sound was down. "Well, then don't," he said.

"Don't?"

"Move in here."

"Ford, I can't," she said. "I have Samantha."

"She can come too. We can all live together."

Diana hesitated, and then she went to the couch, sat down beside him, turning sideways and pulling one leg up beneath her. "Do you mean that? I mean, I don't think there's enough room."

On the television, Ester had arrived, positioning herself between Fred and Lamont, staring Fred down, one eye shut and her chin jutting forward, lips pursed. Diana looked at Fred, reading his lips. "'Cause you so ugly," he said to Ester.

"We can make room," said Ford, "and then after we save a little money, we can look for a new place. A bigger place." He took her hand. "Just for us."

4

Ford got up, bare-chested and still in his briefs, and looked out the back window over the graveyard. A canopy was up in the distance, the artificial carpet of grass, draped over an empty hole. A funeral coming later. A woman was out there jogging—blue sweatpants, gray sweatshirt, headphones. You didn't see many people out there this time of year. Sometimes in the summer he liked to sit on the back porch, or out on the balcony, and people watch, sip a little scotch. There were often people out there then—exercising, pushing baby strollers, or vacationers stopping to look at the weather-worn graves from the century before—but not much this time of year. The jogger stopped, hands on her hips to catch her breath. She was young, blonde, hair in ponytail. Probably kind of hot—it was hard to tell from the distance.

He went to his bureau, checked his reflection in the mirror, ran his fingers up through his hair, and then squirted some Visine in his eyes. He lit a cigarette and placed it on the rim of the ashtray on the bureau—surprised it was still there; every time he brought one up, Diana moved it back out, didn't want him smoking in the bedroom, she said, and dropped hints about not smoking in the house in general. Funniest thing he had ever heard—his bedroom, his house, and she was going to tell him, try to tell him, he couldn't smoke in it. Call the cigarette police. There was a note from her on the bureau weighted down with his bottle of Aqua Velva.

Picking Sam up from school, then need to run a few errands
in Vineyard Haven.
Hope you had a good sleep.
Love, Me.

Signed with a lipstick kiss.

Running a few errands. The female code for spending money. That's all she did—he made it, she spent it. It wasn't just her though. He knew that. They were all like that. Tara before her had been like that, too. But Tara had been special. A voice that melted his heart when she sang. That short cropped hair and brown puppy dog eyes. And such great tits. He had loved those tits. He loved her, too, but it wasn't meant to be—they could never get along. They had gone through too much together. But he had *really* loved her.

And he loved Diana, too. If he didn't, they never would have come this far.

And he liked her, usually. He had liked her the moment he met her. She was quiet at first, but she was casually watching him, figuring him out. He could tell. He was playing cards with her brother and his boyfriend, and some fat guy from New Orleans, the first time they met. The fat guy had a girlfriend who was even fatter than he was, and supposedly the two of them liked to strap on some leather and whip each other and shit like that. Ford had met him a few times, and he talked like that a lot, but he didn't talk like this in front of Diana; when she was there, he just sort of looked at her the way a serial killer might size up his prey, or maybe a rapist. He was having dirty thoughts at least, and it bothered Ford a little—fucking fat scumbag—and it was then that Ford realized that he himself liked her. He liked her a lot. And he wanted to protect her.

Diana didn't laugh when Ford said something funny, or at least when he was trying to be funny, but she did smile, and he liked that. If she laughed too much, he would have probably questioned whether she was sincere, or was just trying to make an impression. Being phony. No, the little smile was better, and then later, when they were alone, she looked like she was really listening to him, like she really cared. She didn't even know him then, but she seemed like she cared.

He wondered if he would have even hooked up with her if they hadn't met when they did. All the shit just falling through the floor with his family, and his old man on the lam. And of course, he and Tara had broken up not long before. He and Tara were like fire and ice—things were getting heated and he loved her way too much. That was his problem half the time—he loved people too much, too much, and then expected too much from them, expected them to love him just as much in return. He realized this; he prided himself on being insightful. Raw intelligence, his old aunt had once said. Anyway, that's probably why it went bad with Tara, he figured, what pushed him to the brink, the love. And when people loved each other that much, that shit sometimes happened. It got out of control sometimes. He knew that, and he didn't want it to come to that with her. Didn't want to be like his father, Big Daddy. And with Diana, he knew, he would be able to keep his cool. He liked her, and he loved her, but it wasn't a love that whacked him in the face every time he saw her like it did with Tara. It could be more comfortable. Quiet. And that's what he needed, quiet. And besides, she liked to please him. At least she said she did. And he deserved that at this point in his life, all he had been through.

And he did love Samantha.

She might not be his blood, but he loved her, and she loved him. Ever since they met, he had tried to do whatever he had to do, to be a good father. And once a father and daughter created a bond, it could be pretty tough to break. And he would never let that happen.

But Diana's family thing was bothering him again a little lately, too. She didn't have to see all of them, didn't miss all of them. But she wanted to see some of them. It was only fair that she could see some of them, she said, and maybe she was right, a little bit. But her mother was a crazy bitch—he had pegged her for one from day one—and he knew in his heart that if he gave her the okay to see some of them, sooner or later it would lead to all of them. And that wouldn't be good. They were all better off away from them. He sometimes felt bad about it, but he knew it in his heart to be true. It was just fortunate that he could spot a pedophile like her little brother coming a mile away—having spent the first eighteen years of his life in a house with that and worse pretty much made him an expert—and all he needed was ten minutes with her brother Stephen, and he had that whole little situation summed up pretty neatly. It was a toxic atmosphere, and one better left behind them. Better for him, better for Diana. And better for Samantha, of course. The way it worked out, none of them even came to the wedding. Nobody from either of their families was there—just their friends. And it didn't matter. Not then. Not now. It was all for the better. As was the island.

Ford wasn't stupid, he knew the separation from her family was bound to bother her, but he could make up for it. Once she saw the house here, he knew that would make up for everything. It was like the house was meant for them. He figured he would look the other way if she wanted to stay in touch with her brother Phillip and her little cousin, allow her a little contact, and maybe even his sister Cybil, but that would be enough. They had their own little family now. And that was all they needed. They just needed one another.

He looked at the note a minute longer and then dropped it in the trash. He liked an uncluttered room. Liked things neat. Liked them to stay just the way that they were. Order. Life only worked when you had order. That was one thing he liked about the PO, separating the mail. It gave you a sense of order.

He pulled on a T-shirt and shorts—the house was warm, the heat cranking; he was going to have to talk to her again about cranking the heat—and then he stopped in the doorway and listened. He thought he heard a scraping noise. A chair on the floor? Diana? Sam? And then hurried footsteps on the old hardwood floor, bowed up in the middle, in the back parlor. A door closing. Going by the note, he didn't think Diana would be back yet. But maybe she was, maybe she was back. But it didn't make sense. And if not . . . ?

He picked up the baseball bat Diana kept behind the bedroom door—she sometimes got scared on the nights when he was working—and he stepped quietly, carefully, as he made his way down the stairs to the first floor. Always better to step quietly, senses on alert. If there was someone in the house, someone other than Diana or Sam, he was going to surprise them, and not the other way around. But when he reached the first floor, listened, there was nothing. The only sound was the quiet hum of the dishwasher still running in the kitchen; and if the dishwasher was still going, Diana couldn't have been gone that long. He made a tour of the house, quietly, checked the closets and empty rooms, checked outside the windows. Nothing. The doors were all locked and there was nothing. The bolt on the cellar door was still pulled tight, too, and that was good. The last thing he wanted to see, that he could handle, was seeing the cellar door unlocked and open. He didn't need that. Not now.

Ford's heart was just beginning to slow. He cut back past the dining room, glanced inside. The long table, and the chandelier above—Diana didn't like the chandelier, but Ford loved it. The lights were off, but with the light coming in from the windows around the front door, he could see clearly. Four of the six chairs, all high-backed and antique, red velvet cushions, were pulled out.

With a China Doll sitting on each one.

Small plastic teacups on the table before them.

Samantha. Must've been fucking with the dolls again. He swallowed his breath. It really put him over the edge. He gave her everything, and all he asked in return was one simple thing. One simple thing, one simple request, and she couldn't control herself. He knew she was little—he got that—but was it really that fucking hard? She had every toy under the sun, more than she needed, but still, she . . . had . . . to . . . go . . . and. . . fuck . . . with . . . the . . . dolls. He felt his blood beginning to boil, both wishing she was home, and glad she was not. He wanted to finish this, clear it up—one more time—needed to snap, but then again it was better she wasn't here. Give him a little time to compose himself—a little distance—calm down a little. Then he could be reasonable. Explain it clearly, one more time. He didn't even have to yell.

Wouldn't yell.

And he could show Diana how reasonable he could be.

He wondered if he *should* just sell the dolls outright before they were ruined. There were six of them, but only four here now in the dining room. Two with blonde hair, one with jet-black, and one with dark auburn hair; she had a green velvet dress, her hair up under a green hat with a white feather. Empty glass eyes. They all had the empty glass eyes—one of many things that had always unnerved him a little about dolls. One of the blondes wore a red dress, ballroom style, and the other baby blue, white apron, and matching blue bonnet. The black-haired one sat in the chair closest to the mantle, at the side of the table. She had a black dress to match, a black veil, now pushed back over her head, and a small bible clutched in her hands. A doll in mourning. He never would have thought they'd make a doll in mourning, but then again, Victorians were strange about death. They romanticized it somehow, and it was so common back then, an everyday part of life. Both for the old and the young, the weak and strong. Even children. Little kids were always dying. How many children's headstones had he seen in the cemetery out back? Surmounted with sleeping lambs, or sometimes even a sleeping child—hands folded beneath their heads. All ages. eight years, three years, and sometimes just a matter of months. Ford never liked the graves of children.

He wondered what the odds were that all his brothers and sisters would have lived to see adulthood if born a century earlier. Probably slim, and probably for the better. Fewer punching bags, less fodder for the old man. Nine of them, and as far as he could tell, he was the only one who wasn't royally fucked up. Everybody, everywhere, had their issues, but he had always prided himself on staying a step ahead, always within earshot, just around the corner. People couldn't one-up him. Lord knew enough had tried.

He didn't like looking at the dolls, but he couldn't let Samantha just destroy them. It was getting ridiculous. They were antiques. Worth a lot of money.

And the house wouldn't like it.

What had his aunt said? Something like that. Way back when.

Ford stepped into the room. Picked the first doll up, wanted to gather them all, and put them back where they belonged in the back parlor, but then thought better of it. He needed to leave them where she had left them. Evidence. Exhibit A, for when he talked to her—"Look—kid, dolls. This is the kid, and these are the dolls, and the kid, you, doesn't touch the goddamn dolls."

He supposed, maybe he was making too big a deal out of it, but they were antiques; he knew that for fact. That was that, and they had to be worth something. And if he were honest with himself, if truth be told, he wouldn't mind getting rid of them. He was kind of fascinated by them, but he had never really liked them, not even when he was small. His aunt used to move them all about the house, and it seemed that when he visited, each day he would walk into a different room and there they would be. Always staring—at him or one another. They unsettled him for some reason, and it never seemed a stretch to imagine them talking. Especially when his aunt would arrange them on the window seat in the alcove off the back parlor, a clear view of the cemetery beyond, watching the dead. It seemed the perfect place for them, the perfect background. The dolls inside, and the dead beyond. And for that reason, when she put them there, they frightened him all the more.

"You should sell them," he remembered suggesting to his aunt. He was seventeen, down for Columbus Day weekend. Raking leaves, and patching a hole in the roof above the upstairs bedroom. It had rained the week before and his aunt had said that water had come in.

"Sell them?" the old lady had said. "Oh no, I couldn't sell them. That wouldn't go over well at all. I would hear about that, and that is for certain. They are as much a part of the house as I am. Maybe more—they've been here longer than me." She had stared at him a moment, a look in her eyes half-smiling, half-measuring. "And the others would not be pleased."

The others would not be pleased.

That's what she had said.

His aunt had wispy white hair, and was already crooked by then, walking with a cane. But her eyes were beautiful. Sky blue and always looking amused. He had started coming down on his own in junior high school, taking the bus to the ferry at Woods Hole, and after he would do odd jobs for her, in the house and around the yard, she would always have treats for him. Cookies and candy or soda when he was young, sometimes ordering a pizza, and later, when he was a junior or senior in high school, she would keep a six-pack of beer in the fridge for him. And even back then the house had made him a little uneasy. He would never have admitted it to anyone—he would have sounded like a pussy—but he didn't like being alone in the house, even alone in some of the rooms, and sometimes he would follow his aunt about, casually, coming into a room after she had already settled in there, pick up the Rubik's Cube she used to have, or open a beer, pretend to do something, always keeping an eye over his shoulder, his ears open for sounds.

Whispers.

Sometimes even back then he swore he could hear whispers.

And his aunt would read his eyes, see it.

"Spooking you, are they?" she said.

"Spooking me?"

"You get used to it," she said. "Every house has its history, just like people. We all have our pasts, and you can't just sweep them away. You just learn to live with them."

Ford had tried to smile. "Who is 'them'?" he asked, but his aunt didn't answer, or at least she didn't seem to.

"I like you, Ford," she said. "You're a good boy, and you even have the potential to turn into a fine man, if you don't give in."

"Give in to what?"

"Life. And your weaknesses—you do have a few. But you can't let them beat you. Too many of the men in our family have let them beat them. And once that happens, forget it, you're of no use to anyone. And it is the people around you who end up suffering. Just look at your father. I suppose he may have almost been a good man once, but look at him now. No use to anyone."

But Ford was of use to her, and she had made him feel good. Even at sixteen or seventeen, he didn't mind coming down by himself and spending time with her. Any respite away from his home, away from Big Daddy, would have been a welcome one, but the old lady made him feel needed, and she made him feel loved. With all the kids in the house at home, and the way things were, it was pretty much impossible to feel loved, he always thought, and of course, his mother being a corn husk shell of the woman she once might have been, and Big Daddy being Big Daddy, just made it worse.

But his aunt, the old lady, was different. It was hard to believe they were all related to her sometimes. Even when he wasn't on the island, she was always sending him cards. Five dollars here. Ten. Twenty. And other than birthdays, he was the only one. She loved his brothers and sisters, too, she once told him, but he was special.

Now he flicked off the light and went to the kitchen. Took out a beer, some butter, two eggs, and an English muffin. He loved beer and eggs. He greased a frying pan with some butter, and then cracked the eggs. The yolk broke on the second egg. He hated it when the yolk broke; Diana broke one nearly every time she cooked him some, and it made him crazy. But he always just bit his tongue. She was lucky he was so good at biting his tongue—a lot of guys wouldn't be, but she didn't always understand that. He took out another egg. Perfect. Took a sip from his beer, and then popped the English muffin in the toaster. She wouldn't be home for at least an hour, he figured, at least an hour. He reached up into the cabinet above the sink and took down the bottle of Jameson. His boss at the PO had given it to him two weeks before—for his birthday—and he still had almost half left. That was pretty good.

It was expensive though, and he wanted to make it last, but his nerves were still shot, a little on end. The noises. The footsteps.

He poured himself a shot, threw it back quick. The whiskey burned in his throat for a moment, and then warmed in his belly. The warmth rushed immediately up through his face, temples, tingling. He took another sip from the bottle, just a small one.

Ford looked out the back window while he waited for the eggs to finish cooking. A line of cars, pulled over onto the grass, and a crowd of people. Gathering beneath the canopy. It didn't look like it would rain though; there were a few clouds, but the rest of the sky was a deep blue like it could only be in early to mid-fall. He could see it like pieces of a jigsaw puzzle through the branches of the enormous oak tree. He wondered who had died. They didn't' have many burials out there this late in the year, didn't have many period anymore. They used to have quite a few, and he and his aunt would watch from the back window, and his aunt would quietly pray.

Now people were crying, he could tell from here, and there was a woman sitting in a chair before the casket, all dressed in black, her head down. The mother or the wife. Had to be. She reminded him of the doll in the dining room. He wondered what it would be like to be loved that much. Diana loved him, he knew, but not that much. Not enough to understand him. He reached up into the cabinet, and poured himself another shot.

On his way back upstairs, something caught his eye as he passed the dining room. The light was back on—he could have sworn he shut it off. He stepped inside and reached for the switch, and as he did, he felt a jolt to his heart. The doll that had been sitting closest to the mantle—the doll in mourning—was now sitting in the chair at the head of the table, and the doll that had been there, was flat on her back on the floor beside the chair. And the chair was turned out, facing the door.

5

The business with Stephen escalated not long after Diana had introduced Ford to her parents. Diana and Ford had a small Christmas party with her siblings, a few friends, and her cousin Freddie just a few days before Christmas. They served hors d'oeuvres and beer and wine, and after dinner they had a toast of champagne. Ford hung his dartboard in the living room, and he and her brothers played a few games. He was sipping whiskey, but he had been in a good mood from the start of the evening, and she was happy to see him getting along well with her brothers. After the incident with Charlotte the Saturday after Thanksgiving, she had been walking on egg shells leading up to the party, not sure if her brothers would come, and if they did, how it would go between them and Ford.

Phillip had assured Ford a few weeks back while playing cards that he shouldn't pay much attention to their mother—"I love her dearly," he said, "dearly, but she's a pathological liar and she's nuts"—and tonight he had been arguing with Ford a little bit about music from the early eighties, drunker than usual and spittle gathering about his lips, but it was good-natured and everything seemed to be going well until Stephen disappeared into their bedroom.

It was late. Their friends had all gone home, and Freddie, and Diana's brothers Roger and Eddie, were on the couch playing video games. Samantha was sleeping, and since Ford's room was farther down the hall than the spare room, farther from the noise,

Diana had put her in there. Phillip's roommate Barry was playing DJ, all eighties new wave, and only Phillip and Ford were left playing darts. Diana had decorated the apartment—with wreaths and lights, tinsel and old-fashioned-looking Thomas Nast Santa Clauses—but Ford had insisted that they wait until Christmas Eve to put up the tree. It was his family's tradition, he said, to wait until Christmas Eve to put up the tree.

The coffee table was covered in bottles and cans, and the music was blaring—Men at Work, "Who Can it Be Now?"—when Ford looked around the room, put his drink down on the stereo and disappeared down the hall. Diana barely had a chance to move herself, when she heard voices rising. Mostly Ford's, and then Stephen saying something, arguing back. And then there was a loud knock against the wall, something falling over, crashing, and the two of them were in the hall, Ford pushing. Stephen tried to take a swing at him, but Ford grabbed him by the front of his shirt and clocked him in the face. Phillip stood frozen, but Eddie and Roger were right on their feet, Freddie not far behind. And then Eddie and Ford were getting into it, both struggling and both exchanging blows, and Diana was screaming.

Diana had them all out the door less than five minutes later, and Ford collapsed back on the couch, his eye already beginning to swell. He took a shot of whiskey, and was silent, staring at the wall. Sam had awoken and was crying, and when Diana demanded from Ford to know what had happened, all he would say was "He was in our room. I don't want that maggot in our room."

⤳

He refused to talk about it over the course of the next few days and on Christmas Eve. Diana and Samantha had gone to her grandmother's, but Ford had stayed home, refusing to go.

Diana was home by nine; it never ran any later, and by the time they arrived Ford was loaded.

He had just finished putting up his tree.

"I thought you were going to wait for us to decorate," Diana said, slipping out of her coat. She had figured she would stay here until midnight, let Samantha fall asleep, and then whisk her off home. Maybe come back for a few hours if it looked like Ford was going to be able to stay awake—he had finally started at the post office, and had worked the night shift the night before.

He turned and flicked his cigarette in the ashtray. A small tin tray he had taken from the pizza place down the street. There was a quart of Jack Daniels out on the coffee table, half gone, but he was using a glass tonight. Water and ice.

"Can't wait forever," he said without looking at her when she commented. "I didn't know what time you guys planned on showing up. It's a shame you had to stay over your mother's so late. If not we could have all decorated it together. That's what I was hoping. Maybe next year we can all do it together." He took a step back. "It's a beautiful tree though, isn't it? I think I did a good job."

It was the next morning as he was cooking breakfast—French toast—that he told her he had to talk to her. He had an apron on, standing at the stove, wearing a starched white shirt with green stripes beneath. His Christmas shirt. Ford had been the first one up, already showered—his hair combed perfect—and dressed by the time even Samantha awoke. He had given Samantha his presents—a Miss Piggy doll, and a framed photograph of the three of them taken outside a haunted house in Salem the previous Halloween—and Samantha had happily opened them, but then looked around the room, a little confused, looking for more.

"Santa brought the rest to Grandma's," Diana said, immediately feeling guilty. She had meant to leave in the middle of the night, to carry the little girl back to her mother's, but then, after the way Ford had responded to their missing most of Christmas Eve with him, she wasn't sure what he would do. "You'll have a lot more there," she said to Sam

"Did Santa bring me a stocking?" Samantha asked.

"Sure, he did," said Diana, "but it's at Grandma's. He can't bring you stockings to two different houses, you silly."

"Can we go now?" Samantha asked.

The smirk waned then, and Ford crouched down beside the little girl. Leaned over and kissed the top of her head. "Maybe Mummy can go pick them up for you after breakfast," Ford said. Diana shot him a look, but he didn't meet with her eyes.

"We all can go," Diana said, but Ford still didn't look at her.

After he finished making the French toast, he set Samantha down with a plate in the dining area off the kitchen, orange carpet, and a dusty seventies chandelier hanging low above the table. He covered the toast with syrup and powdered sugar, and then asked Diana to come into the bedroom so he could tell her what he needed to tell her.

He sat on the edge of the bed, sipping some tomato juice. Diana wondered if there was vodka in it. He patted the bed for her to come sit beside him.

"I think I'm getting my period, " she said.

"No. It's not that." He reached over and put his hand over hers. Diana could hear the Barney song starting up in the living room. "*I love you . . . You know it's true . . .*" Samantha loved Barney, and Ford had even gone out and bought several of the video tapes so she could watch while she was visiting. "I need to talk to you about Samantha," he said.

Diana's senses suddenly jumped to alert. "What about her?"

"I didn't want to ruin Christmas, and that's why I was waiting to tell you. But I'm not sure you should take her to your mother's today."

"Well, why not?" Diana asked. "I understand if you don't want to go. My mother was rude to you last month, and after what happened the other night with Stephen, I don't blame you. But she's Samantha's grandmother, and it's Christmas."

"It's not because of your mother." He took a breath. "It's because of Stephen."

"What about him?"

Ford sighed. "Well, Samantha was in the bedroom."

"And?"

"She saw him."

"Saw him?"

"Yeah. She saw him."

"Saw him what, Ford? Stop being so evasive. Just tell me." Diana felt something dropping inside her. Something dropping and something rising. A sickness meeting in the middle and brewing in her abdomen. A tightness in her throat. She knew what was coming—the realization came like a blow across the head—and she didn't want to hear it. She wasn't sure she could. Ford was sitting there with the worst of all possible responses waiting on his lips, waiting for her to ask. And she didn't want to ask. Didn't want to know. But she was Samantha's mother. Her caretaker and guardian. She had to know. "What?" she said at last. "What did she see, Ford?"

Ford sighed again. Then he looked her in the eye, put his hand on her knee. "He was masturbating, Diana. He was in the room alone with her, he was watching her sleeping, and he was masturbating."

The story that followed left her speechless. Ford explaining how Stephen was struggling to pull up his pants just before Ford started swinging. And that was when they stumbled out into the hall. He didn't want to tell her right off, didn't want to ruin Christmas, he said again, but it was eating at him, and he couldn't hold it back anymore. Diana was silent. Her thoughts racing, and her head, her body, feeling empty all at once. It couldn't be true. But why would Ford say it if it wasn't true? She wasn't sure whether to call the police, or just head over to her mother's house herself. Put Stephen on the spot. Demand an explanation. An answer. And hopefully, she prayed, a denial. A sincere denial. But Ford just brushed that off. Of course he would deny it, he said. How could he not? You couldn't go by that.

"And Diana," he said, "I saw him."

When the wave of nausea started to subside, Diana's body began to shake, and then she had started to cry. Ford pulled his chair close to hers, and took her into his arms, rubbing her back. It happened a lot more than she knew, he said. It was happening everywhere. An epidemic. Schools, day cares. Boy Scout meetings. Churches. Homes, he added. But it could have been worse. They were lucky he got in there when he did. Who knows what would have happened, he said, if he hadn't got into the bedroom when he did.

It was irrelevant, she told him. Samantha was her child, and she had failed to protect her. That was her main function in the little girl's life, to protect her, and she had failed. Failed in the most horrible way.

She should have never invited him over, she said. She should have known. Stephen was sick. He only went out to get high, and then he was home. Sometimes flying. Sometimes withdrawing. Always crazy. And her mother didn't see it. Her mother didn't see anything that she didn't want to. The neighbors had been complaining about Stephen since he was small, she told Ford. Awful things. They tried to confront Charlotte but got nowhere. There were the run of the mill complaints—broken windows, eggings on Halloween. Bikes stolen from the yard. But then it got worse. They told her he was torturing their pets. Cats and dogs. Doing things to them. Obscene things.

"I know." Ford sighed. "You told me."

But Diana kept rambling. She had to let it out. The only way to make the nightmare even a little better, to try and understand it, was to let it out. She had gone to her mother in the past, she told him, but she wouldn't listen. It was always the same response. "Boys will be boys." Diana wasn't a boy, so she didn't understand, Charlotte said. "They all get like that," her mother said. "Hormones," she said, shaking her head.

Hormones, Diana remembered thinking. Stephen then had been twelve years old back then. Drugs had yet to even enter the picture. She had gone to her father, who finally convinced Charlotte to take him to a counselor, a psychiatrist. And then after three supposed visits, Charlotte had brought him back to the house and said the psychiatrist declared him cured. What was more, she said, the psychiatrist didn't think there was really anything wrong with him to begin with. He was just experimenting, Charlotte said.

And now apparently he was trying to take the experiment to Diana's little girl. She needed to bring it to Charlotte, to hear it for herself, but not now, not as upset as she was. If Samantha saw her upset like this it would just make it worse for her. Just make her even more frightened. And ruin her Christmas.

"Are you sure?" she asked Ford, trying to compose herself. "I mean, I know you said you saw him, but are you sure that's what he was doing? Because if I'm going to confront my mother about this, you need to be sure because it's going to start World War Three."

"Do you think I would have upset you like this if I wasn't sure?" he said. "I love you too much, Diana. I love Samantha too much, and believe me, I know about these things. You can even ask Samantha, see what she says? Just ask her what she saw. How's that expression go—From the mouths of babes?"

❧

Diana didn't want to confront Charlotte. She knew Charlotte too well, and confronting her wouldn't change anything, wouldn't make it any more real, not for Charlotte. But she had to confront Charlotte even with full knowledge that it would just tatter the little that remained of their relationship, the little that remained since she got pregnant with Sam. She stopped at Saint Rocco's to say a prayer for guidance the day after Christmas. She was on her way over to talk with her parents. The church where she was baptized, made her First Communion, was confirmed. The church where she met with the old priest to confess to fornicating, to confess to her pregnancy.

Her pregnancy. The memory of it all probably scorched her more than any of the others, up until now. Diana had been saving for college for three years—she had been accepted into the nursing program at St. Elizabeth's, been assigned a dorm— and then a month out of high school she was pregnant. She hadn't wanted to tell her mother, but she hadn't much choice. She had missed her period, and gone to see the family's pediatrician, family insurance card in hand, and it wasn't until after her parents received the insurance bill that she had to come clean. It was late August then. Diana had just finished vomiting one morning and had begun packing her things for school, when her mother walked in, and held up the statement. Eyes empty. Empty wasn't good. Empty meant crazy and crazy meant rage. Her mother asked what it was about, and Diana didn't bother trying to lie.

Her mother sighed.

"Well," she said at last, "I guess we'll just have to work through this."

Diana's thoughts, feelings, all came to a sudden halt; she couldn't believe what was happening. Her mother was still looking at the insurance statement, calm and composed. "We'll just have to work through this," she said again, and this time she looked up herself, the emptiness gone, and Diana felt herself beginning to cry.

"Do you mean that?" she asked.

Charlotte looked perplexed. "Of course I do. I'm not happy about it, but you're our daughter, and I love you. And it's at times like this that families need to stick together."

Diana had gone to her then, sobbing, and her mother had held her. She hadn't held her in years, and for the first time in years, Diana felt safe.

And it wasn't until later the next day that her mother called the family meeting.

Diana, her parents, her grandmother, Phillip and his room-mate Barry, and her other five siblings, were all at the table. The table was made from sawhorses her brother Eddie had stolen from a construction site. A long piece of plywood, and a red checkered cloth. Diana's father had nailed the plywood into the sawhorses and sometimes if you pressed your hands too hard against the cloth you would end up with a splinter. Diana had been given a seat at the head of the table, directly across from her father, and her mother right beside her, holding her hand.

Charlotte stood and banged her spoon against her water glass as if about to give a toast. "Can I have your attention? Attention please."

Everyone was talking at once. Everybody was always talking at once, loud and never listening. Diana figured they were all expecting food. Anytime they all got together there always was food.

"Attention," Charlotte said again. "This family meeting is being called to order." There were mumblings, last words, and a bunched-up napkin thrown across the table. Diana's younger sister Bibi, eleven, had something red and sticky smeared across her face. Diana's grandmother was leaning forward on her cane.

"I know we usually conduct the family meeting on the first Friday of every month, after attending the adoration of the Sacrament," Charlotte said. Diana looked up at her, antennae rising; her mother was in her element—lying. Diana couldn't remember the last time they had a family meeting, nor when all of them had attended the adoration. "And you're all probably wondering why we're having this special one on Sunday, and the reason is because we have some special news. And I want to make the announcement official." Diana watched her carefully. She was both smiling, and struggling not to smile—no one else could hold their mouth so tight in the line between the two. Things were suddenly going very wrong; she could feel it. Her mother had acted as if she had taken it well, but Diana should have known better—there was no way she was going to take it well. Her mother took nothing well. Diana's heart began to race, and she wrenched her hands together under the table. Why had she told her?

"By now some of you know," Charlotte said, "—although some of you little ones might be too young to understand—that your sister, my daughter, and your granddaughter," she said, looking at her mother, "is a slut."

Diana went to speak. Couldn't. But the shock lasted less than a few seconds, and then she felt the cords of her neck beginning to tighten, and she was afraid she might start to scream. She stood to leave the room, but her mother stood with her, hand tight on her shoulder, and pushed her back down. Her mother was much bigger, stronger. Two of the boys started to snicker and Diana's grandmother's hand shot out and belted one across the back of the head.

"Now, sluts happen to a lot of families," Charlotte continued, "and not just ours. As long as there is repentance, then there is forgiveness, but when you lead a life of lust, when you stray from the Lord and behave like a whore, there are consequences. There has to be consequences, and that is what your sister is about to learn."

Diana heard the click of a lighter, smelled a whiff of smoke. Her grandmother was staring her down. Paper-thin skin, and watery blue eyes with bloodred lids. She was only in her mid-sixties, but hadn't moved far from her own dining room table, two blocks over, in fifteen years. Most days she sat and smoked, did crossword puzzles, and said the rosary. She was much too unwell to travel far, she said, and it wouldn't be long before she would be seeing her savior.

"What got into you?" The old woman dragged on her cigarette. Despite not lending much credence to her grandmother's ailments, Diana had always gotten on well with her. She would clean her house, and wash her dishes. Massage her back and sometimes her feet, listening to the old woman moan with delight as she did. "I'm talking to you," she said now.

Diana just looked down. She didn't want to answer to her. To any of them.

"The good Lord gives you looks and brains and a cute little figure, and what do you do with them? You throw them back in his face. And in the face of your poor mother. And for what? A quick little slap and tickle. And where has it gotten you? A baby. And you not even yet married. You ought to be ashamed."

"We're going to have a baby?!" spouted Bibi. Big dark eyes and hair in a ponytail. "What kind of baby? A boy or girl?! I have to tell Melissa!"

"We're not telling anybody," Charlotte said. "Not yet. And this is nothing to be proud of, Bibi, nothing to celebrate. What your sister has done is a very bad thing. She's thumbed her nose at our Lord and Savior."

"Thumbed her nose and pulled down her pants," said Diana's grandmother. "It's really very sad, if you ask me. Very, very sad. You had the whole world ahead of you—full of noble ideas about college—and now what do you have? Nothing. Ashamed. I'm telling you—you should be ashamed."

Diana had looked up then. "I'm still going to college," she said.

All eyes, all around the table were on her. And all except the children, seemed to know something. Something she did not.

Charlotte had just looked at her. "No, dear. I'm afraid you're not."

And she hadn't, not at St. Elizabeth's. But she had done it on her own, despite her mother. It took a little longer, but she had gone part-time, pushed herself through, commuting to the community college in Quincy. And earned her RN. Despite her mother.

Now, Diana looked toward the altar, the lights down except for a few dim electric candles up near the altar. The wreaths illuminated, along with the poinsettias. Christ nailed to cross, bleeding, his eyes turned to the heavens. The Blessed Mother, head bowed in prayer in an illuminated alcove off to the right. Saint Rocco himself, the patron saint of the sick, down on one knee and off to the right, a small white dog beside him. And high above it all, the Angel Gabriel, sounding the trumpet, heralding the Annunciation. And later the judgement.

⌒

"I don't believe it," Charlotte said. "He has a girlfriend. He always has a girlfriend." Diana was with her in the kitchen. Roger was in the living room watching a football game, and her sister Lucy was upstairs playing, but the other kids had gone out. Diana had avoided Christmas dinner, dessert. Called and told her mother that she needed to talk, but didn't want to ruin the holiday. It was all she could do to keep her composure over the phone.

Phillip was with her now. Diana had gone upstairs at the apartment to see Phillip, asked him, pleaded with him to come.

Phillip was the golden child. Tall and handsome. Tall and broad-chested, small blue eyes and hair parted neatly to the side, looking as if he had just graduated from a prep academy. Could do no wrong in Charlotte's eyes. And Diana thought, hoped, that if there was to be any chance her mother would listen to her, she needed Phillip on her side.

His jaw had dropped when she told him. He had volunteered to go first alone, but Diana had thought better of it. She loved Phillip, but deep down inside, she knew he didn't have much of a spine, and if she wasn't there he could just as easily slip onto Charlotte's side, away from Diana. Despite the fact that he was her older brother, throughout their childhood Diana had spent her time sticking up for Phillip, taking on the neighborhood bullies, much as she had for Freddie. Clocking them with round-houses, and then rolling down the hill of the sidewalk, or off somewhere in the dirt. Phillip would usually run for the house— sometimes bloody but at other times just sweaty and trembling, always crying—as soon as she started in, and Diana preferred it that way; someone had to stick up for him, but she figured it was demeaning for him to have to sit and watch when that someone was his little sister. There was always someone teasing him, calling him a blubber ball or a gaybo, and Phillip never forgot how she had looked out for him. Now he said he was more than happy to go to bat for her, for Samantha.

Diana stared at the lights strung along the perimeter of the picture window in the kitchen. White lights, starting to blink. The entire house was decorated—holly, and mistletoe, and Saint Nicholas's likeness from nearly every culture on every table, available space—making what she had to say seem all the more obscene.

Phillip stood, nervous, drinking, and her father sat at the head of the table. Staring at her. He hadn't said a word. It wasn't unusual for her father to be quiet, but when he was loud, he was the loudest in the house. "We have the same tempers," he used to tell Diana when she was small, rubbing her head. "Poor kid," he'd say. But he wasn't yelling now, nor did he look as if he were going to. He just looked confused. His relationship with Stephen had always been strained. He could never understand the drugs. The craziness. The lack of ambition. Diana's mother, of course, was different.

"I don't think Stephen even recognizes her," Charlotte said now, "I don't think he even knows she exists."

Diana's father shot her a look, cleared his throat. "He was just playing with her in the living room a few weeks ago."

"And I was right there with them!" Charlotte snapped. Diana's father opened his mouth, looking only further confused, but no words came through.

"But the thing is, Ma," Phillip said, "if he's using, it's not good for him to be around little kids." He dropped his voice to his best baritone. "It's just *too* dangerous."

"He's not using anymore," Charlotte said. "He's been clean for . . . six months. I take him every week to have his blood tested."

Diana's insides were turning again. She would have rather heard her mother say that she wasn't with Samantha constantly for at least then she would have known she wasn't up against the complete wall of a lie. And if her mother was sure he was completely innocent, there would be no need for the wall. No need to pretend Stephen was clean. Would there? But if somewhere inside, she herself wasn't sure . . .

"You need to get him to see someone," Diana said. "Or I'm going to kill him, Ma. I swear, I'll kill him."

"You," Charlotte said, "will do no such thing."

"Just an evaluation," Phillip said. "That's all we're asking."

"No," Diana said. "He needs help. He needs to see someone."

Charlotte's face flushed. "Oh, he's seen plenty of people. He's been seeing specialists since he was small—every time someone complained about something—and you know what they all say? They all say he's completely—"

"I don't want to hear it." Diana started to cry then. "If he did this, you can't protect him."

"I have to protect him," Charlotte said. "He is my child."

"And Samantha is your grandchild."

Charlotte just stared.

"She's your grandchild," Diana said again. "And she still *is* a child. Stephen is not."

"He's eighteen years old," Charlotte said. "And he is my child."

"Nineteen," said Diana. "And he has serious problems."

Charlotte put her hands on the table, making to stand. "We're just going to have to finish this conversation another time. I'm not going to sit here and listen to the two of you yell at me."

Diana looked at her father again, her eyes pleading. He covered for her mother constantly, whenever she lied, but he couldn't now. He couldn't possibly now. It was too much. Too far.

"Charlotte, you should at least talk to him," he said. "See what he says. If he did do this, he's going to need help."

"If he did do this, so what?" Charlotte said at last. "All boys do it. It's a stage they go through. Experimenting. The rest of your brothers all did it, all the time" she said to Diana. "And your uncles."

"Not in front of people!" Diana said. "Not in front of little kids!"

"Yes, they did," said Charlotte.

Diana reared back. "Who?"

"You," said Charlotte. "And your little sister. You were all in therapy for it. You just don't remember."

Phillip was standing with his mouth hanging open. "What . . . are . . . you . . . talking . . . about?"

Diana shook her head. "That never happened, Ma."

Charlotte's jaw dropped open. "You just don't remember. That's the problem with you. You remember things that never happened, and you don't remember things that did." She looked at Phillip. "And now you have this one covering for you."

"I've never done anything like that, Ma," Phillip said. "That's not fair."

"You just don't remember," Charlotte said. "The therapist hypnotized you. He thought it would be for the best. Everyone hypnotized, no one remembers, no one is hurt. No harm done."

Diana was sobbing now, wanting to run, afraid to move. She wondered if her mother had given Stephen a heads-up, told him to get out of the house for a while. Diana had hinted at what was coming on the phone, but not told her the whole thing. But her mother was intuitive when she wanted to be.

Her father took another breath. "You at least need to talk to him."

Charlotte cut him with her eyes. "I've talked to him plenty of times. He tells me everything."

"Not everything," said Diana.

"He tells me enough." Charlotte stood. Her eyes had switched again, even a bit emptier than they had been before, and Diana suddenly realized there would be no getting through. Nobody was home now. Charlotte was gone. "And I'm not going to stand here and listen to this in my own house. And I'm not going to have this asshole you're shacking up with coming around and accusing my children of awful things."

"He was trying to help," said Diana.

"My ass," said Charlotte. "He's filling her head with lies."

Diana shook her head. "No. He's not."

"He is not welcome here, Diana."

"We're going to be married," Diana said, and even as she did, she wondered if it were really true.

Charlotte was silent a moment. "Then you need to choose," she said at last.

"What?" Diana said.

"You need to choose, Diana. Him or me. Us," she said looking at Diana's father.

"Don't make me," Diana said.

Charlotte shook her head. "I'm not making you do anything, dear."

"Then I can't stay here," Diana said.

Charlotte hesitated. "You do what you have to do, dear. I'll pray for you."

She walked out of the room then, and Diana's father stared down at his hands, flat out on the table. Phillip had his head down. Diana glanced at the cuckoo clock on the wall. The bird hadn't come out since she was small, and now she wondered if it had ever worked, or she just thought she remembered it working. Her mother had hung a garland of pine around the clock, and above it a picture of the Baby Jesus. Floating in the air and swaddled in a diaper. Palms open to the sky. The angels forming the words in the sky above him. *Joy to the World.*

6

Ford had caught the ferry out of Woods Hole. It wasn't any trouble getting his car over this time of year, and the boat was almost empty. The old lady had been ninety-five years old. Imagine that, he thought. Even he didn't know she was that old. Sections of the harbor were still frozen, and he saw an ice cutter in the distance when he stepped outside on the top deck. The cold didn't bother him much, not even out here with the wind and the sea. Ford reached inside coat and took out his flask.

He wondered if any of his siblings would be here—the old lady wasn't subtle when it came to her feelings about Big Daddy, so he doubted he would see his mother and father—but he was too late for the church, and when he got to the cemetery behind the old house, he recognized no one. And there weren't many to recognize. Just a few old codgers in heavy coats and hats, more than likely distant cousins he had never met or friends from another time. Diana had wanted to come with him, but he had said no. He had been nice about it. This was something he had to do alone. He had spent most of his time with the old lady alone, so it was only fitting, he say goodbye to her alone.

The barren tree limbs were still lined with snow from the week before, as were the headstones, the tombs. The minister was small and round with thick glasses and his face red in the cold, and his voice boomed in the thin winter air. His aunt's name had already been chiseled beneath that of her husband's, Edward, but just the beginning date, not the end. Not yet. *Dorothy Evelyn Barlow,*

November 23, 1898–. They had draped the ground around the casket with artificial green carpet, and Ford was a little surprised when he saw the backhoe waiting in the distance, engine quietly rumbling. He wouldn't have thought they could break the earth this time of year, but then again he supposed that was a thing of the past. Storing bodies in the squat stone building in the corner of the graveyard to wait out the winter. The newly dead whispering back and forth to one another throughout the cold dark nights.

Whispering.

Ford looked over the headstones at the house in the distance, and even though he knew it was now empty, he couldn't help feeling there was someone in there watching them, watching this. *One more added to the ranks.* The thought was crazy. Stupid. There was no one in there, and other than the occasional visitor, there had been no one except the old lady for the past sixty years. All the more reason to give it a quick walk through after this was over.

Ford tried to pray, but it felt false, phony. He couldn't believe there was anyone listening. Couldn't believe there was anyone out there anywhere.

The minister said his final words, and as he did, his face to the sky, it started to snow. Ford waited until the old people had cleared away, and once they did he walked over and placed a single rose on the casket. A rose like the rose of the wolf in the lattice. The house. His house. Now. It was going to be just what they needed.

7

The house had been in his family forever, he told Diana. He used to visit in the summer, and the old aunt had taken a liking to him, saying that he looked like her brother. Despite the work he had done for her though, he hadn't been expecting anything when she died, and so the house came as something of a shock. But it was a shock they needed, he said, since they couldn't yet afford a house on their own. And there was a hospital on the island, and Diana could eventually look into getting a job there. Ford himself had already requested a transfer to the post office in Vineyard Haven, and it looked as if it were going to go through.

"It will be for the best," he said. "That way it can be just the three of us. We don't need anybody else. And if we don't take her away from here, Diana, away from that environment, we would be as bad as he is. It would be criminal."

Criminal. Diana didn't mind moving, but the fact that it was an island made it seem all that more distant, and it unsettled her some to cut away from her family completely. She still hadn't spoken to her mother, but she would miss her father, she thought, her elderly aunt, and a few of her brothers and Ford's sister Cybil. But she rationalized that the ride to the ferry was only an hour or so down 495 and Route 28, and then another forty minutes or so on the water. It wasn't like moving to the other side of the world.

"It's not," Cybil had agreed. She had given Diana a gift certificate for a manicure and pedicure for her birthday, and the two of them sat side by side in the salon with two small sisters painting their toes. "We used to get down there in a about an hour and a half, including the ferry. I think it just feels that way because it is an island. I felt bad that I couldn't make the funeral service, but I couldn't get coverage for my shift."

Cybil was a nurse, too, and she had a fierce independent streak. She had put herself through college, and through grad school and had been supporting herself since she was eighteen. She and Diana had got close quickly shortly after she had met Ford, and she had attached herself to Samantha nearly immediately, always around to keep a watchful eye on things. She was a year older than Diana with auburn hair, breasts that still turned up, a thin waist and just enough hips. Picture-blue eyes and a small scar on her chin. She said she got the scar sledding as a child, but the more Diana learned about her family, the more she wondered. She had a slight sneer to her lip that might make a lip reader maybe think much of what she said was said with sarcasm, and sometimes it was.

"That's the thing," Diana said. "It's an island. I'm just worried that I don't know anybody. I mean, it's probably going to get lonely."

"Believe me," Cybil had said. "You get a house on the Vineyard, you're going to have people wanting to visit you all the time—more than you want to deal with. And besides, my boyfriend Norman's family has a house down in Hyannis. We're down there all the time in the summer, so we can just jump on the ferry and come over and visit as much as you want. We'll make sure you're not lonely. And with everything that has happened, with my family and your family, I think it will be the best thing for you to create a little distance. For both you and Ford." Cybil was quiet a moment. "I think you've been good for him," she said. "And I think he can be a good man if given the chance."

Diana smiled. "Can be?" she said.

Cybil had turned and looked into her eyes. "Yes," she said. "Can be."

8

1994

Saturday. Ford hadn't come home for lunch the night before—at least not that Diana had heard—and she was up before he got home for good. He passed her in the back parlor before heading upstairs but he hadn't said anything. Just threw his new chart book onto the stairs, and then kept moving. He always said it was a great thing about the night shift—if things were slow, he got to study his books. And on the island in the winter, everything was slow.

Diana took Samantha out to push on the swing Ford had hung from the oak in their backyard early last summer. The tree was enormous and beautiful, nearly perfectly shaped, with ancient initials and dates carved into the trunk some ten feet off the ground, the letters and numbers risen in the bark and healed over like scars. Diana loved the tree, perfectly placed between the house and the cemetery, and Samantha would stay on the swing for an hour at a time if she let her. Now she was talking about the dolls again, the china dolls. Diana's heart sinking a little more as she recited the name she had given each—Claudia, Sabrina, Ariel, Jewel, Cinderella, and Diana, named after her Mummy, she said. Diana knew nothing good would come of the dolls, the more she played with them, the more it would give Ford something to complain, rant, about—but the little girl loved the dolls, and keeping her away from them just seemed cruel. When she started to get loud, squealing as she swung higher, Diana gazed up at the house, and then she took Samantha to the cemetery to run about. Preserving the quiet.

The cemetery was flat and open and it made it easy to keep an eye on her. Samantha had been an early reader, and she would often read the names of the graves, ask Diana questions, and sometimes make up stories about the people beneath. Now she ran ahead of Diana, and vaulted the iron pipe fence, broken and sagging, that separated their yard from the graves.

There was a wind today, shaking what little remained of the leaves in the trees, blowing the little girl's hair across her face, and Diana hugged her arms tight about herself to ward off the chill. The grass was brown and dead, and even the potted flowers left among the headstones had frozen and wilted. The cemetery stretched far into the distance, and was spotted with oak trees. Diana heard a tree limb creaking above her, and when she turned back to the house she thought she saw a shadow pass in the rear window, overlooking the outdoor shower. Samantha's room. There for a moment, and then it was gone. Ford, she thought, but Ford usually didn't get up once he was down to sleep for the day, not this early. It was more likely her mind playing tricks on her. Samantha called out to her and Diana turned back to the cemetery.

Samantha peeked around the tomb of Captain Isaiah Hawes Norton.

"How it the captain today?" Diana asked.

"He says you're very pretty, Mummy."

"He does?" said Diana. "Well, tell the captain I said thank you."

"Okay." Sam looked off into the distance for a moment, then looked at Diana and smiled. "I told him. But, he's in a bad mood, Mummy."

"He is?" said Diana. "Why is that?"

"Because," she said. "He's mad at Mr. Fallon."

"And who pray tell is Mr. Fallon?" Diana asked.

"He's a varmint. A filthy little pig."

"Oh, my goodness." Diana laughed a little. "What did he do?"

"Well, he's the recruiter."

"The recruiter.?"

"It's his job to get men for the ship and negotiate their pay. They are supposed to sail this Tuesday, but they're still short seven men."

Diana hesitated. She opened her mouth to speak, looking at the little girl, trying to read her eyes. Negotiate? Recruiter? Sam was precocious, but as much as she liked to make up stories, they were stories that usually involved fairies and leprechauns, elves, and small animals. Sometimes princesses. Maybe Ford had said something to her. Talk about whaling ships? It was possible, but if Ford talked to her at all these days, it was usually to scold her for something, explaining why what she did was wrong.

"Well, I think the captain's sailing days are probably long behind him," Diana said at last.

Sam looked at the tombstone again, silent, and then turned back to Diana.

She smiled. "He can never leave the sea, Mummy."

Sam reached out and pressed her open palm against the tomb, and then she turned and scurried away. Probably hoping Diana would chase her. And maybe she would, maybe in a minute, but right now she was thinking. The little girl had friends in her preschool, but she wondered if she was lonely. Making up friends, carrying on conversations. Or maybe it was anxiety. Listening to Diana and Ford argue, listening to Ford lose his temper. That could do it, she had read about it. This was the first time she had pretended she was actually talking to someone in the cemetery, but it was becoming more and more frequent in the house. The house. She would often clam up when she was talking to her imaginary friend and Diana walked in, but lately she seemed less guarded about it, more comfortable, and sometimes when Diana did walk in, even she herself couldn't help feeling something. Eyes on her. Someone watching.

Something.

And it had been just a few days before that Sam had found the journal.

Diana had been down the cellar doing laundry and cleaning up a bit, and Sam had been investigating some of the boxes on the shelves—antique small appliances, faded statues, knick-knacks, and postcards. She had even found an old pamphlet from the mid-nineteenth century Methodist camp meetings at Trinity Park. Yellow with time and torn at the binding. Drawings inside of people in Victorian garb—women with wide dresses cinched tight and hats with feathers and men in shirt vests or suits. There were also several dusty old books, all hardcover, ancient and faded and coming apart at the seams: *The Second Great Awakening*, *The Book of Offices*, *A Pictorial History of the Island of Martha's Vineyard*, and *Reverend Dr. Thomas Coke—A Life in Worship*. *The Night Side of Nature, or Ghosts and Ghost-Seers*, by Catherine Crowe, and three by a man named Paschal Beverly Randolph: *The Grand Secret*, *Seership! The Magnetic Mirror*, and *Love and the Master Passion*. But it had been in an ancient nineteenth-century atlas, the binding broken and middle pages cut out to hide a treasure, that she had found the journal.

Samantha had pulled it out and flipped through the pages. "This one isn't a real book."

Diana put down her broom, and tussled the little girl's hair. "No?"

"No," she said. "Somebody wrote the words in it. There's a couple of pictures though, there aren't many pictures in the others."

Diana lifted the journal from Samantha's lap. Hardened brown leather, the pages browned, and the smell immediately musty and old. Diana flipped quickly through it. Along with the written entries, it also contained sketches. Drawings of the island. The house here, or what looked to be their house, minus the trees, half of the front porch. Houses in the Trinity Park, and an enormous hotel by the water, and people strolling along the peer. And glued to the inside cover was a photograph. A woman in a long, dark dress, and her hair parted tight in the middle and pulled up in a bun in back. Hands folded in her lap. A high white collar. She was a pretty woman with the same lost eyes as the woman in the wedding picture above the work-bench. Had to be the same woman, except here she was a little older, maybe thirty.

The name was written in longhand on the first page. *Elizabeth Veronica Steebe*. And then the year, *1871*.

Sam looked at the picture and smiled. "Cassie," she said.

Cassie.

Diana had asked who Cassie was, but Sam had gone quiet for a minute, staring at the well, and then told Diana she didn't want to talk about it anymore.

Now, ahead of her, she ran down the main road of the cemetery, her footsteps loud in the quiet. Everything had been so quiet the past month or so that it was hard to believe it was the same island as it was in the summer. Samantha looked back, eyes playful, and then she turned and dashed off to the left. Diana followed her with her eyes as long as she could, but the cemetery sloped slightly down and her view was blocked by a tree.

She called out to her, but Samantha didn't come back. Diana picked up her pace, but she hadn't hit the point of worry. Samantha played this game often with her, and this time of year, the cemetery was mostly empty except for the occasional groundskeeper. But something felt different about today, and she wasn't sure what. She called out her name again, and then she broke into a jog, the cold air biting her hands, already chapped. She made it past the tree, and could see clearly down the slope, but Samantha was still nowhere in sight. Diana called her name out, louder, and now broke into a full run, her thoughts spinning. Panic setting in. Foolish to be daydreaming, foolish to let her out of her sight. Even for a second. That's all it took—one second—isn't that what they were always saying? One second, then gone. A hand from the bushes, a car on the side of the road. She raced between the graves, still calling out to her and now almost crying, and she had almost reached the far side of the cemetery, when she heard giggling from behind her. She spun around. Samantha was sitting there, not twenty feet away, her knees up, and her back to a large headstone, rounded on the top. Diana felt the relief flood through her body.

"I scared you, Mummy," she said.

Diana struggled to catch her breath. She started toward her. Wanting to hug her, but also wanting to spank her. Threaten her life.

"Don't," she said, "Ever. Do that again. I call out to you? You answer me. You understand me?!" she shouted. The little girl nodded, eyes wide. And then her lips trembled and she started to cry. Diana got down on her knees, the earth frozen beneath her, and pulled her close. "I love you too much," she said.

Samantha wiped her nose on Diana's coat, and Diana hugged her tighter.

"It's okay," Diana said. "Okay." She stroked the back of the little girl's head. She looked at the headstone behind Sam, and was taken aback a moment. Dorothy and Edward Barlow. The old aunt, and her husband, dead almost sixty years before her. Diana had never visited the grave with the girl before—she knew it was out here, but not exactly where—and she wondered if Ford had. She looked up then and she realized they weren't alone. There was a man in the distance, standing in the middle of the cemetery, in between them and the house. Dark coat, hemmed in at the ribs, white shirt and black tie. From the distance he looked to have a beard, or at least some sort of whiskers, and it looked like he was holding a pocket watch in his hand, the chain clipped to his vest. But he wasn't looking at the watch, he was looking at Samantha and Diana. He almost looked like something out of an old cartoon, a carpetbagger or traveling snake oil salesman. She must have passed him while she was running, but she couldn't have passed him without seeing him. Could she? She had been looking all about her, and it would have taken him several minutes to get to where he was standing. But she must have passed him. And he *was* watching them. She didn't like him watching them. Diana lowered her chin, and kissed Samantha's head—the girl getting her sobs under control—and when Diana looked up again the man was gone.

9

The Journal of Elizabeth Veronica Steebe

June 16, 1871

Sin City. Or so Hiram and the others have dubbed it. The company broke ground on a new building. They call themselves The Oak Bluffs Land and Wharf Company, and four of the owners are islanders, none of the them strangers to Trinity Park here—Captain Grafton Norton Collins, William Bradley, Captain Ira Darrow, and, of course, Captain Shubael Lyman Norton. Mr. William S. Hills is from Boston, and the "Honorable" Erastus P. Carpenter is from Foxborough. Their fortunes dwindling with the sorrowful plight of the whaling industry, these men, no longer able to harvest the seas, apparently see fit to harvest our community. They have already erected several buildings, more than one questionable in nature, in and around Cottage City, and now they are building an enormous hotel down near Ocean Park, overlooking the water—the Sea View they plan on calling it—and Hiram reached out to the people during the camp meeting in an emotional appeal for soul searching, imploring upon everyone to band together and take a stand against it. It was bad enough that one house of ill repute after another was going up so close to Trinity Park, but now they were building them, breaking ground, here on a Sunday, scraping the filth from their shoes upon the day of the Lord.

Hiram had fire in his eyes as he spoke. His anger, frustration, has been rising for years now, but to be honest there doesn't seem much hope of turning things around. There were a few halle-lujahs and Mrs. James Cowley fainted in her chair in a state of heightened ecstasy, but the majority of our brethren appear given in, believing we need to learn to live with the new people. But Hiram will not count himself as one of them. "The Lord called us to this island, this woods, this 'Place of Great Trees,' overlooking Nantucket Sound," he said, "to make this place holy and to keep it so, and to share our love and conviction, proudly and openly, among one another. And not," he said, "to allow these imposters, these men who had once called themselves our brothers, to waltz over our faith and to create a Sin City. It has been that way ever since the first circuit rider, the Reverend Jesse Lee, pulled ashore to the island, to preach the ministry of John Wesley himself. Since Reformation John Adams organized his sparsely attended camp meeting high on West Chop. And," Hiram added, "since the venerable Reverend Pease held our first camp meeting here among the towering oaks. And now," Hiram said, "the burden is upon us to honor and protect their vision. And to see it through 'til judgment."

The people listened attentively, but all the while we could hear the hammers, the noise causing Hiram to shout all the louder, his voice carrying and shaking through the trees, tents, and cottages. The buildings on Circuit Avenue have all sprung up quicker—it seems as if there is a new one every day—than any of us ever could have ever imagined, and the company has already built its own church—an interdenominational building—they have dubbed "The Union Chapel" but Hiram says it is a ruse, a ploy from the Devil to pry the good from the hands of God. The Sea View Hotel is being built to serve as his domain, to house the transitory faithless all under one roof. "They will come from far and wide," Hiram says, "to partake in the debauchery that is now becoming Circuit Avenue—the once honorable Circuit Avenue—and the Devil will be pleased. Already the tavern down on Lake Avenue is being worked by women who have fallen from Christ," he says, "lifting their petticoats for any man with a coin."

I have seen these women, sitting precariously on the rail of the balcony high above the tavern, on the evenings when Hiram and I have taken a walk to the water's edge, "bluffing" as it is known, on our moonlight stroll to view the moon and the sea, and the picturesque Lover's Rock as it swallowed by the tide. These women always smile and wave, and always seem quite friendly, but Hiram has insisted we not acknowledge them at all. For just one look, just one connection with the eyes, can be the downfall of any man. "The Devil's powers are strong," he says. And despite the ten p.m. curfew here in Trinity Park, the fence gate closing at ten, Hiram likes to walk to the water later at night sometimes, too, after the builders are gone, to monitor the progress the sinners have made. He says nothing would please him more to stroll down there one evening and find the entire thing engulfed in flames. Burning to the ground. A modern day Gomorrah, he calls it, and he says he is beginning to wonder if God is now setting the final stage, the final stage for the final battle. Armageddon, he whispers.

July 2, 1871

Hiram had an altercation with a man on the wharf late this morning, the architect of the hotel. A Mr. Samuel Freedman Pratt, a fellow Bostonian. The island is now much more crowded than it has been in months, throngs of people arriving on the ferry boats, some for the services, others for the upcoming holiday and the recreation land that is springing up all around us. Hiram was not well when he woke—I could tell by his eyes— and he refused any breakfast, informing me that he was fasting. He prayed for an hour before collapsing to the floor, so full of the spirit that he was apparently unable to speak or to move , and then when he finally rose, he told me he had some business in town. He told me he wished me to remain inside the cottage today, and wash all the linen, and then he spent a good five minutes gazing in the mirror, at first not moving again, not at all, just staring—an empty gaze—and then adjusting his tie and his hat before heading out the door toward Circuit Avenue.

He had me quite anxious, watching from the window, so once he had begun to round the circle, close to exiting the campground, I grabbed my umbrella and decided to follow. Hiram says he likes to think while he walks, to commune with the Lord, and despite his impressive height, he never moves very quickly. He walks with a limp, his leg lame from the war, and always looking straight ahead, and the people clear a path for him as he makes his way. He is a commanding figure and the people that know him know better than to interrupt him while he is walking in communion with the Lord, but there were many people out and about today, the cottages all bustling—the camp dwellers fanning themselves and taking cool drinks on their porches and front lawns—and twice as I followed, I lost sight of him.

Everything is in bloom now, the flowers bright and matching the many colors of the cottages, and it is my favorite time of year. Nearly all of the camp dwellers come and go with the season, either back to Edgartown or back to the mainland, but Hiram and I recently winterized our cottage, selling his family home on South Water Street in Edgartown, and now plan to stay here year round. It is our business to stay, he has told me, to remain through the darkest days of winter to watch over things and keep this place sacred, shrouding ourselves in pleasing grief and mournful joy.

Hiram stopped inside the Arcade Bldg.—where the offices of Oak Bluffs Land and Wharf Company are located on the first floor—but after less than a minute, he was back out the door, and crossing Circuit Avenue. At that point, I was quite certain I knew where he was heading. The hotel by the sea.

Even from the distance, I was amazed to see the structure towering as high as it is, wooden beams and scaffolding climbing into the sky. It is a magnificent sight to behold from the distance, and I found my heart fluttering in awe, but Hiram has warned me not to be fooled. The Devil comes in many packages, he has said, some grand and some small, and nearly all initially enticing to behold. Enticing until you look closely, he says, to see his things for just what they are, to see them once stripped of their pomp and their grandeur, to see the bare workings of what would be their soul if indeed their soul were to exist. I see, he has told me, tapping his temples. The Lord has given me the gift of sight, and I see clearly through men, machines, structures and nature, to the essence of what exists within. Some may consider it a curse to carry such a burden, he says, but I consider it a blessing. The trust of God placed in my head, my eyes and my hands, to see through it all, and make it all right. Hiram has told me many times, and told the people at large, that he had his first vision late in the war while he was convalescing following the battle at Chancellorsville. He had been severely wounded, twice in the leg, and once in the chest, and he spiked a high fever while his wounds fought infection. The doctors later told him he came close to losing his leg—the beginning signs of gangrene—and more than likely would have lost his life, but Hiram says it was then that the Lord intervened. Here was Glory himself, magnificent red robes and bathed in white light, Hiram said. He stood at the foot of Hiram's bed, and raised his scepter high above him. He had a higher calling for Hiram to answer, the Lord said, than that of the war. His time would come, but it had not come yet, and with that he breathed a great wind down upon him, a wind that roared through Hiram's body, cleaning as it did, and within a day, his fever had broken, and within a week his feet were on the floor, the hand of God beckoning from the door of the old schoolhouse they were using for a hospital. A miracle, the doctor said, but Hiram said no. With the Lord there were no such things as miracles for with the Lord, anything was possible. It just was.

Hiram returned to the battlefield, but this time with no fear, and until the war's end never was he grazed by a bullet, nor touched by the shrapnel of a cannonball exploding, again. While others around him fell by the dozens, Hiram marched on from the final battle of Appomattox Courthouse, to his studies in Methodism off island at Boston University. And here he marched still, as I watched from behind, down the worn path that bisects Ocean Park, and on to the Sea View. God marching with him.

Hiram was no stranger to Mr. Pratt. He has been to see him several times at the company offices dating back to the day when the offices stood in the old storehouse building where now they construct the Sea View, and he has implored upon him for years, at first civilly, pragmatically, and later with the fire leaping from the tip of his tongue, the need to see the error of his ways, the evil he is bringing to Wesleyan Grove. Mr. Pratt does not see it, and constantly reverts to the Union Chapel to prove his case in point. An octagonal house of God, he says, with four doors, facing east, south, north, and west, welcoming everyone. And such is the problem, Hiram has reminded him, he welcomes everyone, both the good and the wicked.

In the distance, I could see the crowds passing along the plank walk that runs along the shore—men, women, and children, some stopping for refreshment at the pagoda building, taking a moment to escape the sun, others bustling about at Tivoli Dance and Recreation Hall, and others still continuing on along the beach in the direction of Old Edgartown, all looking happy, at peace—and I must admit that for a moment, I stopped, something feeling to drop deep inside me, wondering why it can't be so for myself and for Hiram. Why the search for the higher good cannot in itself, ever take a holiday. But never would I utter these thoughts to Hiram. For a holiday with the Devil will lead to torment for eternity. Of this, he says, we must be certain.

Hiram found Mr. Pratt near the water's edge, the head of the wharf, the framework of the structure rising high above them. Mr. Pratt was leaning over a table, presumably spread with the plans for the building, and he at first appeared to be paying Hiram no mind. Mr. Pratt is a man small in stature, and Hiram towered over him. Mr. Pratt was down to his vest, his tie gone, and his collar undone, his sleeves rolled to his elbow. His hat was pushed high at an angle as he studied his prints, and his eyeglasses had slipped to the end of his nose. I was near the pagoda building, mixing in among the crowd, and though I could hear Hiram's voice, steady at first and then beginning to tremble, gradually getting louder, I could not clearly decipher all of his words. A crowd had begun to gather about the men—workers and tourists and members of the campground—and yet Mr. Pratt still appeared to be paying Hiram no mind. If he spoke at all, and I believe he did not, I could not hear him, and his silence only appeared to be provoking Hiram all the more. Hiram slammed an open hand down upon the table, and though he was a distance away, his back turned to me, I could see his eyes, I knew the look that burned inside them—I have seen them like this enough times before, the rage consuming him completely, leaving him with nothing left inside. Mr. Pratt first turned his gaze to the hand, the fingers splayed upon the table, and only then did he look up and confront Hiram. What he said, I know not, but whatever it was, it set Hiram's words into actions, and he raised his hand as if to strike, shouting as he did, and now I could hear him quoting Scripture, Corinthians 11:13-15—"For such men are false apostles, deceitful workmen, disguising themselves as apostles of Christ. And no wonder, for even Satan disguises himself as an angel of light. So it is no surprise if his servants, also, disguise themselves as servants of righteousness. Their end will correspond to their deeds." He finished the verse and then he smote his open hand forward.

He did not get far. Mr. Pratt leapt backward, and Hiram, on his bad leg, lost his balance. Two of the workers lunged forward, coming between Hiram and the man, and one brought a clenched fist up from his side, striking Hiram in the abdomen, and when Hiram doubled over, this man hit him again, this time in the jaw. This man was as tall as Hiram, but well-muscled, and wide across the shoulders, quick in his movements, leaving Hiram not a second to respond, he hit him a third time in the side of the head. People were running about, and some of them were shouting, and Mr. Pratt had stepped in front of the worker, his hands on his shoulders, pressing him backward, and he, shouting, too. Hiram was now down on his knees, and soon disappeared behind the swarm of the crowd.

Mr. Pratt was still shouting at the man who had struck Hiram, and the man was looking down as if in shame, a dog to its master. It was necessary to push my way through to get to Hiram—two men from the camp were down on one knee beside him—one holding up fingers before Hiram's eyes and asking him to count. He looked in a daze, and his eyes looked unfocused, but the focus returned as soon as he saw me. The confusion was instantly replaced with fury. He got to his feet, unsteady at first, brushing the men from the camp aside, and brushing the dust from the sleeves of his jacket, he stepped forward and took hold of my arm, pulling me along as we pushed out of the crowd. "I told you to stay home," he told me.

It all happened very quickly, and though people with whom we were familiar called out regarding our well-being, Hiram paid them no mind. He was staring straight ahead but muttering words beneath his breath. Words directed at me. Disobedient. Insubordinate. Filthy.

He directed me to sit in the chair in our bedroom when we returned to our cottage, dolls on the chair and dolls by the windowsill, watching me. And then shutting curtains and the window that looked out upon the tabernacle, he removed his strap.

10

What happened in the cellar had probably been his own fault, Ford figured. But still, he didn't want to go down there anymore. Not unless he absolutely had to. It wasn't that he was scared, he didn't scare easy, and he had never been one to believe in any paranormal bullshit—not usually—but still, the house seemed different, had always seemed *different*, and the whole thing just left him a little unsettled, his nerves jumping all around. He had been drinking for a few days before it happened back last September, so that might have caused it, he figured. Touch of the DTs. And besides, old houses made noises, they settled. Moved in the earth.

Diana wasn't home when it happened, and he had the day off, so he had figured he would go down there and work on his telescope stand. It was going to be a thing of beauty. Sometimes he brought the scope out to the backyard, and sometimes he used it on their balcony—but Diana complained when he did that in the winter, the cold air following him every time he came in and out of the bedroom. He had been working on the stand on and off for a couple months, and he had just started sanding the sides—held tight in the vise on the workbench. He had been drinking that day, too, but he was only on his seventh or eighth beer when he heard it.

The whispering.

He had thought he had heard it a few times since they moved in, heard something, but it was never this clear. At first it was just one voice, a woman's, sounding as if it were calling from a long tunnel, distant and fading. He had spun around, but there was no one there. Other than the sound of water dripping in the well, the cellar was silent. But he knew he had heard something.

Maybe Diana. Maybe upstairs. She had come home, he figured, and was up there talking to Sam, and her voice was just traveling through the floor. Distorting it a bit. Had to be. She could be pretty loud. Ford went to the bottom of the stairs and called up to her, but there was no answer. He called out once more, and looked up, and then the door creaked open. Fucking with him, he thought. She must have been fucking with him, thinking she was funny, but he called out her name a third time and still there was nothing.

"You're a regular laugh riot," he had called up. Waited. Nothing. He went up the stairs, hesitated and listened. Nothing. A silence with a hum. And suddenly he knew he was wrong—the house was empty, he could feel it. He called up to the second floor, just in case, hoping for a second maybe he would hear Samantha giggle—a joke—he might be a little irritated, ha-ha very funny and all that, but at least it would explain it. But still no answer. He went to the cellar door, swung it back and forth a little—it moved easily enough, but he did need to oil it. That was the problem around here, he was expected to do everything.

Ford grabbed two more beers from the refrigerator and headed back down the cellar. This time leaving the door wide open. The draft would come up, but that was okay—at least he would hear them when they came home, it wouldn't take him by surprise. He didn't need any more surprises; he was feeling jittery enough as it was.

He went to the workbench and ran his hand across the surface of the stand. Blew away the dust. Perfectly smooth. Sometimes he thought he missed his calling, should have been a carpenter. Should have done something with his hands. Something skilled. He cracked a beer and took a long slip. Refreshing and cold.

And then the door slammed shut above him.

The sound echoed throughout the cellar, and then slowly faded. So there was a draft. He couldn't feel it, but there had to be a draft. That was all. Better to leave the door shut now because if it happened again, it was just going to unnerve him all the more, and he didn't need that. He had work to do, needed to get the project completed before the best skies arrived. Winter skies, thriving off the darkness that covered the earth for sixteen hours a day. And Jupiter would be visible after Halloween. You could see it nearly all night long in November. And the Orion constellation was beautiful that time of year, too. Ford sipped again—another beer or two would probably straighten it all out, settle his nerves. He picked up his sandpaper. And then he heard it again.

The hairs stood up on the back of his neck, and he was suddenly afraid to turn. The voices came from behind him, distant again, sounding as if they had traveled through a tunnel. Two voices now, a man and a woman, arguing—asking each other who he was, what he wanted, growing louder and louder, and then progressively receding. At first just the two, and then several others, joining in, all talking at once. Chaos. Separate conversations but all focused on him. They were there. He had heard them. Now he had no doubt. And they spoke as if they were observing him, seeing him while remaining unseen, and believing they were hearing him without being heard. Until he turned. And then the voice of the woman.

He knows, she said.

And another. *The little girl. He heard it from the girl.*

Ford crumpled the sandpaper in his hand, and hurried for the stairs.

Look at him, watch him.

Does he hear us?

Of course he hears us.

Should never have been here.

A long time ago.

But you'll never understand that. It wasn't, it just simply wasn't. Not his.

He's just like him.

No.

Yes.

He'll do it. He'll do it again.

And then someone screamed.

Ford turned and hurried up the stairs, dropping the sandpaper behind him. His hands were shaking. Heart racing. He took the key from his pocket. A skeleton key, as old as the house. He dropped it once—it felt electric in his hand—and picked it quickly back up. He needed to get the door locked. Locked. Just for now. Give him a little time to think about this. He couldn't hear them now. That was good. They were down there. Not in his head. That was good. But they had to be in his head, made no sense otherwise. Had to be in his head. Just all the booze—the house?—playing with his nerves? Had to be. That was it. It. He put the key in the lock, turned it, pushed the dead bolt for extra security, and took a step back. Staring at the door. Waited. Almost expected for someone to come knocking. But there was nothing. Just the silence. And then a car passed by on the gravel road out front. Moving slowly, but there. Solid. Reality. Ford clenched his fingers tight. He had left his beer down there. He needed a beer.

11

Freddie stopped by on the Thursday before Thanksgiving while Ford was still sleeping. Diana looked out the back window and saw the Pepsi truck pulling up across the street, and then she dressed Samantha in a hat, scarf, and gloves, and they ran over to meet him. Samantha loved riding in the truck, being up so high in a vehicle with the Pepsi logos on the doors of the cab, and it was always a big thrill for her when he took them for a drive about the island; and every now and then, especially in the winter, Freddie had some time to kill in between ferries.

"Prince Charming still asleep?" he asked as Diana opened the door and boosted Samantha inside.

Samantha crawled forward, wrapping her arms about his neck and kissing his cheek. "Who's Prince Charming?" she asked.

"Oh," said Freddie, catching himself. "Prince Charming? You know who that is. That's my dad. That's your mummy's and my code name for my dad."

"But he's bald," said Samantha.

"That's right," said Freddie. "But so am I. And you think I'm charming, right?" He checked his mirrors, and put the truck into gear as Diana buckled Sam in, and then herself. Freddie reached over and handed Sam a Reese's Peanut Butter Cup.

"Maybe," Sam said. "Maybe if you wear a hat. Or maybe a wig. A black wig that goes straight across the front."

Freddie rubbed her head. "Ohhh . . . I know who you mean. That's not Prince Charming. That's Prince Valiant."

And Sam, chocolate already all over her face and hands, turned and looked up at him. "Yup. That's you."

They drove over through Vineyard Haven, across the drawbridge spanning the channel between the lagoon and Vineyard Haven Harbor, onto State Road and then on up into Menemsha, winding hills and valleys moving through long patches of woods and fields of tall grass with horses, llamas, and sheep, and then panoramic views of water all around. Ponds and marshes, small sheltered bays with boats moored for the winter, and then the open sea. And then on into Aquinnah. Gay Head.

Freddie pulled the truck over at the top of the hill just below the lighthouse, a field of cut grass sloping down beneath. Peeling white benches. Freddie pulled on a knit cap with the New England Patriots logo on it.

"It says thirty-minute parking, but they won't really ticket me, will they?" Freddie asked.

Diana shook her head. "Not this time of year. I haven't been out this way since summer. Ford used to come out here sometimes to fish at dusk."

"He ever catch anything?" Freddie asked.

Samantha climbed out of the cab, Diana waiting on the pavement to help her down.

"We caught some crabs once," Sam said, "but they kept trying to pinch us so we let them go. Then it was dark, and we couldn't see anything anyway, except for the lighthouse, and so then we went home. Daddy says he caught a striped fish once, though, but it was as big as me so he threw it back in the ocean because he was afraid it might eat me."

"Well, it's a good thing he's looking out for you, then," Freddie said.

The sea was loud in the distance. Diana could hear the waves crashing and retreating, and hear the cries of the gulls circling above the beach. They started up the worn path to the lighthouse, the earth hard and dusty beneath, the brush and shrubbery to either side brown and dead, awaiting spring in the moisture coming in off the sea, and Samantha ran up ahead.

Freddie stuffed his hands in his pockets, and tucked his chin to his chest against the wind. "Isn't this where the nude beach is at?"

"Not this time of year," Diana said, "unless maybe you're a wacko." She looked out over the water. "It's all the same beach. You just have to walk for a while before you get to the nude section."

She and Ford had gone out there once. His idea. Early last summer, shortly after the solstice. It was still a lot less crowded than it would be once July hit, and he talked her into it. It was very warm, and they had found a babysitter through postings at the library across the street, and drove out here later in the afternoon. You had to park at the top of the hill, and then make your way down the path that wound through the beach grass and brush, and there were people on the beach, but the numbers dwindled as they moved along, walking at the edge of the surf, and soon enough it almost seemed deserted. Almost. Just a few couples, a few solo old men—standing proud with their hands on their hips as they gazed out upon the sea—and small groups of tanners, sitting about with coolers and blanket, wearing sunglasses and beach hats and little, if anything more.

"It's always the old people who want to be naked the most," she remembered Ford said. "It's kind of funny." And he was right. Nearly everyone they passed was sixty or above. Ford was being nice though, had been nice nearly all day, and he held her hand as they walked along the surf. Diana couldn't remember the last time he had held her hand.

They walked nearly as far as they could. The red clay cliffs towering high behind them, shifting, and crumbling, eroding. The beach was small, lapped with the tide, and spotted with enormous boulders jutting up from out of the sand and smaller, smooth rocks all about, almost giving the cove they chose the look of ruins, the remnants of a temple uncovered from the earth. One of the boulders was tall and narrow, the top resembling a head. A profile. Chin, nose, and brow.

"Lot's wife," Diana said, pointing. She lay her towel flat on the sand, and then took Ford's from him to do the same.

Ford looked at her quizzically.

"You know? Sodom and Gomorrah? God turned her into a pillar of salt because she wasn't supposed to look back."

"Look back at what?"

"The destruction of the city."

"Oh." Ford looked away. "I knew that. I just forgot. I just don't see it though. In the rock I mean." He was quiet for a minute, and Diana felt immediately bad for embarrassing him. He was very proud. And he hated to be called out. On anything.

"The only reason I knew it is because I went to Catholic school," Diana said, taking a seat.

Ford smiled. "They bible you up, all good and clean?"

Diana pulled her T-shirt over her head, shimmied out of her shorts. A white-and-green-striped string bikini beneath. "Good maybe. Maybe not always so clean. Maybe a little bit dirty. Maybe."

"The old God, the angry God, probably wouldn't like that too much, would he?" Ford said.

Diana cocked her head. "Probably not."

"Probably turn you into a pillar of salt or some shit like that."

"Probably."

"Well, maybe we should test him and see." He sat down beside her. Reached over and began to play with the band on her bikini bottoms.

Diana looked down at his fingers. "I don't want to be stuck down here on earth forever."

"Forever probably isn't so bad," Ford said. "Beats the alternative."

"What's the alternative?" Diana asked.

"Nothing," he said. "We just stumble right on into nothing."

Diana looked around. The only people in sight were farther down the beach. Small in the distance, except for a woman on a large rock some fifty feet out in the surf. Facing the ocean. She reclined back, supporting herself with her hands. Long blonde hair and a sheer white dress.

"When did she get there?" Diana asked.

"I don't know," Ford said. "I was just thinking the same thing. Maybe we missed her in the glare of the sun. Or she could have been swimming."

"Could have been."

Ford smiled again. "She looks kind of hot. Maybe we should ask her to join us."

Diana tossed some sand at him, and then he tackled her on the towel and began to kiss her. "You ready to take your clothes off?" he said, pulling back and looking down into her eyes.

She reared up and kissed him. "Maybe."

"You want me to do it, or you want to do it?"

"Well, if you do it, someone might call the cops. I think they look the other way if you're naked, but probably not if you look like you're about to have sex."

"Okay," he said. "Well, I'll count to three and then we'll both do it."

Diana nodded. "And if you tell anybody, I'll kill you."

Climbing to his feet, Ford shook his bathing trunks free from his leg, and then Diana unsnapped her top, looped her thumbs of the hip strings of her bikini and pulled it right down. Ford had made a dash for the water first, and Diana quickly followed.

The sea was cold, but the water was beautiful, and once their bodies adjusted, they stayed in for a half hour or more. Ford had pulled her close and kissed her at one point, pushing her hair back from her forehead.

"You're beautiful, you know?" he said. "Did I ever tell you that?"

Diana shook her head. "Nope."

"Well," he said. "I'm telling you now."

They had brought sandwiches and a bottle of chilled white wine, and after warming in the sun returned to the water. And the rest of the day had been beautiful. Maybe, she thought, thinking back now, the most perfect day they had had together since they moved to the island. The seals had come close to the shore. Small heads bobbing up and down throughout the breakers. There for a moment, then gone. Snouts and whiskers. At least four or five

of them—it was amazing how many had come back to the area—
and Ford had waded out and snapped a few pictures.

They had stayed until close to sunset, and the girl on the rock
didn't move except to occasionally glance their way and smile.
And then, as they were gathering their things together to go,
Diana looked up, and the rock was empty, and the woman was
gone. The rising sea breaking over the top, and leaving a spray in
its wake.

↜

"Well, I'll have to come back out in the summer and check it out,"
Freddie said now, in reference to the beach. Samantha opened
the weatherworn gate, and then scrambled up the path toward
the lighthouse.

"Everything is better in the summer," Diana said.

"That's true," Freddie said. "I like to snowboard a few times
a year though. You should come up for the weekend sometime
this winter with Samantha. We can go to Attitash or maybe even
Wachusett Mountain or something more local. I bet she would
pick skiing right up. It's amazing how quickly kids that age pick
things up."

"I'm sure she'd love it," Diana said.

"You still have your skis?" Freddie asked.

Diana nodded. "At my mother's."

"Uh-oh," Freddie said, laughing a little. "Well, maybe I can
pick them up for you."

"If Stephen hasn't sold them for drug money."

Freddie nodded. "That's highly possible. If he did, I can smack
him for ya. But in all honesty, you should come up."

"Just a matter of getting there."

Freddie laughed a little. "Just take the car and leave a note."

"Yeah, that would go over big. Once I start working again, the
first thing I'm going to do is buy my own car."

"How is everything else going? He's not acting like an asswipe
again, is he?"

"He's okay, I guess. All things considered. He tries, I think. Been better, been worse."

"Well, I only say it because I can, Cousin, but when it comes to you, it should just be better."

Diana put her arm around him then, pulled him close and kissed his head.

At the top of the hill Samantha stood outside the door to the lighthouse. The conical-shaped tower was made of red brick and rose some fifty feet above the lawn. Two steel platforms, one surrounding the rotating beacon and one just below. Alternate flashes of red and white. Since the day it was built in 1856, they had to keep moving the tower back every few decades, the clay cliffs it surmounted constantly eroding and dropping 130 feet to the ocean below. Diana wondered if there would ever come a day when the campaigns to move the tower would fall short, and if it would tumble, lost to the sea like so many wrecks.

She doubted the tower would be open, not this time of year, but when Freddie knocked, and then tested the door, she was surprised to hear a voice from inside.

A small old man sat behind a wooden desk covered with post-cards and keepsakes, brochures and books on the history of the light and the history of the Vineyard. The man wore a knit hat, and had dark skin and long gray hair. Thick black-rimmed glasses, magnifying his dark eyes behind them. There was a small green shaded lamp on the desk casting dim light upon the brochures, but other than that the small round room was dark, the only light filtering down from the windows high above.

The man asked them to shut the door, and held up a bag of butterscotch candy, offering them each one. "It's too cold out there for me," he said. "You invite the cold in for too long, and she never wants to leave."

"I didn't even think you would be open," Diana said. Sam clung to her leg, staring.

The old man smiled. Remarkably straight white teeth, that Diana imagined had to be dentures. "Sometimes we are," he said.

"And sometimes we ain't. I ain't got nothing better to do. You get to be my age, you won't have nothing better to do either."

"How old are you?" Sam asked.

The old man shifted his eyes slightly to the left. "My mother says that I'm eighty-seven, but I'm not sure I believe her. She likes to tell tall tales. I'm not as old as the lighthouse here, though. That much I know. You see the cliffs out there, little lady?" he asked Sam, his eyes smiling. "You know why they're red?"

Samantha shook her head.

"They are red because a long time ago, before the white people came, Moshup, a giant of the Wampanoag people—some say he was a God, and some say he was a devil with super-great powers—loved to cook whales. He also liked to feed the people, so each day he would wade out into the sea—back then whales used to come close to the shore—and he would grab a whale by the tail and throw it against the cliff. Then he would pull a tree from the ground, and build a fire to roast the whale for supper, and everyone would have a feast. The cliffs are red because of the blood of the whales, and that's why there are no trees out this way. No big ones at least."

"Poor whales," Samantha said.

"Maybe," said the old man, "but the people gotta eat. And if you dug in the clay you would still find coals from the burnt trees, bones from the whales, and sharks' teeth, too. That's what they say. Moshup used to use sharks' teeth to pick his own teeth clean after he was done eating. We still call that beach at the bottom of the cliffs Moshup Beach. Moshup shaped all these islands out here. The Elizabeth Islands, Noman's Land, Nanucket, and Noepe."

"Noepe?" Diana said.

"The Wampanoag people call this island Noepe. You know what Noepe means?" he asked Samantha. He kept his chin high as he spoke, looking down at Samantha from the bottom corners of his glasses.

Samantha shook her head.

"It means 'in the midst of the sea.' But nobody much calls it that anymore. They had to build this lighthouse because of all the wrecks down there. There's a big ridge coming from the bed of the sea out there—they call it the Devil's Bridge—and boats would smash on it all the time. There was a big one in 1884. A ship called the *City of Columbus* ran aground out there, and the lightkeeper and a bunch of the Wampanoag people went out in a lifeboat to try and save them, but they were too late, and weren't able to save too many. A hundred of them drowned." He nodded. "I still see them sometimes, usually in bad weather, or sometimes close to dusk, out there trying to swim in the waves."

"You see them?" Diana asked.

The old man smiled. "That's the funny thing about this island. A lot of ghosts. Seems like people never want to leave. A lot of the lightkeepers have said they have seen them over the years."

"How long have you been a lightkeeper?" Freddie asked him.

"Oh, I'm not a lightkeeper. I'm just a tour guy. I sell the books and open the place up. The light is all automated now. They tore the lightkeeper's house down in 1956, and there hasn't been a lightkeeper since then. Although, most of them that did work here, I'm willing to bet they're still here, too." The old man smiled. "Once a keeper, always a keeper."

Diana held Samantha's hand going up the winding iron stair-case, and Freddie followed behind them, keeping an eye on the little girl's feet in case she tripped. They stopped at the level of the lower platform—Samantha was afraid to climb the narrow ladder into the lens room—and squeezed through the small iron door. The wind had picked up, and Diana almost believed she could hear the tower creaking, shifting, but the view was breathtaking. The cliffs stretching into the distance, the sea breaking on the rocks below. Cold and blue. White breakers rolling to the shore. She rarely made it out to this part of the island, and she had never been up here before. She put her hands on Sam's shoulders and held her close; there wasn't much separating them from a drop to the ground. A narrow rail and iron bars, spaced some six to eight inches apart, nothing more.

Samantha looked left to right, scanning the water, the wind blowing her hair across her face. Diana thought of what the old man had said about the wrecks. The *City of Columbus.* The surf, the bodies, the rescuers, and the souls. If you focused hard enough you could almost picture it. Maybe he was right. What he said about the island. She thought again of the day on the beach with Ford, the girl on the rocks. But it was crazy to even think of it, she supposed. Crazy.

"What are you looking for?" she asked Sam.

"Whales," she said.

"I don't think they come that close to the island anymore," Diana said. "That was in the old days."

"I hope that giant didn't kill them all," Samantha said.

"That's all you need," whispered Freddie in Diana's ear. "Now she's going to be having nightmares about giants, ghosts, and devils."

The little girl turned her head slightly and looked up at him. "No," she said. "Just devils."

12

Diana had just stepped out of the shower when she once again heard Sam talking in the room next door. It was an overcast Sunday, and Ford was out. Said he was going into town to pick up a few things—maybe a leaf blower at the hardware store on Circuit Avenue, if it didn't cost too much. That was the biggest problem with living on the island, he said, things cost too much, but worst-case scenario, they at least needed a new rake; the entire backyard was covered in a carpet of leaves from the big oak tree and more blowing in from the cemetery beyond.

Diana wrapped a towel around her, and stepped quietly over to her doorway, her hair still wet and cold against her bare shoulders. She heard Sam get up and walk across her room, and then the bed creak as she must have sat down upon it.

"She's not a little girl," Sam said.

Her words were followed by silence.

"Oh. Well, maybe a long, long time ago, but she's not anymore. She's my Mummy's age. She's very nice."

Silence again.

"She bought me a Malibu Barbie Beach House once for Christmas, and she took me to see Disney on Ice once for my birthday. She's pretty. Her hair is long."

Diana stepped closer. Shivered a little. There was a draft coming in from somewhere.

"Umm . . . it's still that color," Sam said. "I think. I haven't seen her in a couple little while. Mummy says she is coming down for

Thanksgiving. Maybe we can get new dresses for Claudia and Sabrina." Silence. "Ummm . . . no. I don't know her. Mummy says she used to live in this house, and she was a very old lady. My grandma is an old lady, but not wicked old. She isn't covered with seven thousand hundred wrinkles and she doesn't walk with a cane. And her hair isn't white."

Diana inched her way closer to Sam's door. She felt a chill again.

"My grandma? Sometimes she was nice, but sometimes she would yell a lot, and then she would slam a pot down on the stove and scream, 'I'm sick of this shit!' And then after she did that, she would have to go take some headache medicine and lie down on the couch while my grandpa watched the news in the other room. And then it started to snow, so he went outside to shovel. Daddy yells a lot, too. Especially if he needs a beer."

Silence.

"No," Sam said. "I like him sometimes."

Diana peeked in the room. Sam was on her knees in the middle of the floor, the white-and-pink braided oval rug. Surrounded by the dolls. Two in her small rocking chair, and two more at her small play tea table in the corner of the room. A fifth on the floor beside her. The blonde in the red velvet dress. The only one missing was the doll all dressed in black, the doll in mourning. Claudia. Sam picked up the blonde and began to brush her hair.

"I used to like him more when he wasn't always grouchy." She looked up at the bed. "Do you like him?"

Diana poked her head in the door. "Hi, Angel."

Sam turned her gaze toward her. "Hi, Mummy."

Diana looked around the room. "Who were you talking to?"

"Well, we were having a tea party."

"I guess. I hope the tea wasn't too hot."

"We put it in the freezer to cool it down."

Diana stepped into the room. The draft came again. It was even colder in here than out in the hall. She walked over and checked the windows. Ran her hand around the perimeter. Felt nothing, but she pushed her hand against the window and it rattled a little.

They would need to be replaced within the next few years, she thought.

"It's chilly in here, honey." She turned back around. Sam now had the doll she was holding quietly talking to one in the chair, her voice barely whisper.

"Sam honey," Diana said. "What do you think Daddy will say if he comes home and finds you with all these ladies upstairs?"

Sam looked up. "It will be . . . okay, Mummy." She put the blonde in an empty chair at the table. "It will be . . . all right."

"Sam . . ."

"Claudia is downstairs on the lookout. She's going to let us know when Daddy gets home."

"But, Sam, I know it shouldn't be a big deal, but you know how Daddy gets when you play with his dolls."

Sam shook her head. "The dolls don't belong to Daddy, Mummy."

Diana felt the chill again. She wrapped her arms tight around her, hands on her shoulders. "Well, who do they belong to, then?"

"Cassie."

13

Maybe nothing more would have happened with Ford if she hadn't invited Norman and Cybil down for Thanksgiving. Maybe, she thought, but in her heart she knew it wasn't true. It had been building—in both Ford and in the house—and it was coming one way or the other.

Ford had worked the night before, and slept throughout the morning as Diana prepared the food. She had brined the turkey for two days prior, under the advice of her brother Phillip, and she had also made twice-baked potatoes along with butternut squash lasagna. A honey baked ham. Asparagus and goat cheese. Stuffing, and corn. Cranberry sauce, shrimp cocktail. An apple pie, and a chocolate torte for dessert. Diana had opened a bottle of wine while she cooked—a Sebastiani Cabernet—and Samantha helped her in the kitchen, frosting some cupcakes. Diana had dressed her in a long, festive dress, and her hair done up with yellow ribbons. Cybil and Norman were staying at a B&B down near Ocean Park, and Sam was happy when she heard they were coming. Cybil was always nice, she said, and usually brought her presents, and Norman, sometimes gave her money. Samantha had kept her money in a pink elephant piggy bank for the past two years, but the elephant was gone now, she said. It was missing. Or maybe someone had stolen it. Or maybe Daddy had taken it because her room was a mess, she said to Diana. He went over the edge when her room was a mess, and once, last year he had filled three bags with her toys and thrown them in the trash. Then later that night after he had gone to work, Diana had taken her outside and gone through the bags, letting her keep a few things she really wanted, and hiding the rest in Tupperware bins in the cellar.

"You can't keep everything, or he'll know. Then we'll both be in trouble. But you need to try and keep the room clean."

"But if the room's not clean," Samantha said, "he might not notice what we pulled from the trash."

And her room was a mess now, so maybe the elephant was still in there somewhere, Diana figured. Ford had given her the piggy bank last year—he usually wouldn't throw out anything he gave her himself—with a five-dollar bill for her birthday, saying he wanted her to learn to appreciate money. To save. But the piggy bank wasn't the only thing to go missing lately. After the shirt, there had a been a wristwatch with a built-in stop watch that Diana liked to use when she went for a run, and there had been an expensive corkscrew from the kitchen, a picture of Diana and her father—taken when she was in kindergarten—that she kept on the mantle, and even a pair of pajama bottoms that Ford sometimes wore to bed. Along with the James Taylor biography; he had flipped his lid when the book went missing.

Now Samantha licked the frosting from the butter knife. "I think a robber might have come in and taken it." .

"The piggy bank?" Diana asked. She finished kneading the top of the pie crust, and slipped it in between two sheets of wax paper. Preparing to roll it flat.

"Yeah," Samantha said. "If he climbed up onto the outdoor shower, he could jump up and grab hold of the balcony outside of you and Daddy's room, and then climb in through the window. And then if I was asleep I would probably never hear him. Unless he tripped and fell, and then he would make a lot of noise."

"Well, if he tripped and fell, we all would hear him," Diana said, "especially with all that junk you have all over your floor."

"Cassie says she never even had many toys when she was little." Samantha licked at the knife again. "And that she didn't even get toys for Christmas."

Diana began to roll. "She didn't, huh?"

"Yup. She said all they did on Christmas was sit and pray."

"You know, I've been wondering, honey, just who exactly is this Cassie, anyway?"

"She's a lady," Samantha said.

"A lady?"

"Yeah. A lady."

"And where did you meet her?"

"In my room." Samantha peeled another cupcake wrapper. "She sleeps with me at night."

"Sleeps with you?" Diana asked.

"Yeah," said Samantha, "at night."

"Isn't Cassie your little stuffed dinosaur?" Diana opened the oven, a blast of heat rising as she did. She squinted, backed her face away, eyed the turkey.

"She's Cassie, too. They're both Cassie. This Cassie is a lot older. She lived here a long time ago."

Diana shut the oven. The little girl was frosting another cupcake. Frosting smeared all over the counter.

"A long time ago?"

"Yeah." Samantha nodded, took a bite. "Now she's dead."

Diana felt her heart jump.

"Dead?" she said, deciding to make light of it. "Well, that's silly. How can she be dead?"

"I don't know," Sam said. "But that's what she told me."

Diana just looked at her a moment. Nodded. "Well, tell your friend Cassie she is silly."

Diana turned back to the oven. Dead, she thought. It had to be an imaginary friend, of course it did—plenty of little kids had them—but she wondered why Sam had to make her's dead. Maybe the cemetery, she thought, and their game with inventing lives for the people in the tombs. Maybe she was taking it and running with it, in which case it would be better to ease off, play another game. She asked her how often the lady came in to sleep with her, and Samantha had looked at the ceiling a moment, and then told her again she didn't want to talk about it anymore. And with that Diana hadn't pushed. Imaginary friend or not, if she pushed it too much, she was afraid she might scare her.

Cybil brought a box of fudge, two bottles of Pinot noir and a bottle of sauvignon blanc. She wore a tight black skirt, and low-cut red blouse. Red lipstick. Cybil always looked good, always ready for a night on the town. Samantha had run and jumped into her arms. Cybil pulled her close, kissed both of her cheeks.

Samantha giggled. "Both cheeks?"

"That's how they do it in Italy," Cybil said, and then she gazed hesitantly up the stairs. "Is Ford still sleeping?"

"I told him I'd wake him at three," Diana said. "I figure three would be good."

Cybil raised her eyebrows, nodded. As much as Diana liked Cybil, wanted her to come, it always made her nervous. Cybil didn't always care much what she had to say in front of her brother, and that could set him off. And the last thing Diana wanted to do was set him off, ruin the holiday. She took their coats and hung them in the closet beneath the stairs. There was always a strange smell coming from the closet—something old and not quite right—but she had cleaned it out front to back and had never found anything, couldn't figure out what it was. But there it was, still there.

"I can't believe how dead Circuit Ave is," said Cybil.

"It's a summer island," Diana said. "Everything is dead this time of year."

"Oh, I know," said Cybil. "I just figured that things would pick up a little with the holidays. I was never down here much in the winter before."

Norman went to the cabinet, pulled down some wineglasses and opened the bottle of sauvignon blanc. Norman liked to drink, but it never seemed to affect him adversely. Not in the way it affected Ford. Norman might get silly, and a little more lovey, flirty, and maybe a little obnoxious, but that was usually it. Diana had never seen him get angry with it. Never any rage.

The parade was still on television, and Samantha was in front of it, opening the first of two presents Cybil had brought for her.

Struggling with the ribbon. Cybil knelt down beside her to pull at the knot. First her fingers, then her teeth. Cybil could make anything sexy, it seemed—even pulling at a ribbon with her teeth.

Samantha ripped off the paper, her face lighting up. A board game. Operation.

"Ah, it's not Christmas yet, Aunt Cybil," said Diana. She was back in the kitchen now. Shoestringing the beans.

Cybil pursed her lip, looking at Samantha. "I know, but she deserves it, and besides she's so cute"—she reached out and pulled her cheek—"chipmunk cheeks, and . . . I think I missed her birthday."

"You got me Malibu Barbie for my birthday," said Samantha.

Cybil feigned ignorance. "Did I? Hmmm . . . I must have forgot."

Underdog was floating down Madison Avenue, filling the screen. Confetti flying.

"Well, you should have waited until Christmas," Diana now said to Cybil. "You're going to spoil her."

Cybil smirked. "Just think—I could have got her a Ouija board. Hah!"

"What's a Ouija board?" Samantha asked.

"Hmmm," said Cybil. "Well, it's a just board, you know like a Monopoly board, but you use it to talk to people you care about but haven't seen in a while."

"Can you use it to talk to people you don't care about?" Samantha asked.

Cybil lowered her chin. "Like who?"

"Like George Washington."

Cybil smiled. "Absolutely. You can talk to him, too."

Diana was watching them, Norman beside her—picking at some little spinach turnovers she had made as an appetizer. Diana sipped her wine. "Except in this house," she said.

Cybil made a face. "I know, can you imagine? My sister Sheila said they used one in this place once when they were back in high school—she and a couple of her friends stayed over for the weekend—and she said the thing went wild. She said pictures started falling off the walls, and then they heard this banging upstairs like a foot was coming through the floor.

"They kept my great-aunt up all night."

"Did you ever meet the aunt?" Norman asked Diana.

"No," she said.

"She looked like a raisin," Norman said. "Or like one of those apples you carve as a kid, and leave on the windowsill to dry. Just like that. They must have left her on the windowsill a little too long."

"Stop it," said Cybil, standing up, and smoothing her skirt. "She was very old. I'd love to live to be that old. And besides, she was a sweetheart. I miss her." Cybil came over and took her wine. Diana heard movement upstairs, footsteps, and felt her heart sink a little. She was hoping he would sleep until at least three. Three would be better. Maybe make him less grouchy, confrontational, and give them time to be foolish, maybe gossip a little. Samantha had the doctors equipment spread out all over the floor. She banged the man's nose with the reflex hammer. A bulbous, flashing red nose. The man was a drunk.

"Don't tell her about Ouija boards," Diana whispered. "You'll give her nightmares."

Cybil sipped. Took a cracker and pushed it through some crab dip. "I know. I was just kidding. I wouldn't get one of those things if my life depended on it. Bad stuff happens."

Diana heard the pipes turn on, water running, and then more footsteps. Slow, measured. Across the second floor and then down the stairs. Diana pulled out the turkey, and began to baste it some more. Ford walked in with bedhead, eyes at half-mast. A white tank top, and still wearing his postal pants. Everyone was quiet. Cybil gave him a quick hug, which Ford half received, half ignored. He went to the refrigerator, took out a carton of Tropicana orange juice, undid the cap and then took a long swig. After he did, he turned, orange juice still in hand, smiled, and extended his free hand to Norman.

"What's up, pal?" he said.

He had gone upstairs to shower after that, come down a half hour later with his hair combed neat. A button-down Oxford and pleated baby-blue corduroy pants an inch too short on the ankle. Polo cologne. The turkey had been ready for some time and Diana was worrying that even out of the oven it would overcook with the foil still on it, and that wouldn't be good. She needed it to be good—she needed it to be perfect. They sat in the dining room, the chandelier with curved glass bulbs above them. The room was long and narrow and fairly dark—just one window at the back of the room, long red drapes that had come with the house; Ford had insisted she leave them up—and the bricks on the hearth were covered in green enamel. There was a lot about the house that Diana would have changed, would have renovated, to make it hers, to make it new if it were just up to her. But much of the decor reminded Ford of the time he spent down here when he was young, he said, and it gave the house character. Antiques, he said. Nobody gets rid of antiques.

On one wall was an oval gilded mirror with a gilded candle holder on either side, and on the opposite was a framed reproduction of John Singer Sargent's painting *The Daughters of Edward Darly Boit*. Four young Victorian girls, two—twins—chatting in the background, in the shadows, another in a red dress and white apron standing alone, and the fourth, the smallest, sitting splay-legged with a doll on the floor, staring at the artist. The mirror had come with the house, but Diana had brought the picture, had always loved it, making a point to go visit it each time she went into the Museum of Fine Arts since she had been in high school. She had taken art classes up until she was sixteen, and they made several trips to the museum. She had even thought about studying art in college, if even just as a minor, but then of course all that had all fallen through. She had read that the girls in the painting had gone mad upon reaching adulthood, which just made the piece a little more haunting. Ford didn't like the picture, but she had won out on that one. A rare victory, but as a concession she had been forced to allow a poster of the Milky Way in their bedroom. Ford said he liked to look at it while falling asleep in the morning. He said it comforted him.

He stood at the head of the table, sleeves rolled up to his elbows as he carved the turkey, taking over the show. But Diana didn't mind. At least he was socializing, being friendly. He had switched from champagne to whiskey, but she, Cybil, and Norman had stuck to the wine. Now Cybil's cheeks and her nose had turned pink.

"Do you remember all the skunks down here when we were little?" she asked Ford.

"There was like an army of them," Ford said, forking some mashed potatoes.

"Melanie used to call them 'kunks," Cybil said. "She couldn't say the skunks."

"Who is Melanie?" Samantha asked.

Cybil patted her head. "Our little sister."

Ford kept eating, appearing not to acknowledge the name.

"Didn't they tree you once?" Cybil said. "You climbed up the oak tree."

Ford stopped eating. "I had no choice. There was like three or four of them. I was playing wiffle ball in the backyard, and it was almost dark, and they were all coming out of the bushes, marching right at me. It was either climb the tree or get sprayed." He looked at Samantha, rubbed her head and winked. "Little stinkers."

"How old were you?" Diana asked.

"I don't know. Eleven or twelve. Something like that. They were probably heading for the trash, but it seemed like they were just circling the tree for like forever."

"You were so cute, trying to scramble higher and higher," Cybil said. We were watching from the window, and then Auntie peeked out and saw you, and she disappeared into the pantry and then goes marching out into the backyard, blowing a whistle, and waving this umbrella around. It was hysterical. This little hunched, eighty-year-old lady, blowing a whistle to scare away skunks."

"I know," Ford said. "She saved me." He winked at Samantha again, and then poured himself another half glass of whiskey.

When they finished eating, Diana served the pies and the torte and coffee—a glass of Coke for Samantha. Ford stared across the table, toward Diana, but he didn't appear to be looking at her, rather past her. Looking into the mirror on the wall behind her. His face was flushed, his eyes taking on the empty glaze they reached when he had way too much to drink, and Diana was beginning to get nervous. Samantha had been rambling, talking about a boy in her preschool class—Ronald Mooney, who was always sitting in the corner, always in trouble—and the bow atop her head was coming undone.

"He was crawling on the floor on Tuesday, barking like a dog," she said. "He thinks he's a dog."

"Maybe he is," said Cybil.

"No," said Samantha. "His nose isn't wet, and he doesn't have a tail. Dogs have tails."

"Not all of them," said Cybil, "Sometimes they clip them off."

"Well, I know he isn't really a dog," said Samantha, "because he doesn't even have fleas. And if he was a dog, Mrs. Kearney wouldn't make him sit in the corner, she'd make him go outside. He told me he's going to shoot Mrs. Kearney someday when she isn't looking."

"Well, he sounds like a fine young man," said Diana.

Norman laughed. "All little boys talk about that stuff, it's completely normal."

"It's not normal," Cybil said to him. "It's wrong. These kids are exposed to it so much, they think nothing of it, and then look what happens. They grow up and walk into a mall and go on a shooting spree."

"He doesn't have a gun." Samantha looked down and adjusted something on her lap. Diana hadn't noticed her bringing anything in, and she wondered if she had some food down there, something she didn't want to eat. But she had told her she didn't have to eat anything she didn't want to, so she didn't understand why she would go and hide it. Diana had dimmed the chandelier when they started dessert, and now they had candles going. "He has a bow and arrow," Samantha said.

"There you go," said Norman. "He's going to go on an archery spree."

"You're missing the point," Cybil said to him.

"No, I'm not," said Norman, "I know what you're saying. I'm just saying kids are going to be kids, and you shouldn't sound the alarm every time they say something that might be a little concerning if said by an adult." He looked at Ford. "Now if somebody at your work said something like that, I'd think everyone's ears would light up." He laughed a little. "Am I right?"

Ford was still staring into the mirror, and for Diana, it was beginning to feel even more disquieting. Up until ten minutes before, things had felt to be going as well as could be hoped. He had been talking to Norman about football some more, and then politics, the past election. And he had even been laughing a little.

Now he turned and looked at Norman. "My work?"

"I mean because of all the postal rampages. It seems every time you open the paper you read about some postal carrier, Vietnam vet, shooting up all his co-workers. It's like an epidemic."

"Norman," Cybil said, "stop."

Ford sipped his whiskey. "That's okay. We just had one of those last week. I'm lucky I work the night shift or I'd be dead right now."

Norman hesitated. "I was just joking."

Cybil put her hand over his. "Norman always carries a joke a little too far."

"I didn't mean anything by it," said Norman. "Besides, Ford can take a joke, just because you can't."

"I can take lots of jokes," Ford said. "I've been taking them my whole life." He put the glass down and looked at Norman. "I'm taking one right now."

The table was silent, and Diana struggled to think of something to change the subject. She had been prepared for anything uncomfortable that might come up, ready with other topics to switch to, but now she could think of nothing. Her mind a blank, her fingertips tight against the bottom of the table.

"Well, Ronald Mooney wouldn't like mailmen, either," said Samantha.

"Why not?" asked Cybil.

"Because," said Samantha, "he's a dog." She lifted what she had on her lap now.

A doll.

One of the china dolls.

Black hair and blue velvet dress. Jewel.

She ran her hand back over the doll's head, and Diana felt her heart begin to stutter. She tried to catch the little girl's eyes, to send her a message before Ford looked her way, but Samantha wasn't looking at Dianna.

Ford did look at her now, up and down, hesitation in his eyes. "Hey, Sam? Where did you get that doll?"

Samantha looked at him, a deer in the headlights. She put the doll back down on her lap.

"I asked you a question," Ford said.

Samantha didn't answer.

Diana started to speak, but Ford held his hand up in her face. "Sam," he said again, "I asked you a question. Where did you get that doll?"

"In the back parlor," she said quietly.

"And what's the rule about the dolls?" Ford asked.

"I don't get it," said Cybil. "What's the rule about the dolls?"

"Sam knows the rule, don't you, Sam?" Ford asked.

Samantha was still staring at him, wide-eyed.

"Ford doesn't like her playing with them because he says they're antiques," Diana said. "Sam, just put the doll back."

Samantha nodded, and started to slide off her chair.

"No," said Ford. "Sam still hasn't answered me. What's the rule, Sam?"

"Oh, Ford," said Cybil, "give me a break. Those dolls are a thousand years old. We played with them all the time when we were kids. She's only little. Leave her alone."

"That was then, this is now," Ford said. "This is my house now, and if I want your opinion, you'll be the first one to know. Sam, I asked you a question."

"Cassie said I could," Samantha whispered.

"Cassie?" Ford asked, looking confused. "Who the hell is Cassie?"

"Ford, I told her she can play with it," broke in Diana.

"Cassie upstairs," said Samantha.

Ford scowled. "What are you talking about?"

"Cassie is her imaginary friend," said Diana. "Jesus, Ford, I told you I told her she can play with it—it's not her fault—let's not make a big deal out of it. Samantha, just put the doll back."

Ford turned to Diana, his eyes slightly more alive. "How can I expect her to listen to me when you won't? She's sees that you don't listen to me, Diana, and what do you think she does?"

Diana took a breath. "Ford. Enough." She turned to Sam. "Honey, just put the doll back."

"Those dolls are well over a hundred years old, and worth a lot of money," Ford said, "and once they're broken, once she breaks them, do you know how much they're going to be worth then?"

"Ford, you're being ridiculous," said Cybil.

Ford shook his head. "That's me. Mr. Ridiculous. I have everyone laughing."

"Sam," Diana said again, and with that the little girl jumped from the chair and hurried out of the room.

"Ford, honestly," Cybil said, "I don't see what the big deal is either. She's a little girl, they like to play with dolls. That's what they're there for. Besides there's like ten of them, right? Why don't you just let her have one, and you can keep the others safe so you can play with them yourself."

Ford nodded. "And why don't you just mind your own goddamn fucking business?"

"She's my niece," said Cybil, "it is my business."

Ford looked into his whiskey. "You know the problem with you, Cybil? You don't know what is your business, and what's not. Ever since we were kids, you've always been sticking your nose where it doesn't belong. It gets a little annoying. You're kind of a cunt."

Diana felt her heart seize.

"Hey!" snapped Norman. "Jesus Christ!"

"I'm not Jesus Christ," said Ford, "and neither is she. Mary Magdalene maybe. She was a slut when we were young."

"Enough." Norman jumped up at the table, and as he did, Diana moved with him, standing between him and Ford.

"Okay," Diana said, her voice beginning to shake. "Let's just end this now. This is ridiculous. It was just a doll. Ford, come on, we were having a nice time. It's Thanksgiving."

Ford hadn't moved from his seat. "What are you going to do, *Norman*?" Ford asked. "Beat me up? Are you going to fight me in my own house?"

"I'm not going to let you talk to her that way," Norman said.

Ford shrugged. "Then don't." He sipped his drink again. "Let's see what you've got."

Norman didn't move. Ford locked with his eyes. Waited. After a moment, he sighed. "So much for the cavalry." He stood up. "Now get the fuck out of my house."

Norman still didn't move.

Ford stepped forward quickly, and Norman flinched, drawing his head back. Ford stopped, still staring him down.

"Ford, calm down," Diana said. "You're being an ass."

"I said get the fuck out of my house, Norman."

Cybil started to cry. "You're just like Daddy," she said to Ford. "I swear to God. You don't deserve these two. You're a drunk."

Ford nodded. "Yeah, that's right. I'm a drunk. Me. I'm the only one drinking here."

"You're the only one acting like a asshole," said Cybil.

"Out." Ford looked at Cybil. "You, too. Don't come back. Ever."

Diana shook her head. "Why do you have to do this? We were having a nice time."

Ford shrugged. "Because I'm a postal worker, right? Isn't that what we do? Go psycho. That's what Norman thinks. Right, *Norman*?"

Cybil took Norman's arm, pulling him gently away, saying "Let's just go." Diana kept her ground between the two men, just in case Ford decided to lunge. She didn't think he would, not unless Norman moved first, but she couldn't be sure. He had only called Norman on because he had sensed fear in him, that was all; otherwise, he never would have pushed it so far.

Ford took his seat back at the head of the table. Diana looked around for Samantha, but the little girl was nowhere in sight. She figured she was upstairs. Afraid to come down. Ford was staring at Diana.

"You're acting like a child," Diana said. "And you're out of control."

She walked Norman and Cybil to the foyer, the door, apologizing all the way. Cybil pulled her into an embrace. She whispered in her ear, told her to not to stay there for the night, to come back with them to the bed-and-breakfast. Both herself and Samantha.

Diana shook her head. "I can't," she whispered. "It will just make it worse. He'll calm down. He always does. He's just being obnoxious because he had too much to drink."

"I'm worried about you," said Cybil.

"He'll be fine," said Diana. "I'll call you in the morning. I'm sorry this happened. I'm mortified."

"Don't be mortified," said Norman. "Just come with us. Just for the night."

Diana hugged them both again quick. "I'll call you," she said, and then she was shutting the door. Wanting it shut, needing it shut, before Ford got up again. She could hear their voices outside. There for the moment, then getting smaller and smaller as they made their way off the property. Diana passed the stairs again, but there was still no sign of Samantha.

She was tempted just to head to the kitchen, or maybe just upstairs, but first she needed to make sure the girl hadn't come back down. Diana went back to the dining room and Ford was still sitting at the head of the table, his face half-illuminated in the candlelight. He had a cigarette going, sitting on the edge of the table, the smoke curling up before him. She would confront him about this, she wasn't going to let it go, but not now. Now wouldn't be good. But she could feel everything building inside her, burning, making her want to scream, want to cry, tell him to leave. He didn't look at her as she approached the table to begin to clear away the dishes. Stacking one plate upon the other. As few trips as possible would be best, she figured. With any luck he would go to his den, or better yet to the back porch with his Walkman, and listen to his music. He did that sometimes, maybe even knowing he had to defuse himself, she figured. But now he looked up at her.

"Hey, Diana?" he said.

Diana froze, the plates chest high. "What?"

"Don't ever do that again."

"Do what?"

"Side with someone else over me."

"Go to hell, Ford," she said, and as she did, he jumped, raised his hand and smacked her. Diana stumbled backward, the china still held tight, and her back to the mantle, and then he jumped closer. A closed fist. He caught her in the ribs. She winced with pain and doubled over, and then he got her in the face again, the cheek, his fist still closed, and this time she did drop the plates, sending them scattering. One skittering across the table, flipping up as it hit the gravy saucer, the others going over her shoulder, shattering on the floor. She flew backward, and he hit her one more time and she was on the floor, facedown. She could feel her face beginning to swell, the taste of iron on her lip. She shut her eyes tight. She could hear him breathing, the squeak of him snubbing out the cigarette, and then his footsteps going by her to the closet to get his coat, and then out the front door. Diana still didn't move, afraid he would come right back in, but she opened her eyes and when she did she could see the doll—the doll Samantha had carried upstairs—sitting on the floor, propped in the doorway.

14

Diana waited until she was sure he was gone, and then she pushed herself up off the floor. Ran upstairs to check on Samantha. Asleep, curled up at the foot of her bed, still in her dress, her ribbons, holding one of her own dolls. A bald baby whose face she had scribbled with purple marker two years before. Baby Poussie. Diana could feel her cheek beginning to throb. She checked herself in the bathroom mirror—split lip, cheek swollen.

She hurried downstairs and filled a Ziplock bag with some ice, wrapped it in a cloth napkin, and then she grabbed a change of clothes, her purse, a few toiletries and a few toys, coloring books and crayons, and then she grabbed the journal. She woke Sam and dressed her in her hat, and they ran out into the night.

She wasn't sure where Ford would have gone—maybe the bar down on Circuit Avenue where he sometimes hung out, or maybe just to buy a bottle and sit by the water, but she didn't think he would be heading back in this direction. Not yet. And she knew she just had to get out. Check in somewhere for the night. She wasn't even worried about herself, not anymore, but she was worried about Sam. Ford had never touched Sam, never hit her, but the possibility of it occurring was beginning to worry her more and more. His temper, rage, growing stronger as the days grew shorter, light dwindling. Working the night shift, he saw barely any daylight this time of year, and she wondered if that affected who he was, what he was becoming. Along with the alcohol. Depression turned outward, refined into fury. She hated him right now.

15

Ford could feel his knuckles swelling. He hadn't hit anyone in a while, not with a closed fist, and he had forgotten the damage it could do to your hand.

Bitch.

She had to push him, just had to do it.

He cut down the dirt road through the trees heading toward the harbor. He should have grabbed a pint before leaving, and then he could just sit on the bench on the hill and look at the lights on the sea. Think. But he couldn't even pick anything up now—liquor stores were closed because of the holiday. He shouted out, "Fuck!" and his voice echoed back to him, empty.

Why had she gone and made him hit her? She just never knew when to keep her mouth shut. Making him look foolish, siding with Cybil. Norman. Pathetic little Norman. Maybe he shouldn't have hit her, but you don't do that—you don't side with someone else against your husband, not in front of them. It was a matter of pride. Made you look disloyal. Sure, maybe if she wanted to talk about it later, in private, share her side. Sure. He would have listened. He was reasonable. But not in front of people. Not in front of Cybil. Not in front of the mirror.

The mirror.

What had been in the fucking mirror? He kept catching it from the corner of his eye. There, then gone, and then he'd look back and it would be there again. The same face. Older. Not his. Or not really. It was distorted. Dark, empty eyes. There for a second, then gone. Only if he stared directly into the mirror, kept staring, did it keep it gone. His mind playing tricks on him. Had to be. Booze. And anxiety just being around Cybil. All the memories.

He hated Cybil, hated his whole family. As soon as he heard she was coming, he knew there would be trouble. Always was. Couldn't mind her own fucking business. They had a nice, quiet, happy little life here, and then there was Cybil. "Let's invite them for Thanksgiving," Diana had said. And Ford had felt like clapping his hands together. *Why yes! Let's! Let's just invite my whole fucked up family into our lives so they can fuck up ours, too!* Didn't she see that there was a reason he had left them? All of them? Was she that fucking stupid? That was Diana's problem—she was stupid. Maybe book smart, a little, but when it came to life, she was just fucking stupid. Dumb as a bucket full of rocks. She didn't understand people. Not a slither of insight. She didn't see the . . . big . . . picture. *I adopt her kid, save her from her fucked-up family, move her to an upscale island, set her up in a beautiful home, with a house that would probably go for, what? Four hundred, maybe even as much as five on the market, and she has to turn around and embarrass me in front of my fucking sister? Really, Diana? Then she turns me into the bad guy, provoking me to the point where I lose control—just for a second—and hit her. Never would have happened if she hadn't provoked me.*

I am not my father.

Never will be.

The harbor was empty, and the crests of the waves white in the moonlight. The sky so bright above. He loved the winter skies, better down here with so many fewer lights on the ground, the open sea all around. That's what he could have done—just brought out his telescope, taken a few deep breaths, relaxed. Smoked a cigarette, and had a few more drinks until he got tired enough to sleep, put it all behind him.

Or he could kill himself.

The thought, the voice, entered his head and hung there for a second, thin like a whisper.

Kill himself. Quick, painless. A hose in the exhaust, the driveway in the dark. And make them see. Pay. *They'll be sorry*, someone said, a distant voice—not quite a man's and not quite a woman's, just very old, timeless—that felt like a nibble at the inside of ear. A painful small biting.

Sorry, it said, *they will be sorry.*

Make them sorry.

Ford shut his eyes, took a breath. No. That wasn't him. He wasn't sure where that was coming from, but that wasn't him. He didn't think that way. Thinking that way meant defeat. Not him. He would decide how things would end. His terms. No retreat. No, he just needed a few more drinks. Forget about them. Cybil. Diana. Samantha. That was what started it all. Samantha. The little shit. How many times had he told her not to touch the dolls? For chrissakes. He wasn't an asshole—he would buy her a fucking doll, get her one for Christmas. An expensive one. He had just asked her not to touch the china dolls. Who knew how much money they were worth? And she wouldn't have done it except she knew she could get away with it because Diana would let her. That was the story. *Always the same story.*

Spoiling the kid rotten, letting her get away with everything. She would be a good kid—he loved her—if there was someone to say no to her once in a while, set some limits, have some rules. The way it was now, you said no to her once, and she got that look on her face, starting to shake and then starting to cry, her nose, her whole face, blowing up like a balloon. You would think you just beat the hell out of her the way she responded, and all for what? For saying no? Because she couldn't hear it. The kid had no idea how good she had it either. Didn't know what it was like to grow up with a son of a bitch for an old man, the things he did. She thought hearing the word no was bad? How about being four years old and hearing a three-hundred-pound fat fucker's fist come cracking into the side of your head? Didn't know what that was like, did she?

She was lucky to have him. Both of them were. They just didn't see it.

They don't see it.
Show them.

No, he thought. Drunken thoughts. Stupid. How many times did he think/plan something stupid while drunk, and then wake up just to realize how stupid and foolish it was? Happy he didn't do it. How many times had he thanked God he didn't follow through with something stupid while drunk, wasting his pride? Calling Tara. Calling Big Daddy.

Putting a gun to your head.

He tripped on the hill. Coming down hard on the frozen earth, skinning his palm as he reached out to break his fall. He cursed once, and then found his feet. Cuts always hurt more in the cold. He made a fist, attempting to squeeze out the pain, and then warmed his palm against his jeans. Maybe it would be better to turn and go home, he thought. Maybe he was drunker than he realized. He'd fall again, hit his head, and then that would be it—he'd freeze to death out here. And then she'd be sorry.

Sorry.

16

The wind came in raw and cold off the water as Diana and Sam hurried down the hill above Sunset Pond. Most of the harbor was empty, the water a black mass in the dark—the boats stored for the winter, and just a few still in their slips, rocking gently in the wind—but she could see the lights of the ferry moving in the distance.

She wasn't looking to catch the ferry—not just yet. She couldn't leave the island without at least a few more of their things, but she couldn't stay in the house and wait until he got home either. She wasn't sure if he had taken the whole weekend off. He didn't like to tell her when he did, but the big rush was coming—Christmas—and she knew the PO discouraged the employees from taking time off this time of year. And if he were working, maybe they could go back then and get a few more things and go for good. Maybe. Right now they just needed to get away, even if just for a few days, think things through before making any sort of life-altering move. Stay somewhere downtown while she made a decision. She took Samantha's hand as they started down the worn path that cut across the brown grass of the hill.

She could hear a buoy clang in the distance, the whitecaps riding in from the sea. The little girl had her scarf up over her face, but she was awake now and talking. Always talking. And Diana nodded, quick yes's and no's. Samantha carried her doll—Louie, raggedy dreadlocks and bald in some spots, one lazy eye—by the foot, its head bouncing off the ground as they went.

They cut up the street toward the Wesley Hotel, across from the wharf, the rose and hydrangea bushes that ran the length of the front porch promenade so colorful in the summer, now all wilted, dead. Brittle and hollow. But it was Thanksgiving weekend, and she was hoping that maybe the hotel opened up at least partially—there had to be guests on the island for the holiday, and the rates would be much cheaper than in season— and maybe they could get a room. A big place was better—the employees less concerned, more apt to let you be. It might not be like that at a bed-and-breakfast, she figured.

The Wesley was the last of the grand hotels from the nineteenth century. At one point there had been several—the Highland House, the Pawnee House, the Sea View—but the others had all burned at one point or another. Even the Wesley had been set afire by its founder, Augustus C. Wesley, for insurance reasons, but he had been caught. Tried, convicted, tainted. The hotel was repaired, and climbed back up out of the earth to overlook the sea. Augustus, she had heard, was actually a French Canadian cook with the last name of Goupee but he changed his name to Wesley for subliminal reasons to attract the business of the Methodists; the founder of Methodism was named John Wesley.

They walked along the promenade, the floorboards of the porch creaking beneath them. You could taste the salt in the air, and the wind blew their hair across their faces. There was a light on outside the front door, and a bell clanged somewhere up ahead. The Wesley climbed five stories, four fronted with porches, and stairs climbing between, the top of the building surmounted by an enclosed Victorian turret. Shingled. In the summer, at any time, morning or night, you could come by and see guests of all walks of life—young couples, old, tourists in T-shirts and shorts, and bikers with big bellies and leather, children—rocking in the chairs, lining the porches, but now there was no one. Diana stepped to the front door, Samantha close to her side, and cupped her eyes to peer through the window, hoping to see someone, anyone. A dim light was on, and she could see the sitting area by the front desk. The round stone fireplace against the far wall, and all the furniture. The chairs all wingbacked and framed in wood, and the small round tables with curved, ornamental legs. Lifted from the late nineteenth century and set down here in 1994. Everything dark. Diana rang the bell.

She had never stayed at the hotel, but she had stopped inside once with Sam during the good weather. Got a Coke from the bar, and took a seat in the lobby on the claw-footed maroon sofa and pretended they were guests. Just for a few minutes, watching the real guests pass by on the promenade. They had just come from Illumination Night—the lighting of the Chinese lanterns throughout Trinity Park. Every porch on every gingerbread house was decked with the paper lanterns, and a band played inside the tabernacle, a chorus of singers; the music carried across the night. It was evening, but still very hot, and the lobby was cool but bustling with people, life. Guests, and maids, and bellboys. A family had come by, the parents not much older than Diana, with two children in tow. Everyone tan from the beach. The father carrying the smallest of the children, a boy sleeping with his head on his shoulder, while the mother whispered to the girl, smiling. And the sight of them had made Diana happy at the time. It was what the island was about. Should be. And the night had been wonderful, Samantha had her face painted by an artist outside the tabernacle, and now she was a Dalmatian, a long red tongue painted over her chin. She sipped her Coke, and babbled on about a turtle they had seen down by Sunset Pond. His name, she said, was Sweetie Pie.

Now Diana rang the bell one more time. She was about to turn, to start back down the promenade when she saw movement at the desk. First just a shadow. And then the muted image of a man as her eyes adjusted to the dim light, his hand reaching over the guest ledger with a pen, and scribbling something. A name or a date. The figure becoming clearer, but bent over the ledger as he was, she couldn't see his face. Bald on top, with a thin peninsula of hair climbing out toward his forehead. Diana focused, her heart picking up, rang the bell again, and tapped upon the glass of the door. The man didn't appear to have heard her, so she tapped one more time. And then he looked up. He wore a long walrus mustache, and bow tie and vest. He stared at Diana a moment, and then he put down the pen and came around the side of the desk, marching toward her, the door. His stride so pronounced, angry and quick, that she took a step back, bracing herself for the confrontation. But then as soon as he was there, he was suddenly gone. The door never opened. Diana looked inside one more time, but there was no one at the desk, no one in the lobby. It was completely silent, empty. It was impossible. The man had been there, she was sure of it. He had stared right at her.

17

Hiram has taken to his bed. It has been four days now, the curtains drawn. He is not taking food. I would like to believe that he is in communion with the Lord, silently, at prayer, perhaps searching, perhaps repenting, but I do not know that to be the case. It has happened before, and when it does, I'm not sure there is anyone left inside of him to commune with anybody at all. Certainly not with me. Nor am I in any state to let him with the way things have gone.

He took to his bed the day immediately after the incident on the wharf. His rage had gone on for hours, straight into the night, and he destroyed much of our china.

And one of the dolls—its head broken on the hearth.

Hiram used to bring me back a doll each time he went away, traveling to Boston, but it has been more than a year since he returned with one. Better days. During his rage he also destroyed a crystal vase my father had bought us for our wedding, and a picture I kept hanging on the wall in the back parlor. The picture was of a woman in the snow, walking across the Long Wharf in Boston. I had saved my money and bought the picture in a gallery near Boylston Street not long before I moved down to the island to be with Hiram. It reminded me of the city, reminded me of home, and I think deep down that is the reason he destroyed it. He has said, many times, it was improper—a woman walking about the city by herself, especially near the waterfront—suggestive of her intentions, and he repeated these words as he screamed. Intentions! These words and many more he should never repeat, and probably will not when the Devil leaves his soul. I pray he will not repeat them. Hiram has told me, in moments of clarity, that the Devil can do more damage, quickly and severely, to the soul of a good man than that of a common man when he gets him in his grip because there is that much more to ruin, that much more to compromise and pollute, and I fear he may be right. I have seen him angry often, but never as angry as this. It will be some days before I myself go out in public, before I can let the people of the campgrounds see me. There would be too many questions, too much concern, and people are already having difficulty understanding a man as complicated as Hiram.

I sleep in the spare room at the front of the house. The room where Hiram's younger brother Thomas slept when he came to visit last summer, before he left for San Francisco. Thomas is such a kind man, confident and happy, without always feeling the need to push for more, to demand more, demand better. I am sure both men once set out upon this same path, on this same island, so where did my husband veer off so terribly in a different direction?

August 11, 1871

Hiram led a group of camp dwellers back down to the hotel today. There were nine of us in all, walking in single-file procession, our hymnals tight to our chest, and our heads bent in prayer as we walked from the campground, across Circuit Avenue, and then out and across Ocean Park. Only Hiram held his head high as we went. At one time, Hiram would have led a group of fifty or more to approach the hotel builders and perform the Lord's chore, but that is no longer the case—not since the incident on the wharf. Now people whisper, and walk hurriedly away as Hiram approaches.

The day was dark, the skies threatening and the seas rough, and Hiram said that was how the Lord would have it. He says the people must see the Lord's fury, as well as his love, kindness, and benevolence if ever they are to find him. The men on the construction site moved hurriedly, trying to get a day's work in before the storm. We all dropped to our knees on the beach and began to sing "A Mighty Fortress is My God," and some of the workers did stop on the scaffolding for a moment to look down and observe—a few looking on with sincere curiosity, but one or two were laughing. I thought the laughter may once again awake the Devil in Hiram, but ever since he arose from his bed, he has been behaving like a new man. He has told me the light of Christ now burns in his heart, and Jesus himself took his hand while he was in bed, carried him to the ends of the world and offered him visions. He says Jesus showed him the Pit, and the sinners burning within, and then he brought him just outside the gates of Heaven, and handed him the key. Hiram said he could still feel the key in his hand even as he woke, and he knew what it meant, he knew what he had to do. Jesus had put the light in his heart, he said, and offered him his blessing. And now his face is indeed alight, his eyes wide and as excited as the sea itself. He has been sleeping very little, and spends most of his nights communing loudly with the Lord, or sitting at his writing table, furiously writing pages and pages of what he has seen and what he has deemed his own personal covenant. He says it is his agreement he made with the Lord, a pact, promising that he will continue to bring him his minions or die trying. And now I fear, he may do just that.

Mrs. Rhodes from across the campground was with us. She is a round, older woman with a long nose and small eyeglasses, and she is one of the few people left who still listen intently when Hiram goes to speak. Many feel that Hiram has gone too far, and are beginning to question as to whether we can possibly live peacefully with the new people pouring into the hotels and elaborate cottages going up almost daily around Ocean Park. Mrs. Rhodes has told me that she harbors no judgment upon Hiram for the incident at the wharf, and sometimes the Lord raises our hands to strike when all else has failed. A wolf among the sheep must be dealt with quickly, and severely, she has told me, and that is just what Mr. Pratt is, indeed—a wolf, she says—but I myself am not so sure. Despite Hiram's ongoing disruptions at the building site, Mr. Pratt never appears all too riled, and he still, from time to time, attempts to speak with Hiram regarding the hotel, and what he says will be the quality of the guests they allow to rent its rooms. Christian people, he says, but Hiram will not hear it. He sees what has happened at the Pawnee House on Circuit Avenue, he says, and the class of people—men and women—coming and going from the saloon on the first floor, and he believes the Sea View only rises because the Devil is running out of room in the Pawnee House. The Devil needs more room, he says.

The problem, I fear, is that no matter how much we sing, how much we pray, our efforts will prove futile. The building is going up so quickly, and really is becoming an impressive structure, surmounted with a tower that looks upon the sea. They have completed the roof.

Mrs. Stephens and her nephew were with us also. Her nephew is tall with sloped shoulders, and walks with a limp. A club foot, I once heard somebody say. He is a simple man, often unwashed, and today there was much of his breakfast still left in his mustache. He does not speak, as far as I know, and neither did he sing, but he sways back and forth, following along. But Mrs. Stephens sang quite loudly, and she says she must do so because she is singing for the both of them. The nephew's parents were reportedly lost at sea when he was still a boy, and Mrs. Stephens, now long a widow, has been caring for him ever since.

There were still many people patrolling the wharf today despite the darkness of skies, many stopping for refreshment at the pagoda, and a band played in the bandstand in the center of the park. The Oak Bluffs Land and Wharf Company likes to keep up the illusion of a festive air despite our protests, and I have heard that it was Mr. Pratt himself, who commissioned the band—they hail from Fitchburg—their trumpets and horns and thundering bass drums drowning out our voices. But louder, Hiram kept shouting, we must sing louder. It was when the thunder finally cracked, lightning breaking the sky, that Mrs. Stephen's nephew got up and began to run. Mrs. Stephens was soon in pursuit of him, as were the others when they noted her efforts to be futile, but when I went to stand, Hiram pressed his hand firm on my shoulder, whispering to me that we must go on. And then there we were, just the two of us singing, and the sky soon flooding down upon us. It wasn't long before I could no longer turn the pages of my hymnal; the pages had all stuck together.

18

The bed-and-breakfast where Norman and Cybil were staying was a Victorian nestled on Samoset Avenue behind Ocean Park. There was a tower surmounting it, a cupola, and Cybil said it offered a great view of the sea. The couple that ran it had purchased the house after the husband had struck some money with a software company, sold his shares and bailed ship, and not long after the company had gone under. They had restored the inn to match its original splendor, refinishing the woodwork and balconies and mahogany rail on the staircase, and much of the furniture and artwork had been there for a hundred years or more.

Diana had shown up with Sam sleeping in her arms shortly after eleven o'clock, asking for Cybil. The woman had looked at her suspiciously for a moment, the side of her face, but it was cold and it was late and she had a small child. She had asked Diana to wait in the foyer and then gone up the stairs.

When Cybil pulled her close, Diana's body heaved, and then she started to cry. Just for a second, and then she pulled away, wiping her eyes. "I must look like a fool," she said.

Cybil took her hands. "Don't say that. This isn't your fault. I'm going to call the police."

Diana shook her head. "No. Don't. It will just make it worse. You were right. I shouldn't have stayed. He was obviously in a bad way, and staying just made it worse. If I hadn't of stayed it never would have happened. Everything would have been fine."

"You can't go back there," Cybil said. "He needs to be arrested. I'm going to call the police. You can stay here for a few days. There's five bedrooms, and three of them are empty right now. I can explain what happened. And I'm sure she'll give you a break on the cost."

"No, Cybil, honestly. I don't need the pity wagon. I brought this on myself, and I'm going to have to deal with it. He just needs some help. I just want him to get some help, and then he'll be fine."

"No." Cybil shook her head. "He's my brother, but he's a monster. He's just like our father. And he's not going to get help unless it's something he decides to do, and he won't do that. He can't. Look what he did to you. There's no excuse for that, Diana. None."

Sam was asleep on the couch. Diana walked over to the fire, looked at her daughter. "I just need to go back to get some of our things. That's it. And then I have to think things through."

"You've already thought things through. You need to leave him. Now."

"And where am I going to go?" Diana asked. "Back to my mother's? No way. I have too much pride to go crawling back to her. And I don't have a job right now, so it's not like I can afford a place of our own, and besides, Samantha is in school. She has friends here." And she did, it was true. And as desolate as it could be in the winter, Diana had grown to love the island, the quiet and the beauty.

"You're just looking for excuses to stay," Cybil said, "and you can't do that. Sam will get over it. It's better that she's safe, and then she can make new friends."

"Oh, he wouldn't touch her. He knows better than that. He knows I'd kill him. I would. I would kill him."

"You don't know what he would do," said Cybil. "You don't know what he's capable of." She put her fingers to her chest, her heart. "I do. Believe me. I grew up with this. And besides, this is about you. You need to be safe. If you go back, it's just going to get worse. He'll apologize, while subtly blaming you, and then it might be better for a while, but then it will just get worse. I've seen it, Diana. Listen, after you get your things, you can come back up to Salem and stay with us. The apartment isn't huge, but we have room. We can make room." She reached over and took her hand. "Just until you get back on your feet. Okay?"

ᔦ

The following day they drove to Edgartown to get some lunch, away from Oak Bluffs so Diana could relax. In the good weather, parking in town was nearly impossible, but now there were spaces all along Main and North and South Water Streets. Just a few art galleries still open, the lights soft and warm in the windows. They ate at David Ryan's, downstairs in the pub, sports shows playing on the televisions, highlighting the football games from the day before. Diana's stomach was in knots. She ordered a Reuben, broke it into pieces and pushed it about her plate, and Samantha ate her French fries.

Cybil had asked Samantha if she would like to come and stay with them, with Diana, for a few days, and the little girl seemed excited, but Diana sidestepped the conversation again, saying, "We'll see." She wanted to leave, and yet she did not. Before Ford, she had always been independent, even in high school, and the thought of being dependent on somebody now, being a handout, even for a short period of time, was making the hollow feeling inside just swell all the more. And maybe if he did stop drinking, he could be different, she thought, not such a jackass. Maybe it was just a matter of getting him to stop. But she couldn't say that to Cybil. She wouldn't understand—would call it battered woman syndrome. And what if Diana told Cybil that the stress was getting to be too much, that she feared she might be having a breakdown, that she had begun to see things. People? Ghosts? And that Sam was making up people to have conversations with? What would Cybil say then? She would look at her as weak, troubled, and then what? Would she report her to DSS as an unfit mother? Unable to care for Sam? If she did, Diana had no doubt she would do it in the belief that she were doing the right thing, for Sam, and for Diana, that she would be doing it to help them, because she loved them, but it wasn't that simple, wasn't that easy, and Diana couldn't bear the thought of being separated from Samantha. Maybe Cybil wouldn't do anything at all, nothing besides offer her support. But you never knew—she had already been through too much trauma herself.

Now, leaving the restaurant, Cybil was walking up ahead, holding Samantha's hand. Diana was with Norman, some twenty feet behind, and she couldn't hear what they were saying, but Samantha's lips were going, talking and talking, and she looked happy, and Cybil was listening. They headed toward North Water Street, which led to the lighthouse. As old as Oak Bluffs was, Edgartown made it seem young. Especially here on North Water Street, the white colonial mansions, Georgian in style, lining the brick sidewalks, close together and so close to the street, towering above you and seeming to look down. To Diana it seemed as if you almost never saw anyone coming in and out of these buildings, even in the good weather, and it was almost as if each had been frozen in time, its occupants from that bygone era gone one day, never to return, leaving the shells of these grand homes, untouched and silent, waiting, not even the dust allowed to pervade inside.

Many of the homes had been owned by sea captains, whalers, who for every six months they spent at home, spent three years at sea. Children growing, and wives quietly tending to the homes, every once in a while looking out upon the sea, never really sure if their husbands would ever return. A ship on the harbor could very well be them, and it could very well not be; there was always a chance that their ship already rested at the bottom of the ocean. Diana wondered what life was like then? Never knowing. Some women probably missing their husbands terribly, bombarded with the echoes of the empty spaces around them, and others maybe praying they would in fact never return. Their hearts slowly sinking as they saw the weathered men walking up the then streets of cobblestone, chins high and carriages erect, cabin boys in tow, dragging the captains' sea trunks behind them. Home for now, another six months. The peace gone. Her life, his will.

His will.

"As a matter of fact," Norman said to Diana, "we were going to stop by the house today regardless, even if nothing happened, and invite you up for a few days. After yesterday, we were kind of getting the feeling that a little distance for all of you might not be such a bad thing."

"He's not always bad," Diana said quietly, the words feeling heavy, false, but somehow still necessary. He was her husband, and she had taken her vows seriously, and despite everything, there had to be some loyalty. Hadn't there? But she hated him right now, hated him.

"Oh, don't get me wrong," Norman said, backtracking a little. "I've seen him act like a great guy. Funny and all that." He chuckled a little. "The trouble is the other ninety-five percent of the time when he's acting like a total asshole. He can get pretty scary. They all have their baggage in that family, Cybil included. She's been seeing a shrink for years. That old man incurred more damage in a few short years than most fathers could do in a lifetime. And believe me, I bet his father did the same thing to him. Probably beat the hell out of him. That's how it works. It's all cyclical. It never ends."

"Well, it could end if they wanted it to. Anything can end if you want it to." The wind came in off the water, sharp and cold.

"Do you think so?" Norman asked. "I'm not sure. Think of how you feel when you lose your temper, how you react. Whether you scream, slam your palm against the table, throw things or sulk. When your emotions get away from you, you do what you do. And anger is one of the most controlling and debilitating emotions we have. Rage can consume you. Just think how hard it would be to change how we react. We react as we do because that's who we are. It's ingrained in us—both before and after we're born."

"You sound like a psychologist," Diana said.

"Well, I'm trying to think like one. Just to put it in perspective, I mean."

"So you think anyone who is born of an abused parent will be an abuser themselves."

"No. Not necessarily. I think the wiring for that sort of temperament has to be there to begin with, but then that person would have to be abused, too. And if that happens? Forget it. No shot."

Diana looked ahead again at Samantha. She wondered how much Sam processed what was going on, how much she thought about it. Diana knew that Ford scared Samantha at times, but it hadn't been like that early on. She had been quite attached to him at first, her eyes lighting up every time she saw him. Diana thought of days gone past, better days. Ford taking her to the planetarium at the Museum of Science, playing Frisbee in the park, D.W. Fields. Climbing the Blue Hills, and feeding the reindeer at the bottom in the November chill. He was capable of being a good man. She had once been sure of it, and now, at least had to hope for it. He was just . . . a mess. And now it had been some time since Diana had seen that light in Sam's eyes. She wondered what he was doing to her, psychologically, emotionally, what she was doing to her, the two of them living together, and yet whenever she thought of leaving for good, she found herself racked with guilt. Never marrying Samantha's biological father, then marrying Ford, then taking her away? Leaving her with just one parent? Again? Ford had never touched her, never hit her, she was sure of it, so maybe he had some self-control. Maybe he had something.

"No shot, huh?" Diana said to Norman. "Thanks for making me feel good."

"Well, I'm not trying to make you feel bad," he said, "but I am trying to make you see that it's not your fault, and unfortunately, there's probably not much you can do about it."

"Can I ask you something?"

"What?"

"Have you ever hit Cybil?"

Norman grinned. "Are you kidding? She'd kill me."

They passed an old whaling church. Early mid-nineteenth century. Greek Revival. The enormous white pillars, and the clock tower high above. It was a beautiful church, solid and proud, and it was amazing to think it had stood here so long. Voices were coming from inside now, singing. And the sound of organ keeping time. The voices sounded to be soft at first, gradually growing louder. And then the voice of a man rising above them, a man shouting, and then again the singing. All seeming distant somehow, thin. It startled Diana for a moment as there were very few cars parked out on the street, none in front of the church. She stopped and looked at the doors, sealed tight. She could picture the captains, the crewmen, and their wives passing through them, way back when, and the minister offering comfort to the families in times of grief, disaster, or just voyages gone too long. Diana had read once that Herman Melville's inspiration for Ahab was a sea captain from Martha's Vineyard. Captain Pease. She wondered if it were true. The name was still everywhere on this island, even a street here named after him.

"I wonder what's going on in there," she said to Norman.

"In where?" Norman asked.

"The church," she said.

Norman just shrugged. "I don't think anything is. It looks closed."

"I know," Diana said, "but with the singing, I mean."

"Singing?"

She hesitated, looked at his eyes. Trying to determine if he was having her on. He wasn't the type to do that much, but you never knew. He might have wanted to make a joke, spook her a little and lighten the mood.

Diana swallowed her breath. "The singing. The singing from inside."

Norman shook his head. "I'm not hearing it. Maybe somebody has a CD playing somewhere. You must have dog hearing though because mine is pretty good. At least it used to be. I'm not getting any younger though."

Diana turned back to the church again, but the singing was growing quieter, more distant, and then from the corner of her eye she thought she saw a man walking around the side of the church. Tall with stooped shoulders, head down and dressed in black. But as soon as she looked he was gone. No one there. Just a few dried leaves being blown across the brick walkway, one clinging to the old lamppost. A lamppost they had once filled with whale oil.

19

Hiram addressed the community from the pulpit today. Asking the Reverend Hightower if he could share a word at the end of the service. "The Spirit will speak when the heart is open, Reverend," Hiram said to him, "and are we not all part of the service? All one body in the eyes of the Lord?"

The reverend was hesitant. I could see it in his eyes, and his words in response came slowly, in a whisper meant only for Hiram, before he took a seat on the stage beside the pulpit. his arms folded, and his head bent forward, eyes shut and lips pursed, as if in engaged in heavy thought or prayer. Hiram used to address the congregation quite regularly, preaching the word, but now it has been some time, and today he wasted little time. He read from the Book of Genesis—"Then the Lord rained brimstone and fire on Sodom and Gomorrah, from the Lord out of the heavens. Turning the cities of Sodom and Gomorrah into ashes, condemned them to destruction, making them an example to those who afterward would live ungodly."

"How do we all find ourselves with the Lord this week?" Hiram asked.

There were a few shouts, one or two hallelujahs, and a woman up front swooned a bit, and cried out for Jesus.

"Yes," Hiram repeated, "Hallelujah." And then he shouted it. He shut the book. "Will we find ourselves in his paradise one day?" he asked. "Or will lose ourselves in Sodom? Gomorrah?

Rained upon by brimstone and fire? Brimstone and fire," he repeated. "Would the Lord do this again? Brimstone and fire? I tell you he will. And why?" he asked the crowd. "Why would he punish his minions in such severe, unforgiving measures? Well, why did he before? The answer is right there, in need of little to no interpretation. It is because the people of the cities of Sodom and Gomorrah had turned ungodly, and he wished, he needed, to make an example of these wretched souls, so that those who came after would fear to live so ungodly. So that other people, other cities, would not fall to the same temptations.

"The same temptations that man falls for today!"

Hiram held the book high in his right hand. "Some people forget," he said, "and others . . . merely choose not to listen. They choose to scorn the Lord, to live as they please, and not as he pleases. And we, my friends, need to look no further than our own Wesleyan Grove."

"You need not try and convince me that not all the souls who perished in the fires of these two cities were guilty of the crimes—lust, fornication, adultery, murder, theft, and sodomy being just a few—but they all were guilty of one thing." Hiram paused, and when he resumed his speech, he started to shout. "They all were guilty of turning their back on the Lord! They all were—at least, and I do say at least—guilty of turning the other way while their fellow man, their fellow citizens, engaged in debauchery! And I say to you, all of you here today, a sea of faces, a sea of eyes, floating before me, some bored, some enthralled, and some annoyed, that you, too—I, too—will be just as guilty as the non-sinning souls of Sodom and Gomorrah, if we continue to sit idly by while the Devil continues to build his playland by the sea! Sin City! It will be on all of us! And the Lord God will call us all to answer!"

With this a few of the people stood—one being Dr. Mortimer from the town of Concord, along with his wife, and one being Mr. Wendell, who runs the livery over in Edgartown—and took their leave of the tabernacle, ignoring Hiram as he continued to shout. Even the family of Thomas Mayhew took leave, and with that, the others followed, the entire tent began to empty, out of the shade, and into the sun. The service for them was over.

"And when he calls," Hiram yelled, "his justice will be swift, and his justice will be without mercy! You can either take a stand as a soldier of the Lord, or you can frolic in this world and burn in the next! You can turn your back on me, but you cannot turn your back on the Lord! You cannot forsake Him! For it is He who speaks through me!"

In the end, I was left in the audience with only two other souls—Mrs. Stephens and her nephew, but now the nephew lay flat on the ground, staring at the beams of the roof high above us.

20

Diana didn't want to call Charlotte, but she had no other choice. She needed somewhere to go, at least for now, and as kind as Norman and Cybil's offer was, she couldn't intrude upon them indefinitely like that. It wouldn't be fair, and there was still something about it that didn't feel right. Cybil was her friend, but she was still Ford's sister. And even in the worst of circumstances, that always meant something—blood was thicker than water, wasn't it? And besides, if she did go with them, Ford would know right where to find her. He might figure she had gone back to her mother's, too, but he wouldn't go there looking for her. Wouldn't dare. He would look for her at Cybil's.

For now they were spending another night at the bed-and-breakfast, and Samantha was downstairs by the fire with Norman and Cybil, playing a game. *The Muppet Show* board game. Norman had stopped in the toy store down on Circuit Avenue on the way home and bought it for her.

Diana stared at the phone, trying to gather the courage to call. She had told herself she'd never go back. Promised. She didn't want to risk having Samantha near her brother Stephen in the event that anything Ford had accused him of was even remotely close to true, but also she had too much pride. Going back meant defeat. Victory for her mother. "I knew you'd come around to my way of thinking"—she wouldn't say it, but it would be there. Victory harbored in those otherwise empty eyes, and then again she would have Diana under her thumb. There was too much water under the bridge: The fighting about Ford, the nightmare with Stephen. The lies, delusions. Rejection of her friends, boyfriends, her mouth washed out with soap when she was young—dirty words, filthy mouth—and face dunked, held, in the font full of holy water that her mother kept beneath the painting on the Blessed Mother in the parlor. The beating she had taken at four years old when she was showing her friend Emily the hole in her yellow bathing suit. "Show you my hole," she had said. Her mother had heard, lost her mind. Filthy. She remembered not even knowing what she had done wrong. It was just a hole in her bathing suit. Then of course Billy, the end of her dream to go away to school. Her pregnancy.

Her pregnancy. The memory of it all probably scorched more than any of the others. The family meeting, the following exile to her uncle's house in Connecticut, Charlotte's call to the college, St. Elizabeth's, to tell them that Diana would not be attending, and her whole life taking a sudden detour. It had just been the beginning of a quick ride downhill. Things could never be right with her mother. She knew that.

She stared at the phone again. Go back? How could she go back? Crawling. That's what she was doing. Pathetic. It would kill her but she had to do something, she was stuck, had to think of Samantha. Couldn't let the little girl grow up around that kind of violence if Ford kept it up. Or worse become a victim herself. Just a few weeks, she told herself, at tops a couple months. She could handle that, she told herself, would have to. What other choice did she have?

The room she was in had a window overlooking Ocean Park in the distance, lit from the lampposts. The room was pretty. Lace curtains, a queen-size bed, a mirrored armoire against the far wall—a scrolled top and clawed feet—and a pitcher and wash basin just outside the bathroom door. There were a few prints in the room, tasteful: one of the harbor at what was once known as Holmes Hole, now Vineyard Haven; one of old Edgartown, horses and buggies in the street, and a man carrying an armful of firewood up the hill to his home above the sea; and the third an old portrait of a handsome-looking man with a high collar and goatee. Black hair and dark eyes. Eyes that almost seemed to reflect the vastness of immortality, of God and the sea, staring back at Diana as she dialed the phone, piercing into her soul.

She hoped her father would answer, hoped that she could talk to him first.

He did not.

Charlotte picked up.

Diana's tongue froze.

"Hello," Charlotte said. "Hello." She was about to hang up, Diana could feel it, when she finally pushed out the word.

"Ma," she said.

Her mother was silent for a moment. And then she sighed. "I had a feeling it was you."

"I just figured I'd call to wish you a happy Thanksgiving," Diana said. The house was creaking in the wind and the cold, and Diana thought she heard footsteps on the stairs. Muffled. And distant voices below. Samantha squealing, happy.

"Oh, thank you," her mother said. "Was it yesterday or the day before? I'm already losing track. This age thing."

"It was yesterday," Diana said. Cybil had poured her a glass of wine, and Diana had brought it upstairs and drank half of it before calling. Getting up the nerve. Now she swirled it about in her glass, the thin red film coating the sides.

"That's right, it was yesterday," Charlotte said. "Everyone was here. It was wonderful. We had three turkeys. Twenty-five pounds each."

Diana sipped. "What did you do with seventy-five pounds of turkey?"

"We ate it," Charlotte said. "Every last bit of it. It was a feast. Stuffing. Twice-baked potatoes. Stuffed mushrooms. Shrimp cocktail. Sweet potatoes. Seven different kinds of pie. Fresh cranberries I picked myself on Wednesday."

Diana tried to ignore the remark. "How's Grandma doing?"

Charlotte sighed. Heavy. Dramatic. "Not very well. I think this is going to be her last year. Probably her last Christmas. She just doesn't look very good, and she's really in a great deal of pain. She's suffering terribly, but you know her, she's like me, never complains. It takes a strong woman to deal with everything she has to, and still never forget to smile, to continually spread her love of God and love of her family day after day. Not asking for help nor sympathy. Nothing. Some people can deal with the obstacles life places before us, the challenges, and some people just . . . can't."

"Well, I hope she's okay," Diana said again.

"I'm just afraid she's riddled with cancer. Head to toe. Her color is just gray, absolutely gray." She sighed. "I wish we had someone medical in the family."

"Well, I'm a nurse."

Charlotte was silent.

"How's Dad doing?" Diana asked.

"Oh, he's fine. Been doing a lot of reading."

"How about everyone else?"

"Well, Bibi just was voted class valedictorian," Charlotte said. "It was very exciting. The principal himself called to tell me."

"But she's only a freshman," Diana said. "They don't usually do that until senior year."

"Well, he said she's doing so well, it was unanimous. And I think it is just for the freshman class."

"That's weird. I never heard of them picking it in November before."

Charlotte paused. "Well, like I said, it was unanimous, and I guess her grades are so good that she's out there all alone. Away from the pack. We're so proud of her."

"Well, it's good she's not flunking anymore." Diana wondered where it all came from. Wondered if Charlotte actually thought about this stuff, believed it, or if the lies just slipped right off the tip of her tongue. Bibi had been held back in first grade, and then was pushed from one grade to the next, year after year.

"Oh, that was just in elementary school. And you know what the school psychologist told me?"

"What?"

"He said that that was just because she was bored. All those subjects just didn't interest her because she was too smart. Been there, done that. It couldn't hold her interest." Charlotte took a breath. "So now they have her taking advanced college courses. She's studying at the level of a junior in college. Advanced placement. They say at this rate she'll be able to get her bachelor's and PhD, or doctorate if she chooses, within two years after high school. And then, who knows? The sky is the limit."

The conversation was quickly getting off-track, but it was better to just play along, you had to play along, and Diana figured if she were going to ask, she needed to ask quickly. Swallow her pride, get it over with. Tell Charlotte it would just be temporary. She would find a job, immediately. Pay for her their own food. Temporary.

"Well, that's fantastic," Diana said. "Tell her I said congratulations."

"I will." Charlotte took a deep breath. "And you'll have to congratulate your brother, too."

"Which one?" Diana asked.

"Stephen." Charlotte paused, waited, but Diana didn't respond. "He's back in college. He's going to Boston College."

"BC?" Diana said. Through the window she could see the lampposts of Ocean Park. The only lights out there in the night. She put her head in her hand. Why did it have to be like this? Crazy. Crazy before, crazier now. Charlotte's delusional world building and building, a bubble expanding that was bound to explode. And what then? What would happen when it exploded?

"Yes, Boston College," Charlotte said. "He has a 4.0, and he's doing so well that the dean has asked him to be a guest lecturer. It's quite an honor. I guess they only ask one student from each class, and this year it was Stephen. He's ecstatic. I can just picture him, walking building to building, in a tweed coat and smoking a pipe."

"Maybe," Diana said, "but it wouldn't be filled with tobacco."

"I don't know what you mean," Charlotte said.

"Oh, come on, Ma," Diana said. She couldn't hold back anymore. It was too much. "The kid's not a college lecturer, he's an addict."

"An addict?"

"A drug addict, Ma. You know this. Crack, heroin, you name it."

"Stephen has been drug-free for almost a year."

"Oh, please, Ma, he has no interest in getting clean."

"Diana, you haven't even seen him in how long now? Two years? I'm not going to talk to you if you're going to speak to me this way."

"Of course not, because you can't face the truth."

"I won't."

"I know you won't."

"The problem with you, Diana, is you think you know everything. Always have. That and you're selfish. And ever since you met . . . you met . . . that asshole, it's just been worse. You know if you could just think of someone else for once, for once in your life, I think I would drop to my knees right out in the street and start saying the rosary. Is this why you called me? To insult me? The truth. Why don't you tell me about the truth, Diana?"

Diana heard the phone click, but it was some time before she took it away from her ear. She didn't want to move, didn't think she could, and she wondered if she had ever before felt so alone, helpless. She wondered where you went when even your own mother turned her back on you. The one person in the world who was supposed to always look out for you, protect you. Gone. The wind was louder outside, rattling the panes of the glass on the windows. The sea looking to come closer, to be let in. On an island like this, it was always looking to be let in. The sea owned the island, and the people who inhabited it, and there was always a need to remind them of that. If she wanted it, them, they were hers. Diana looked back at the portrait of the man on the wall. Eyes so dark and empty, and somehow still watching.

21

In the morning with Samantha still sleeping, Diana snuck downstairs to get a cup of tea. She had fallen asleep in her clothes the night before, and now in her stocking feet, she passed Cybil and Norman's room. The door was shut, the only noise, Norman's muffled snores. It was just before seven, and the entire house was quiet. Diana peeked outside. It looked as if it would be a nice weather day, the dark blue of the night sky beginning to lighten, and the rising sun springing forth from the sea. She turned into the parlor, heading toward the dining room to look for some tea—she had seen the breakfast serving dishes set up in there the night before—and then stopped, glancing back toward the stairs, thinking she heard something. Samantha? But, no, the house was quiet again. Nothing. She started forward and as she did she jumped. There was a man sitting in the parlor with his feet up, reading, a mug of coffee in hand. She hadn't seen him at first—would have sworn there was no one there—but now he, too, jumped, spilling a bit of coffee over the arm of the chair.

He put his feet quickly on the floor, started to apologize.

"No, I'm sorry," Diana said. "I startled you. I didn't think anyone was up yet."

The man waved her off. "No, no. I'm too blame. I startled you." He stood, surveyed the area around him. Stalled.

The coffee was running down the side of the leather chair.

"Let me give you a hand." Diana hurried over to the highboy, grabbed a small stack of napkins, and then crouched down beside his chair, sopping up the coffee. "These are beautiful chairs," she said. "I'd hate to see them ruined."

"Well if there is a man who could ruin them, that man would be me," the man said. "I'm beginning to fear I'll never have the grace of a dancer."

Diana balled the napkins up in her hand. "Well, it wasn't much. I'm sure it will be fine." She stood and took a quick step back, feeling suddenly self-conscious, remembering the bruise on the side of her face. She hadn't realized how close she was to the man. He was right in front of her, still hadn't moved much. He looked to be a little older than her. Early thirties? Late? It was hard to tell. He was dressed for the day—faded jeans, and a faded blue sweatshirt—"VINEYARD" in big white letters written across the front. He was handsome, she thought, not overly handsome, but enough so as to make you look twice. Slightly exotic. His hair dark, curly but short, and he had a square jaw and amused eyes, remarkably dark and fluid A Mediterranean complexion, she thought, and he looked familiar. She had seen him before—she must have—but she couldn't picture where. He stared down at the floor. Her feet. Diana followed his gaze. There was a large hole in the sock on her right foot, the heel missing.

"Well, that's embarrassing," she said. "I didn't even notice that. I must look like I just walked out of the poorhouse. We didn't plan on staying, so I didn't bring much clothes."

The man sat down, and started to remove his shoe. "Listen, don't be embarrassed." He pulled the shoe off, and held up his foot. "You see? Two holes. I've got you beat." He was looking at the side of her face now, had paused, noticed it. He hadn't noticed right off—she would have known if he did. Maybe the shadows in the room, poor light, or maybe it was already starting to heal, the swelling receding.

"You might want to put some more ice on that," he said.

"Ice?"

"Your face." Diana blushed, the shame rising again. "Oh, that? It's nothing. You think you'll never be a dancer? I can't even walk through my house without bumping into a wall. I'm going to get some tea. Do you want more coffee? I can get you more coffee. I feel bad."

The man stood again. "No, no, that's fine. I can get it. The owner finds out I have the other guests waiting on me, she'll probably force me out the door."

Diana was quiet.

"I'm' joking," he said. "I actually stay down here fairly regularly, so she gives me a good deal as long as she has an open room—it's usually easier in the winter." He held out his hand. "I'm Michael, by the way. Michael Chiaro."

Diana held her hand out. "Diana," she said. "Barlow."

He shook his head. "You don't look like a Barlow."

"Barlow is my married name," she said.

He nodded, this time a bit slower. "I see. Are you just down for the weekend?"

Diana wondered if the owner had mentioned them to him, or how much the owner even knew. Diana knew that Cybil had talked to her about their situation, but wasn't sure how much she had told her.

"No," Diana said. "I live here."

⤸

They sat at the dining room table, Diana sipping her tea and nibbling at a scone. Chocolate chip. He said he lived in Boston, that he came down here to paint.

"You're an artist?" she said.

He laughed a little. "Well, that wholly depends on who's doing the viewing. I do a number of things, actually. I spent some time studying history, a little philosophy. I teach, too, when I can, and when I can I sell my paintings. It makes me a little extra money. Enough to pay the landlord anyway. And it's nice to be able to spend time down here."

"What do you paint?" Diana asked.

"Spirits."

"Spirits?"

"Ghosts," he said. "You know. The dead."

Diana held her teacup halfway to her lips, wondering if he were just having her on.

The man smiled. "I'm joking again," he said. "My subject matter is mostly period work though. Nineteenth-century people, places. Mostly from around the island, so I have to rely on a lot of old photographs and things. I spend a lot of time at the historical museum. Exciting, huh?"

"I like the museum." Diana sipped her tea, thinking of the Wesley, the desk clerk, and the bell ringing in the distance. "Do you ever paint any of the old hotels?"

"I love the hotels," he said. "I can show you."

He brought down some of his canvases then—he said the owner let him keep them upstairs—and leaned them against the wall in the parlor. He *had* painted the Wesley Hotel, people in Victorian garb lining the veranda, but the entire facade looking quite different than it did today, the balconies on the successive stories all much smaller, and no fourth floor. A man stood on the dusty street below, bowler and suit coat pulled together with one button in the middle. He had his arms folded, and appeared to be leaning back on his heels. There were others, too. The Arcade Building on Circuit Avenue, The Willard Hotel, the steamboats, the Edgartown train, and the Highland House. Then he pulled out the last one from the bottom of the stack, and there it was. The Sea View.

The hotel was beautiful, but it looked nothing like the scaffolding shell Diana had been reading about in the journal. Here it was complete. High and magnificent, and perched upon the edge of the sea as if calling her on. Daring her to try and bring it down. There were people in this painting too, but they were just small black shadows, milling about Ocean Park, and holding umbrellas to the sun on the beach below. Diana couldn't make out any of their faces—the focus of the painting was the hotel, detailed and glorified, and the colors magnificent. The colors grabbed her first. All of the photos that she had seen of the actual building were all black-and-white, of course, and made it all seem like a black-and-white world. But to add color . . . It somehow made it all seem that much more real. The people real. Not just ghosts.

He had portraits, too. Men and women. Mostly in Victorian dress. One was of a man with a white beard and rolled-up pant legs walking through the surf. It was a very Homer-like painting, Diana thought, and the paintings brought back memories from when she was young. Her art classes. Her mother's one concession while she was growing up. She remembered the long narrow room with the track lighting, the students' paintings on the wall, and her teacher. A disheveled old man with sapphire-blue eyes and curls of gray hair. A stained cashmere sweater, and pipe tobacco stale on his breath. He would approach from behind, lean over, his face an inch away from the canvas. "What's happening here?" he would say. And more than once he had brought Diana's work to the front of the class to show them how to do it right.

"Our budding little Georgia O'Keefe," he had said with a sparkle in his eye.

Diana had liked him.

"Do you get them all from photographs?" she now asked Michael, viewing the man on the beach. "Some," said Michael. "You would not be able to get a photograph like the man in the surf, not from that era. People needed to pose, holding extremely still, or the photograph would fail. It wasn't like a photographer could walk down the beach with his camera. He would need time to stop, set it up, shoot. Look for the right light. I wanted to try and capture the light in that one—so you could see it was dawn, the sun rising in the distance, without seeing the actual sun. And I wanted to capture how it was. The time, I mean."

"I can see it." Diana held her hand up, fingers splayed before the canvas. "You have a lot of talent."

"Well, thank you. It's kind of you to say so, but the subject matter certainly isn't hard to find. There are ghosts all over the island. Houses, landscapes, the reflection in the eyes of the gulls on the beach. I sometimes think the fact that it is such a beautiful island is what keeps them here." He smiled. "Even the ghosts never want to leave."

"Never?"

Michael shook his head. "Never." He looked back at the painting of the man in the surf. "Anyway, once I get enough of them completed, I hope to have a show." He was quiet a moment. "Maybe in Edgartown. Or maybe over in Holmes Hole. There are a few galleries over there."

Diana looked at him from the corner of her eye. "Holmes Hole?"

He laughed. "Vineyard Haven, I mean. It used to be called Holmes Hole, and some of the old-timers still call it that. An old friend of mine has a few connections there."

22

Hiram has bought several acres of land on the hill above Squash Meadow Pond. It didn't come about quietly. The people of the campgrounds have asked him to leave. Summer is now nearly gone, as soon will be most of the camp dwellers, and we sleep in a canvas tent at the top of the highlands, looking down upon Trinity Circle, as we watch our new home rising before us. We have "crossed the Jordan" as the people from the circle like to say, moving further from the wayward ways of the ever-expanding Oak Bluffs, across Squash Meadow Pond, but unlike the others, we have not done so on our own volition; Hiram was not nearly ready to give up his ground, to give up the fight, to give in to the Land and Wharf Company, and I need to seriously wonder if he ever really would; I'm not sure the fire and the soldier, and indeed sometimes the madness, in him would ever allow it.

The builder Frederic Carl is constructing our home in the manner of the cottages but on a larger scale. He had worked for Mr. Pratt for a time, but confided in Hiram that he could no longer abide by the intent of the man's ways—building nondenominational churches to quiet the masses, and presenting himself to be a service-going Christian while paying his laborers quite unfairly and promoting his playland to undesirables of all walks of life. Indeed, Hiram agreed, the Devil excludes no one willing to walk with cloven shoes, and with that he signed the man on.

Our prayers rise to the Lord that the house will be completed before the winter arrives, and if not, I shall have to implore upon Hiram to travel to the mainland, to spend the season with my family in Boston. It will not be easy. Hiram is making a stand. He won't be driven from his home, his island, not by heathens, and not by the disciples of Lucifer, parading about the campgrounds, disguised as Christians. These are Hiram's words, not mine. I hold no judgment against our former friends, nor the neighbors, both the seasonal and year-round residents, those who sat beside us each Sunday as we worshipped. Hiram is no longer able to live among them and keep any semblance of composure, and it is not their fault. Were he to find these words, penned by me, I fear what consequences might arise, but I hide my journal well, only scribble when he is sleeping, in town, or down on the bluffs beyond Lake Anthony.

He will no longer walk through Trinity Park, and forbids me to do so also—not that I would after all that has transpired. I can still see him in the tabernacle, overturning a pew, screeching, but even then our neighbors, the good people that they are, may have been willing to forgive him, may have looked the other way, if Hiram had not unleashed his fury upon Dr. Mortimer's daughter.

Dr. Mortimer's daughter was only visiting for the week. It is said she cannot abide too much sun and when her parents arrive to spend the summer she stays with an elderly aunt who lives in Lexington. Hiram has heard this, too, and he informed me that he knows for fact for this to be false. He says the Lord set upon him and showed him in a vision the way the young woman conducts herself while her parents are here on Martha's Vineyard, showed him the activities she delights in to fill her day.

I must admit that Hiram's disdain for Dr. Mortimer's daughter, Mary, took me by surprise at first as I remember their first meeting last summer, and none of it was apparent then. Indeed, Hiram, in an unusual showing for him, went out of his way to make the girl feel welcome. Taking off his hat, and bowing to her at their introduction, and then spending some time sitting and talking to her after the last meeting of the day on Sunday, each of them sipping a cool glass of lemonade, and the girl with an umbrella spread open above her, despite the sun already breaking in reds as it set upon the western side of the island.

I remember him telling her then that he was not prone to take in a great deal of sun himself as it brought on headaches and made him tired. There was too much that needed to be done during the day to spend all his time idling in the sun, he said, and he laughed loudly as he did so. It was good to see Hiram laugh, and it was also rare, though not as rare at it would be now, but he was different then, still enveloped in the light of the Lord but not as closed to the thoughts of others.

The Mortimer girl is a pretty girl with fair skin and wide green eyes—wide as if everything she hears is completely new and comes as surprise. Her bosom is ample, and she is narrow in the waist. She has a small voice that you must sometimes strain to hear, and it is because of this voice, I imagine, that she is prone to whisper, leaning close to her audience's ear as she did with Hiram that day, all that time Hiram listening intently, nodding. She couldn't be more than twenty-three or twenty-four, though some have already begun to whisper the word "spinster" when she retires to her parent's cottage for the evening, so perhaps she is older. Hiram, last summer, took umbrage to this and said there was no shame in a girl waiting for the right man to find her, the man who would lead her down the path of the Lord, and I remember him returning to our cottage that evening and speaking of her happily but quietly, telling me that he had never met a young woman who shines so with Jesus before. "Radiant," he said. "Simply radiant." As far as I have seen though there were never many suitors about on any of the occasions where Mary Mortimer has come to visit, although Louisa Teal had told me this in fact was out of respect for Dr. Mortimer as he is stern on approach, carries himself with a quiet air of dignity, and many of the young men on the island have no wish to offend him. And offending him is precisely what Hiram did.

I fear I will never know what exactly ignited his fury, but it was within the first hour of Sunday services, and after coming face-to-face with Mary Mortimer, recently returned to the island. Hiram and I had taken a bench near the back, and Dr. Mortimer, as usual, sat in the front row, standing aside to let Mrs. Mortimer and Mary pass before him. Upon sight of Mary Mortimer, I felt the change in Hiram, sitting beside me—a tension rippling and a rising in temperature—even before I saw the change on his face. He began to murmur, and then he bowed his head, and the reverend began his service. He was deep in the Scripture—John 2:13-25—when Hiram stood and began to shout. He pointed at the Mortimer girl and called her Salome. "She would take us all down to burrow in her little nest full of sin if she had her way!" he shouted. "Invite us to burrow and then deliver us to the Devil!"

Dr. Mortimer stood and turned, looked at him, facing him head-on, but Hiram kept going. "Wallowing with the Devil," Hiram said, now a shade quieter. "Parading about and flaunting her breasts, like a proud little robin. Tempting weak men to succumb to the flesh. Tempting here, merely tempting, in the midst of our tabernacle." He paused. "But forfeiting freely in her relative's home far away in Lexington!"

"Stop," said Dr. Mortimer.

"Forfeiting and indulging," said Hiram.

"Stop," Dr. Mortimer said again.

"While her mother and father come ashore to our island and worship among us. Who is this young woman worshipping? I ask you!"

I reached for Hiram's sleeve, hoping to pull him back down in his chair beside me, but he neither brushed me away nor succumbed to my wishes. He stood perfectly still. "I have it on fact from a dear friend who travels off island in August every year. Travels to Lexington. He has seen this woman, and the company she keeps. Spending time on the town common, and even now and then, time in the public house. Alone, unchaperoned, and waiting."

Dr. Mortimer began to move toward the end of his aisle, intent on meeting Hiram face-to-face. The congregation was nearly silent, just a few whispers, and the reverend had a look on his face as if he were lost in the woods, mouth open and eyes frightened. The Mortimer girl had not turned, she had her head down, hiding, and my heart suddenly broke for her. Hiram was ill. I now knew he was ill, but she did not. All she could possibly see was the cruelty, and there I could not blame her. There was no friend who traveled to Lexington, not that I was aware of.

"How many men have nestled their heads in her bosom?! Can you stand before us now and come forth?!" Hiram shouted. "I have spoken with the Lord and he has told me you are legion! Legion they are, and many more coming! For this woman comes to our retreat to lead as many as she can in, and lead as many as she can out! Merging with the sinful land springing up all about us. A spy from Satan, leaving a trail of bread crumbs to the hotels, the saloons." He paused again. "And the brothels."

Dr. Mortimer was nearly upon him now as were several young men of the congregation, following suit. But Dr. Mortimer turned to them, raising a quieting hand. "Not before the altar of the Lord," he said.

He raised his chin as he came within arm's reach of Hiram. Hiram is much taller than Dr. Mortimer, but the man did not seem intimidated in the least, and despite everything, he was doing a remarkable job of maintaining his countenance. Hiram continued to spew a volley of words, and he seemed to be yelling at the sky more than anything else. I reached up again to take his elbow, to try and pull him back down beside me, to settle him.

"I won't tolerate this insolence, Hiram," said Dr. Mortimer.

Hiram opened his eyes. Glared. "You, sir, speak to me of insolence? You?"

"I could speak to you about a lot of things, many of which are unsettling, but not here, not now. It is neither the time nor the venue, and you, I fear, are not well. I fear you pose a danger to our community, Hiram."

"The spawn of your flesh leads our young men down the road to hell, good sir, and you will speak to me about danger? Who masks you? In whose name do you come?"

"I come in the name of my family," Dr. Mortimer said, "and in the name of our Savior, and I'm asking you to leave."

I feared then that Hiram would strike out at him, so I stood, prepared to position myself between them if need be, although I must confess my concerns grew more toward Dr. Mortimer than they did toward Hiram. I knew Hiram's strength, knew the power he wielded when he closed his fist, and I couldn't bear to think of anyone else getting hurt. Hiram was still glaring, but Dr. Mortimer glared right back.

"Spare your wife the spectacle, good sir," he said. "She is a good woman, a lovely woman, and she deserves better than this."

"Do not speak to me of my wife," said Hiram. "Her name is soiled for coming off your tongue."

"Hiram," I said, "please let's go. Maybe we can meet later, when tempers have cooled, and talk then."

"There will be no more meetings with your husband," Dr. Mortimer said, "not before this altar, not in this congregation."

At that point I feared it might all go very badly, worse than it did, but several more men from the congregation did come and stand behind Dr. Mortimer then and even Hiram, I believe, could not believe his eyes. He looked about the sea of heads, some turned watching, and others still turned away, facing the pulpit.

"Will no one stand with me?" he asked, his eyes still searching, but his voice suddenly quiet. A few people whispered, a few others stirred, but no one else stood. Not Mrs. Stephens, not even her nephew. For a moment, I believed the nephew was going to get up, and Hiram, I believe, saw this, too, but then the old woman put her hand firm upon the simple boy's shoulder.

I stood, but not to confront the crowd, but rather to attempt to reason some more with Hiram, talking quietly and encouraging him to come with me so we could go home. The silence, the tension, seemed to spread throughout the park like water up a cloth, only to be broken by the clock on the church tower striking noon. I put my arm through his, and something changed in his eyes again then. Something went out, emptied, but then within seconds was filled with something else, something beyond rage and beyond reason.

"I curse you all," he whispered, "I curse you all, and the Lord permitting, I'll see you to hell." With that he pulled free from my arm, and walked toward the crowd. Dr. Mortimer looked startled for a moment, and several of the men tightened their shoulders, ready, but then they must have seen something in his eyes as he was looking past them, not at them, and with a nod from Dr. Mortimer, they all stepped aside, parting like the Red Sea to let Moses through, and Hiram paid them no mind as they did. He walked very slowly, his head high, and departed the tabernacle, disappearing beneath the tall oaks and off toward our little painted cottage. A proud but beaten soldier, his faculties gone awry.

It was the next day I found the petition, taped to the door.

23

The lights were all out on the house on the hill, and Ford's car wasn't in the driveway. The gravel crunched beneath the tires, Norman's car, as Diana pulled onto the side of the road in front of the neighbor's house, a summer house, and Diana hoped the sound didn't carry. She didn't want to be heard, seen. The street-light above turned on, reacting to her movement, as she stepped out of the vehicle, startling her for a moment. It was nearly midnight, the best time to come. It was too early into his shift for Ford to come home for lunch, or even for a break, and he never overslept when it came time to go in. Punctuality was as important to him as keeping his hair neat, his clothes pressed. Appearances were everything. Norman had tried to come with her, insisted, but she assured him Ford wouldn't be home, that no crisis was too big for Ford to miss work. But the reality was, even if by some slim chance, Ford was home, it would be better to come without Norman. Bringing Norman might only send things escalating again, and although she couldn't tell him—for fear of wounding his pride—she didn't want him to get hurt.

The lawn was covered in frost, silver in the light from the moon. Diana stepped onto the porch. The wind picked up, and the rocker to her left began to move. She pressed her face against the stained glass panel of the door, but the house was completely dark, and she could see nothing. She closed her eyes and said a quick prayer, and then she shoved as she turned the key, the chimes above her ringing out as she did.

She shut the door quietly behind her and looked up the stairs. No movement, no nothing. Everything was shadows, the dark deepening around her. She could hear the grandfather clock ticking in the dining room, and she could see her breath; the house was cold, and maybe that was good. Maybe he had left for a few days, turned off the heat. She had given in and agreed to stay with Cybil and Norman—what choice did she have?—just for a week or two, she said, and now all she needed was a few minutes to pack two suitcases, a few more toys for Sam, and that was all. The rest could stay, at least for now, maybe for good. In her heart she didn't care if he kept it all. It was all attached to memories and if you were going to sever the relationship, you needed to sever the memory. She believed that. She listened again, frightened for the moment that she might hear the voice she sometimes heard upstairs talking to Samantha, but still there was nothing. Just the clock. She took a step forward, and flicked on the light switch.

Ford was sitting in the dining room.

Diana jumped, her heart seizing, tightening, and then immediately sinking. Everything lost. "You scared me," she said.

He had his feet flat on the floor. His hands tightly gripping the wood scrolled arms on the winged back chair. He had positioned himself facing the door. Waiting.

Diana's mouth felt dry, the hairs on her neck standing on end, but she didn't want to let him see she was scared. He was like a dog—if he sensed fear, you were done. She didn't want to overreact, didn't want to make a big deal out of it. Big deals could turn into huge deals all too quickly. She hurried past him and turned on the side table lamp.

"You can't see a thing in here." She glanced around the room, everything was clean. The dishes, glasses gone. The mess cleaned up from the floor. Ford was clean, too. Showered, his hair combed back. But his eyes were still yellow, broken with red, and his face was pale.

"Your eyes adjust to the dark pretty quickly," he said.

"Well, I don't like the dark."

He was watching her, but she didn't want to look at him, not directly. "I know," he said, "but I figured if I had the lights on, if I didn't hide the car, you'd never come in."

She stopped, did look directly at him now, trying to read him. A trap. Had he seen her drive up? Was he drunk? She couldn't smell any booze, but if he *was* drunk, it would be best to get out quick. Just head to the kitchen, out the back door and keep on going.

"I haven't been able to sleep since you left," he said, his voice suddenly small. She listened for an edge, but there was none that she could discern.

"Well, get used to it. I just came back to pick up a few things. We're not staying, Ford. It's over. I'm done."

He looked down at his hands, his fingernails, and then when he looked up he had tears in his eyes. "Please don't go."

"It's gone way beyond please, Ford," Diana said. "You need help, and I can't help you. I can't live like this. I won't."

"Please," he said again. "I'm sorry for what happened. Just let me explain. Please. I need to explain."

"No."

"Please."

"No. I'm tired of the explaining. Every time you act like an asshole, you always want the chance to explain. And I'm tired of giving it. You need help."

"I'll get help. I promise. I just need to talk to you. I love you." He started to cry. "And I love Samantha. Just five minutes, that's all I ask."

Diana hesitated, her head telling her to go. He looked pathetic, sitting there like that. Nothing like the monster with the rage in his eyes that had knocked her to the floor just forty-eight hours earlier. But she knew that monster was still in there, always in there, sometimes hiding, sometimes exploding, but mostly, just there, right below the surface, waiting. She didn't want to listen to him, he didn't deserve to have her listen to him, but at least, she thought, if she did, she could say that she did, gave him a chance, and then that would be that. It would make it that much easier packing their things—she wouldn't have to watch her back. Not so much. He wouldn't hit her again, not now, not in contrition mode. Not with everything at stake. He might follow her about, crying, pleading—he did that well—but that would be it. And God, why did he have to look so pathetic?

Ford got up and came to her, tried to hug her, but Diana stepped back, held her hand up, and shook her head. "Stop," she said. "Back off."

"Please."

"No. Do not touch me. I don't want you touching me. Just the thought of you really makes me ill right now."

His hands were shaking. "I'm sorry."

"Sorry doesn't mean crap with you, Ford. It's not enough."

"I know it's not. I never should have done that to you. I need to make it up to you. I don't know why I act like I do sometimes. It's like everything I've gone through in the past comes crashing down on me at once, and I take it out on you." He started crying again, this time harder, his chest heaving. She hated seeing him cry, and while part of her pitied him, part of her really did just find him sickening, wanting to be away from him, and part of her realized, somehow, that part of her, a very small part, still loved him. In some way. Maybe not the way she had in the past, maybe not with the passion. But something. In a small, sad way. Her heart began to sink again, hating herself for caving, even before she knew she would cave.

"I never told you everything," he sobbed. "Never explained. Not about growing up. Not about my father, and the way he treated us, me."

"You told me enough. He was a bastard just like you. I get it."

"But I never explained it all. How bad it got. I need help, I know I do, and I bang my head against the wall trying to under-stand why I do some of the awful things I do, treat you the way I do, and every time I do I just keep coming back to him, the things he did. I just want a chance to explain. Please. "

Diana locked with his eyes, stared him down.

"Please," he said again.

"Five minutes," she said. "That's all I'm giving you."

Ford nodded. He stepped back, and took a seat again in the chair. And then he looked towards the window and took a deep breath.

"Big Daddy was just that," Ford said, "big—well over six feet tall, with an enormous belly and his pants always slipping down. He had to wear suspenders to hold them up. He wore glasses—thick glasses with thick black rims—when he had to read something close up, and he always kept his hair in a crew cut. Like he just walked out of the fifties or early sixties. He worked as a trucker, and he drove cross country, sometimes as far as California, Washington, and Oregon. He could be gone sometimes for a week or more at a time, and when he came back, he usually had little presents for me and my siblings. Stuff from the road. Once he brought me back a little tepee, and a little wood-carved Indian from a reservation in Nevada, and I had thought the Indian was the greatest thing ever because my father told me it had been carved by a real Indian.

"I still have it somewhere in that house," he told Diana, "probably in my old bedroom. I never had much, and I loved the little Indian because it was something, something that meant that maybe my father gave a shit after all. But I knew he didn't. The good times would usually only last a day or so after my father got back—he always had three or four days off between long trips—and he would start drinking the second he got home. Beers in the morning—Schaefer's—sometimes as early as six a.m., and then by noontime he was drinking whiskey, the country radio station he liked to listen to blaring in the kitchen. He would dance sometimes with my mother, listening to the music, and while he was doing that, he was funny, trying to make us all laugh, square dancing.

"But if you were smart," Ford said, "you got out of there almost immediately after the fun started because you always knew it wasn't going to last, wasn't going to end well. My older brothers and sisters figured this out pretty quickly, and they would go upstairs, out in the yard, or down the street, but I was only little.

And besides, he was my father, and all I wanted was for him to love me.

"Big Daddy loved the fifties," Ford continued, "and I remembered him always saying that maybe the world should have stopped back then. Maybe someone should have pressed the button. He said that was the last time things were the way they should have been. A world full of black-and-white beer commercials. Before civil rights, and before the women's lib movement. He loved to joke about women's lib, and I remember a picture he kept in the basement down where he and his buddies played cards. A naked woman, legs spread, reclined on a couch, a picture of Gloria Steinman's head taped over her face."

Diana was now sitting on the foot of the stairs, still near the door, her coat still on. She had told Ford she would only listen if he stayed in the chair, stayed at a distance, and he did. She kept looking at her watch. She wanted to remind him that the clock was ticking.

"He kept porn pictures hanging on the walls of your house with kids inside?" she said. "Nice."

"Oh, he didn't care. And besides it was in the basement. He always told us we had no business in the basement. The only time any of us went down there was when he was out on the road. We had all sorts of rules when he was at home that made it almost impossible to be a kid. I was always trying to help out. Mowing the lawn, shoveling snow, vacuuming, and doing the dishes. Dusting all the Hummels. And I even helped him clean out the septic tank once when I was like twelve. And it was what happened then that I first realized what a monster he really was, how much I hated him. It was then I knew he would kill me if he felt like it. That I could die, and he wouldn't care.

"The septic tank was always overflowing," Ford said, "and it should have been pumped every couple years, but my father wouldn't pay the money to have that done, so instead he got this idea—I was small enough that he could send me down into the well. He handed me a five-gallon bucket and a shovel, and lowered me down. I thought I was going to cry from the start, but I held it in, figuring my father would lose it if I did, call me a crybaby. I started shoveling, standing up to my chest in shit and piss and toilet paper, while all the while my father sat up there on the grass in his lawn chair in the summer heat, drinking his whiskey and smoking cigarettes. I had to climb out of the hole and carry the buckets of shit to a little stream that ran by our house and dump it all in there, being careful the whole time that none of the neighbors saw so we wouldn't get reported. I hated climbing into the hole, but dumping the shit into the stream wasn't much better because of the rats.

"The rats were always in the stream. They swam around, propelling themselves with their tails, their eyes and snouts just barely above the surface, and sometimes they'd just float there and stare at you, not even a little scared, waiting for you to slip, or make a mistake. Waiting to come after you. I tried not to look at them, but I knew they were always watching." Ford pulled at his chin a bit.

"The work in the tank went on for three days, and when I still wasn't done, my father started to get pissed, calling me a lazy good for nothing, wasting his time, and moving too slow. And then I was still down in the tank when my father did it."

"Did what?" Diana asked.

"He told me that shit belongs with shit," Ford said, "and then he stood up and slid the cover over the tank. A heavy concrete cover that must have weighed a hundred pounds."

Diana studied his eyes, trying to decide whether she should believe him or not. Or whether now was the time to go. Out the door, and don't look back. His story sounded horrible, and maybe it hadn't happened, or maybe it had. But Ford was too far gone. He wasn't her problem. Couldn't be. Not anymore. So why was something pulling at her? Telling her to stay.

"He put the cover on, and then he just left," Ford said. "I kept screaming, but out there in the middle of the yard like that, in the middle of summer, most of the neighbors away on vacation, there wasn't anyone around to hear me. I thought I was going to die down there. If I didn't suffocate or bake in the heat, I figured

I'd starve to death. Starve to death lying in a big pool of that fat old man's shit. And then I started thinking about the rats. Making their way through the pipes, or burrowing through the earth, coming from the stream. And it was so dark, I wouldn't ever even see them. But I would hear them, getting closer, squeaking, and have absolutely no way out."

"So what happened?"

"My brother Jimmy found me eventually. Hours later. He came out in the yard after getting home from work—it must have been six or seven o'clock—to hit some balls because he didn't want to be inside that house, and by that time my voice was almost gone, but I heard the crack of the bat on the balls, and I tried to start yelling again, and it took him about ten minutes to figure out where the hell the yelling was coming from. Then when he finally got the cover off and pulled me up, it was almost dark. I tried to run—there was no way I was going back in that house— but Jimmy was a lot bigger, and he tackled me, and then he was pissed because the two of us were covered in shit. I fought him a little, but then he pushed me inside, and when my mother got a look at me, and asked what happened, you know what my old man said?"

Ford looked down at his ashtray, snubbed out his cigarette, grinned a little. He said, "I was going to let him out. I just had to teach him a lesson."

"And what did your mother do?"

"Nothing. What could she do? She mumbled something about him being rotten, and he laughed a little, and then she told me to get into the shower, but that was about it. If she ever spoke up, really spoke up, he beat the crap out of her. So when I didn't move right away she just yelled at me a little for being fresh, and then she marched me into the shower herself. I could tell she was trying not to cry, but all she said was, 'For godsakes, you're stinking up the whole house.'" Ford looked down at his hands. "And she was right. I was. For months after, that's all I could smell. I can still smell it. I swear it soaked into my skin, into my pores, and every time I went to school I was embarrassed as hell. And then the next day, he told me we—we, he said—had to finish, and you know what I said?"

"What?"

"I said no. I said no, and then the guy just looked at me, his mouth curling up on one side the way it used to, and his eyes staring down at me, like he was trying to remember who I was, and then he pulled off his belt, real slow like he was trying to think things over, and he folded it in two and whacked me across the side of the head. I wouldn't go down—I didn't want to give him the victory—so then he whacked me again, and again, and again. And once I finally did go down, I curled up in a ball on the kitchen floor, and I could hear him above me, all out of breath. And then he got down on his knees—he couldn't crouch, he was too fat—and he lifted my head off the floor by the hair, and said, 'Don't you ever say no to me again,' and then he knocked it back against the floor." Ford was quiet a minute.

"You see," he said. "I don't understand why I do some of the things I do sometimes—why I act like an asshole—but I know he has a lot to do with it. It's because of him. Flashbacks. All that PTSD shit. After the septic tank I swore I would kill him someday. I was always swearing that I'd kill him, but I never did." Ford's chest heaved again. "I still fantasize about it. And now the fat bastard is almost sixty years old, and just sitting there getting older and fatter, and I still haven't said boo to him."

Diana felt on the verge of crying herself now. "Instead you've become just like him."

"No," Ford said.

"Yes, you are, Ford."

"No. I'm not. I've slipped up, but I'm not like him."

"Maybe you don't see it. Not fully. But you are."

Ford got up, approached her slowly again, and got down on one knee, took her hand in his. Diana looked down at his hand. Didn't move.

"I'll stop," he said. "I swear to it. Just please don't leave me. If you leave me, I don't know what I'll do—I'll probably kill myself."

"Don't pull that, Ford."

"Pull what?" he sobbed.

"The suicide card. It's a load of crap, and you know it is."

"It's not."

"It is."

"I've tried before. When I was younger. And if you guys leave now, I don't know what I'll do. Probably drink myself to death."

"What else is new?"

"I love you too much. And I love Samantha. I don't want to live if you guys aren't here."

"But why do you want us here, Ford? It makes no sense. You're never happy when we're around—you can tell we just irritate you. And you're miserable."

"I am happy, Diana. I just don't show it. You've made me happy, you and Sam. I love that little kid so much. Please don't go."

Diana ran through the last year in her head. All the days since they moved to the island. The summer, the blue skies and salt water. People all about. Souls abundant. Despite the crowds, the traffic, she liked the island better when the summer people arrived. Everything came to life then.

And Ford was better then. Wasn't he? Before the fall?

And who was she kidding? Leaving? Where would she go after Cybil's? She had no money, none that was her own, and at least here they had a house. A house of their own. And if she left? She had no job. Not right now. She could get one, she was sure, but it would take a little while. And she had a five-year-old little girl she had to take care of. Food, clothes, shelter. And most importantly, love.

"You need to stop drinking," she said at last.

"I will," he said, nodding. "I will. I'll start going to meetings again—I used to go back when I was with Tara. She wanted me to go. And they have meetings here on the island—a guy I work with goes. I'll start. Right after the holidays."

Diana stood. "No," she said. "Now. Or me and Sam are out of here, Ford. I swear it."

Ford took a breath. Looked up into her eyes. He never looked into her eyes anymore. "Okay. I will. I promise I will."

"And I am not your property. I can do what I want."

Ford was silent, blank-eyed.

"You understand that, Ford? Because if you don't, we *are* leaving."

"I do," he said at last. "You deserve that."

"And," she said. "You hit me again, or worse, you ever lay a finger on Sam, and I'll have your ass in jail, I swear it."

"Diana—"

"You got that, Ford?"

"I would never hurt Sam, Diana, you know that."

"I need to know that you understand that, Ford. That part of our lives is over."

"I do. And it is. You're right. It's over. I swear." He paused. "I love you."

24

He took them to the antique carousel down by the wharf, the Flying Horses, the following Sunday. The carousel had been around for well over a century, boasting to be the oldest in the country. Built in the 1870s, moved to the Vineyard from Coney Island. The horses were all hand carved, and their tails were made of authentic horse hair. Hair from long-forgotten beasts that had moved through a wholly different time, and now in a sense still moved. At least part of them. The carousel was closed for the season, but Ford knew the man who ran it, and he had lent him the key. It was going to be a special ride, he said to Samantha. The horses all to herself. She could ride any one she wanted. Diana had been hesitant, thinking the whole idea a little unnerving, riding it alone, but she had bit her tongue; he had been doting on Samantha, maybe a bit too openly, awkwardly, she thought, but he was trying, at least making an attempt to connect with them again, and that was the important thing. If he tried, and she road-blocked him, then what would that say about her?

It hadn't gone well with Cybil when Diana had returned from the church, but Diana had expected that. Cybil had started to cry a little. Told Diana she was nuts. She couldn't go back to him, couldn't bring Samantha back near him.

"But he's never laid a hand on her," Diana said. And it was true, he never had. And if he had that in him, wouldn't he have done that by now? "If he did, I would never go back," she said to Cybil. "Never. He knows that, so he wouldn't dare."

"He will though," Cybil said. "Believe me. He will. I've seen this, Diana. I've lived it."

"And he has, too, that's why I think he's willing to change," Diana said, and even as she did, the words felt stagnant in her throat, false, leaving her wondering what she now believed herself.

Cybil just shook her head. "They don't change. Not for good."

She had given her some phone numbers. Support groups. Names of therapists. And then Diana and Samantha had left before Cybil and Norman got back on the ferry. Diana went over the entire scenario in her head, over and over, on their way back to the house. History. Options. Lies, love, and forgiveness. She had told herself it would be wrong to uproot Samantha yet another time. She wanted to believe that. If nothing else, Samantha needed stability. She had never had stability. One more incident, and they definitely would go. Would have to. That would be it. She promised herself. Promised Samantha. And if push came to shove, she could protect her—she would die before she let anyone hurt her. And he promised things would get better. They would give him one more chance, and that was all.

Now, Ford flicked on the lights, the horses suddenly bright, alive and surreal. Everything inside was surreal, the night surrounding the building, dark and cold and void of all life. There was no heat in the building, and their breath fogged before them. Ford was going out of his way with all this, doing it to try and make up for things, maybe to be more of a father, more of a husband, but something about it felt all wrong. Carousels were meant to be cluttered with children—waving, squealing, and smiling wide at their parents each time they came around—and ridden in the summer. Warm air, stuffy air. High humidity. The spinning of the machine bringing a cool, welcome breeze.

But it was far from summer.

Ford told Samantha to step back as he opened the gate, the enormous key ring the manager lent him dangling from his fingers. He liked holding the key ring, and he liked Diana seeing him hold it. He wanted to send her a message. Wanted her to know. People liked him. People trusted him.

He had crouched down before Samantha when they returned from the bed-and-breakfast, looked into her eyes, and had told her that what Daddy had done was very, very bad, but sometimes good people make bad mistakes. Samantha just looked at him with a blank stare in her eye and nodded. And then Ford swallowed his breath and hugged her.

"Everybody makes mistakes," he said, "both Mummy and Daddy, and it is important to remember that. And maybe," he said, "if Mummy and Daddy didn't fight so much, didn't get each other so angry, things like what had happened the other night, never would have to happen at all."

Diana had just looked at him with that, a cool anger rising. She tried to trace her footsteps. Her part. But most of it was a blur. And maybe she had said some things. Maybe. Things she didn't realize she was saying, things he misinterpreted. Maybe in the heat of the moment, things she didn't remember. She had talked to Samantha after they left Norman and Cybil, asked her how she felt about going back to the house, going back to live with Daddy, and the little girl had barely flinched.

"It's okay," she said.

"Are you sure?" Diana asked, hugging her tight.

"I knew we were going back anyway," Samantha said.

Diana hesitated a moment, wondering if Cybil had guessed, had said something. "How did you know that?" she asked.

Samantha brushed her doll's hair back over her head. The knotted dreadlocks. Louie. "Cassie told me," she said.

Now she ran inside the gated circle, around the perimeter, trying to pick the perfect horse. A white one with a purple mane. Tiny little animals embedded in his glass eyes. They all had the glass eyes. Ford helped her up.

"How is it going to move if it's not summer, Dad?" Samantha asked.

"Daddy's going to make it move," Ford said. "Daddy has the key to the controls. Daddy's the boss. I just put in the key and then I pull the lever. Then the music starts and everything. It will be just like summer, but instead, you'll have it all to yourself."

"Do you want me to ride with you?" Diana called out to her.

Ford was busy buckling Samantha onto the horse. "I need you to take pictures, while I work the controls. Besides Sam wants to ride herself. She's a big girl—she wants to be the queen of the carousel, don't you, Sam?"

"Mummy can ride if she wants," Samantha said.

"Mummy can't ride," Ford said. "She has to take pictures. Just think, in all the years this merry-go-round has been running, over a hundred years, and thousands and thousands of kids, I bet no little girl has ever had it all to herself, and now you do because you're the best, and that's what I told the owner, and there's no way he could say no. Not to your dad." He leaned forward, and kissed her on top of the head before stepping off the platform, heading to the gate. He looked at Diana, smirked a little, and tossed her the camera he pulled out of his pocket. "Think quick!" he said.

Diana jumped, grabbing the camera just before it thumped against her chest.

At least he was being playful, she thought. Even Ford, as bad as his temper could be, had trouble switching gears when feeling playful, so that much was good. She tried to smile at him. She had told herself that she would withhold sex from him, at least for a while, something to hold over his head, but he asked her to talk to him for a moment upstairs after dinner tonight. He put his back to the door and pulled her close, and then he was caressing, then pawing, slipping a finger down the side of her jeans, her hip, beneath the elastic band of her panties, and then that was it. They were on the bed, and he was crying again, apologizing, and then pushing inside as he did. And she didn't bother to fight. She was back here with him, and he was trying, so what was the point of fighting? If they were going to live together, she told herself, they had to get along.

Now he climbed up into the booth with the high stool at the far side of the room. Called out and asked Samantha if she were ready. Samantha nodded. Diana waved to her. How many times had she been inside this building? How many times and paid little attention to everything around her? The wooden beams above the horses, the rainbow-colored chariots. Painted pictures of island steamships. Horses and buggies and old hotels. And the rings.

"Remember to try and get the gold ring," Ford said.

The rings, mostly brass during the summer, came out of a dispenser just within arm's reach of the children each time they came full circle. One hand holding onto the horse, they would reach out with the other to grab for the rings, placing them on the horn atop of their horse's head after they did, and the child who caught the gold ring automatically received a free ride.

Ford flicked a switch and the music started. Time bending and surreal. And then the machine began to move. Slow at first, then picking up speed. Samantha was clinging to the post. She freed a hand for the flash of a second to wave to Diana, but she didn't reach for the rings. Ford was sitting on the stool, inside the booth, his hand on the ring distributor, silently watching. Two turns, then three.

Snap. Diana took a picture.

"If you don't reach for the rings, Sam," he called out over the music, "you can't win."

The little girl didn't flinch. Didn't hear him, or didn't care. Or maybe she was scared. Waving still but not smiling. The building suddenly felt colder, a draft seeping inside. It wasn't designed for winter, especially so close to the sea. Diana huddled her arms about her chest, and shivered a little. She wondered how long Ford would let the ride go.

Samantha passed again, and Diana took another. *Snap.*

Diana remembered the carousel at Paragon Park when she was small. Nantasket Beach. That one almost as old as this. Certainly more elaborate—the lights and sounds and hand-carved horses. Painted murals of Victorians playing in the surf. Diana's father would take them to the beach, Diana and Phillip. The other children were too small to go then, or at least too small for her father to juggle them all at once, and her mother never went to the beach. Diana loved the water, she loved her father, and she loved the water more when her father would come in with her. And then sometimes after they would stop on the boardwalk for fried clams, and her father would get a beer. He would only have one, but they always had to promise not to tell their mother about the fried clams, and they couldn't tell her about the beer; it was their special treat. And then always after, they would head to the carousel, the sun beginning its descent in the breaking reds of the summer night sky, and from the park the noise of the barkers and the music, the rides, the crashing of the roller coaster, the haunted laughter from Kooky Kastle—a ride with a wax-like green Frankenstein chasing a screaming woman in a white dress, around and around, revolving in and out of the castle, forever through eternity—was loud all around them.

It was important to have a father. Have someone. And she had to believe that. Ford could change. She just needed maybe to love him more, be more compassionate. Understanding. Her own mother was difficult, but her father had loved her, and at least she had had that. What had Ford had? Nothing except a nightmare of a childhood. She had to be more understanding, empathetic, and then he would change. Anyone could change. And somewhere deep inside, she thought, she didn't want to be alone. Not again. It was worse to be alone, wasn't it? It would have to be.

Diana lifted the camera. *Snap.*

She looked up at him now, the lights shining into the booth. He was watching Samantha, growing impatient. She could tell he was trying—he didn't want to lose his patience—but Samantha just didn't want to reach for the rings, and she was no longer waving as she came around. She was staring at the horse just ahead and to the right of her, staring at something, but she wasn't waving. Just clinging to the horse. She had had enough, and Diana called out to Ford, told him he thought she had had enough. It was cold. But Ford ignored her.

"Come on, Sam," he said. "Don't be a party pooper, just reach for the ring. You won't fall. I promise."

The music seemed suddenly louder, deafening, and Ford called out something again, but Diana couldn't hear him. She stepped back, and snapped a picture, taking in the whole carousel. Ford's lips were moving, and his face was slipping, just a little more angry, but Diana couldn't make out anything he was saying. Then Samantha came around again, and Diana saw it through the viewfinder as she snapped another picture.

Saw what Samantha was seeing.

Another little girl, in a long blue dress and blue ribbons in her hair, white stockings, was riding up and down on the horse just ahead of her, just to the right. Riding, but turned sideways in the saddle, turned so she could look back at Samantha, and waving to her, beckoning. Calling her on to join her. Diana went to scream, to yell at Ford to make it stop, and then they came around again, and this time, the little girl wasn't alone. There was a man standing beside her. Shirt vest and boating hat, a scar running the length of his cheek. Diana felt her heart rising in her throat. She screamed again, and then the man and the little girl turned and looked at her. There for a moment, and the horse passed by again, and then they were gone.

Diana hopped over the fence, and jumped up on the rotating ramp. Ford said something, but the music was still loud, colors spinning, and she couldn't hear him, didn't want to hear him. She reached Samantha and pulled her off the horse, looking right and left for the man and the little girl. But there was no one else inside. There was only Ford.

25

November 1, 1871

The house is complete, and just in time as a dusting of snow arrived early this morning. There is still some painting to be done, a few odds and ends, but all in all the work is finished, and Hiram says the rest can wait until spring. I myself welcome the quiet, and am happy to have the winter to harbor us before the crowds arrive again next summer. Maybe by then feelings will have changed, things best left forgotten. Nearly all of the camp dwellers from Trinity Park are gone for the season, and chances are better we will see no more confrontations, at least for now. The house we have built is warm and sturdy and should be fine withstanding the weather. Hiram had Mr. Carl build the well in the cellar, which will make obtaining fresh water during the weather that much easier as I just need to travel up and down the stairs rather than out into the yard. I like the yard though, and the house lies adjacent to the graveyard, and though the tombs are few, some are nearly a hundred years in age, and there are many nice spots to rest beneath the shade in the warm weather. Hiram, in a rare mood of good spirits, chuckled while sipping his morning tea in our new kitchen and discussed the graveyard.

"I don't mind living beside the dead," he said. "The dead tend to be much more reasonable than the living." It is so unusual to see him light in spirit, that I cherished the moment, and am recording it nearly immediately. This house will be good for him, good for us. I can feel it.

January 6, 1872

There is more than two and a half feet of snow covering the island. This year it seems we're averaging a storm a week. The back parlor of the house has a small alcove at the back, overlooking the graveyard, and Hiram has designated it as a spot for prayer. He sits there for hours at a time watching the graves and watching the snow. Spirits appreciate the snow, he has told me, as they feel much freer to arise from the graves and move about, quietly whispering in the wind. At one time, I would never have believed I would hear Hiram speak this way—of spirits left to wander the earth—but I do not question him on his new thoughts or new ideas, nor do I tell him that I have read up on the spiritualist movement a great deal myself. The whole concept for me is fascinating, but I fear of how he may respond should I bring it up. His temper has quieted with the winter, but his mood still remains dark, and sometimes I go three days or more without hearing him speak. On these days he retires to his bedroom, and it gets so quiet within that I have to wonder at times if he is still breathing. He won't come out to eat or wash, and I fear his temper should I ever disturb him.

The island is so deserted now that you see few souls even on a walk into town to pick up some dry goods and groceries at Otis Foss and Company. Even the majority of the cottages—all those not winterized—on the campground are closed, shuttered up and the balconies empty, and when I do gather the nerve to pass through, it feels like a ghost town with not a soul within view. Hiram successfully sold our old little cottage near the tabernacle, but as far as I can see the new owners have yet to even visit. In late spring, I imagine, I will see them, and the thought of it brings me a dull pain in the pit of my stomach. Despite some of the dark days, and the turmoil of this past summer, I loved our little cottage, even more so than our old house proper in Edgartown.

January 24, 1872

Hiram has begun to speak to me again about having a child. We have tried before but to no avail, and my deepest fear is that I am barren—he has suggested this before, in the midst of fits of rage, and called me worthless. What good is a woman, he has said, if she cannot bear you children? But even if I can, I'm not convinced it would be the best decision. Who is to say what effect having a child might have on Hiram? But with his melancholy and moods—and at his worst, the hysteria—I might fear for any child brought into this house. I have learned to navigate my way about—taking my cues from his different behaviors, reading his eyes—and I have learned when to speak and when to keep quiet, and although I still find myself beneath his open hand now and then, I can't say it happens as much as it has in the past. As long as things are kept in order and to his liking, I give him less reason to succumb to his temper. A child though would not know these things. And how do you teach a child to fear his father?

He came to my room two nights back and we did have relations. He kept his eyes shut tight and his lips were muttering words I could not comprehend as he moved on top of me, and it was over quickly. When he was finished, he adjusted his suspenders up over his shoulders, and mopped at his brow. He would not look at me as I lay on the bed, but he did say something about it being a necessary sin, and sometimes we must succumb to the Devil to work in the name of the Lord, and then he was gone from the room. I blew out the lamp beside my bed, and then rolled onto my side to watch the snow falling beyond the window. It doesn't seem as if it will stop this year.

February 7, 1872

He comes to my bed now almost nightly, and has, on several mornings inquired upon me as to whether there is anything he should know. I have told him that it is too soon to tell, but I know that is not true. I feel no different. Nothing. My body has not changed, and even for the short period I was with child before, a few years back, I could feel the difference, and even the awareness itself—that you are suddenly more than just you—is rather startling. I have no such awareness now. It is just me. I am sure of it.

February 14, 1872

Hiram is planning on journeying to the mainland. He has come into more property—bequeathed to him by an elderly uncle in Abington—and he says he has no use for it, nor for the town in which the house and plot of land sit, and so he is traveling to finalize the sale with a bank in town; bankers cannot be trusted when you deal with them from afar, he has said, as they are not required to look you in the eyes. A look into a man's eyes will tell you everything, he has said, what he will, and will not, stand for. The plot of land is substantial, and the sum of money he will receive is not small. Hiram, for one reason or other, has always seemed to have a fair share of luck when it comes to land, property, and money. It just seems to come to him.

He has not asked me to accompany him, nor have I asked to go. Crossing frightens me this time of year, the biting wind, the endless snow, and half of the harbor frozen. You could catch your death riding by carriage up the coast, and I, myself, am in no hurry.

March 3, 1872

A trance lecturer is coming to Edgartown, and I may be in luck as the event is scheduled for an evening while Hiram is away on the mainland, completing his transaction. I have read much about this man, and his name, Paschal Beverly Randolph, has been in all the papers. It could be quite a show. I will have to travel by coach, and perhaps spend the night at an Edgartown inn, but the snow has begun to recede and the journey may not be wholly unpleasant. Unless of course, Hiram were to learn of it—then of course "unpleasant" may prove to be the understatement of the century. He would not be pleased.

26

Diana stopped at the pharmacy on the way back from picking Samantha up at preschool. One-hour photo that they promised would be ready within two days. The store was mostly empty. The girl at the film counter was heavy with long, straight blonde hair and glasses. Chomping gum. She rang the price up wrong twice, and then Diana, with Samantha in hand, took the photos to the car. Tore open the package as Frank Sinatra sang on the radio. "The Summer Wind."

The photos went all the way back to summer. She hadn't developed any in some time. She hurriedly flipped through them. Last summer. State Beach. Norman and Cybil. Norman standing atop the "*Jaws* Bridge"—used in the movie—holding Sam's hand, waving to the camera, just before jumping. A photo of Ford standing on the balcony with his telescope—one she had taken from the yard—and photos of Samantha hiding behind graves in the cemetery. Pictures with Frankie, sitting outside at the Brew House. The harbor at sunset in October. Then Thanksgiving. She hesitated a moment. A dinner table image, of Cybil holding a wineglass to her lips, staring at her brother.

There was a shot of the street buried in snow. Several snow shots. A snowman in the yard. And then the pictures of the carousel. Samantha, wide-eyed and staring, clinging to her horse. Ford in the control booth. Bright spinning lights, some blurred, and the rest of the room, empty, lost to shadows. And then Samantha coming around again, this time crying. And that was all. No man, no child. There was no one else there.

27

Christmas had come and gone, and Phillip was coming to visit, bringing Barry along with him. Diana could tell that Ford wasn't happy, but he had been continuing on best behavior ever since she returned with Sam—a few eruptions with shouting, pouting, but nothing more—and he wasn't about to say no. Not yet. And Diana knew that she had to seize the moment while she could.

Besides, she figured, Phillip and Barry were safe. Ford and the two of them had seemed like pretty good friends when Diana and Ford had first met, and along with the card games, they were always going out to the bars, and Ford had gone fishing with Barry a few times, and talked Barry into playing on his softball team two summers before. Diana remembered Ford teasing him—"He looks like he's swatting at flies up there at the plate"—but it was all good-natured, and even Barry had laughed. And Ford was always willing to help with whatever was going on. Diana remembered Ford changing Phillip's oil, and helping the two of them refinish their floors once they got the okay from the landlord. And then the parties. Late nights, and early morning cleanups. It had all been good, at least until he and Diana had started dating—"He's a great guy," Phillip had said. "He's had a hard life, but he's come out remarkably unscathed, and believe me, you and I know how hard that is to do. Unscathed," he repeated. "But I mean it, both me and Barry really like him"—and then nearly overnight, Ford seemed as if he wanted little to nothing to do with them.

Now they were scheduled to arrive on a Friday afternoon, and Diana had been cleaning for three days. One of the reasons Phillip had moved out of their parents' house as young as he did, he said, was because of the filth. "I just couldn't take it," he had told Diana, "On every surface, in every corner. It never seemed to end." And this was partially true, Diana conceded privately; there was the filth but there also was Barry. And if Phillip lived at home, he could not live with Barry, and although she would never admit it to Ford, she knew in her heart, that Phillip wanted nothing more than to live with, be with, Barry.

She and Sam met them at the ferry in Vineyard Haven. Ford was sleeping. It was still early February, but the past few days had been warm, low forties, and the snow had begun to recede. Diana and Sam watched the boat in the distance, blowing its horn as it approached the wharf.

Phillip came rushing, nearly stumbling, down the ramp, excited, in a fleece vest and knee-length denim shorts.

"You know how I overheat," he said. "As soon as January is over, that's it. I'm done with long pants. One month out of the year, that's it." He did have a slight sweat broken on his brow, his lips wet with spittle, and he already smelled like alcohol. "For a commuter ferry, their gin and tonics aren't all that bad."

Barry was two steps behind him, dragging on a cigarette and much more bundled for the elements. Lanky and tall, he worked as a roofer. He wasn't quite thirty, but his hair was already gray, heavy bags and dark circles beneath his eyes—he always looked as if he hadn't slept in months. His skin was yellow from three packs a day, and he still wore his mullet from the eighties. Barry loved the eighties.

Diana hugged Phillip—awkward, her family had never been big on hugs—and then she hugged Barry, just a little bit tighter. She had once had a crush on Barry, briefly, actually dated him a couple times when he first moved in with Phillip, and if he wasn't so intent on killing himself prematurely with the cigarettes, she thought he still would be attractive. Phillip hugged Sam, and patted her head.

"My favorite niece," he said. "You look like you've grown."

"I'm your only niece," Sam said.

"For now, you're right. Grandma said she had a bag of Christmas presents for you guys that she wanted me to bring down, but when she came by yesterday, she forgot to bring them."

"Yeah, well," Diana said, "she lied."

Phillip grimaced a bit. He had always been their mother's favorite, and as long as he stayed in the closet, Diana imagined he would stay that way. Though even if he did come out, her mother probably had enough denial saved up in her arsenal of bullshit to cover it all up, nice and clean. Convince herself it wasn't true. Phillip could be whatever she wanted him to be, and that was that.

"I don't think she lies so much as she . . . enhances the truth."

Diana took one of his bags, slung it over her shoulder. "No. She lies."

Phillip giggled. "Okay, you're right. She lies." He gazed toward the car parked in the corner of the empty lot, hesitantly. "Where's Ford?"

"Home," she said. "Sleeping."

"Oh, good. Maybe we'll have time to get a couple drinks in before he gets up."

"A couple?" said Barry. "A couple for you was about three hours back."

Regardless of Barry's remarks, Diana thought, he seemed more amused by it than anything else. He was used to Phillip's drinking, obviously—he had to be as Phillip rarely stopped. He was a sloppy drinker but never a mean or angry one. Maybe only mean to himself, perhaps when alone, beating himself up, but then again, he probably had enough of their mother in him that he could pretend to be anything he wanted, or pretend not to be.

Barry had only brought a tiny duffel bag with him, and Diana wondered what he planned on wearing all weekend. If he hadn't lived with Phillip for so long the way he did, she would never think he was gay. She wondered what it was that tipped Phillip off whenever it had, although when they first met, moved in with each other, they had both had girlfriends. So maybe she was wrong . . .

Phillip turned to him in the car. "Did you remember to pack your wool socks? I left them out on the foot of your bed this morning."

Nope, she thought, definitely not wrong.

"Are you kidding me?" Barry said. "That room is such a mess, I can never find anything."

Phillip sighed. Looked over at Diana. "I clean it once a week for him."

They crossed the drawbridge from Vineyard Haven into Oak Bluffs, and then took the road curving up past the hospital. Sails down on the few boats left moored in the harbor. Samantha was telling Barry about some of her classmates at preschool—Lydia who had three hamsters, and Edwin who told her he had a booger collection on the wall of his room at home. "He's disgusting," she said. "Even Mrs. Abrams told him so."

Barry smiled. "Well, I think I had a booger collection when I was his age, too. Everybody does, right? It's only disgusting if he eats them."

"He does," said Sam.

Phillip gasped a little as they surmounted the hill overlooking Oak Bluffs. The harbor, the clock tower, and Sunset—once known as Squash Meadow—Pond.

"You know," he said, "it's still beautiful even this time of year. I've never been down here in the winter. How long has it been since we came down here for the weekend, Bar? Two or three years at least."

"At least," Barry said.

When they pulled into the driveway, Barry lit up a cigarette right out of the car, cupped it in his hand to block it from the wind. Sam was already up on the porch, reaching for the doorknob, as if in a hurry to see someone inside. Phillip stopped in the driveway, staring up at the house before him, the porch swing slowly moving back and forth, and the graveyard behind.

"You don't like it," Diana said.

"No," said Phillip. "I love it."

They were both talking at once as they came through the house. It was a thing with their family—everybody talking at once—and although an outsider might find it hard to follow the threads of the conversation, for them it was easy. Something of an art form. Diana had just started telling him about the color—a burgundy— she hoped to paint the dining room when she stopped short upon entering the kitchen. Ford was awake. Already showered, and sitting at the table, drinking his coffee, reading the paper. He never got up this early the day after working and she wasn't expecting him to be now.

He looked up at Phillip, and Phillip forced a smile, nervous, and then Ford stood, and casually stepped over, reaching out to shake his hand. He smiled wide, beaming.

"Hey, Phil," Ford said. "It's been a long time." And then he pulled him into a tight embrace, Diana watching on, cautious. Ford finished hugging Phillip and stepped over to shake Barry's hand. "I'd hug you, too," he said, still smiling, "but you're not family."

Barry waved his hand in protest. "That's okay. I don't need to be hugged."

"How about something to drink, then?" Ford asked. "Must've been a long trip."

"A drink," said Phillip, "sounds awesome."

Ford went to the fridge, pulled out three Budweisers, tossed one to Phillip, one to Barry, and then cracked the third himself. "What do you guys think about the color Diana's going to paint the dining room?" he asked after a moment. Diana was ready for the criticism, the sarcasm, but Ford just sipped his beer.

"I think it's going to look awesome," he said.

Almost immediately they were reminiscing, people they had known in Brockton—Ford had heard their old landlord passed away—and laughing about the late-night card games. Phillip downed two beers in ten minutes and suggested cosmopolitans. He had brought his own martini shaker—stainless steel and shaped like a penguin—and a bottle of vodka. He asked Barry to go down to the store at the bottom of the hill for the triple sec, lime juice, and cranberry juice, and Ford jumped right up and offered to give him a ride.

"I can point out a few good fishing spots for you, on the way back," Ford said. "We can take a detour. You still fish?"

Barry pointed at Phillip. "When this one will let me."

Ford took two beers for the ride, and they were still chatting as they set off out the door. Phillip looked at Diana as soon as they were gone. No baritone, no theatrics.

"Is it any better?" he asked.

Diana hesitated. "How do you know it had gone bad?"

"Well, it didn't seem that good to begin with," he said, "not from pretty early on. And then running off usually doesn't make things better. And that's basically what you did, right?"

"Mum drove me away. I would have stayed."

"I've told her that." He gulped his beer.

"You did?"

"Absolutely." He giggled. "In no uncertain terms. Don't worry, she didn't listen. I don't believe she even pretended to hear."

"She was probably overmedicated."

"Probably. I told her it didn't matter what he said about Stephen, either. That she needed to get over that, to let it go."

"I don't want to talk about Stephen," Diana said.

"He's changed."

"I don't want to hear it."

"He's still your brother."

"No," she said. "He's not."

Phillip just stared at her a moment, nodded.

Diana took a breath, composing herself. She didn't want to start crying again. Not with Phillip just arriving. That would do no one any good. "Anyway, it is better," she said. "Ford's trying, I think, and at this point that's about all I can ask for."

"He does seem like a different guy. I'm not sure I've ever seen him that welcoming."

"Well, Sam and I did almost leave. It came very close. And I think that really shook him up a little. Maybe got through to him. I don't think he ever believed I really would."

"And why didn't you?"

"Well, I married him, you know? And I take my vows seriously. For better or for worse—I think it hit the point where I figured it could only get better. At least, it couldn't get worse. And he loves Sam. Maybe not me, maybe not all the time, but he loves Sam. The problem is, I really don't know how much I love him, anymore."

"Oh boy." Phillip reached for the wine bottle in the middle of the table, filled her glass and pushed it toward her. "Drink."

"I don't need to drink. That's not going to help anything."

"It's not going to hurt either."

Diana sipped, and then Phillip held his beer mug up for a toast.

"To the old days," he said, "before you and Ma hated each other." But then before he clicked her glass, he cocked his head, as if listening to something somewhere else in the house, or perhaps the car pulling into the driveway. But Diana couldn't hear the car, just Samantha, upstairs.

Phillip laughed a bit. "Who *is* she talking to?"

Diana took a deep breath. "Cassie," she said.

It was after dinner and several drinks—and a few stories from Diana about the things that had happened in the house—that Barry had come up with the idea to run the séance. Diana tried to make light of it, but she felt something stiffen inside of her as soon it was suggested; it wasn't something she wanted to test, but Barry kept coming back to it. Ford had been quiet throughout most of the talk regarding the house. He hadn't been drinking the cosmopolitans with them, but he had been drinking the vodka. Diluted with a little cranberry juice, Ford stirred the drink with the tip of his finger while talking to Barry but watching Diana and Phillip. He wasn't looking directly at them, but Diana could tell he was watching—he always was whenever she got together with someone from her family, always listening, always on guard.

But he still had been in good form. Making jokes about the old man down the road who spied on their house with binoculars—watching Diana in the summer when she was out back in her bikini—and talking to Barry about the Red Sox, and darts, challenging him to a game before the night was through. Diana had been trying to keep tabs on how much he was drinking, but with her back turned to the sink, it wasn't easy, and each time she turned, his glass was at the same level. The change hadn't come over him yet, the automatic pilot settling into his eyes, nobody home, and that was good. He hadn't drunk *that* much since he promised to quit—not nearly as much as he had been drinking before—but she knew he snuck a few shots here and there. Or the occasional six-pack. As long as it was just a few, she could look the other way. She could tolerate a few, and if that kept him happy, it was worthwhile. He had also been talking to Barry about the roof over the porch. Asking Barry if he could help him fix it. A few of the beams were rotted—probably the originals—and needed to be replaced. Maybe in the summer. That would be great if they could come down in the summer, he said, they could stay the whole week. The island was beautiful in the summer, and he would show them all the best spots.

Barry changed the subject—because he worked construction, people were always trying to get free jobs out of him, Diana knew. People figured because that was what he did, he liked to spend his free time doing it also, enjoying it perpetually.

"So what about this ghost?" Barry said again now.

"I didn't say it was a ghost," Diana said. She had gotten up to do the dishes, Phillip giving her a hand.

"Sounds like one to me," Barry said, smiling. "And if you have a ghost, I want to see it."

"Well, I do not." Diana pulled a towel from the stove handle to dry off the pasta pot. "And besides, that's not what it is."

Phillip's face was flushed from the vodka and he had broken a sweat again on his forehead. "Then who is Sam talking to upstairs?" he asked Diana quietly.

"I told you," Diana said. "Cassie. It's her imaginary friend. And shhh . . . Don't say it too loud. I don't want her to hear. She might still be awake."

Ford had still been silent on the subject, but he suddenly looked unsettled, and it was rare for Ford to show anything like that. She thought of the cellar, his refusal to go down there.

"But you yourself said you've heard things," Barry said to Diana, his eyes alight.

"I said I've thought I've heard things," Diana said. "It's an old house, you can hear a lot of things. Old houses make noises." She sipped her wine. She was beginning to feel light-headed. She thought of the man she had seen in the campground, and the man in the hotel. The carousel. Nothing, she reminded herself. Stress. Imagination. Nothing. Just like the noises. The singing upstairs. Nothing. "They settle," she said. "They make noises."

Phillip lowered his chin. "But they don't make voices."

Ford looked into his glass, finished his drink. His pallor was changing, going gray. Some people turned pink, red, when they drank, but Ford turned gray. His soul draining out of him, Diana thought. Please don't let his soul drain out of him. Not now, not tonight. She wondered what he was thinking. His threats about what he would do if she left just a few months before? Maybe. And if he was thinking that way, if it started to bother him, embarrass him? It might not be good.

"Well, I want to talk to the ghost," Barry said. "Let's do this. We'll ask a question, and then we'll pick a person to recite the alphabet, slowly, and then we'll ask the spirit to make a noise, knock or something, when the person reciting the alphabet gets to the letter he needs to make a word."

"She," Diana said.

"What?" said Barry.

"The ghost," Diana said. "If it does exist, and I'm not saying it does—it's a she. And I don't want to do this."

Ford stared over at her. His eyes empty. She couldn't read him. If he was frightened, lost, or maybe not even interested. It was impossible to read him when his eyes got like that. Diana looked at the clock. Almost eleven. How did it get to be almost eleven? He had been drinking steadily, along with Phillip, for almost eight hours. It was no wonder the change was coming on.

Ford wet his lips a little. "What's the big deal?" he said at last. "It will be fun."

⤺

Diana checked upstairs on Samantha. Sound asleep, sitting in her red Elmo chair, her head tilted, resting on her shoulder. Diana put her in her pajamas, and slipped her into bed, the covers up to her chin. Then she kissed her forehead and turned on her Winnie the Pooh nightlight. Pooh, constructed like a paper lantern with a small light inside.

Downstairs, Phillip had lit the candles in the dining room, and they were all sitting around the table. It seemed more appropriate to have it in the dining room. The room was darker, older, some of the furnishings fifty years old or more. Diana still wasn't crazy about the idea. She didn't think anything would really happen. But what if it did? From what she could tell, so far the ghost, if there really was a ghost, hadn't been hostile, but what if they had disturbed her. Invited others in? She had read about what happened sometimes when you invited others in.

"I'm not sure we should do this," she said, pulling up a seat next to Ford.

"Come on," Barry said. "It's just for fun. We'll give it ten minutes, and then if we don't get anything, we'll call it quits."

"Promise?" Diana said.

"I promise."

"He's good for his word. One thing about Barrr . . ." Phillip said, rolling the name off his tongue, "he's always good for his word."

Ford lit a cigarette, let the first exhale of smoke out through closed lips. It looked blue in the low light of the room. "You never know," he said. "We could get two thousand of them."

"Two thousand?" said Phillip.

Ford shrugged. "We've got a cemetery right out back."

Phillip cringed. "That's right. I forgot about that. Let's not do this."

"Come on." Barry lit his own cigarette. "We're doing it." He reached over and took Diana's free hand, fingers rough, callused. Diana was still holding Ford's, and with his other, Ford took Phillip's.

"No getting fresh," he said.

"We all need to shut our eyes," Barry said. "What's the spirit's name again?"

Elizabeth, Diana thought, but she couldn't say that. Not now. Maybe not ever. "I have no idea," she said.

"Well, what did you say Samantha calls her?" Barry asked.

"Cassie," Diana said, and she was glad for the moment that she couldn't see Ford. She had never told him about Samantha talking to anyone. She wasn't sure how he would take it, especially secondhand. Especially considering what had happened in the basement. And she was worried that he might blame the little girl. Forbid her from playing. And what if it were her imagination? How would you forbid a small child from using their imagination?

"Cassie?" Ford said now. "That's what she used to call that little pink dinosaur she plays with. The one I bought her the Christmas before last."

"That's what she calls her invisible friend, too," Diana said quietly.

"I think she's having you on, Diana," he said. "She's talking to her stuffed dinosaur."

"Let's make another drink," said Phillip.

Barry let go of Diana's hand, and she heard him take a drag off his cigarette. Exhale. "Five minutes," he said. "Just give it five minutes, and if we get nothing we'll stop. Cassie," he said. "We're looking for someone named Cassie. Is there anyone here? If there is, can you knock so that we know you're here. Twice for yes, once for no. Anybody? This is a very old house, there must be somebody here."

"Yeah," said Ford. "Built in 1871."

"Anybody?" Barry said. "Once for no, twice for yes."

"You're going to confuse her," said Ford.

"We don't mean you any harm," Barry said. "We just want to talk to you. Anybody."

Diana felt fingers, lightly racing up her arm. She swatted out at Barry. "Stop it!"

"Stop what?"

"Tickling me."

"I didn't touch you."

She opened her eyes, looked at Ford. Poker face. He reached down, his eyes still shut, and dragged again on the cigarette, seeping the smoke out through tight lips. Then again he took Phillip's hand.

"Anybody?" Barry asked. "Is there anybody out there?"

Diana felt it again on her arms, watched as the hairs stood on end. But it wasn't fingers, it was a chill. A draft. The entire room felt suddenly cold.

"Is there anyone in this house, besides us?" said Barry.

"Yeah," said Ford, "Sam's upstairs."

"Anybody?" Barry asked again, and the temperature felt to drop just a little bit more. A cold, stale air. Empty.

Diana's heart began to race—we shouldn't be doing this, she thought, it wasn't good to be doing this—and Barry gripped her hand tighter.

"Anyone at all?" he asked.

There was a small sound. Faint. A rapping against wood. Once, then twice. Diana jumped. Opened her eyes. Phillip had opened his eyes, too, but Ford and Barry had not. Ford just dragged on his cigarette again, showing no expression.

"Can you tell us who you are?" Barry asked.

One knock, now slightly louder.

"Who did that?" Phillip said. "Somebody did that."

"I'm going to start to recite the alphabet," Barry said, "and when I get to the first letter of your name, knock once." He smiled, looking like he was enjoying this. "ABCDEFGHIJKL—"

One knock.

Diana let go of his hand. "Okay, enough. You guys get to go home, but we have to live here."

"ABCDEFGHI—"

A knock again, this one sounding closer. On or under the table.

"L-I," said Phillip. "Doesn't sound like a Cassie to me."

Diana stood up quickly. "You guys can finish. I'm going to the kitchen to finish cleaning up."

Both Barry and Ford opened their eyes. Diana started away from the table, but had only moved two steps when the room went dark, the candle blown. Diana stopped short. She couldn't see any of them, anything, and the temperature dropped again. Cold, colder. And then it was instantly frigid. Like stepping outside of a warm house in January. The cold was there for but a second and then began to dissipate.

"What the hell?" somebody mumbled. Barry.

"One of you did that," Diana said. "And it's not funny. I can't see a thing."

Someone let a small cry, a gasp. Someone struck a match, and then Ford leaned over, relighting the candle. He used the rest of the match to light another cigarette, shaking it twice before dropping it in the ashtray.

"Which one of you did it?" Diana asked.

Phillip looked pale. He stared at Diana with his mouth open. "Nobody did it." He raised his hand, the Boy Scout he once was, returning. "I swear to God. How could we make the temperature change like that?"

Barry smiled, looked up toward the ceiling. "Did you do that?" He waited. "Do it again."

"That's enough." Diana went to the doorway, flicked on the light switch, turning up the dimmer on the chandelier above the table.

Barry looked at her appealing with his eyes. "Come on . . . We were so close."

Phillip pushed back his chair. "I'm with her. I'm sorry, but I admit it—I'm a wuss. That was enough for me."

Ford just rounded the cigarette head in the ashtray, staring at it as he did.

Diana went to the kitchen and took two more pots off the stove and put them into the sink, squirted in some dish liquid, and then filled them with warm water so they could soak. She could hear Phillip, still in the dining room. His voice seemed far off, separate somehow, coming from a different house, and she heard Barry respond. She went to push the cork back into the bottle of wine, hoping they would all agree to call it a night, and then she felt a hand on her shoulder.

Diana spun around to find herself alone in the kitchen, and as she did, the lights went out. Once again, complete darkness. Cold. A knock came then, but she couldn't tell if it was on the wall, or the kitchen table. Or where. And then she heard whispering. No, not whispering. Just a voice, a woman's voice, distant but clear.

"Diana."

Diana felt her heart jump against the wall of her chest, her mouth suddenly metallic and dry. One of the men shouted something, and then she heard Samantha crying, immediately followed by footsteps running up the stairs. Ford? Phillip? Diana ran out through the back parlor, tripping on the hassock as she did, and bracing herself against the wall before turning up the stairs. Samantha was still crying. The cry of an infant, followed by her calling for Diana. One of the men called out to light a candle. Diana raced up the stairs and into Samantha's room. She could hear Samantha sobbing. It was lighter in her room, the moon coming through the window, and there was a man in there with her.

Ford.

Crouched down before the bed and holding her in his arms. Quieting her.

As soon as she saw Diana, Sam struggled to break free from Ford, but he held her tight. "Shh . . ." he said. "I got you. Daddy's got you."

Ford struggled with her a little, but Sam still squirmed, pushed him off and then reached for Diana. Diana hurried over to her and pulled her into her arms.

"It's okay, sweetie," she said, "it's okay. You just had a bad dream. Mummy's here. It was just a dream."

Samantha pressed her face against Diana's shoulder. "I want him to leave."

"Who? Daddy? Daddy was being nice—he just wanted to protect you."

"It wasn't me, Diana," Ford said. She could hear the resentment, anger, rising in his voice. "For chrissakes, I had it all taken care of."

"No, not Daddy." Samantha wiped her nose on Diana's shoulder. "The man."

Diana glanced at Ford, his outline in the dark. His eyes dark shadows. He was sitting completely still, looking at them, staring.

"There's no man," said Diana. "It was just Daddy. You just had a bad dream. You were asleep."

"No," said Samantha between sobs. "No, I was drawing a picture."

Diana looked down at the bed. Children's books, paper. Crayons. And three magic markers without covers. Everything blue in the light of the moon. None of it had been there when she tucked her in.

"I think you probably fell asleep again while you were coloring," she said.

"No, I wasn't asleep. I woke up. He was in the doorway, and he started walking towards me, and then the lights went out, and everything was dark."

"Maybe it was Cassie," Diana said, trying to divert her.

Samantha pressed her face tighter against her. "No. It was the man."

The lights flickered then, suddenly coming back on. The red digits of the little girl's alarm clock, blinking. All the power. Diana held the little girl tighter, and looked out the window. No rain, wind, lightning. Nothing.

Ford turned his head and looked toward the window.

28

I have been to Edgartown to see the medium, the trance lecturer Paschal Beverly Randolph. Hiram left on a Wednesday and did not return until the following Monday. I offered to accompany him down to the ferry despite the early hour and the sun not yet risen, but he refused, saying it would do no good for the fellow islanders to see me returning to the house on my own. Furthermore, he said, I was not to leave the house except to care for the animals in the barn while he was gone. I was not to be seen.

The lecture was on Saturday. I hired a boy who sleeps in a room above the stable down near the wharf to tend to the animals—telling him it would be our secret—and then I hired a carriage to transport me as planned, taking the new road along the beach and past Sengekontacket Pond. As the sun had already set I saw few fellow travelers en route, and it was not until I arrived at the lecture hall that I encountered any familiar faces. I was secretly hoping that I would not recognize anyone, nor they me, and perhaps the audience would be small. But in reality it was quite the opposite. The hall was crowded, heads bobbing as they searched for seats and voices rising into the emptiness above us, and I immediately recognized both Mr. Pratt—the Mr. Pratt of the Oak Bluffs Land and Wharf Company—and Dr. Mortimer and his wife. I prayed that neither man had seen me, and being that they were on the floor, near the front, I quickly moved to the balcony just as the lights began to dim.

I took a seat beside an elderly couple in the third row. I recognized neither the man nor woman, and I don't believe they recognized me. The red velvet curtains were still closed, and the crowd was whispering, but the noise soon dropped like a curtain. A sudden sea of silence. And then the lamps lining the walls of the theater began to dim and we were all left in a room of complete darkness. I heard several women gasp, and then someone lit a candle on a table in the center of the stage. I heard no footsteps nor saw anyone retreating after the candle was lit, but there it was, nothing else, and the entire audience, still silent, stared at it, the tiny flame quietly flickering, in anticipation of what was to come. And then, from the left-hand side of the stage came a voice, a man's voice, deep and severe.

"Good evening," he said.

Paschal Beverly Randolph. The name still rings like poetry coming off my tongue. He is a tall man with dark eyes, his hair combed back neatly and his beard fashioned into a goatee. He was younger than I imagined, and I placed him at maybe forty. He remained silent again for a moment, his eyes trained upon the audience, and theirs upon him, before he once again spoke. I have read that he is of mixed race—his mother, a descendant of Madagascan royalty—and I must admit he appeared quite dark, but I had also read that he is a trained physician, which he soon went on to confirm. Also before the war, he was quite involved in the abolitionist cause. He is many things—a sailor, a scientist, an orator, an author, a magician, and a gentleman—but tonight he was with us as trance medium, he was with us, he said, to tell us of the other world, the one waiting for us beyond this one, and of course, to speak to the dead. He raised the water glass, chest high, and gazed out into the darkness, up into the balcony— although it is questionable as to whether he could see any of our faces—hesitated a moment, and then he sipped.

"Noepe," he said. "The name the aboriginal people, the Native Americans—the Wampanoag people—gave your little island, before the white man arrived. Noepe. Translated it means 'In the midst of the sea.' I have spent a great deal of my life at sea, traveling to far-off lands, communing with different cultures, learning their ways and respecting their traditions, and they are all so very, very different, so unique, except for one thing. "He held up a finger. "There is one thing they, we, all have in common." He paused, sipped again. "And that is . . . the belief in the spirit world. The belief in the afterlife."

He paced the stage, his chin down, and his hands folded behind his back, a man in the midst of great thought, great contemplation.

"The sea is awash with spirits," he said. "I have seen them off the coast of Africa, and I have seen them while in port at Shang Hai. In the San Francisco Bay, floating through the wondrous Golden Gate, and in Trinidad. In New York," he said. "Boston. I have seen them, heard them, and felt them, and it is no wonder there should be so many alive out there knowing that so many souls, many we have known—whalers, sailors, fisherman, and pilgrims—have been lost at sea. I have contemplated this a great deal, especially at night, aboard a lonely ship, adrift in the middle of the Atlantic, with no noise except the wind, the mainsail flapping, a whale sounding, and what could only possibly be the cries of the distant, drowned sailors." He stopped, lowered his chin, and looked out upon us from under his brow. "I have contemplated this, and then I have asked myself, is it all so different on land? All so different anywhere? For what are we there, here? On the water or in the Catskills, on the soil of this great young land, or on the soil once roamed by the ancient Egyptians, but a family, a sea, of souls. All bound together by one thing." He raised his finger again. "One thing. And that is that we will be together in the afterlife. We will all move to the next realm. The spirit world."

He spoke more at length, now and again causing a ripple of hushed whispers, and then he removed his coat, down to his vest, and he rolled up his sleeves. He repeated again that we would all be together, for though he himself a Christian, he said, he does not believe that neither faith nor works during this brief lifetime are enough to assign a person to eternal bliss, or eternal damnation. No, he said, there has to be more. More experiences, more challenges, and some might say, he said, more chances. There are many spheres we must ascend through following our time in this one. The afterlife is not a static place, but rather one where the spirit evolves, learning and growing, and then moving on. His assistant came forth with a silver pitcher and refilled his water, and then Paschal Beverly Randolph took a seat at the table.

The gentleman to my right was soon fast asleep, his lips sputtering as he snored, but his wife appeared enthralled, hanging upon each of Mr. Randolph's words, gasping when his lecture grazed the periphery of polite conversation, alluding to the acts of a man and wife in the marital bed, and describing how such acts can prove to be both a "metaphysical and holy ritual." There was much shuffling following this, and several audience members rose to depart. I could not see who due to the low lighting. Mr. Randolph made no acknowledgment to these sudden departures until the room was once again quiet, and then he stated that he bore these people no ill will, and that as much was to be expected. Not everyone is ready, he said, to hear the truth.

He stood again then, stepping closer to the foot of the stage and asked if there was anyone in the audience who had a loved one, now deceased, whom they would like to speak to. He waited, staring intently, his eyes deep, dark pools, and when there was still no answer, he waited some more. Then after a moment, a hand rose in the fifth row. Mr. Randolph nodded and motioned for the volunteer to come forward.

A woman approached the side of the stage, and Mr. Randolph greeted her there, offering her a hand as she ascended the stairs. She was a heavyset woman in her middle years of life, and she did not look familiar. Mr. Randolph asked her name, and she said it was Rebecca Cushing, and that she came from Nantucket, the wife of a whaler. It was her husband, Jacob Cushing, she said, whom she wished to speak with, and then she started to cry. Mr. Randolph offered her a chair, and then he offered her a glass of water.

"It is a sad thing to lose a loved one," he told the woman, "but the important thing to remember is that even when they are lost—at least to us, beyond our sphere—they are never really gone. And although our sphere may not incorporate theirs, their sphere incorporates ours, and although, they may not be with us, we are with them. They can see, feel, hear us, and if it is a spouse, we mourn, they can lie beside us as we turn the lights down before slipping away to our dreams. And sometimes, he added, it is within our dreams that we meet them. He asked her in what year she lost her husband, and how it came to be. 1858, she said, and he had, as far as she knew, been one of those of whom Mr. Randolph spoke, one of those lost at sea. His ship had been gone for three years, due back in 1857, but by 1858, it had still not returned. No wreck, no word, no nothing. The ship had last been seen rounding the Cape of Good Hope.

1858, I thought, and still she grieved. I wondered what it would be like to have a husband whom you could love so much, miss so dearly.

"The Cape of Good Hope," said Mr. Randolph, and then for the first time since his lecture began, I saw him smile. "Lost like the Dutchman. But is he lost? Or is he in this room with us now as we speak? Watching your tears, his heart breaking as he does, but unable to reach out to you, speak to you, soothe you. He may be lost to you, for now, but I assure you, my good woman, you are not lost to him."

His trance, Mr. Randolph said, was not exactly like that of other mediums. For he believed strongly in the concept of "will." Most mediums, he said, abandoned their will while in the trance state, and so left themselves open to be influenced by countless entities around them, and as such, their results could often prove unreliable, sometimes even, contradictory. But his method involved what he termed "blending." While blending he would not lose himself completely to the trancelike state, but rather would identify with the soul of the departed while still exerting his own personal will. This would result in a "knowing" without a vacation of self, of will.

The gas lamps came on at either side of the stage then, the lights still low and bathing the stage in what I can only describe as a distant shade of yellow, and then Mr. Randolph turned to the audience and asked for two more volunteers.

"Witnesses," he said.

Several hands rose, and after carefully scanning the crowd, he quickly made his decision. One was a woman, probably in her late twenties, not much younger than me, and one, shockingly, was Mr. Pratt. The woman gave her name as Eleanor Mayhew. She was a pretty woman with a long-lipped smile and rosy cheeks, and she stated her occupation as a seamstress. Mr. Pratt stood off to the side until Mr. Randolph turned, seemingly sizing him up just a little bit more, and shook his hand, asking his name and occupation.

"Samuel Pratt," he said. "Architect." He cleared his throat. "And builder."

Mr. Randolph paused. "The Samuel Pratt?"

Mr. Pratt nodded. "That's right."

Mr. Randolph made a small side nod with his head. "Excellent."

His assistant brought forth two more chairs, and he asked Mr. Pratt and Miss Mayhew to have a seat at the table with Mrs. Cushing. Miss Mayhew sat at the center of the table, facing the audience, and Mr. Pratt sat across from Mrs. Cushing. Mr. Randolph then explained that he would remain standing a short distance from the table and all that may transpire. He wanted the audience to be comfortable with the fact that there would be no trickery. As he said this a long horn, attached to a wire, descended from above, stopping short a few feet above the heads of the volunteers, its mouthpiece angled. A spirit trumpet. I have read of them.

"It is not common that we engage deeply enough to receive actual voice transmissions from the dead," said Mr. Randolph, "but it is also not unheard of. More often than not, the spirits, if they speak at all, speak through me, but there has been occasion . . ." He paused. "Yes, there has been occasion . . ."

The lighting of the stage appeared to enhance his features even more. I hadn't quite realized just how handsome, commanding, and confident, he really looked. Miss Mayhew seemed to have realized it before I, however, and she kept looking over at him, shyly, blushing. He seemed to pick up on this rather quickly.

"Now I am going to need your full concentration, young lady," he said. "Indeed, the full concentration of everyone present." The woman beside me gave her husband a subtle elbow. He shuddered a little, but then went right on sleeping.

"The souls in the next realm are much like the souls here in this room," continued Mr. Randolph, "composed of energy, and for the energy to come forth the receiving area must be focused, and of course—and this is a big of course—welcoming. We all must focus on thoughts on whom we are looking for, and why." He paused again. "We are looking for Mr. Jacob Cushing."

He asked the volunteers at the table to hold hands, and if comfortable, for each of us in the audience to take the hand of our neighbors beside us. The woman beside me did not look at me, but she reached over and placed her hand over mine, taking her sleeping husband's in her other. Mr. Randolph said he needed everyone present to close their eyes and to take a deep breath, hold it briefly, and then exhale. We did this several times, with Mr. Randolph, speaking in a calm, soothing manner as we did. He wanted us all to think pleasant thoughts, he said, to imagine ourselves somewhere pleasant, somewhere warm—perhaps even summer right here on our private little paradise, in the midst of the sea—somewhere relaxing. He wanted us all to feel relaxed, to feel it in our fingers and in our toes, flowing gently through our bloodstream, down our arms, legs, moving gently in our chest, up through our necks, and settling, peacefully, in our heads, soothing our thoughts. We were all at peace, he said, as were our visitors, at peace. All one, our spheres separated by a thin membrane. Our world theirs, and their world ours. Peace, he said again, relaxed. Breathe. In. Out. Feel our chests rising. In. Out. Breathe. Relax.

"Mr. Jacob Cushing," he said. "I'm looking for Mr. Jacob Cushing. Your wife is here, Mr. Cushing, in this room, on this island not far from your own, and she misses you. She misses you dearly." He paused, waited. Everyone, he said, could open their eyes, and then he continued. He still had his eyes closed. "I can feel you," he said, "But I cannot hear you. I would like to ask something of you if you would be so gracious to help us, help your wife, here this evening. I would like to ask you some questions and if you can, if possible, I would like you to answer these questions with a knock, a rap upon the table or floor. Once for yes, twice for no. Can you hear me?" Mr. Randolph paused again, and I must admit my heart had begun to flutter, my mouth dry. "I said, can you hear me, Mr. Cushing?" Still nothing. Mr. Randolph took a deep breath. "Very well, I shall proceed regardless in hopes that we have in fact made contact. I can feel something, a change in the room, but I would like to be sure that it is in fact you." He took a step forward then, turned his body square. Facing the audience, his back to the volunteers.

"Your wife says she believes that you were lost somewhere near the Cape of Good Hope. She says you were a crewman aboard a whaling vessel. The whole ship, she believes, was lost. Is this true?"

Mr. Randolph waited, his hands behind his back, and standing perfectly still. His eyes remained closed, but as I watched his face began to change, subtly, a shifting in his pallor, his beautiful bronze skin suddenly draining of color, and then once again shifting, gray, then blue. He himself nearly looked like a ghost. "Mr. Cushing," he said, again, and then it was not just he that was changing, but the entire room around us. It was suddenly remarkably cooler, the temperature dropping. I felt a shiver run up my spine, and the old woman beside me let go of my hand to adjust her shawl. People throughout the audience were shifting about, silent but unsettled.

"Mr. Cushing," Mr. Randolph said, "Were you lost upon the Cape of Good Hope?"

There was something then. A small sound, distant and unsure, but carrying enough power to break apart the room. It was a knock, and the sound came from the stage. I am sure of it. A woman down near the front gasped again, and the old woman beside me blessed herself in the sign of the cross. I myself felt my heart rising in my throat, the hairs on my arms standing on end, but Mr. Randolph did not stir.

"Thank you, Mr. Cushing," he said. "I can hear you clearly, here on stage, but I fear that some others further back may not be able to hear you quite so well. Would it be too much of an inconvenience if I asked you to respond a bit louder? If at all possible, of course." He waited again. Another knock. One. Louder.

The young woman at the table, Miss Mayhew, let out a cry, and jumped from her seat. "It came from the table," she exclaimed. "Someone knocked on the table!" Mr. Pratt moved quickly over to her, a hand on her shoulder and a whisper in her ear. Something comforting, I would have to assume. The woman shut her eyes, and nodded a little, and then again took her seat.

Mr. Randolph was still facing away from them, and the whole thing had taken on the effect of a play.

"Thank you, Mr. Cushing," Mr. Randolph said again, "but just to be sure, I would like to clarify. Am I in fact speaking to Jacob Cushing?"

One knock.

"Good. I would like to ask you a few questions. An image of you is forming, over there and in this room, and I would like to say you look very well. Your wife has told me nothing about you except for your name, and where you were lost, that it is all. I know nothing else about you, and I don't want her to tell me. I," he said, "would like you to tell me about you. By the look of you—reddish hair and slightly balding, clean-shaven, barrel-chested, and blue-gray eyes that mirror the sea—I'm guessing that you were probably not yet thirty when you passed."

Now it was Mrs. Cushing's turn to gasp, all eyes instantly upon her.

"Am I correct?" Mr. Randolph asked.

Two knocks.

More whispering.

Mr. Randolph did turn and look at Mrs. Cushing then.

"Had he made it home, my husband would have been thirty-four that year," she said, a tremor to her voice.

Mr. Randolph nodded, and turned back to the audience, again closing his eyes.

"Thirty-four?" he repeated.

One knock.

The woman beside me gave her husband a visible shove then, and the old man awakened, startled, looking around the room as if he was not sure where he was, nor for that matter, where he had been. She pointed at the stage. He made a strange noise with his throat and nodded.

"You did leave behind some children, did you not, Mr. Cushing?"

Knock.

"Four children," said Mr. Randolph. "Three boys—one himself now at sea—and a girl. Now all grown."

Knock. Knock.

Mr. Randolph did not turn this time, but he waited. On the stage, Mr. Pratt looked at Mrs. Cushing. "My daughter died of small pox when she was eleven," she said.

"Yes," said Mr. Randolph. "Now I can see her. She is with him."

Mrs. Cushing began to weep. I heard no noise emit from her. But she bit her lower lip, and her body shuddered slightly, tears moving down her cheeks. A look on her face of both sadness and joy.

"A fair-haired girl," continued Mr. Randolph, "blonde with streaks of red. She's wearing a green dress. Velvet. You want your wife to know that she is with you."

Knock.

Mrs. Cushing let out another cry.

"Mr. Cushing," continued Mr. Randolph, "you had written a letter to your wife, not long before your ship was lost."

Knock.

"And you would like to know if she ever received it."

Knock.

Mrs. Cushing nodded.

"Mrs. Cushing," said Mr. Randolph. "Is there anything in particular you would like to ask?"

She nodded. "Yes, yes, there is. I wonder if he has seen my mother."

Silence. And then a knock. This one loud, almost perturbed.

Mr. Randolph smiled, "The infamous mother-in-law-son-in-law relationship," he said, "it, too, endures through eternity." The audience laughed.

"Can you ask him if . . . if there is a heaven?" the old woman asked. "Is he in heaven?"

The audience sat in silence, but the tension felt to be rippling through the air. I felt my hand tightening on the old woman's beside me, and her's on mine.

"Mr. Cushing?" said Mr. Randolph. "Mr. Cushing. If you can, would you be kind enough to speak through the trumpet. The trumpet is there so the audience can clearly hear you."

Silence.

"Mr. Cushing."

It was then that the rattling began. It was first very faint, nearly imperceptible, but I noticed the looks on the faces of the volunteers. Mrs. Cushing was still staring out in wonder, eyes boring into the back of Mr. Randolph's head, but Miss Mayhew and Mr. Pratt, were looking down, staring at the table. The table moved again just slightly, another quiet rattle. They both removed their hands from the surface, and it moved again, this time slightly more violent, enough to cause the water to splash over the rim of the grass. Someone in the audience gasped again. Miss Mayhew and Mr. Pratt suddenly pushed back their chairs, but Mrs. Cushing stayed put, and then the table before her began to shake, the noise growing louder and louder, impossibly loud for such a small table. The shaking became so aggressive, it almost felt as if the table might explode, breaking into a thousand pieces. But it didn't explode. It stopped quite suddenly, and then as several more members of the audience stood, preparing to leave, it began to rise.

"Mr. Cushing," said Mr. Randolph again.

Miss Mayhew and Mr. Pratt pushed their chairs farther backward. Mr. Pratt's face had drained of all color, but then he suddenly stood, approached the table, swinging his arm through the air above it as if looking for strings, wires. Nothing. And then dropping to his hands and knees, swinging his arm below. Clean. He backed up quickly and landed flat on his rear end. Adjusted his spectacles. The table was left hovering there above the stage, two feet in the air. And Mrs. Cushing still had yet to move.

I watched as Mr. Randolph took a deep breath. "Mr. Cushing," he said. "I would like to respectfully thank you for joining us this evening. It was kind of you to take the time."

The table dropped, banging loudly as it hit the stage, and only now did Mrs. Cushing jump backward, her chair nearly tipping over. Mr. Pratt was quick to her rescue. Grabbing the back of the chair, and lowering it to the floor before it could topple.

Paschal Beverly Randolph, his color now returning to his cheeks, opened his eyes, but he paid no attention to the people who had begun milling toward the exits. I wondered if it happened often.

⌐

Following the demonstration, Mr. Randolph took a seat at the table on the stage, and several people stepped up to speak with him. He had books for sale and was signing them for anyone who wished to purchase one. I was tempted but then worried what would happen should Hiram find it. Even worse things would come to be if he were ever to find this journal. After contacting Jacob Cushing, Mr. Randolph had gone around the audience and offered words from deceased loved ones for several people who had raised their hands. Only once did a man say that he had no idea whom Mr. Randolph was speaking of.

I came down from the balcony and waited at the back of the theater, watching as Mr. Randolph spoke quietly with the people on the stage. I was astounded by what I had witnessed, and merely wished to have a better look at him, closer. This man with the power, the gift, to ease the sorrow that finds all of us sooner or later in our lives. Sometimes throughout. I realize that many of his kind have been labeled frauds, charlatans, but it was not so with him. He cared about people, wanted to comfort them. It came through his voice, the way he moved, carried himself, and the things that he said. He was both a man of science, and a man of faith, compassion. I could feel it.

The lights were much brighter now, and he looked older, tired. It shook me a bit as I moved closer. Later, he would tell me that the communicating experience often drains him considerably, sometimes to the point where he feels too weak to stand.

As the crowd dwindled, a woman, perhaps in her late thirties, sat with him on the stage, their chairs facing each other. At first she was speaking and then sobbing into her hands. Mr. Randolph placed a hand on her shoulder, and then closing his eyes, he began to whisper, and I wondered if he were healing her.

I waited until she left, and then taking several deep breaths, I gathered my nerve and followed him backstage. The door to his dressing room was open, and his assistant was nowhere in sight. The lighting was dim back here, and everything about me seemed coated in dust. Old and long since touched. I almost felt as if I was floating through a dream, and I couldn't quite believe I was approaching him. He was sitting in a chair in the dressing room when I knocked, completely still, and he was looking straight at me, not the least bit startled, almost as if he were expecting someone. Expecting me?

I went to speak, but even I could barely hear my words, my voice so small emerging from my throat. I thanked him for the performance, but he still said nothing, he just sat staring, and then I asked him—despite Hiram—if perhaps I could purchase a book. He smiled a little and shook his head.

"You didn't come see me for a book," he said.

A few wisps of hair fell from my bun, and I brushed them away from my eyes. "I'd love to purchase one."

There was a box beside his dressing table, and he leaned over and pulled out a copy. Scribbled the inscription. *To Elizabeth, Best Wishes, Paschal Beverly Randolph.* I felt a jolt in my chest, my heart. I hadn't told him my name. He handed me the book, and my hands shaking I went to hand him the money, but he brushed it away.

"Compliments of the house." He paused. "I saw you in the balcony. But that wasn't your parents you were with."

"No, I'm not sure who they were."

"Well, in a way that's good," he said. "The gentleman won't be with us much longer. There are several people on the other side waiting for him. His parents, an uncle, and a brother, I think. Maybe more. It was there for a second and then it was gone." He was quiet again, squinting a little as he stared at me. Reading? And then something passed through his eyes, the color again passing from his face. I asked him if everything was all right, and he shook his head a bit, almost as if awakening from a dream. "Fine," he said. "Fine."

My heart was racing again, and I had so many things I wanted to ask, so many things I wanted to say, but my tongue could barely move. I thanked him and turned to head back out through the theater. I had just passed through the doorway when he called out to me.

"Elizabeth."

I turned.

"The name Henry?" he said. "Does it mean anything to you?"

I nodded.

"A paternal figure. But older. Your grandfather?"

Shocked, I nodded again.

"He says to tell you that you have to get away from him," he said. "He's very worried. He's afraid of what might happen."

29

Ford was out in the yard without any shoes. It didn't make any sense that he wouldn't have any shoes on because it was winter, but then he noticed the leaves were back on the trees, bright green, and the air was rippling with waves of humidity. A quiet humming sound that only came in high summer, that only came when you were alone, and everything else was silent around you. But he wasn't alone. There was a woman in the backyard with her back to him, kneeling on the ground, facing the cemetery. She had her hair up, and wore a long dress despite the heat. She sat perfectly still just to the left of the oak tree—the oak tree was tiny, barely a sapling, but he knew what it was—almost as if she were praying, and there was a little girl running about the tree. A bow in her hair, and herself in a long dress tied in back with a bow. White stockings. The little girl looked as if she were trying to catch the woman's attention, but the woman either couldn't see her, or was paying her no mind. And then when Ford looked again, the tree had grown. It was enormous now.

Ford took a step closer, and listened, but he could still hear nothing but the humming sound, and then something breaking in the tree above. An acorn falling. Either a squirrel or a bird moving in the foliage. The house was behind him now. He felt eyes on him, coming from the house, the hairs on his neck standing on end, and his heart picking up its pace. He wanted to turn and see the house, he had to turn, and yet he couldn't. Was terrified to turn. The woman stood slowly then, her back turned toward him. And then she turned slowly to look at him, and Ford tried to scream.

He sat up in bed, his shirt soaked. He looked at the clock. Just after nine—and Diana hadn't yet come up to bed. He wondered if he had really let out a cry, or if it was just in the dream. It was a dream he had repeatedly since they moved in—the woman, the little girl, and the enormous tree, but up until now the woman had never turned. And now he realized he had seen the woman in the dream before. Seen her picture. Down in the cellar.

He lay back, catching his breath, stared at the ceiling.

30

March 24, 1872

If Hiram finds out what I have done, I shiver to think what might happen. I don't believe neither he nor I would be safe, from him.

A storm had come in off the sea Saturday night while we were in the theater, and I waited an hour or more for it to pass but when it did not, I decided it would be better to stay in Edgartown for the night. There could be little harm. I still had a small sum of money tucked away, and certainly enough to get a room at the inn, and Hiram would not return before Monday at the earliest—more than likely even later should the storm on the mainland prove to bring snow. I know how people, islanders, might view a lady staying here on her own, but given the conditions, traveling back home, especially with the road so close to the sea, did not seem to be wise. I had spoken to one coachman who had come that way and he had advised me that much of the road was already nearly impassable, the waves crashing over the land bridge that is Beach Road—connecting Cottage City with Edgartown—and flooding Sengekontacket Pond. It is a tidal pond, and he assured me that waters should have recessed by late morning or early afternoon of the next day, but as of now, he said, it was out of the question.

I had no umbrella. I don't know why I didn't think to bring an umbrella as the temperature had risen and it was surely too warm for snow, but I had not. Nor had I brought a night bag nor a change of clothes. I hurried along South Water Street, the wind and rain blowing in furiously coming in off the sea, and the waves crashing loudly in the distance—I could only imagine the damage they were doing to the wharf. By the time I arrived at the Achelous Inn my clothes were completely drenched, the water dripping in rivers down my cheeks. The inn was an impressive mansion in the Georgian style with Doric columns and an enormous clove leaf window above the porch roof on the second floor. It had been owned by a sea captain with two ships—*The Syren* and the *Pilgrim*—and he had built the home to retire in with his wife, but the town lore stated, she had retired there alone, her husband lost at sea.

Now there was a thin man in a high collar and gray vest waiting inside at the desk. He was bald on top except for a small tuft of dark hair right in the center above his brow. He needed only one look at me to understand my situation, and he explained that his wife could possibly lend me a nightgown to wear while I laid my clothes out to dry. The inn was nearly full, he said, but there were two or three rooms still available. Mine would be on the second floor.

And it was on the second floor that I once again ran into Mr. Randolph.

I was on my way back to the desk to check with the man about obtaining a pitcher and a glass for water—I had already taken off my wet things and wore my overcoat over my nightgown—and Mr. Randolph looked to be just entering his room, two doors down. He stopped and looked at me, but he did not smile, and as his eyes betrayed nothing, for a moment I did not think he recognized me despite just having seen me backstage. But then he bowed his head, slightly.

"Mrs. Steebe," he said.

His voice startled me. I didn't remember telling him my last name either, and I wondered if he were reading my mind. I didn't want him to be reading my mind. I started to blush, and bowed my head slightly in return.

"I imagine more than a few people from the lecture will be spending the night," he said. "The weather being as it is. I, myself, was not planning on leaving until tomorrow regardless. The eleven clock ferry, a coach to Boston, and then the train to Albany, I hope. I usually stay over near Trinity Park—there is a nice little inn there with a wonderful view of Ocean Park and the sea, and that wonderful hotel that is going up—but I heard the road tonight is impassible. The weather in this region is so unpredictable, it is hard to make any plans definitive."

"Usually," I said.

I cannot recall how the rest of the conversation went before I found myself in his room, sitting at the table by the window. I believe I had mentioned going downstairs for water, and I believe he said he had some inside, but how I ended up in there is not clear. I know how it would be looked upon if anyone were to learn that I spent time in his room, and worse, oh, much, much worse if word were ever to get back to Hiram. And normally, under normal circumstances, I never would have followed him. But the circumstances seemed far from normal, and to be truthful they seemed far from real. Nothing seemed real since I first heard his voice in the theater, and then witnessed what followed. It was all a dream. And I almost wonder now if he had put me in a trance.

He poured us each a glass of water, and then he removed his coat, his bow tie, down to his shirt and his vest. He rolled up his sleeves and he took a seat across the table from me. The wind grew louder outside, rattling the panes on the window. We were far enough inland, and up a slope, where we should have been safe from the surf, but on an island in a storm, you could never be sure.

I could feel the man's eyes on me still, but I tried not to look at him. I couldn't be sure what it may imply if I looked at him, what my eyes might betray. He worked searching through the layers of people's minds, their souls, so who could say what he might see that others, anyone else, would surely miss. Possibly it would be something I could not even see myself. But then something inside me stirred, I felt a pull, something magnetic, and I did turn. The black of his eyes, his pupils, already so large, steady and transfixed. And then, as hard as I might try, I couldn't look away.

"The spirits are strong around you," he said at last. "Have you known many people who have passed?"

I shook my head. "Not more than most. I had a brother who died when I was small."

"Jeremy," he said, and as he did my heart jolted as if it might stop. "Short for Jeremiah—although, I suppose it usually is. A small boy, weak, and his skin very pale. I can see him. Was it a lung disease he died of?"

I nodded. How could he know of Jeremy? It made no sense. I had barely ever even mentioned him to Hiram, never mind strangers. It had been so many years earlier, but we had been very close. My older brother—just two years older. He was always looking out for me.

"He is over there with your grandfather," said Mr. Randolph. "They are together. With someone else. A woman. She looks like you, only heavier. Your mother. Your mother is with them. Has your mother passed?"

I nodded.

"Yes, I can see her now. She wasn't coming through before. She has passed, but your father has not. Her name is—"

"Susan," I said.

"Yes, Susan," he said. "But don't tell me next time. Let it come through. From her. She is concerned about you, very concerned, but it is not clear about what. They are all concerned. I see others—several more people standing at the foot of the tunnel, the light. Some you know, and others are ancestors you have yet to even meet. But they know you, love you. You are well loved, over there—the afterlife, the next dimension, is all about love— and they are all concerned. Something to do with your home. Your marriage." He glanced down at my hand. "You are still married?"

I nervously slipped my hand over my ring finger, but I nodded again. I didn't want to nod, I didn't want him to know, and even now, after everything that transpired, I cannot be sure why that was.

"A religious man?" said Mr. Randolph. "Although some might say his perception of God, of Christianity, is somewhat skewed. He doesn't know what to make of it; they don't know what to make of him." He paused. "You don't know what to make of him."

I looked away. Didn't answer. My heart was fluttering again. He couldn't possibly have known who I was, anything about me, and yet, he seemed to know everything. Unless . . . Mr. Pratt . . . Maybe Mr. Pratt had seen me in the audience, said something to him following the lecture. But why would he? By the time I approached the stage, Mr. Pratt was gone, and he would have had no way of knowing that I would come to speak to Mr. Randolph. I was not even sure I was going to speak to him until I stood right before him. And Mr. Pratt, despite the many failings that Hiram has attributed to him, has never impressed me as one for idle gossip. No, it could not have been Mr. Pratt.

Mr. Randolph was quiet again, his eyes boring through me. Then: "And I think that is where the danger lies."

I could hear voices, footsteps, in the hall, but everything seemed distant. I was completely alone with him, and not just in the room. Alone. Everything was far away, and nothing could touch us. I could see him clearly, his outline, but everything else around him had blurred. Muted colors. Shadows.

"How do you do it?" I whispered.

"How do I do what?"

"Everything."

He smiled. "I don't do anything. They do it. They do it through me. I can show you."

He asked me to lie on the floor then. I didn't move at first, but then he reached out and put his hand over mine. "It will be fine," he said. "I wouldn't do anything to hurt you."

I lay on my back at the foot of the table, and kept my arms at my sides as he had instructed, my eyes locked on the ceiling. It seemed very high up, very far away. Clouds. At first just clouds, broken and thin, white and gray, moving together and moving apart. And then thin lines of faces, lines and shadows, fading in and out. I could vaguely hear the wind, the surf, but these things too seemed quite far away as if I were no longer on the island and neither was he. He knelt down on one knee beside me, brushing a wisp of hair away from my eyes, and then he opened his hands, palms to the ceiling. He told me to relax again, shut my eyes.

People were talking around me, but their voices, too, were faint. There were many of them. They were all talking at once, and I could not make out clearly what anyone was saying, but I did hear my name. Then the names of others. Then somebody, quietly, hushed somebody else, and I could only hear the voice of a woman. The voice of my mother. All in an instant it sounded just like her, but somehow, it also did not. I cannot explain it. Not then. Not now. It was a feeling, more than the sound, the tone, I suppose, and the words. The words were hers, ones she would choose. Little Lizzie, she called me, my Little Lizzie. "Sing a song of blackbirds," she began to sing—the nursery rhyme she would sing to me when I was small. No one had called me Lizzie in years. Then her voice began to fade, the others all talking again at once, and then my body began to rise from the floor.

I felt completely relaxed, but unable to move, and I kept going up. Mr. Randolph stood as I did, his palms still open to the ceiling. I shut my eyes, and then, somehow, I was out of my body and looking down upon the whole scene. Myself, floating, eyes shut, and Mr. Randolph standing beside me. I could see the crown of his head—he was beginning to go bald, just a small bare spot in his thick hatch of hair, and his shirt had begun to come untucked in the back. I wondered if he realized I was now above him, and for a second, I wondered if I were dying, if perhaps my heart had stopped. I could see directly into the pitcher of water, see the furniture all about the room, his open bag, full of books, the still-made bed. The voices of the others were louder now, taking turns speaking, my mother again, my grandfather, and the small voice of my older brother, all there for a second, and then gone. And I felt myself being pulled, and then pushed, stuffed, my soul back into my body. It hurt only slightly, but jarred my whole being.

I felt his hands on me then, one on my shoulder and one beneath my hip, my buttocks, steadying me, ready to catch should I begin to fall. But I didn't. I stayed floating there, my eyes still shut. I feared to open my eyes. He ran a finger up my middle. I wanted him to stop—he had to stop, I am a married woman—and yet I didn't want him to. If I kept my eyes shut, did not look into his, it wouldn't be real. It would be like the rest of the entire experience, the entire night. An illusion of some sort. It had to be an illusion. The voices were still there, but now even more distant, talking to one another, but not to me, going back to the tunnel. With my eyes shut, I could see the tunnel, and the shadows moving in, the light emanating from it far too bright to allow me to make out any of their features. I hoped they could not see me, and even in my trance-like state, I began to blush. I felt the man's breath as he leaned over closer. He kissed my cheek, holding his lips against my flesh just for a second, and then I felt myself descending. Settling gently upon the floor. He kissed me one more time, and then I could hear him, settling back into his chair at the table, and everything else was gone. We were back in the room at the inn, and nowhere else. I opened my eyes, glancing down quickly to make sure I was appropriately covered, and then I looked his way.

He sipped his glass of water. "You're a beautiful woman," he said, "amazingly so. If I were not married, you were not married . . . Ah . . . well . . . There are a lot of ifs in this life I think."

It was some time before I moved from the floor. I turned on the my side, my hands beneath my head, looking at him, hoping he would lie down beside me, but not wanting to speak. Not wanting to initiate anything more as it would be wrong, but not wanting to stop him if he initiated it first. But he wasn't going to. A man gets a look in his eye when he is going to advance upon you, and he gets a look in his eye when he is about to surrender, and Mr. Randolph had neither. A complete lack of tension, a complete look of peace.

"It is perhaps none of my business," he said at last, "but the spirits concerns are rarely in vain. If they are worried, you should perhaps think things through. Protect yourself."

"Protect myself?"

"The Lord may have created the institution of marriage." He raised his water glass. "But it is the man who corrupts it. You must be careful, Elizabeth."

When I woke in my room, it was half past three, the wind and the sea still roaring outside my window. I didn't remember returning to my room, and I began to wonder if I had ever left at all. If it were all a dream.

31

Late February. She ran into Michael again down at Ocean Park. Standing on the lawn with an easel in front of him. He was painting the Corbin Cottage. The Corbin "Cottage" was actually an enormous Victorian mansion. Queen Anne style, and three shades of green, it caught your eye as soon as you stepped onto the island from the ferry, impressive enough to stand out among the numerous Victorian mansions and elaborate gingerbread homes. The roof was surmounted with both a turreted tower and a widow's walk behind. Rounded steps leading up to the wrap-around porch.

Ford was sleeping, and Samantha was at preschool, giving Diana three free hours. Despite the chill, the air was surprisingly calm, even coming in off the sea. Little to no wind. The park was mostly empty, and only a few cars lined the boardwalk overlooking the beach. Michael had his back to her. He wore a peacoat, work boots, and faded jeans, and she could tell by the small balding crown on the back of his head that it was him. She stood behind him for five minutes or more, before he realized she was there. He had the full structure outlined on the canvas, most of the color. Working on the detail. Using oils. Thick and alive.

When Michael turned he had one brush in hand and one clenched between his teeth. He smiled, pulled the brush from his teeth, pointed.

"I know you," he said.

Diana stepped closer. "Sorry. I was just watching a bit." She blushed. "Not for long. Just for a few minutes. I like to watch people paint—it always amazes me what they can do. If they're talented I mean." She hesitated, took a step backward. "I'm sorry. I'll go. I don't want to disturb you."

"No," he said, "Don't worry yourself with it. I was looking for an excuse to take a break anyway." He put both brushes down on the easel. Wiped his hands on a rag he pulled from his pocket, looked at the canvas. Diana stepped closer.

"That's amazing," she said. "I can't imagine being able to do anything like that."

"Well, the wonderful thing about buildings is that they don't move. So I can return tomorrow and pick right back up where I left off. The light may be different, but with a painting like this, that isn't as important until I'm near the end."

"You look pretty close," she said.

"I suppose. Still a ways to go."

"I love this house. I can't believe they've kept it in the shape they have for so many years. It's got to be well over a hundred years old, right?"

"In spirit, yes. This house is actually a replica of the original. The owner uses it as summer cottage, believe it or not. He bought it some years back when it was a mess and renovated it, and then it burned and it wasn't old at all."

"You're kidding me?" Diana said.

"No," Michael said. "Burned to the ground. A faulty wire, I heard. Then the owner started from scratch, ground up, using the original plans, everything painstakingly perfect. So what we're looking at is pretty much the same thing that people crossing the park in 1891 would see. Remarkable, isn't it? A wonderful view to the past." He looked back at his picture. "Which reminds me, I was thinking of you recently."

Diana looked at his eyes. "You were?"

"Yes, I was viewing a photograph I took, and it got me thinking about you—the conversation we had. I think I have it with me." He had a saddlebag on the ground beside him—full of his supplies—and he crouched down beside it. Undid the buckle, and began flipping through a stack of pictures.

"What's it a picture of?" Diana asked, but he didn't look up, still scanning.

"This place," he said. "The Corbin Cottage. A lot of times I'll shoot a number of photos of a building before I paint it, different angles, distances, and perspectives. Then if the weather is bad I can use them to work on the piece inside." He stopped. "Here," he said, standing up. The photograph was four by six, taken from approximately the same angle they were standing at now. "I usually take a shot in black-and-white, and a shot in color. I like the black-and-white because it can give me a better feel for the shadows. Anyway, I was looking at this one, and I noticed something I found curious."

Diana gazed at the photo. "What?"

"Well, look at the front porch. What do you see?"

"It looks like a man standing there."

"You're right," he said, "it does, and there wasn't. I'm sure of it. I remember taking the picture quite clearly. It was only about two weeks ago when I was down for the weekend, and there was no one up there, no one in there. As a matter of fact, there was no one around here anywhere. The wind was wild, and the temperature couldn't have been much above twenty. I was the only one mad enough to be out here. Anyway, I took several shots of the house, up close and further back, and there was no one there. I am sure of it."

"He looks like he's wearing a suit," Diana said. "Three-piece."

"Yes, that's what I thought, too. I mean, the image is not very clear, it's too far away, but it certainly looks like a person, I think, some kind of top hat on and one hand resting on the rail. And you don't see too many people around looking like that anymore, now, do you?"

"It looks like he's watching you take the picture."

"I know. I almost wonder if I should place him in the painting." Michael looked at the photo a moment longer, and then crouched down and slipped it back in his bag. "Anyway, it did make me think of you. Who knows? It might just be shadows, or a trick of camera or something."

"Is that what you think?" she asked.

Michael chuckled. Blushed. "Well . . . no, I don't think that at all. But I don't know you very well, and I don't want you thinking I'm nuts."

The wind had picked up now, almost out of nowhere, the crests of the waves rising in the distance, and Diana felt a chill. "I could tell you a few things that would make me think I'm a lot crazier than you," she said.

Michael packed up his supplies, dropped them at the bed-and-breakfast, and they walked over to Circuit Avenue to get a cup of coffee. Diana felt a little uncomfortable, a little nervous. She wasn't doing anything wrong, she kept telling herself. It was just coffee. But if someone who knew her, knew Ford, saw her, she wondered if they would say anything. And if that happened it wouldn't be good. But there were few people about, most of the shops still closed, and the only one in the coffee shop was a ruffled man, scribbling in a notebook. He kept looking at them from time to time. Look, write, look.

She told Michael all about the house, the cellar. The history. The man she had seen on the front porch of the gingerbread cottage, the man in the cemetery, the man she had seen behind the desk in the hotel. Sam's imaginary friend, and the voice upstairs. And she told him about the journal.

Michael mostly just nodded, listened, stirring his coffee with his spoon. He didn't look skeptical, and he didn't look amazed. "And these people you have seen, have they ever spoken to you?"

Diana hesitated. "No. Well, the man in Trinity Park looked to be yelling, but I couldn't hear anything. Maybe the others said things, and I just didn't hear. I'm not sure. My heart was racing so badly each time that anything is possible."

"Possible," he said. "But it almost sounds as if you might be seeing imprints."

"Imprints?" she asked. The man with the notebook looked at her again, but then when she looked away, and looked back, he was still there. Real.

"Yes. Paranormal imprints. We have spirits, and we have imprints, or so I'm told, and they're not the same thing. I've read a little about them, imprints, I mean. People think they're ghosts, but they're not. Well not really—I mean they are not what we would think of as ghosts, watching us, able to interact with us if they wanted to. Imprints are not something active, intelligent. They're oblivious, if you can even refer to an image as oblivious— to everything around them. People say they are just sort of like a residual high energy, often left behind—or traveling back—from some sort of emotional incident or calamitous event. Murders, battles, accidents, acts of violence. Things like that."

"But what would cause that? I mean, it's not like they are all over the place."

"Are they not? I'm not so sure. Maybe we're often seeing people who aren't really there, passing them on the street, but we don't realize it. It sounds mad, but who knows? Some men speculate that the earth's electromagnetic field can serve as a sort of tape recording device. And if given the right conditions, events of the past can be played back. But that's all they are—recordings. Once real but not anymore. Something like a window or door to the past. Times gone by. I mean, we really have no idea how time functions, right? Whether it just exists here—"

"Here? Like the earth?"

"No, this dimension. Or everywhere. And sound can travel out into space and come back, hundreds, thousands of year later, so who's to say that images can't, too?"

"Is that what you think was going on with the man in your photograph?"

"Possibly. There certainly didn't seem to be anything traumatic going on with him—he was just standing there—but you never know. Sometimes apparently mundane events aren't at all what they seem. You don't always know the circumstances. The emotions. Maybe that man had just stepped back outside after murdering somebody."

Diana was silent.

"Or possibly," Michael said, "he is just one of many. Countless people. Countless souls. Maybe most of us just aren't seeing people who really *are* there. Just a few of us, sensitive souls, getting a glimpse of them from time to time, out of the corner of their eye, the peripheral vision. True ghosts of some sort. Maybe they are all around us, living their lives, or post lives, in their own time, but standing right beside us. What did that man Einstein say? The only reason for time is so that everything doesn't happen at once."

Diana hesitated. "What did he mean by that?"

"I think he meant that time is just an illusion—a man-made one—because our brains can't tolerate the fact that everything is going on all the time. We've always been here."

"Always?"

"Always. No beginning. No end. We don't ever really die, in theory at least. Maybe actual death is just an illusion so that our human forms don't get hit with sensory overload. Sounds mad if you think about it, but who is to say?" He was quiet a moment, his eyes back on her now, thinking. "So what does your husband think about your experiences?" he said at last.

Diana sipped. Put her cup carefully back down. "He doesn't."

"He doesn't have an opinion?"

"No, I haven't told him. Not much anyway. And he doesn't think. That's half his problem. He stews but doesn't think, not rationally."

Michael just stared at her.

"I'm sorry," she said, "I shouldn't say that. I barely know you— and I don't want to start venting about my marriage."

"Not a problem. It doesn't bother me. And I might be stepping over my boundaries, but if you don't mind my saying so, it didn't look as if things were going particularly well last time I saw you either."

"No. But it's gotten better. He's trying. He says he's trying."

"Trying to what? Not abuse you anymore?"

Diana pulled at her ear a little. Feeling awkward. She *didn't* know this man. Only knew what he told her, that he liked to stay down here, dabble in several different things. For all she knew he could be just like Ford. Another one out in the fold. Ford could be charming, at least when he wanted to be. Isn't that what people who met him often said? Friends, people who worked with him, people who didn't live with him? She had thought he was charming once, too. She believed that he had saved her, and *he* still believed that, or so he said. But there was a difference between charming and kind. Charming had a glow to it, illuminating the surface, bright enough to hide everything else, but kindness was quieter, deep and still within someone's eyes. Sometimes with charmers, you looked into their eyes, and you saw nothing, an absence of sorts. A void. They were never really listening, always plotting. The next move. One step ahead. And Michael appeared as though he were listening.

"Well, there's that," she said, laughing a little nervously, "but there's other things, too. It's hard being married. A lot of work, a lot of give-and-take."

"I suppose that is true, but usually if someone's hitting you, the giving and taking is no longer going both ways. By that point, there's usually just a lot of taking." He stared at her a moment. "I'm afraid I'm making you uncomfortable, though, you look like I'm making you uncomfortable."

"I do?"

"You're red. It started in your neck and spread right up through your cheeks."

"It's warm in here," Diana said.

"Well, maybe I shouldn't have been so bold, jumping to conclusions, I mean, but if it does happen again, I strongly suggest you take action of some sort. At least speak to someone—these days there are a lot of services, support, for that sort of thing, much different than the old days." He shrugged. "Or maybe, and I say this with all due respect, you should just get out. I knew a woman once—she lived on the island here—whose husband used to beat her pretty badly, and it didn't end very well. She stayed with him despite the fact that he nearly disfigured her, and he actually started, for all intents and purposes, holding her prisoner. He had been hitting her for years, but no one knew it was happening until it was too late."

"What happened to her?"

Michael shrugged. "Well, he locked her in the house for a while, and then he killed her."

Diana felt her chest seize a little, then a tightening down through her limbs. "Oh my God. That's awful. I'm so sorry. Was she a relative of yours?"

"A friend," he said. He sipped. "It was a long time ago."

"I hope the bastard rotted in jail."

"Well, nothing was ever proven. Not in the eyes of the public, anyway, the law.

"But back then laws were more lax—concerning the abuse, I mean, not the murder. People either tended to accept it as part of married life, at least for some people, or they just tended to look the other way. It was quite disturbing."

Diana looked at him. "It couldn't have been that long ago."

He shrugged again. "It was a while back. I was pretty young. And besides, it still happens more often than you think. The husband concocted a story, told people she left him, moved, and people believed him."

"Then how do you know he killed her?"

Michael stared at her. "Because," he said. "I do."

Diana felt something stirring in her stomach. Tightening again.

"In any case, I have a hard time looking the other way, especially now, especially after what happened. I'm not trying to scare you—you just have me worried. And if you ever need a place to stay again, please don't hesitate to go to back to the inn. If Carol doesn't have room, I'm sure she'll make it. She's very good that way. The important thing is that you keep safe, both you and your little girl."

"It won't happen again," Diana said, and even as she did, she wondered if it was true. She pictured Ford. Sobbing. Pathetic and small. Begging forgiveness. He was abused. A victim of abuse. It wasn't his fault, he said. It would never happen again. Never. He promised.

"You sure?"

She hesitated, nodded, her fingers tight on her mug. "I'm sure."

Michael looked at her a moment longer, and then he smiled, hesitantly, and then he nodded.

They said goodbye out on the street, on the corner before the large pink inn with the octagonal turret on top. Michael stood there looking at her for a moment. She liked him, and yet, she had no idea what to make of him. He seemed kind, and he seemed different, and she was afraid for a moment that he might try to kiss her. But then looking as if he had words on the tip of his tongue, he merely cleared his throat.

"Can I ask a favor of you?" he said.

"Sure," she whispered.

"Well, it may sound silly, so if it does, please feel free to say no. I mean if it makes you uncomfortable at all, I mean."

Diana started to smile. "What is it?"

"Well," he said, "I was wondering if you might let me paint you."

32

Ford had started to run to catch up with her as she started across Ocean Park. Diana was heading toward the water, to look at the waves, the boats, he guessed. She liked to do that. And maybe he could surprise her, he thought, grab her by the shoulders and give her a little scare, all just in fun. Hug her after, and then take her hand, and they could walk over there together. A little romance. Maybe that is what they needed—a little romance. And then back at the house, who knew? Anything was possible. But then he stopped. How would he explain himself? Why he was following her. She thought he had been sleeping—he was almost always sleeping this time of day—and he had pretended to be at least until she left. But he needed to know what she did. Where she went. How she spent her time away from the house when Sam was at school, and he was asleep. They hadn't been fighting much, but ever since the incident with Norman and Cybil, the fight they had caused, things hadn't been the same. She was quieter, more distant, and if truth be told, he would rather have her bitching at him than being quiet all the time. At least when she was bitching things were out in the open, he knew what he was dealing with. And lately, that was a problem—he didn't know what he was dealing with. No idea what she was thinking. Or worse, whom she might be spending time with.

He had followed her down through Trinity Park, waiting for her to stop, expecting her to stop, somewhere, anywhere, and now here she was at Ocean Park. Wearing her black leather jacket and her scarf tight around her neck, hands in her pockets. Her beautiful ass. She was moving slowly, hesitantly it seemed. Heading toward . . .

She was heading toward a man on the far side of the park. A man with his back to her standing at an easel. Painting.

She didn't approach the man right away, not even stepping closer until the man turned and saw her. A tall man with dark hair and olive skin. Peacoat and jeans. Ford couldn't make his face out clearly, not from this distance; his features seemed muted, not clear at all. Ford tried to concentrate on what was happening in front of him, but at the same time his head was flashing with pictures. Diana and this man. Talking. Then kissing—he could see it all in his mind's eye. Then somewhere quiet and alone and pulling at each other's clothes. Ford could feel the rage, still just simmering, but building. And that wasn't good. Not yet. No need for that yet. He was exhausted, way overtired, and his imagination was getting the best of him. He took a deep breath, cleared his head. Jumping the gun, he told himself. He practiced his breathing. More deep breaths. Good for the temper. Control. All of life was about self-control. It was just a guy painting a stupid picture, and Ford was jumping the gun. They were talking now, but not even standing close, not that close, and Ford was too far away to hear what they were saying.

But then after a moment, she did move closer, with relaxed body language, and the guy was looking for something in his bag, showing something to her. She knew him, Ford thought. It wasn't just a stranger she had stopped to watch paint. She knew him. Ford tried to think back. How many times had she slipped out without a good excuse as to where she was going? Not many times, he thought, at least not many without Sam. And it didn't make sense, didn't seem like her style. But what was her style? Did she have it in her? And when did she start acting different, getting cold toward him? He had to piece it all together, make sense of it. Needed more to go on before outright accusing her.

Ford's head slipped to tunnel vision then. Nothing else around him. Just Diana, and the man. Now walking ahead. When they approached the bed-and-breakfast, he almost lost it, ran at them and clocked the piece of shit in the jaw. They were getting a room, he was sure of it. Going somewhere to fuck. But then something stopped him. Who went to B&Bs just to fuck? It wasn't like it was a cheap motel. And then Diana didn't go in with the guy, she waited outside, the guy soon coming out, buttoning his peacoat high. And then they were off walking again, heading toward Circuit Avenue The sun had broken free for a moment, but then passed again behind the clouds, casting the street in dark shadows. Ford took a breath and shut his eyes. When he opened them again, Diana was alone. He looked twice, and then again she was with the man. And then she was alone.

33

March 28, 1872

I almost believed a ray of light, of hope, had entered my relationship with Hiram, but then as soon as it appeared it was gone. The madness and darkness and melancholy that has become our lives together overtaking it all. I should know better by now. Know not to hope.

I had met him at the wharf to welcome him home. It was Wednesday, he had been delayed by two days, but his spirits were high; the land transaction had gone well, and as he put it, he had attended a service on Sunday in Boston. We took a carriage home, rather than carrying his bags all that way, and he requested relations nearly immediately after we had passed through the door. This took me by surprise for it was just after three, and the sunlight was still streaming through the window; in the past, Hiram has never requested relations until the sun has long set. He took off his hat, and smoothed over his hair. He felt fertile, he said, strong, and time could not be wasted. He had a vision while he was on the road, he said, a vision of an angel, and the angel had shown him his son, the child we were to conceive, and the angel had said the time was now. Hiram took my hand, his eyes deep, vacant, but happy—I could not remember ever having seen a look in his eyes such as that—and he asked me a question. "And do you know who that angel was, Elizabeth?" he asked.

I tried to look happy myself, but was unable to keep my thoughts from moving back to the Saturday evening before. Mr. Randolph. Shame. I swallowed my breath and shook my head.

"The Angel Gabriel," he said.

"Gabriel?" I said.

"Gabriel," he repeated. "He of the annunciation. The harbinger of the Messiah." He took a breath. "He who will blow the horn to wake the dead on the final day. The time is now."

He took me to his room and asked me to remove my garments while he watched. I hesitated, but he nodded.

"Go on," he said, "it will be all right. It has been written." I removed my dress, and then my brassiere. I felt quite exposed, ashamed. Throughout our entire marriage I had never stood like this in front of him, never in front of anyone. I folded my arms, and looked away, covering myself, and Hiram, for a moment, just stood there, staring, and then, he, too, removed his things, completely. I had never seen him like this either, and it startled me at first, the size. I had felt it many times before but never seen it in the light of day, and it scared me a little. His chest is covered in coarse hair as are his legs, and without his clothes, he just didn't look like Hiram. I've always identified Hiram with his clothes, always neat, proper, covered.

He stepped forward and touched me, his hand going lower, and then he tilted my chin, raising it so he could kiss me. It has been years since Hiram kissed me. I could feel the full length of him pressing against me, throbbing, and he ran his hands down over my shoulders, my back.

"I don't think God will be pleased," I said.

"We are doing it to please Him," Hiram said. "I would not act in such a way unless He directed specifically to do so. The child must be created through love, beauty, not through practicality. The Lord has seen that we are good, innocent, as were the first man and woman to walk this earth, and He has chosen to reward us." He kissed me again.

I had never heard Hiram speak this way. Relations were meant for the dark, most of our clothing still in place, and never ever to be spoken of. To speak of it was to fall to the Devil, and even as he spoke of God, I had to wonder if indeed it was to the Devil we were falling. Perhaps I had opened the door with Mr. Randolph, and now, somehow, Hiram was slipping through with me. I never would have believed any of it, and I wondered if it were a dream, a hallucination. Had Hiram now fully and completely taken leave of his senses, his mind? Or had I ?

He kissed my neck, and then below my ear, and he whispered, "I'd like you to turn around."

I froze.

"Please," he said. "I will be gentle."

When I still didn't move, he placed his hands back on my shoulders, assisting me, and then when I had turned completely, he pushed against my upper back so I leaned over, my hands supporting myself on the foot of the bed.

"A position such as this is conducive to producing male offspring," he said, "and the child must be male. Of course."

He was confusing me, but I did not want to question him, not while his mood was elated. The wrong word, the wrong tone, or movement could make things change quickly, and I knew that all too well. He moved inside of me, and as he did, I bit my lip to stifle a cry. I thought of Mr. Randolph. His eyes, his hands, his touch. I tried not to, tried to clear my head, but I could not help myself. He was everywhere, all around me, and it was him behind me, not Hiram. Hiram, his hands grasping my hips, picked up speed, mumbling something beneath his breath, something that almost sounded to be the words of a prayer, and then suddenly I felt something tensing in my legs. Up through my spine, my shoulders, out through my arms, and flooding my insides. I had never felt anything like it before. I arched my back, and my body bucked as Hiram pushed further. I had lost complete control, but the flooding of warmth, tension building and releasing, was like nothing I had ever experienced, not once. Hiram tensed himself, and then I felt him releasing inside of me. He grunted quietly and then he was done, but I was not. I wanted to be, but could not. I couldn't control my movements. I collapsed on my side on the bed, my muscles still twitching, and I was unable to get up. I felt Hiram take a seat on the bed beside me, and I felt his eyes upon me, but I dared not look at him. I could hear him still catching his breath.

"Elizabeth," he said at last. "Are you not well? I didn't hurt you, did I?"

I shook my head, and my legs twitched again. I wrapped my arms around myself, covering my breasts.

"Are you sure? Are you having any chest pain?"

I shook my head again.

"Are you—?"

I shook my head, and forced a small smile. Hiram was quiet a moment, completely still, and once again I heard his breathing begin to accelerate.

"Dirty," he said at last.

I opened my eyes. He stood now, glaring at me, the rage boiling in his eyes. "You, dirty, dirty whore," he said. He raised his hand, and I started to back away, inching away on the bed. "The Lord entrusts me with a glorious task, sends his messenger to greet me in person, and you turn it into an outing fit for the Devil! Dirty!" He shouted again, and then he swung at me. "You dirty, filthy whore!" Hiram slapped me again, and then he kept slapping, I covered my face and started to cry, and then I backed up so much I fell off the bed to the floor.

April 2, 1872

The worst has happened. Hiram has forbidden me to leave the house, even if to just to step outside to hang the wash on the line. There are outside forces, he says, penetrating me, changing me somehow, and he has become quite concerned. He says it is not like me to behave in the manner in which I have behaved. I have been corrupted, he said, and he wonders if it has anything to do with my passing through Trinity Park, passing by "his" dominions, he says. He says he will need to conduct an investigation, make some inquiries as to whom I have been speaking to, and whom I may have been seeing. I told him no one, but he lowered his eyeglasses, and looked at me skeptically. "I love you too much to ever believe you, my dear," he said. "And I'll do what I have to, take whatever course of action, no matter how severe," he added, "to ensure that you are saved." I volunteered to take another route during my sojourns to town, but he will not have it. "Perhaps it is this island, after all," he said. "Perhaps the Devil has at last taken it for his. And perhaps," he added quietly, "that is why the Lord has chosen to place me here."

I have free reign of the house while he is at home, but while he is out, he has taken to locking me in the cellar, the key in his pocket. I do not like the cellar, the dark, the damp, and the shadows, even the well. But it is a good place to hide my journal as Hiram would never look down here. Since it started, he has not been gone for more than a few hours at a time, but he examines me closely upon each return, looking into my eyes, and asking me to open my mouth as he peers down my throat as if he were a physician. I am not sure what he is looking for and he refuses to say.

April 14, 1872

There was a child. I did not tell Hiram, not even before it was gone. I was not far along. I suppose Hiram may have been pleased, assuming we were successful in our creation, but if nothing else, I now realize it is dangerous to make any assumptions when it comes to Hiram. His thoughts and beliefs, desires, seem to change dramatically from one day to the next, one hour to the next, and what is worse, I'm not entirely convinced it was his. Although I don't clearly remember my entire evening with Mr. Randolph I do know I lay beside him, and anything could have happened. I only remember the lightness of his touch, dancing fingers, but could it have been more? Could he have managed to move somewhere inside me? He is a magician of sorts, and the entire episode felt trance-like in nature, so who is to say for sure?

Whomever the father, the child is gone—breaking my heart and tearing through my womb. I cannot imagine it was a child meant to be—not if it was Hiram's, not if it was Mr. Randolph's. If it survived, it would have either been illegitimate of father, or illegitimate of love, for no matter how much Hiram may insist he wants a child, wants to love a child, I don't believe he is capable. He has become far too detached to give or take anything like love. When the pain started, I took to my bed—thankfully he was out for the afternoon—and pulled the chamber pot close by. I clenched my teeth, and began to perspire, and then when the pain got to be too much, I knew something was happening. It passed quickly, and when it was over, I hurried to the cemetery and dug a small hole before Hiram returned. I wanted the poor child to be buried in hallowed ground. I dropped to my knees and I sobbed and I prayed, promising her, that we would see each other one day. That we would be with each other. And then when I was finished I returned to my yard, and planted an acorn behind the house. Spring is here, and I am hoping the seed will take. I wanted something to be there, always, so I could look out the window and remember the child. Something for me, and secret from Hiram. My child, my baby girl. I am sure I will never have another.

34

Ford stood at the kitchen window, drinking a glass of orange juice and staring at the big tree. Diana would be home soon. He had followed her and the man to the coffee shop, his mind now focused, no longer playing tricks on him, and he stood down the street, in the doorway of the Tibetan store, waiting for them to come out again. There was little to do in a coffee shop, and he didn't want her to see him. He needed to make sense of it all. Find out who the man was, why she was with him. A divorce lawyer? Maybe. But no, that didn't make sense, wouldn't be a lawyer, not painting on the green. Maybe a real estate agent, talking to her about available apartments? But that didn't make sense either. Why would they meet there, like that? Or maybe she was hiring him for a painting? One of Samantha? Or maybe a birthday present for Ford, a surprise? But even that didn't make sense. He had never been big on art, so why waste the money? His money. No, he thought, she had to be doing something with him, had to be fooling around.

But if he accused her without catching her actually doing anything—other than meeting somebody for coffee—all hell was going to break loose again, and then if she were innocent, he was going to end up looking like the bad guy. Again.

Always the bad guy.

He had waited, trying to keep from sight, trying to keep one eye tight on the coffee shop door, but there was more pedestrian traffic than usual out today, more cars, making it difficult, and then a UPS truck had pulled up, blocking his view. By the time the truck pulled away, Diana was standing alone outside the shop, her back turned to him as if she were looking in the window before she turned and left. If there had been any sort of embrace—a kiss?—he missed it, but she did in fact leave on her own. And that could mean everything, or it could mean nothing. Ford slipped down the alley beside the shop, and then rushed home before she could get there. He needed to control his temper. Keep it in check. If she was fooling around, then sure, he could yell and scream all he wanted, and it was in his right, but he had to know for sure. Couldn't let her provoke him. Didn't want to let her make him do things he'd regret. Not again. That wasn't him.

He wasn't his father.

He sipped his orange juice again, and then splashed in some vodka. A little more champagne. He hoped it would help him sleep. He was overstressed. Overtired. All of it closing in at once, getting the best of him, again. He watched the way the oak tree cast a shadow on the cemetery, the swing moving slowly in the breeze.

35

When Diana got home, Ford was in the backyard. She could see him clearly as she walked up the dirt road. She didn't expect him to be awake, never mind outside. Despite the chill, he was wearing the blue-gray postal shorts that he kept for the summer, a stripe up the side, and one of his ribbed white tank tops. Black boots and black dress socks. A tall glass of orange juice on the ground beside him.

He was cutting down the oak tree.

Diana had stopped to pick up a few groceries on the way home, and now she dropped the bags on the front lawn. Ford swung the ax as if looking to hit a line drive. *Thud*, wind up, release, *thud*. Every muscle in his bare arms and shoulders constricted as he connected, and a sweat had broken at his brow. He was more than halfway through.

Diana's thoughts were racing. He was cutting down the tree. It made no sense. Why on earth would he be cutting down the tree?

"What are you doing?" she asked.

Ford stopped, wiped his forearm across his brow. Face red. He was panting, the dead grass littered with bright wet wood chips.

"This thing is solid as a rock," he said. "I've already been at it for almost an hour. I should have tried to borrow a chain saw. Ken at work has one, I think."

"But why are you cutting it?" Diana asked. "It's a beautiful tree."

Ford looked up through the naked branches. Initials carved across the trunk, the higher up the fainter, scarred over, older.

Samantha's swing still hung from the limb—just a board and two pieces of rope, pushed through the holes and knotted to hold it, but she used it all the time.

"It's pretty old," Ford said

Diana scowled. "So that means you have to kill it?"

Ford repositioned himself. Swung the ax. Wooden handle, flecks of rust across the blade. Diana wasn't aware they even owned an ax. The blade connected, got caught in the trunk, and she watched as the impact sent vibrations out through Ford's body. Up through the arms, into the shoulders and finally causing his legs to totter. He fooled with the ax a little, wedging it this way and that, and then finally pulled it free, staggering backward as he did.

"It's not that. I just wanted to let more sunlight into the house—that house seems so dark all the time—and besides, the tree blocks most of our view of the graveyard, and it blocks a lot of the sky when I have my telescope out on the balcony. It's such a pretty view. I hate seeing it go to waste."

"Well, it was a pretty tree, too, Ford. I loved this tree. And Samantha loved her swing."

"You love a lot of things it seems. I can't even keep up with them. All that lovin'."

"What are you talking about?"

"Nothing. Just talking. Didn't you tell me we don't talk enough anymore? I wouldn't want you to go looking for someone else to talk to. Who knows what that might lead to?" He swung. "Anyway, I'm going to buy her a swing set, probably next summer. A nice one. And I can always plant you another tree. A new one, in another spot." He stopped, wiped his brow again, gazed off to his right and pointed. "Maybe over there so it won't block the view. You like new things don't you?"

"You should have asked me before killing it."

"I wanted to ask you, but you weren't home. I had no idea where you were."

Diana was silent.

Ford picked up his drink. Took a long sip. "Where were you?"

She looked at his eyes, something there. He was acting bizarre, and he never usually bothered asking her where she went in the mornings. Why was he asking her? He knew something, or thought he knew something.

"Picking up some groceries," she said quietly.

"That it?"

"First I went for a walk on Ocean Park. And the beach."

"I like that, those walks on the beach. Walks in the park, too." He smiled, he turned, and he raised the ax.

"You shouldn't have cut down the tree without asking me."

Ford swung. Connected. Vibrated again.

"It's my house, Diana. My yard. If I want to cut down a stupid fucking tree, I'll cut down a stupid fucking tree. It's going to make the yard that much prettier. This thing has probably been here for over a hundred years."

"All the more reason to let it live."

He swung. "Do me a favor? If I get to be over a hundred? If you're still around. Don't let me live."

"You're an ass." She walked away, and picked the grocery bags up off the front lawn, the sound of the ax still echoing in her ears. She hadn't seen this coming—had never even heard him complain about the tree, and she wondered why he was doing it. Why he would wake up from his nap, and head out there now? He almost never did anything in the yard in the good weather, never mind February. It made little sense. And the tree had been there nearly as long as the house itself, she knew that. In her heart, she knew it was the tree that Elizabeth had mentioned in the journal. It had to be. And now it was going. And for what? Because her husband was crazy. Nothing more, nothing less.

He knew something. Or thought he knew something. Had to. And she wondered if he had followed her.

Diana put the bags on the counter in the kitchen. She could see him through the window, still out in the yard, and even with the windows and doors shut, she could still hear the thud of the ax. Feel the vibrations. The whole house felt to be vibrating; she swore that it was. Diana closed her eyes, trying hard to clear her head. She thought of Elizabeth, and in the darkness of her thoughts, she could see a woman's face. A young woman, her lips parted in a silent cry.

And then came the roar. The big tree cracking, and the falling to the earth with a thud that shook the floor beneath her. There for a second, then gone. As was the face that had been locked in her head.

36

It is now my third straight day in the cellar. Hiram slaughtered the animals, the pig and the sheep, before he left, making a mess with straw and blood, the entire barn floor soaked in blood. It was unjust to leave them to suffer for my sins, he said, to leave them to go hungry. I fled the barn before he began, but I heard their cries; he had never slaughtered our beasts himself before, and he did not finish them quickly; and then he ordered me to come with him to clean up the mess. He hung the head of the sheep on a nail on the wall.

After forcing me to the cellar, he left me a small amount of food and I knew that wasn't good—he had never left me with food before, so I assumed that meant he would be gone longer than usual. I tried to flee, to run up the stairs when he brought it down—some bread from the bakery, cereal, the remains of a chicken I had cooked two nights earlier, two jars of apples, and a pitcher of water, and two hunks of raw meat—from the pig and the sheep—but he got hold of me, and it did no good despite my struggling. He slapped me twice.

"The Devil has hold of you," he hissed. And then he pushed himself against me, pressing me against the dampness of the cellar wall. He wrapped his arms tight about me, and began to whisper.

"We can't do this," he said. "Not until we get to the bottom of it all, what is happening to you. What they—he—have done to you. I fear what might happen were it to happen again, with God looking on. I fear his wrath. I fear for your soul," he said, "I love you, Elizabeth, I love you too much," and then he kissed the top of my head. He pulled away, and when I once again tried to run, he batted me down. I had dirt in my teeth from when I hit the cellar floor, a tooth chipped, and I could feel the side of my face beginning to swell.

It was the first time he had struck me since we last had relations when he returned from his trip. The act must be holy, he has said, must be seen as holy in the eyes, the light, of God, and it cannot be holy if we risk having me respond the way that I did. He must learn, he said, why I responded the way that I did, and what we can do to prevent it from happening again. I could explain that it was my body responding, not my soul, nothing inherently evil—not that I am aware—but I fear it would just make things worse if I were to take ownership of it. As it stands he views me as a vessel for the evil, but not the evil itself. But sitting here in the dark of the cellar, a candle burning beside me, I have to ask myself, Am I evil?

Perhaps I am.

April 26, 1872

When he returned he unlocked the door. When I came up, he stared at me a moment, and then advised me to fix him some dinner. My food supply had run out the day before, and I was quite hungry, the pains starting in my belly. I wanted to wash, too, feeling covered with the dust of the cellar, but I feared if I did, I would set him off. I lit a fire in the stove and began boiling the water for some potatoes. Hiram had brought back some greens and he tossed them on the table. He took a seat at the table and sat watching me. He did not appear as though he had combed his hair, and it was strange for him—to have been out in the community in such a disheveled state. I could feel his eyes boring a hole through my back as I moved about, but it felt good to see the light from outside, the mist moving between the tombs. I fixed him a cup of tea.

"Do you not wonder where I have been?" he asked at last.

I pressed my teeth into my lip, took a breath. "I would think that if you wished me to know, you would tell me."

"I was up in Boston," he said. "Visiting my cousin. He's doing very well. His practice is bringing him in more money than I think he could have ever expected, but I fear as though he may have lost sight of the Lord. I fear many people, these days, may have lost sight of the Lord. I informed him of this and asked him to move his family out here to be with us, thinking that we could perhaps establish a new community—a new city on the hill, here across the Jordan—but I got the impression that he does not wish to leave Boston. A shame. The city can hide many things, both around us and within us, but even the crowded streets and rising buildings can hide nothing from the Lord. I also stopped to pay a visit to your father."

My body suddenly stiffened. I had no idea that Hiram was traveling to Boston, less still that he might stop to visit my father. He had never had much to say to my father, and had once informed me that he feared he may be somewhat simple. My father was never simple though, he was just very quiet. Never one to push his piety into the faces of others. We had always had a fine time with each other, and now I feared what Hiram, in his current state of mind, might have told him.

As if reading my mind, he suddenly said. "I told him that you have been ill, that he should pray for you. And there was much truth in my words for you haven't been well, haven't been yourself, your old self. You haven't been the good woman I married. I did not get into the details of your sickness, for your father did not look well himself. He's quite frail, and has a terrible cough. A neighbor has been looking in on him, I understand, and the neighbor doesn't think he is doing well either. Consumption, I fear, and I did my best to keep a safe distance. He asked if you could write to him but I let him know that in your current state that would more than likely be out of the question. As soon as she is well, I told him, but I did not offer him a great deal of hope."

Hope. My father. Consumption. I felt my heart beginning to break just a little bit more. Wondering if it were true. Any of it. Although something told me Hiram may have very well stopped by to see him, if nothing else to attempt to extinguish any attempts at communication. I hated him then. Both my love and hate for Hiram have always waxed and waned, but now it was just hate. Pure, simple hate.

"I must go see him," I said at last.

"You will do no such thing." Hiram sipped his tea. "I stopped in Edgartown on my way home," he said at last.

I felt my back tense up again. "If I had known you were going, I would have asked you to pick up some provisions. Coffee and flour and things," I said. "We've nearly run out."

"We will make due," Hiram said. "It is in times like this that we all need to make do. Some of the mystics used to believe that hunger provides visions. Of what is, what will be." He paused again. "What was." I heard him stir his spoon in his tea. "I do not subscribe to the beliefs of the mystics, but being a man of visions myself—of sights and sounds—their experiences intrigue me. Do they intrigue you, Elizabeth?"

"I have never thought much about it," I said.

"No?" I heard him sip, and then when he placed the cup back down upon the table, I heard it rattle. Rattling was not good. Rattling meant his hands were shaking.

I turned and looked at him, forced a smile. "Only what you've told me," I said, "of spirits and such."

"Ah, yes," Hiram said. "Spirits. They can tell us quite a bit, can't they?"

"I wouldn't know, I've never heard them speak."

"Never?"

I shook my head and started in on the potatoes.

"I heard there was a magician in town, Edgartown, a few weeks back. A conjurer. He goes by the name Paschal Beverly Randolph. A negro. Or at least partially so—mixed race—they say his complexion is quite dark. Negroes with the slightest degree of education always like to assign themselves fancy names, these days, it seems. Trying to abolish their past, their histories as slaves. I cannot fault them that, as inferior as their kind may be, slavery was an evil institution. But this one believes himself to be a man of letters. Educated above the others. Believes himself to be one of us, I suppose. Have you heard of him?"

I shook my head again. "Not that I recall."

"He's a spiritualist. He would lead people to believe he can speak to the dead. Some very prominent people, or so I'm told."

I could feel my heart fluttering in my chest. Wondering whom he had spoken to, how much he had been told. Hiram has never been one for idle talk. Both when his mind is deranged and when it is quite clear, conversation has a goal, a purpose. I was pressed to believe that wasn't any different now. He had heard something. How much? I wondered.

"Some of the things they do, what I have read, is quite fascinating," I whispered.

"Fascinating," he repeated. "The Lord is fascinating, as are his prophets, the rest of you are all merely common. Fascinating. How fascinated were you Elizabeth?"

I swallowed my breath, my heart. "Was I?"

"Yes, he must have made an impression one way or other, am I not correct?"

"He?"

"Paschal Beverly Randolph."

"I—"

"Albert Raleigh. The chimney sweep. I ran into him at the dry goods store. He saw you in the audience. Saw you sitting in the balcony."

I shook my head. "I know no one by that name."

"You don't have to. He knows you. At least he recognizes you. I heard Mr. Pratt was there, also, basking in the blasphemy. Randolph, Pratt, tables floating, and spirits thumping. It sounds to me as if the whole gathering was little more than a recruitment evening for the Devil, and who should be seated among the disciples but my dear little wife?"

I turned, the peeler in hand. "It wasn't like that at all."

His eyes had changed now, empty and on fire.

"I listened," I said. "He spoke to my mother!"

Hiram threw the teacup. "He spoke to the Devil!" He came around the table now, began to roll up his sleeves. I backed away. "And where were you when you were supposed to be home, while I was away on business? Where were you, Elizabeth? Did I ever give you permission to travel to Edgartown?!"

"I didn't see the harm, the animals were taken care of."

"The animals? You worry about the animals, after I have dedicated my entire life to"—he pounded his fist on the table—"worrying for your soul!"

"He says he is Christian."

Hiram narrowed his eyes. "And how would you expect the Devil to arrive? Bathed in flames, with wings and horns? Oh no, he is much too clever for that. He will come disguised as prophet. Deceiving the people and making false promises. "And there was given unto him a mouth speaking great things and blasphemies; and power was given unto him to continue forty and two months!'"

I hid the potato peeler behind my back, determined to strike out should he hurt me again. Hiram stopped though, muttering nonsensically, his eyes shut, and a full sweat broken at his brow. The tongues had taken him. Languages I could not decipher. Jumbled and pressured, and spoken in fast frenzied fury. His body trembling. I had seen this happen to him before, but never so violently. He opened his eyes then, but they were completely rolled back. Nothing visible except the whites. I let out a cry and he lunged toward me.

I swung the peeler in hopes of connecting with him before he landed upon me, hoping just to scrape him, startle him, but he caught my wrist in mid-swing, squeezing it tight. His eyes had rolled back into place, and he focused on my hand as he squeezed, looking both mesmerized and enraged, and I could feel the skin bruising, the bones beginning to weaken. I let go of the peeler. It dropped to the floor. I let out another cry. And then he raised his fist. I flew back against the stove, and he came forward, all the while, reciting Scripture, words coming too fast for me to completely understand then. His voice so loud, it echoed throughout the house. But there was no one to hear. No one close by. It was just me and my husband, high above the town, alone on our hill.

37

Ford drove down Route 123, off-island, leaving Brockton and entering Willington, past Eldio's, where they used to go for beers on Friday nights, and past the road to Ames Nowell State Park. He was on his way back from the courthouse. He had a couple speeding tickets he had needed to take care of from before they moved—he had received a summons three weeks earlier—and after he visited his friend Toby, he would still have one more thing on his agenda. An item that needed to be tended to; it had been on his list as long as he could remember.

He didn't like going away and leaving Diana alone on the island—for all he knew she was *entertaining* her friend right at that very moment—but he had to get this done, and besides, it was a good test. If she lied again, he would catch her.

There was more snow up here than on the Vineyard. The banks already high, brown, and crusty, pocked with black holes. He had picked Toby up, and they had gone out to drink a few beers and play a few games of pool. Toby was short and stocky with squinty eyes, big lips, and a cheesy little mustache. He waddled when he walked—his heels pointing inward—but he was tough as hell, and Ford had known him since they were something like five years old. Now he was already divorced, and back living with his mother, running his own salvage business out of her yard. After a few games of pool he bought a gram of coke from a greasy guy at the bar, came back smiling, sniffing exaggeratedly to let Ford in on it. He would leave Ford a line on top of the toilet in a bathroom stall at the bar, and Ford would go in right after him, snorting it up off the cold white porcelain, and it was still early evening when Ford asked him if he wanted to take a ride by the old place with him. He told him he needed to go see his father.

Toby set up four more lines, two each, in the car before they left. He had brought out a Lynyrd Skynyrd mirror—a skull with a cowboy hat and sunglasses, the rebel flag tied into a kerchief around his neck—and tossed it in the car when Ford picked him up. The mirror looked like something Toby had probably won at the Brockton Fair, and he probably had. Back in the eighties, back in high school.

They finished the second gram with the last four lines, and Ford was speeding now. The coke numbing everything and dripping at the back of his throat. Toby had saved a tiny bit to do a freeze, first rubbing some baking soda around their gums, then the coke, and then Toby was making funny faces, lips numb and shifting all over the place like it was hard to speak.

Ford pulled out of the parking lot and started back down 123. It was almost dark now, a gray and foggy late winter dusk. Exhaust fumes clouding in the cold. The town had changed so much in a few short years. GTR Finishing where they painted sheet metal for computers and appliances—Ford had worked there sweeping up on Saturdays and after school in high school—was gone, closed. As was the old Mister Donut. They used to get stoned behind Mister Donut, and then Ellie, dark hair and big eyes and looking for a husband used to give them free coffee, free food. And once in a while, a free blow job. Mr. Bicycle across the street was gone, too, and that had been there since the forties. Mr. Bicycle himself, Ford figured, must have checked out.

Toby had found Black Sabbath on the radio. "Fairies Wear Boots." Toby would never get over Sabbath, never outgrow them. Would never outgrow most things. He was stuck back in time. The seventies and eighties. Ford didn't want to be stuck back in time, he wanted to move forward. That's what it was all about, getting away, moving forward, onto the island. And now, visiting Big Daddy. Moving forward.

The outdoor light was already on above the crumbling front step of Ford's parents' house. The house was tilted at an angle and did look to be sinking. Toby was right. Ford's old man had knocked down most of the walls on the first floor to make it one big open room, and that hadn't helped things. Less structure. Less support. His parents had tried to sell it a few years back, but no one would buy it, no one would touch it.

Now smoke poured out of the side of the house, rising into the cold winter air. Big Daddy had installed a coal stove in the kitchen some years back, kept a coal bin out in the yard. It had been Ford's job to haul in the coal, feed the fire. Everything inside was always covered in a thin layer of soot, tasted that way. Food. Beer. Everything. There was an RV parked on the side of the house, and farther back the big bus they had used for camping when they were small. The bus. A regulation-size school bus, painted baby blue, with silhouettes of giraffes, elephants, and lions painted on the side. Now it looked like something out of a made-for-TV movie—goddamn pedophile, Ford thought, it was too fitting. Ford didn't know whether his father fooled around with other people's little kids, but he doubted it; he didn't have to—he had enough of his own. And Ford didn't know how many of them he had touched. Might have been three, four. Or maybe just one. Didn't matter though. One was enough. And the one wasn't lying.

Ford knew.

Jeannie was older than him. Two years. And she must have been thirteen then, old enough to be beginning to understand it, to want to get away. Most of the kids were out of the house that day—gone with their mother to cash in McDonald's gift certificates the old lady across the street had given them for Christmas. Ford's old man had confiscated his—he had forgotten to take out the trash the night before, and so Ford didn't go, had been up the street shoveling snow instead. And Jeannie hadn't gone either. She didn't like McDonald's, she said, and she had sold four fifty-cent certificates to Cybil for a dollar.

Ford had come into the house, nose running. Gloves soaked, and hands frozen. Everything outside was frozen. Tree branches, windows, fire hydrants. The town was covered in a sheet of ice—he had to use the shovel like an ice pick to break through the crust of snow before shoveling. He had taken his boots and coat off by the door, hung the coat on the rack, and he was warming his hands by the stove when he heard the noises. His parents' bedroom was just off the living room, at the foot of the stairs, and the door was open just a crack. A small slant of light. He could hear the television going inside—a repeat of *Gomer Pyle USMC*, and other voices. His father's. If it was daytime, and his father was home, he was either usually fixing his truck or he was sitting at the kitchen table drinking. Watching everyone come and go. Or he was sleeping. But right now, he wasn't sleeping—Ford could hear his voice. Barely audible above the blaring TV.

"Just like that," he was saying, "just like that. I told you I could make you feel good. You just need to get used to it. " And then there were other noises. The bed. And his father sounded as if he were speaking through clenched teeth, stifling a cry. And then there was more crying, but it wasn't his father. It was Jeannie. Ford almost put his coat and boots back on to go back outside. Better to be gone, better not to know. But then Jeannie was standing in the doorway. Blue-striped panties, and a blue T-shirt with the spaceship logo from the rock band Boston ironed on the front. And behind her, sitting up on the bed, his back turned to Ford, and not a stitch on, was their father. Jeannie's face was streaked with dried tears, but as soon as she saw Ford, any sadness she was feeling moved right to anger.

"What are you looking at, you retard?" she asked. Ford's father turned then, his face flushed and glasses on, belly enormous, and he caught sight of Ford, and then Ford was running. Out of the house.

He grabbed his boots, and his coat, but he didn't get to put them on until he reached the bus. It was almost dark out now, and he hoped his father hadn't seen him run to the bus—he had gone up the street a little ways, then cut back through a neighbor's yard, hopping over the bridge of rocks on the stream that separated their properties, hoping to lose his trail, hide his tracks. But it was cold, he was wet, and he didn't want to be outside anymore. He crouched low once he reached the bus, and watched the yellow windows of the house beginning to stand out against the darkness. Waiting to see his father's silhouette pass by. Either there or at the back door. His black mass contrasting against the gray of the dusk, the white of the snow, as he made his way across the yard. Breath fogging in the cold. Ford would see him and he would be ready. But he didn't see him. Not until he heard the bus door open, and he was standing in the stairwell, looking over the bus monitor's seat. Smiling.

"Hey pal," he had said. "Whatcha doing out here?"

Ford didn't answer, and his father climbed up the steps, his bulk filling the aisle, blocking the light from the house.

"Cat got your tongue?"

Ford shook his head.

"Well, answer the question." His father stepped closer.

Ford pressed his back against the seat. He wanted to jump into the aisle, run. Hit the emergency door at the back of the bus, but there was too much crap blocking the door. Coolers, and lawn chairs, the rain canopy, and the rusty old grill they used on the beach. Flashing Miller High Life signs his father's friend who worked in a bar had given him. Broken. Piles of junk.

"Nothing," he said.

"Nothing." His father stepped a little closer, and Ford could smell the whiskey. "Well, it looks to me like you're hiding. And you know why you're hiding?"

Ford's heart was pounding. He had been here before. Came back here in dreams, and didn't want to be here again. He should've run. Just kept going.

"No."

The cold was fogging his father's glasses. He took them off and wiped them on his T-shirt. "You're hiding," he said, "because you're a snoop." He took a breath. "And you can't mind your own goddamn business." He put his glasses back on then, and before

Ford could flinch, he brought his hand down hard against the side of his head.

When he was finished, Ford lay on the aisle floor, in between the rows of seats. The ridged rubber matt wet with melted snow, mud, beneath him. His father panted heavily, trying to catch his breath. He went to crouch down, to get closer to speak to him, but couldn't squeeze his body between the lower part of the seats. Ford covered his face and head. He didn't want to look at him, and didn't want him to see him crying, didn't want to give him the satisfaction. His side hurt, as did his legs, the side of his head.

"Okay now, pal?" his father asked.

Ford didn't move, and his father kicked him. One last time.

"I said, okay now?" his father asked.

Ford whimpered, nodded.

"Okay, then," his father gasped. "Remember. Nobody likes a snoop. Especially snoops with big mouths."

Now Ford stared again at the house. His mother's car wasn't there—at least the car she used to drive—and that was good. He didn't want her to be home. Didn't want her to see this. She was weak and pathetic, and she disgusted him, but still, he didn't want her to see this. Ford opened the car door, and put one foot on the pavement. He snubbed his cigarette out in the ashtray. Toby opened his own door.

"No." Ford looked at him, tried to focus. He was seeing two of him. "Stay here. It's better if I talk to him alone. I'll be back in a minute."

"You're going to be nice, right? Not do anything stupid?"

"I just want to say hi. Like you said, for old times' sake."

Toby made a clicking noise with his lips, his teeth. Coke mouth. "Don't do anything stupid."

"Don't worry about it. Just wait here." He shut the door, sealing off the radio, and Toby, warm in the car behind him, and then he stepped around to the back of the car and took the bat from the trunk.

Toby rolled down his window. "Ford, don't be an idiot. What do you need that for?"

Ford put his finger to his lips. "Shh..It's not what you think." He stumbled forward a bit, and the house seemed to grow as he sloshed through the snow. Moving like a film taken with an unsteady camcorder. Footsteps loud. The beer and whiskey, his head spinning, but the coke was keeping it a little bit clear, maybe, a little bit steady. That was good.

There was a quagmire of footprints in the slush, the mud, leading to and from the house. Out to the driveway, and around the side. To the trash, the RV. His father's old rig. Footprints everywhere. Ford thought about just going in—he doubted the house would be locked, never was—but then decided against it; it would be better to see the old man's face when he came to the door and saw Ford, standing on the steps.

Shit belongs with shit.

Hey pal, cat got your tongue?

You're hiding because you're a snoop. A snoop.

Crybaby. Always whining. Such a little fucking crybaby. Always . . . whining.

All the noise. The shouting. A knock, his head. His mother on the floor, crying, curled up in a ball, trying to protect herself. There, then gone. It could always be gone unless you wanted to bring it back. And now he wanted, needed, to bring it back.

The house was dark upstairs. He wondered if anyone ever slept up there at all anymore. Wondered if any of them ever visited. No one up there but the ghost, he thought. The goddamn ghost. Ghosts of a lot of things. Bad times, bad energy. But the lights were on in the kitchen, and through the windows of the door he could see the heat coming off the coal stove. Could smell the soot. The sewerage. The house never changed. Nothing here would ever change. Music was playing inside. Something by The Killer. Jerry Lee Lewis. The fat old man was rocking out today.

Ford rapped on the door. Nothing. He waited a minute and then rapped again. He could ring the bell, but he knew it wouldn't work. Never had. He waited. Rapped again.

The SoCo and beer were beginning to defeat the coke. Fog battling clarity. But he had to stay clear, just a few minutes more.

He rapped a fifth time. And then he heard the muffled sound of a toilet flushing. The bathroom door was straight across from his line of sight, and Ford watched as the knob turned. Slowly at first. Then complete. The door flying open, and the fat bastard standing there, staring at the floor as he hitched up his pants. He looked nearly the same, maybe a little shorter, shrinking, fatter, but still no grays. Barely any wrinkles. His hair high and slicked back from his forehead. He squinted through his glasses, staring at the door, and with the front light off outside, Ford knew he couldn't tell who he was.

Not until he was standing there right in front of him. He hesitated a moment. Taller than Ford on the threshold, and then he smiled.

"Well, look who it is," he said. "The prodigal son."

38

May 16, 1872

It is my third week straight residing in the cellar. Hiram has engaged in no more outbursts and he brings me food both in the morning, and late in the afternoon. Sometimes, he sits atop of the old cider barrel and quietly speaks to me. Keeping me down here is the only way he can protect me, he has said. The darkness is gathering, he says. Hiram's eyes, in the shadows of the cellar, look even more empty than before, and his odor has grown strong, his beard long and unruly. He truly appears to be a man who has lost his way. But the only thing that fills the emptiness is the rage, and of the two Hirams, I would certainly prefer to see the former. He learned that Paschal Randolph will once again be returning to the island, and he has been researching the man, he has told me.

The cellar is damp, and the mice are always about, rats. Hiram caught one beneath his foot just two days back, and pressed it with his heel, the little creature screeching all the while, as he flattened it to the floor. When he had finished, he lifted it by its tail, and tossed it to the well. I wonder if he has forgotten that we drink that water. I wonder if he cares.

May 23, 1872

Hiram attended Mr. Randolph's performance. He spoke to me about it. How he took a seat at the back of theater, dressed in all black, so as not to call attention to himself, for if anyone saw him there, recognized him, they would know that a man like himself who walked with Christ would not attend such a spectacle for entertainment purposes. They would know, he said, that he was there for one reason and one reason alone—to call out the Devil. "And call him out, I did," he told me. "The heathen was but ten minutes into his 'performance,'" he said, "calling forth the demons, the damned, to pose as spirits of the loved ones of the pitiful souls in attendance, when I stood and exposed him for what he is, what he was doing. I saw Satan shining in his eyes, and I called him out." Hiram raised a clenched fist. "There was an astonished gasp from the audience, and this man, this Mr. Randolph, called me forward. He said I stood in the shadows, and that he needed me to come forward so that he could see me in the light. So, 'The light of the Devil is no light at all!' I told him, and then he was silent a moment. And then he began to quote Scripture. Revelations 1:18. 'I am he that liveth,' he said, 'and was dead; and, behold, I am alive for evermore, Amen; and have the keys of hell and of death.'"

"But if he could quote Scripture," I said to him, "doesn't that tell you anything?" I was very hungry, and I did not want to upset him, but I still held out a small hope that I could reach him, reason with him. But Hiram just glared at me. "The Devil knows his scripture. He must, for it is Scripture that defines him. It realizes him in all his wickedness for all the world to see. It would not surprise me if this man Randolph could recite Revelations forwards and backwards all the while salivating on his moment. No, that meant little to me at all, except to confirm what I already knew, but still I came forward to face him, standing in the middle aisle, and right then and there, he shut his eyes, held out his hand as if casting a spell, and he tried to read me. Me? Can you imagine that, Elizabeth? This man in all his wretchedness tried to read me! As if he could penetrate the barrier of godliness that surrounds me! And you know what he read? Do you know what he received?!"

"What?" I asked quietly.

"Nothing. Not a thing! He did not even try to pretend, did not make up any messages from spirits of the people who loved me, no words of wisdom. Nothing!"

And that, I thought, is because even the dead do not wish to be near you, my dear husband. For you have no soul for them to comfort. But of course, this I could not say. Not without risking being hurt and left to rot here on the cellar floor.

"After a moment he stopped, and took two steps back, and then he took a slight bow and apologized, both to me and the audience. He had met his match, Elizabeth, and he knew it. I shouted at him then. I called him out for what he is. A sinner and a sorcerer. A spawn of the Devil working his misgivings here upon our beautiful little island. Luring people in to convince them that what he says, what he hears, is real, and convincing them to follow him. Follow him right into the fiery pits of hell itself! And follow him, they would have, had I not been there to save them! Had I not banished him from the theater, from the island itself!"

After a moment, he wiped his forehead, and took a seat on the chair beside the well. He took a moment to catch his breath.

"I should have followed him," he said at last. "I should have made sure he was gone for good—even if it meant taking the wretched demon's life, for there can only be virtue in extinguishing evil—but there was much commotion, people standing, looking about, and all talking at once. A few people demanded their money back, and a few turned to blame me. Me. They asked why I had disrupted the performance. One of the men, a man I did not recognize, grabbed me by my sleeve, and it was all I could do to refrain from striking out at him. But refrain I did, and I told him the truth—I had done what I had done for him, and for the others, and for . . . you. My beautiful little lamb led so far astray. And do you know what this man did?"

"What?" I asked.

"He spat on my shoe, and told me I was mad. Mad? Can you imagine that, Elizabeth? Mad? Me. Here I stood, brimming with the goodness of our Lord and Savior, and this man would call me mad." Hiram took another breath, chuckled a little. He shut his eyes as if drifting off into prayer, and then when he opened them he took out his handkerchief, and leaned over to polish the toe of his shoes. He has never liked the cellar for the dirt and the dust.

"I wish you hadn't brought this all upon us," he told me, "forcing me to keep you safe and secure, for if not we could keep clean of both clothes and soul." He paused after he said this. "And you, my good wife, I fear are clean of neither. I wish I did not have to walk alone. I wish it could be like the days gone past when you would march beside and behind me, head high as we spoke his words, but how can you march beside me when my trust in you has been shattered? There must be a solution, and yet though I lie in bed at night, curtained in the darkness, I can't conclude what it is. Tell me, Elizabeth, he said, do you know what it is?"

"No," I whispered.

"Well, we must pray on it, the two of us. Pray for an answer to restore your virtue." He paused after he said this, and then he asked me to raise my dress. Ordering me to bend over and turn around, supporting myself with my hands on the well. He began to pray and then he removed his belt and smacked it hard against my bottom, my flesh immediately wincing beneath the sting. He struck me again, and then put his hands on my hips, repositioning me, and then he struck me a third time. All the while talking, not to me and not to himself, talking as if there were someone else in the room. Whispers turning to shouts and then turning to nonsense, and then as always, invoking the name of the Lord.

I have not eaten now for several days. I only have water from the well—thank our Lord for the well—and I don't know how long that will be able to sustain me. I fear Hiram has left the island, and I cannot be sure how long he will be gone. There could be a storm, he could have had an accident. An accident would be befitting him now, but as no one knows I am here, and it would truly be the end of me unless I can find a way to get out the door. And even if I do? Then what? If and when he does return, I would surely feel the strength of his wrath, and his wickedness. Yes, wicked. For there is no longer any doubt in my head that I have married a wicked, wicked man, and the sanity of whom I question with each living breath. He has gone in search of Mr. Randolph, I fear, following him on the circuit. He says he will demand answers concerning what transpired between the two of us, and I fear both what he will do if he receives them, and what he will do if he does not. I only wish there was a way to warn the man ahead of time, that he could receive messages from the living as well as the dead.

39

Toby was sweating harder than Ford. Panting, too. Fogging up the windows inside the car. He was talking, babbling. "What the fuck is wrong with you? What the fuck was that about? The guy is almost sixty years old for chrissakes. You might have killed him." But Ford could barely hear him, the voice distant, detached—he was still in the zone. The whole night had shut down around him. The car lights, streetlights, everything distant and small.

Ford could still see his father, lying on the floor. It only took two swings with the bat—he could still hear the crack as it hit the old man's skull—to get him on the floor, and then he was swinging some more, the bat raised over his head, and kicking him as hard as he could. The old man had tried deflecting the blows at first, but then he had stopped, his eyes rolling back in his head, and blood trickling from his eye socket, and from his ear. Ford could have finished it for sure right then, once and for all, but then Toby was suddenly in the house, yelling, and pulling Ford backward. He pushed him across the yard, and then into the car, the old man still flat on the floor, bleeding in the yellow light behind them, soaked in the smell of sewerage, and then Toby slammed the car into drive, sped off down the road. Lighting a cigarette, still babbling.

"Jesus Christ," he said. "What's wrong with you? I think you might have killed him, Ford. Jesus Christ. He might die. Your father."

Ford had no answers for him, but when Toby got out at his house, Ford smiled a little and leaned over and kissed him. Once on the cheek. Toby didn't move. "You're fucked up," he had said again, and then he shook his head. "You need help."

Ford laughed. "Fuck you," he said. "I love you."

He bought a bottle of Jim Beam and rented a room off 495. The road was doubling before him, and he knew it wouldn't be good to try and get all the way back to Woods Hole, never mind Oak Bluffs. And he needed to get back in one piece. His family needed him.

40

Diana met Michael the following Friday at the bed-and-break-fast, her heart pounding as she climbed the stairs to the porch, rang the doorbell. There was something about meeting him that made her feel both excited and guilty. He was a painter, an artist, and he was painting her. Nothing more. He didn't think of it as anything more, and neither did she—she had to believe that. She was married. But did she want it to be more? She had been thinking about him since that day at Ocean Park, then and before, their meeting at the B&B. But it couldn't be wrong just to think, to daydream. She had to convince herself she wasn't doing anything wrong, but she hadn't told Ford where she was going. Of course she couldn't tell Ford—he'd lose his mind. He was sleeping again when she left. Had come home at seven and started drinking. Passed out cold by nine thirty, so she guessed he wouldn't wake again until close to supper. She hoped. It was dark inside the house, and for a moment she heard nothing, almost turned and walked away. But then the door opened, and Michael stepped aside to let her in. There was a light on in the kitchen, but she couldn't hear any voices.

"Does anyone else ever stay here this time of year?" she asked.

"Not many." He took her coat, hung it on the rack by the door. The house felt different than it had the first time she was here. Older. Quieter. Bigger. Even when they whispered, their voices seemed to echo. The staircase was beautiful, she noticed now, mahogany and ornate. Halfway up there was a stained glass window, light coming in from over the sea. A picture of Saint Anthony, down on one knee, one hand lifted with a dove perched upon it.

"Do you want something to drink before we get started?" Michael asked. "Water?"

"How about a shot of tequila?" she said, laughing a little.

He nodded. "I think there might be some whiskey. Possibly cognac. Tequila, I'm not sure."

"I'm just joking. I've never done anything like this before. I usually don't even like getting my picture taken."

"Well, you should. Believe me, a lot of people would be very happy to take your picture."

"You're just saying that to be nice. And *believe* me, I take the worst pictures in the world." She raised a finger, pointed, drew it back quick. "However, if the painting comes out bad, I get to blame you."

He looked into her eyes, and then he shook his head. "It won't," he whispered.

He was staying in the top room, the octagonal cupola. It was much bigger on the inside than it looked from the street. Eight windows, one on each wall. Light coming from everywhere. The view was magnificent. The town, the harbor, the open sea. Ocean Park, and in the distance, Sengekontacket Pond. Diana wrapped her arms tight about her, already feeling slightly exposed. Her anxiety was building. She wondered why she was doing this. Why she was really doing this. He seemed nice, but she knew the relationship could never go beyond casual friends, and she wondered if by asking her to sit for him, it implied anything else? Anything further? Or was he just short on models? If it was the former, she didn't want to lead him on; it wouldn't be right to lead him on. But then again, what kind of guy would be looking for someone like her anyway—a jobless twenty-four-year-old with a five-year-old kid, and the baggage of a crazy husband?

He set up his easel, his back to the sun. Diana took a seat on the stool in the middle of the room, hands on her knees, and her knees close together. She wore a black skirt and a red sweater.

"How many people have you painted before?" she asked him.

He was attaching a sketch pad to the easel.

"None for a while. I mean, none that have sat for a portrait. There are people in my landscapes, and in the pictures of the old houses, but I haven't had anyone sit since school, and that was a very long time ago. Back then, my instructor used to bring them in off the street. Elderly, overweight, often unwashed. I think he recruited them down by the wharf. A lot of them looked mad."

"Is that why you asked me?" she asked, smiling. "Because you thought I looked crazy? Or am I just fat and old? I promise you that I've washed."

He had begun sketching. Quick movements, like a conductor with a baton. He was looking at her, and looking at the page, but he wasn't looking at her when he spoke to her.

"No," he said, "I asked you because you're beautiful."

Diana felt her face go flush.

"And you're modest," he said, smiling.

"Well, I don't know about that. Do you lie to all your subjects?" she asked, wanting to make light of it.

"No." And then he did look at her. Eye contact. He shrugged. "I've never been very good at it." He started sketching again. "That being said, I've always been impressed by people who can lie well. It requires a certain amount of detachment. The only way a person can truly lie well, I think, is if they first convince themselves that whatever they are saying is true. It's an art form all itself."

"Well, you'd really be impressed by my mother then," Diana said.

"Yes?"

"Yes. Start each day—lie early, lie often, and then by bedtime you've created a whole new little world for yourself. One you can control."

"Well, I suppose there is something wonderful in that. We all want to control our worlds, right?"

"I suppose, but—"

"I mean, that is what art is all about, creating a world of our own, a representation of what we see, feel, remember, how we interpret it. And once we do it, it's ours alone. Kind of like memory—the past is another country, right? Once the past is the past, if it is really the past, if it doesn't really exist, there is no tangibility to it. You can never touch *it*, not really, but you can make it whatever you want it to be here in the present. And who's to say what was real, and what was not? What is real? Even with photographs, imprints. Kind of wonderful in that regard, I think. Or at least liberating."

"Well, my mother does it without lifting a paint brush or pen."

"How about your husband?"

"He doesn't have an artistic bone in his body. He doesn't have to make things up to control them."

"You never can be sure."

"What do you mean?"

"Maybe he makes things up in his head. Reasons, justifications. Maybe he just doesn't share them."

"Maybe. But I don't think so. There would have to be a fair amount of paranoia going on for that to be the case though, right? And I don't think he seems very paranoid."

"Well, how do you think he seems?"

Diana swallowed her breath. Was he digging? Looking for some kind of in? He wouldn't have to look far, she thought—she needed to vent, talk to someone, it helped to vent, and ever since Cybil had left, she had no one. And Cybil wouldn't be back, not after what had happened last time. Diana had had her chance. Could have left then, renounced it all, but she didn't. Couldn't. And now, just the other day, Cybil had called about her father. He had been found unconscious in his home, apparently the victim of an attempted burglary. His head cracked open, he was still in a coma. She wanted Diana to tell Ford, and when she had, he had just looked at her and shrugged. It couldn't have been Ford, despite being off island when it happened and the history he had with his father, he wasn't capable of that kind of violence. But even still, his absence of any kind of reaction had just left her even more unsettled than she had been to date.

"I think he seems unhappy," she said at last to Michael. "Miserable even. I think his life revolves around this tight little ball of anger and misery that spins around somewhere deep inside him, just getting tighter and tighter, and that's what makes him take it all out on others. It just explodes. He doesn't know of any other way to release the tension."

"And what do you do?" He flipped the sheet over. Started on another. "To release the tension, I mean?"

"Oh, I don't know. I run."

"You run?"

"Yeah, usually just a few miles though. Sometimes four or five. And I read. Spend time with Samantha. Sometimes drink a glass of wine. I used to smoke a little pot."

He smiled again, looking on the verge of laughter. "Pot? Like a pipe?"

"Sometimes," she said, laughing with him. "What do you do?"

He shrugged. "I paint. I read. I walk around and look at the old houses. I like wine, too. But I've never been much of a smoker."

"Never?" she asked. She didn't think she knew anyone their age who had never tried pot. And him being an artist . . .

"Never," he said.

"And what about sex?" she asked, and as soon as she did, she couldn't believe the words had left her mouth. And this time he blushed.

"That one," he said, "has always been my weakness. Sex, and magic, and spirituality. I think they all go hand in hand."

"Really?"

"Really. And how about you?"

"How about me what?"

"Does sex work for you like that?"

Diana felt her heart stutter, rising in her throat. "I'm not sure sex works for me at all anymore."

Michael smiled. "Okay. Well, let me ask you one more thing."

Diana pulled at her earlobe. "What's that?"

"Do you ever lie to yourself, Diana?"

The painting was half-finished, maybe a little bit more, and

Diana's heart jumped when she looked at it. He had her just as she was where she stood, her arms about her as if she were cold, but in the painting, she wasn't looking at him, but was looking off toward something distant. And going by the background, she imagined he had her looking off toward the sea. For she was standing on a wharf, and rising up behind her was an outline, ill defined but there all the same, of the Sea View Hotel.

41

May 2, 1872

Still in the cellar. The earth is growing warmer outside—I can feel it—and in the morning, even through the stone foundation, I can hear the birds. I wish I could see them. Wish I could see anything. But there is nothing. Not even Hiram.

It was not always this way. If anyone is ever to find this, I wish them to know that. When I met him, back in Boston, he was a good man. Perhaps a bit overly righteous, but he seemed so resolute in his beliefs that I couldn't help but admire him. My father admired him, too. His war record, his piety. My father had introduced us, having met Hiram at a lecture on John and Charles Wesley at Boston University. He comes from an old family, he said, a good family—my father had looked into it. Oh, Papa, if you could see him now. But even if he could, would it be any different? Papa is older now, his wits long behind him, and even when I have been able to get him a letter these last two years, he has rarely answered, making little sense when he does. And now I am more Hiram's wife, than I am my father's daughter. What say would he have? In anything? But back then, of course, it was different. Hiram would come to my father's house on Court Street in mid-spring, walking with me past the golden dome of the State House, and down the hill, through the common, and past the flowers of the public gardens, across the bridge and above the swans, my aunt Cecilia never far behind. We had great plans, once he proposed. He had mentioned the camp meetings once or twice, but never dwelled on them, only on his house in Edgartown down on North Water Street. He kept an apartment in Boston then, too, and did so throughout the courtship. He brought me flowers and he read me poems, and then he asked if on Saturdays, I would be good enough to sit with him and read the Scripture.

And of course I said yes. He was so kind back then, so charming, that if it happened again, if I didn't know what I know now, I am sure I would say yes again. And now where are we? Locked away, locked together, possibly forever. And I fear forever is coming too soon. I am so hungry. Weak.

Please Lord, do not forget me.

May 5, 1872

I am now nearing the end of the tenth day without food. Just water. I feel dizzy, and am having trouble standing to my feet. Does he know this? Does he realize what he has done? As cruel as Hiram can be, I can't believe he would leave me here to starve, not to die like this. Something must have happened. I thought I heard a voice today, coming through walls, and then up through the well. A distant voice, calling my name, and sounding as if trying to speak through water. I felt seen without being able to see, and I then realized it was my mind playing tricks on me. The tricks of hunger are causing me to hear and see things that were never really there. I thought of my parents, my departed brother, and of people who had lived on this land before. Had anyone ever lived on this land before? But even if they did, that made no sense, for how would they know my name? No one knows my name anymore. Hiram has taken it, crushed it, and crushed me right along with it. There is a stream beneath the house that feeds the well—he has told me that before. So perhaps the voices come from the stream. Water. The sea. Spirits.

And now he is leaving me to join them.

May 7, 1872

I have seen them, they come and sit with me at night after it gets darker, and even sometimes throughout the course of the day. Yet, one day blurs into another now. Time keeps going, but has also somehow stopped. Or maybe it just is not. The spirits are women, but sometimes I look twice, and they seem more like children. Small, lithe, and their image not quite clear. I think I recognize them, and then I do not. And then I see my mother, my grandfather, and my brother, still a child,, the city landscape behind them. But these things I know I am not seeing. Unless maybe it is the cellar I am not seeing. Which is real? The illusion or the nightmare? I can commune with everyone now, the living and the dead, and the pain from my hunger has all but faded. The water sustains me.

May 8, 1872

Much noise upstairs now. Bangings. And a voice shouting for the Lord, shouting at the Lord. Cursing. It seems so distant, but I know it must be Hiram. He must have returned from his quest. Successful or not, I don't think I will ever know. The best thing to do would be to hide, pretend that I've fled, but I'm not sure I have the strength nor the will. And as one world has opened up upon the other, I'm not sure it matters. I can't think clearly. He is calling out again now. Screaming my name.

The journal ended there, and Diana had to wonder if Elizabeth had ended along with it. Or what may have happened to her. If she got away. She liked to think that she got away, but something in her heart told her she did not. For if she did, why would she come back to this place to spend eternity. If it was in fact her, Cassie, that she heard. But maybe it wasn't her at all, maybe it wasn't at all. Maybe it was just Sam's imagination, and Diana's unraveling mind. Noises and fatigue getting the best of her. But she had to know, had to find out. She supposed she could ask Ford if he knew any family history involving the house. She doubted it, but even if he did, would he tell her?

It was late now, nearly two a.m., Ford at work and Samantha sound asleep, the lights down and the house quietly creaking around her. If nothing else, she had wished for the journal to be hidden, and Diana wouldn't want to chance Ford stumbling across it. She stepped slowly down the stairs, and quickly into the cellar. Back to the atlas, hiding the journal inside. And then quickly back up. She was shutting the door, locking and dead-bolting it behind her, when the sound of the wind in the trees picked up outside, and then something else. The distant voice of a woman, softly singing, a sad, sweet song, the words too far off to come clear.

42

April. Diana couldn't sleep. She could hear the radio playing downstairs. Pink Floyd—"Welcome to the Machine." The vibrations coming through the floor. Ford was down there with his friend Al from work. She looked at the clock. Another two hours and they would be gone. They would have to be. Like vampires, they needed to be back before the day shift started dwindling in.

Ford was drinking again daily. He had been building toward it up until Barry and Phillip's visit, and then the day-long binge had set the snowball in motion. She shouldn't have invited them to visit, she thought, should have known, but then again, she figured, if it wasn't then, it would just be another time, another occasion, another excuse. There was always an excuse. He had stuck to beer the first few days after they left, then moved to vodka, then whiskey. And it had picked up just all the more since he had returned from off island. He didn't tell her where he had been, and she didn't ask. It was better not to ask. He did ask her what she had been up to, which was unusual, and his eyes seemed to follow her a little bit more, making her suspicious. He had been even more sullen than usual since he got back, and more detached, drinking straight from the bottle on the balcony as he stared at the stars. And maybe it did have something to do with the news about his father, but the thing was, she had yet to see him really drunk, stumbling. Just the heavy red eyelids, glassy, empty eyes. And then when he woke, irritable, a full pot of coffee, and two to three nips before going into work. He didn't drink the nips in front of her, but she had been finding them in the trash, buried.

She had been thinking about Michael. It wasn't good to think about Michael, wasn't right, and still, she couldn't help herself. Before she left, on the day of their painting, he had gone downstairs and fixed them a drink. Some sort of martini, cold and delicious, tasting like apples, and almost immediately putting her at ease. She liked being up in the octagonal room, surrounded by the views, the park, Circuit, the pond, and the sea—the tempest quieting with the coming of spring—she liked being up there with him.

When the alcohol started going to her head, she had looked at her watch again, saying she really had to leave, which was true, but she was also beginning to wonder if she trusted herself alone with him. And if she couldn't trust herself, then who could she trust? With each passing year it felt as if the list grew shorter. Michael said he was leaving on Sunday, but before she went out the door, he said he would give her his address. Scribbling on a piece of paper, he folded it in two and slipped it in her pocket. "If you ever need anything," he said, "don't hesitate to get in touch."

Diana had leaned up and kissed his cheek, lingering just for a moment.

"And, Diana?" he said as she started down the walkway. He looked up toward the sky, and then he looked at her and nodded. "Be careful," he said.

She wondered again what she would have done if he had tried to touch her, how she would have handled it. It had been so long since anyone had tried to touch her other than Ford, that the whole thing seemed foreign, and yet she was sure he wanted to touch her. She had thought of him now, and he was there for a moment in that murky state between consciousness and dreams, voices and images mixing what was fantastic with what was still quite real, the wind outside and clock downstairs, and she had felt herself responding, wet, aroused. Wanting someone to touch her. It hadn't been like that with anyone for a long time, certainly not with Ford; his touch now just made her tense. If he was in a good mood he might laugh and tell her she was a prude, that she was old before her time. But she wasn't old and she wasn't a prude, she just didn't like him, couldn't, and what was worse, she now realized, she no longer loved him. And it seemed absurd, because she barely knew him, but she could, she thought, love Michael.

She wondered what it would take to move back. Not to Brockton. She never wanted to return to Brockton. But maybe somewhere close to Boston. Weymouth, or Braintree, or Quincy. Or maybe in Boston itself. Michael said he had a place in Boston. Samantha was young enough where they could live there for a few years, and then maybe move back out to the suburbs. Buy a house. Their own house. She could get a nursing job quick enough, she was sure of it. She imagined she could even get a job out here on the island, the hospital, but if she stayed on the island, Ford would never let her be. She was sure of that, too. He would haunt her.

Now she heard Al jabbering downstairs, and knew they were drunk. She figured they were playing darts. Usually if Ford brought someone home from work during the middle of his shift, they would drink and play darts. If there were more than two of them playing, it could get fairly loud, but now she could only hear Al—a muffled, slightly high-pitched voice, losing its power as it came through the floor—but no sound from Ford. They must have been down there two hours or more when he came upstairs. The door opening and a slant of light spreading across the room. Diana feigned sleep; she wasn't in the mood to get up and fix them something to eat.

She felt him watching her, though, and as he moved closer she could smell his breath. Whiskey. He put his hand on her shoulder and whispered in her ear.

"Hi, sweetie. Are you awake?"

Diana didn't move. He shook her shoulder a little, then with his other hand, cupped her buttocks beneath the blanket. "Are you awake?" he said again.

"No, I'm not." She shook him off, shifting on the bed, moving away from him. Ford took a seat on the edge. Reached out for her shoulder again.

"Why don't you come downstairs for a little while? I have my friend Al over. You remember Al?"

"No," she said, lying. Of course she remembered Al. Obnoxious Al. Late thirties, potbelly. Thin little mustache. Hair slicked over the top of his scalp with long curls around his neckline. He laughed at everything Ford said, and he smelled like Aqua Velva.

"Sure, you do," Ford said. "He was over here with me a few weeks ago. I was thinking you might want to have a drink with us."

"Well, you can forget it," she said. "I have to get up with Sam in the morning, and then I have a dentist appointment. I can't."

"Yeah, but you can go back to bed after, right? The dentist shouldn't come before your husband. Come on."

"No, Ford!" she snapped. "I need to sleep!"

"Come on."

"No!"

Ford sighed. He was quiet for a moment. Diana hated the quiet with him. She could suddenly hear her heart.

"Well, I wasn't going to bring it up," he said at last, "but you know, I did you a big favor when your brother and his boyfriend were over a little while back. I could have been a real jerk, been antisocial and everything, but I stayed up and socialized all night. I didn't even say anything about them being gay or anything like that. I didn't even make fun of the stupid séance stuff. I went right along with it." He hesitated again. "I actually had a really good time with them, and that got me thinking that maybe that's been the problem all along. Maybe we don't spend enough time together, socially, doing things with each other's friends, trying to please each other. Maybe if we did, we'd be that much closer, and not fight so much. I know Phillip and his little friend there are your family, not technically friends, but you're like friends when you hang out together, and you get to cook together and gossip, talk about flowers and show tunes and all that stuff." He was quiet again, waiting. "Come on. Just one drink? You won't even have to get dressed—Al doesn't care—you can just put on your bathrobe or something."

"Why do you even want me down there?" She looked at the clock. "It's after three in the morning. If you want something to eat, there's leftovers in the fridge."

"It's not that. I'm not even hungry." Ford caressed her shoulder. "Al was saying how much fun he had with you last time, so I thought I'd come get you."

"I cooked you guys some grilled cheese and went back to bed."

"Yeah, but he really liked you. He thought you were cool."

"That's great. Lie to him—tell him I think he's cool, too, and we'll call it a day." She moved away again.

"Come on, one drink?"

"Ford—"

"Just one drink, and you can go back to bed. I promise."

Diana squeezed her eyes tight. He wasn't going to leave, and if he wasn't going to leave, she wasn't going to sleep. It might be quicker, better, she thought, to just go down, fix the drink, weak, slug it and go back to bed. Make him happy. She assumed once she got down there he *would* ask her to fix them something to eat again—put her on the spot in front of Al—and then that would be that. Al would think she was "cool" again. Over and out.

"One drink?" she said.

"Just one," he said, "I promise."

She sat up on the bed, swinging her legs to the floor, Ford beside her, and her nightgown up around her middle. Ford looked down. He reached over and put a hand on her bare thigh, slipping down and inside and holding it there. He put the fingers of his other hand under her chin, and turned her head to face him, leaning in to kiss her. A ripple of tension ran up Diana's back, her neck sinking into her shoulders. Everything tight. He moved his hand farther up along the inside of her thigh, pushing and probing. If she was going downstairs, she thought, she was going to have to put her underwear on. Ford drew back, his eyes at half-mast, and his lips barely parted. A bit of spittle she could see in the light coming in from the moon.

"You look really sexy in that nightgown," he said.

"It's an old Red Sox jersey."

"I know, but I like that look. It's playful. You look really sexy in it."

"I thought you wanted to go downstairs," she whispered.

"I do. But first I just want to sit here and look at you. Kiss you." He leaned closer again. "I love kissing you."

Maybe he was drunker than she thought. This wasn't Ford. Ever. They used to kiss a lot when they were dating, but now that seemed too far back to remember. She didn't want to remember. The smell on him was beginning to make her feel sick to her stomach again.

"I love you so much," he said, "I've been thinking about that lately. How awesome you are, what a jerk I've been. And you're so hot. I don't think I've ever really appreciated how hot you are. It's almost like greedy that I get to keep you all to myself." He tilted her head, began kissing her neck. She hadn't reciprocated. Couldn't. Not yet. Everything from a few months back still felt much too close. She felt nothing for him, and yet she didn't want to be cruel. She put her arms around him, rubbed his back a little. Mechanical.

"Listen," she said, "you're getting yourself all going. We should stop. If your friend is down there, you can't just leave him down there."

"I know." Another kiss. "I was thinking maybe we don't have to."

Diana stopped. "What?"

"I was thinking maybe we could invite him up."

She didn't pull away. Didn't look at him. She didn't want to look at him. "Invite him up for what?"

"You know, to fool around a little."

"You're kidding me, right? You're joking."

"Come on," he whispered, "kissing her neck again. She still hadn't moved. "Just this one time. He's a nice guy. I think it will be fun. He needs something. It's been like forever for him. I think it's been ten years or something like that. I feel wicked bad for him."

She did draw back now, pulled her arms away from him, and looked him in the eye. "You're not serious."

"Just this once. If you don't want to have sex with him, maybe you can just do fellatio on him."

Diana nodded. "Fellatio?"

"Yeah."

Diana's thoughts had stopped racing, her mind blank, fury rising. "And what are you going to do?" She could tell by his eyes he was trying hard to focus. Blank eyes. Automatic pilot.

"I can just watch, I suppose," he said. "I'd kind of like that. Or I can do you while you're doing him, you know? Like all three of us—I can get you from behind. All the attention will be on you, two guys making love to you at once, worshipping you—I think it would be really cool."

Diana nodded again. "Yeah, unbelievably cool. Who wouldn't want that—with you and Al? You're a real piece of work, you know that?"

"Come on, you're my princess. One little favor. He's waiting downstairs. I told him I'd come talk to you. He's a nice guy—he didn't want to impose—"

"Well, God forbid," she said. "I wouldn't want him to think he was imposing."

"But I told him you probably wouldn't mind. I said it wouldn't be a big deal. I told him you're great at it. He's like been going crazy it's been so long. He hasn't had a girlfriend since he was like in his twenties." Ford leaned forward again, but she moved out of reach. Stood up, stepped away from him. She needed to be away from him. Far.

"You're crazy," she said. "You are really crazy."

He sighed. "You owe me."

"What . . . the hell . . . do . . . I . . . owe . . . you . . . for? For cooking for you? Waiting on you? For kissing your ass just so you don't blow a gasket and bust up the house every time you get pissy?"

"You owe me for when your brother was down," he said. She could already hear his tone changing, the sugary sweetness draining. "I was really hospitable."

She nodded. "So you think that means I should blow your friend? Nice, Ford, that's real nice."

"Well, there's more to it than that Diana, and you know it. And you know what I'm talking about."

"No, Ford. I don't. If your friend needs a blow job that bad, then I suggest you go take care of it yourself. Show your humanitarian side, Ford. Go suck him off. What's the big deal?"

"Don't lie to me, Diana. I know."

"Know what?"

"You know what I'm talking about."

"No, I don't, Ford. I have no idea. And I really don't want to."

He sneered. "Your little painter friend? Listen, I never ask anything from you—never—and I practically saved you from your family. Saved Samantha from your brother. Gave you guys this beautiful house, a nice place to live. I wouldn't think this was such a big deal. You like sex. How do you know you wouldn't like it with two guys at once? You should at least give it a try." He raised his hands. "Then if you don't like it, fine. Never again. I won't even mention it."

"You can keep your fucking house, Ford. I'm done." She started toward her dresser, antennae up. Waiting, expecting, to feel him move. She'd have to be ready. Dodge him. Grab Samantha. Out the door. But first she needed clothes. Just something to change into. Couldn't go running into the night, the cold, in her nightgown. She'd look like a lunatic. Maybe if she kept talking, quietly arguing, he wouldn't act yet. Might think he still had a chance of convincing her. Then she could move quickly. But no, if he saw her getting her clothes, he would know she was going. She had to go.

"You're being a bitch," he said.

"And you're unbelievable."

"No," he said, pointing at her. "You're unbelievable. I'm the one trying to make this marriage work."

She spun around. Ford was still on the bed. Looking faintly blue in the moonlight. "I can see that." She flicked on the light switch. Everything instantly bright, hard, real. Ford blinked a couple times, eyes adjusting. "Asking me to suck off your friend," she said. "You really go above and beyond."

"This is about more than a blow job and you know it, Diana."

"I do. Maybe you should become like a marriage counselor or something, Ford. Maybe you missed your calling."

"You're sucking off everyone else." He was getting louder. "You don't think I know?"

Diana stopped. He thought she was cheating, and if he thought that, there was no going back. Not tonight, probably not ever—she knew him too well. He wouldn't let her live it down, wouldn't let her forget it. And what had she done? Nothing. A cup of coffee, sitting for a painting, nothing. She gazed at the door, just beyond Ford, measured the distance. She needed to get out the door, get Samantha. Go. He wouldn't hit her in front of his friend—at least she didn't think so—it was important to Ford for his friends to think he was wonderful. Think he suffered. A cold, selfish wife. He was the victim. She opened her drawer, grabbed a pair of jeans, a sweatshirt.

"You're drunk," she said.

"Well, maybe I am. I don't deny that. But I'm also forgiving. At least I can be. Come on," he said, his voice softening. "Please."

Everything flooded in upon her then. Everything from the past three years, since she first met him, and from before. High school, her dreams, her mother, and then her pregnancy. And then Ford. Leaping from the fire to the frying pan. People like him who waited in the woods, the lurch. Predators. Picking you up when you were down, comforting you, just so they could knock you down themselves. She thought of their first dates. His crying, then hers. Opening his door to let them move in; they needed to move in. And then, subtle, quiet insults, dishes thrown, shattering against the kitchen wall, and tantrums over things out of place. The back of his hand against her cheek or a fist in the ribs, falling back and knocking her head. And control. Control. It had always been about control. Slowly acquiring more and more, isolating her on an island, until she was what? What did he expect her to be?

What did he expect?

There was someone in the room with them then. She could feel it. Someone. And a voice. Soft and distant. "Run," it said.

Ford must have heard it, too, for he startled a bit. Looked around quick. But then he composed himself, and patted the edge of the bed again. "You're so beautiful that I just want to share you. Just this once. I promise. Things will be good."

Good.

Diana took a deep breath, struggling not to cry. "You know something, Ford?"

"What?"

"You can go to hell."

She grabbed her clothes and pocketbook, and she headed out the door. She heard him stand up from the bed.

"Diana," he said. "Stop."

"I'm done, Ford," she said, "It's over." But she didn't turn back. She went to Samantha's room. The girl was already awake, sitting up in bed. Diana grabbed her coat and shoes, and swept her up in her arms. Ford was in the hallway now, the threshold to their bedroom.

"Diana," he said; he was starting to get loud. "You leave again, you better not bother coming back."

"Not planning on it," she said, and even as she did, she knew the clock had begun to tick, his rage building. She had to get out, fast. He stopped her at the top of the stairs, put a hand out. Hissing, whispering through clenched tips.

"You better not embarrass me like this," he said, "not in front of my friend. We can drop it right now, everything. I'm willing to let it go. The whole thing."

"Me, too, Ford," she said. "The whole thing. That's what you don't get." He bumped the two of them with his chest. Diana staggered backward a bit. She looked down to see Al, standing at the bottom of the stairs. Ford knew he was there, too. Diana ducked with Samantha, pushed by Ford, moving toward the stairs.

He tried to step in front of them again. "Don't push me, Diana. I mean it. I'm not fucking around this time."

"Neither am I, Ford," she said, covering Sam's head with her hand just in case he did strike out at her. But he didn't. Not with Al watching. Instead he just glared, whispered the word *stop* under his breath, and then she pushed past him one last time. Ford stepped quickly, one last move, but then something happened. Something was there, something he couldn't see and neither could she, blocking his way, and he couldn't move any farther. Diana turned once to see the look of bewilderment—and something else, fear?—cross over his face, and then he took a step back, and Diana kept going.

"Diana!" he yelled, and then when she didn't answer, he started to scream, his voice rising behind them, calling her a bitch and shouting, "Run to your little boyfriend, you no good fucking cunt!" Diana picked up her pace, and nearly ran over Al as she reached the bottom. He looked both drunk and confused. Face flushed, he smiled a little, uncomfortable. He looked up the stairs.

"He okay?" he asked Diana as she reached the landing.

"No," she said. "He's not. I think he's waiting for you." Diana ran through the kitchen, grabbing her coat, and out the back door. Ford had grown louder, his language more obscene. Diana could picture him. Red in the face, shaking, sweating.

They crossed the dirt road, and started across the cemetery and when she turned back, she could see the yellow square of light in their bedroom. A shadow inside, a shadow that must have been Ford, standing at the window and watching them take flight.

43

Sunset pond glistened in the moonlight below them. Diana carried Samantha halfway down the hill, encouraged her to walk, and then carried her again. Samantha clung to her tight. Diana was afraid to turn around. If she turned around and saw him, she would freeze up, knowing that was it—she could never outrun him carrying the little girl. Samantha buried her head into Diana's shoulder.

"I saw him again," Sam whispered.

"Saw who, honey?" Diana asked.

"The man with the bushy face."

"Sam, honey, there is no man with a bushy face."

"Yes there is." Sam started to cry.

Diana wondered what they were doing to her. She knew how powerful stress could be, could make you hear things, see things—she had learned that during her psych rotation. It could have an impact on everything. That was what PTSD was all about, stress of the past controlling the mind, controlling everything. And maybe that's what it was doing, to both of them. Or maybe it was in fact just what Michael had talked to her about. Imprints. Maybe they were just seeing imprints.

Nothing ever really dies, nothing ever really goes away.

"Sam? How many times have you seen him? The man with the bushy face?"

"Maybe seven."

Diana nodded. "Seven."

"Yeah, once in your room when you were getting dressed, standing in your underwear. And once when you were in the kitchen having a cup of tea, he was in the dining room, sitting in the almost dark." Diana felt the hairs on her body again standing on end, everything on alert, senses heightened. Smells, sounds—noises, faint and distant, upstairs—and something else. Something she couldn't put her finger on. An awareness. Eyes watching. They weren't alone. She was sure of it.

"And a couple few days ago, I saw him in the room at the back of the house," Sam continued, "staring out the window. And a wicked long time ago, he was in the graveyard. Remember you were chasing me?"

Diana remembered. Chasing her. November. She thought she had lost her. And then the man in the distance, watching them. Solid and real, and then suddenly gone.

"You've seen him a lot, then, huh?" Diana asked.

Samantha nodded.

"And I bet he seems really real, to you, doesn't he?"

"He is real," Samantha said, "because if he wasn't he would be like a dream."

"Well in a way," she said, "he is kind of like a dream, I think. You can see him, but he can't see you because he's not really there. Not anymore."

"But I saw him there."

"I know you did, sweetie. I believe you. But what you're seeing is like a picture, or a movie. When you watch a movie, you can see the people in it, but they can't see you back, because it's just a recording. A recording of pictures. That's all the man is. I think he's just a recording of someone who lived here once a long time ago, but doesn't live here anymore. He's been gone a long time, and he's not really there. It's just like a movie. So even though you can see him, he can't see you, and he can't ever hurt you."

"I know," Sam said. She wiped at her eye. "Cassie said she's not going to let him. And she's not going to let Daddy."

Diana passed the Wesley Hotel, the lights all still down, not yet open for the season, but she didn't want to look up at it. Was afraid to see shadows on the porch, movement in the windows. Afraid to see anything she didn't want to see. There was only a slight breeze, but she could hear a buoy clanking somewhere on the water. She took a left at the Island Theatre, and started up Circuit Avenue.

She thought about heading back to the bed-and-breakfast, but then decided against it. Michael wouldn't be there—she was fairly certain he was still up in Boston—but the owner would, and how would she look at Diana now? Having gone back after what had happened before, and now fleeing in the middle of the night? A weak woman, a dependent woman. Stupid to have ever gotten involved with Ford to begin with, and stupider still for going back to him. The woman might not say anything, but Diana knew what she would be thinking. *You'll go back again. Your type always does.*

No, it would be better to stay somewhere else. Stay for the night and develop a plan. Then leave the island completely. Tomorrow at the latest. And go where? Maybe to stay with Phillip? Frankie? Or if worse came to worst, back to her mother's. Somewhere on the mainland, leaving the island behind. She started to cry. Fuck him, she thought. Fuck his house, and fuck this island.

Other than the streetlights, everything was dark, everything closed, but there was a light still on outside the pink inn at the top of the street. Diana tried the door, but it was locked, of course. She rang the buzzer, waited a moment, and then rang it again. Sam was back asleep now, her head on Diana's shoulder. After a moment, Diana saw a shadow behind the desk, and then a man followed. Squinting at her, in his pajamas—striped pajamas circa 1955, she thought—but he looked real. Had to be real. Please be real, she thought. He opened the door, and looked her once over. Looked at Sam, sleeping in her arms.

"We're not used to people checking in this time of night, especially this time of year," he said, sounding somewhat suspicious.

"We weren't planning on staying," Diana said. "But we missed our ferry."

The man blinked his eyes, adjusting to the light. Diana had seen him about the island. He was fairly young, maybe early thirties, and during the summer you would see him riding about on a skateboard, maneuvering in and out of the crowds, denim shorts and a Red Sox baseball cap. His hair was cropped short, a part on the side, and his right eye was lazy to the left. And he was real.

He stepped aside to let them in, and ran her credit card. Ford would be able to trace the card, find out they had been here, but not until they had already come and gone.

"The place is pretty much empty," the man said, looking up smiling. "So you can have your pick."

Diana took a room on the top floor. Sloped ceilings, and a balcony that overlooked the street. Blue walls, and a four-poster bed. Antiques of blue-and-white china. She put Samantha on the bed and under the covers, took a seat herself, and slipped off her shoes. Her heart was still beating rapidly. She put her head in her hand. Feeling hopeless. Panic crawling over her skin. He wouldn't find her here—probably wouldn't bother to look yet—not tonight, but still she doubted she would sleep. It all seemed a blur now. Surreal. And what had Samantha said? Cassie won't let him. Cassie. Elizabeth? Something had been there, she was sure of it. Something preventing him from going after them. The woman she had seen, thought she had seen, kneeling in the backyard, planting the tree? It wasn't possible, but nothing else made sense anymore. She knew what she was seeing, as did Sam. Even if things had been good with Ford, she doubted she could go back to that house now. Whether it was Elizabeth or not, she couldn't be sure, but she did know one thing—there was something, someone there.

Diana put on her coat, and went out to the balcony, pulling the door quietly shut behind her. The night air was cold, but it felt good, and she could see up and down Circuit Avenue, and beyond. Down to the docks, the bay—what had once been Lake Anthony. Everything seemed so still, props, and to a certain extent that's all they were this time of year. Most of this street, most of this island. Empty homes, empty streets, empty restaurants, empty stores, and empty hotels. Everything waiting to be inhabited, waiting for life. It was no wonder the spirits lingered. They could take the island back for themselves—at least for seven to eight months a year—moving about unencumbered, unmolested, and few people would bother them. A separate community, she thought—just as Oak Bluffs, Cottage City had originally been meant to be—displaced from another time.

Part of her loved it out here—she loved the landscape, loved the sea—and part of her wanted to leave it behind so badly, she was crawling out of her skin. But she couldn't have the island without the price tag of Ford. She knew that for certain—he would never give her peace, never let her rest. The only thing to do was get away. Collect the few things she needed, and leave the rest for him to do with as he pleased. So little was hers to begin with—he made sure of that. Everything belonged to either the house, or to him, and she wanted nothing to do with either. Ford couldn't have her, and neither could the house. She was not going to be part of its history, locked inside the past. Now she looked up at the sky, dark, blue, and immeasurably distant, and she listened to the sound of the sea.

She was going to need a plan.

44

Ford sat in the dining room, waiting. It was dark out now. He poured himself another glass of Jim Beam, stirred what was left of the ice with his finger, and then looked at it a moment before taking a sip. He liked the dining room. He liked the candles and he liked the mirror. He liked it when they ate their meals in here together, sealed off and quiet from the rest of the house. A family together. It was how things should have been, if only she had allowed it to be. Not been so pigheaded about everything. Stubborn. Selfish. So fucking selfish. Bitch. So much like the rest of them. No one ever cared what he thought. Wanted. Needed. He invited them into his life, and they turned around and back-handed him. Always the same outcome, always the same story. He gave, and they took. He wasn't stupid. He knew that the thing with Al was maybe pushing things a little too far, but so what? All she had to do was say no, and that was it. Everything done, every-thing forgotten. But she could never do that. Everything always had to blow up, become bigger than it was. She was only happy when things were going bad, things were going wrong. That was her problem.

Things had to be a little clearer.

She needed to understand.

Ford sipped his whiskey. He hadn't slept. He had dropped Al off to finish the shift alone. If anyone asked, Al was instructed to say he didn't feel well. He had rushed back to the house. There was a chance, slight, that she would come right back to get her things, figuring he had gone back to work. Slight. And it didn't happen. He thought about checking the local inns downtown in the morning, but that wouldn't work either. She would cause a scene, and there was no need to call attention to things.

No need.

At all.

No. She wouldn't leave the island with nothing at all. Couldn't. She didn't have it in her to start all over with nothing but the clothes on her back. And besides, one thing with Diana, she always needed to have the last word, to foil him, somehow. She didn't necessarily even need to see him, speak to him, but she would need him to know—she had the last word, finished on her terms.

No, he thought, she would be back.

He had sat out on the back porch until dusk, wondering if she might come walking up the road. He knew it was unlikely—she wouldn't trust herself to be quiet enough while he was sleeping—but there was a chance, and from up on the hill, he would see her coming before she would see him. He drank a bottle of champagne, and then a few PBRs, and then he finished what was left of the vodka, listening to his Walkman. The Eagles, "Wasted Time," and Sinead O'Connor's "Nothing Compares 2 U." That used to be his song for her, and now that it had come to all this, it just made the song all that much sadder.

As soon as it was dark, he had retreated to the dining room, and started in on the whiskey. It felt safe in the dining room tonight. And it was the only room in the house right now where he felt truly alone. The house was bothering him, more than usual. He had been hearing voices. Whisperings. Each time he went to turn a corner, he felt as if there was someone on the other side. Waiting. Some voices muffled, impossible to understand, and others seeming to come from a great distance. Echoing as if being carried down a great tunnel, fleeting and hollow. But then he would turn the corner and there would be no one there. The house the same. But it was his house. His. They needed to understand that. She needed to understand that. And he would make things clear.

But first things first.

He needed to think.

And he needed to deal with Diana.

It was just after seven when the phone rang.

The lights were all down. They needed to be down—he needed to keep the illusion of an empty house—and Ford stumbled through the dark to get to the kitchen. The phone was hanging by the back door. He reached about, put his hand on the phone, not sure if he should answer it. If it was her, she might be calling to see if he was home, and if he answered, she would know. But no, it wouldn't be her. Not this time of night. She would assume he was home. If it was later, maybe. Not now. Not this early. The moon had risen above the cemetery, and everything was silver and blue. Trees, tombs, and the worn path across the lawn where he sometimes walked with Samantha.

The phone stopped ringing. Ford waited a moment. And then it rang again.

"Yeah," he answered.

"Is this Ford?" said the voice on the other end. A man's voice. Slightly gravely.

"Who wants to know?" Ford said.

"Hey, Ford, don't be an ass," the man said. "This is Freddie."

"Freddie who?" Ford searched his head, but his memory was shutting down. Everything was shutting down.

"What do you mean Freddie who? Freddie Palmero, Diana's cousin. I need to talk to you."

Freddie, Ford thought, his head switching back on. Freddie was calling. If Freddie was calling, looking for him, then Diana *was* gone. Already off the island. Ford had underestimated her. Fuck, he thought. Fuck, fuck, fuck. And now this little shit was calling to what? Threaten him or some shit like that, give him an ultimatum. Please.

"What do you want?" Ford said.

"It's Diana. She's got me worried. She's not acting right. She's acting crazy."

Ford sipped. "Oh, yeah? I haven't seen her tonight. I was wondering where she is."

"You gotta talk to her," Freddie said. "Talk some sense into her."

"You think so, huh?"

"Yeah. I can't do it anymore. I got too much shit on my plate already, you know what I'm saying?"

Ford paused. "She with you?"

"No. Not yet. She wants me to drive to Woods Hole to get her. She's at the ferry."

"At Woods Hole?" Ford asked.

"No, Oak Bluffs. She hasn't left yet. She's taking the eight thirty-five, I think. Listen, this is all crazy. I don't know what's going on with you two, but you have to work it out. She's not making any sense."

"They rarely do," Ford said.

"She wants to come stay with me, but to be honest, I barely have room for me in this place—it's a tiny little one-bedroom—never mind both her and Samantha. And I got a chick, now, you know? I just don't want to get her pissed at me—you know what I'm saying? I want to say no, but I can't. She isn't talking rational. I know you guys have some stuff going on, but most marriages do. There's always two sides to every coin, and the truth is Diana doesn't understand that. Nine times out of ten the truth is usually in the middle, but Diana always thinks she is the victim. Don't get me wrong, I love her, I love her to death. She's my favorite cousin, hands down, but Diana's problem isn't you. Diana's problem is herself. She always runs away from everything. First that kid who was Sam's natural father, then her mother, her whole fucking family practically."

Ford heard him light a cigarette on the other end.

"And now this," Freddie said.

Ford hesitated. "Well, she knows where we live," he said at last. "There's not much I can do, chief."

"She's your wife. Sam is your kid."

Ford sighed. "Yeah."

"Well, can you do me a favor?" Freddie said.

Ford lit a cigarette himself. "What?"

"Can you at least go talk to her? Before I get on the road, I mean."

When Ford hung up the phone, he snubbed out his cigarette. He went to the sink and poured himself a glass of water, snubbed out his cigarette, and looked out the window. The moon was higher now, and the house was quiet. The quietest it had been in an awful long time.

45

The car was gone. Diana checked twice, up and down the road, nothing. Looked out over the cemetery but it was too dark to see if he had parked out there. Ford had left the porch light on, but the rest of the house was dark. Nevertheless, she was cautious— he had tricked her before.

Freddie had called her back the moment he hung up the phone with him.

"Clock is ticking, Cousin," he said.

"You think he believed you?" she said.

"Hook, line, and sinker."

Diana looked at the clock. She should have just enough time to get over to the house, get a few things, and then get out before Ford figured out they weren't at the ferry at all. Before he figured out what had happened. And then with a little luck, she could get over to the boat to catch the ten thirty, the last one out. But it had to be timed perfectly. She told Freddie she could stay at an inn on the mainland for the night, and would call him first thing in the morning.

"And hey," she said. "Thanks."

"Don't mention it, or even worry about it a little," he said. "The dude is an asshole. I'm just happy to finally be able to say it."

She went over everything again in her head. Mental inventory. She just needed to pack two small suitcases, toiletries, cash, credit card, coloring book and a few toys, and that was all. The rest could stay. She had debated leaving Samantha at the inn, but then thought better of it—it would just mean losing more time, racing back to get her, and she couldn't risk missing the ferry. She had to be off the island. Tonight.

She put her hand on the front door, listening, and trying to feel for a presence, a body inside, a vibration, but there was nothing. She still had an old can of mace in her purse from when she lived in Brockton, and she was prepared to use it if need be, but she was hoping it wouldn't come to that. Please God, she prayed now, please don't make me have to use it.

Sam had asked her where they were going, and Diana had tried to keep it brief, direct. Back to Cousin Freddie's, just for a while. Freddie had told her they could stay with him as long as they wanted, but she told him it wouldn't be too long. Two months, maybe three tops. Out by mid to late summer. She could get a job, then an apartment, do what she needed to do through the courts, and leave Ford in her past.

Now, she pushed her shoulder against the door, cringing as she did, the wind chimes singing. Nothing.

Stillness.

Dark.

She flicked on the light, and pulled Samantha in behind her. She didn't want to turn the corner. But after taking a deep breath, she did. Past the dining room, through the kitchen, and then into the back parlor. She lifted Samantha, and hurried up the stairs. Seeing the house for the last time, she thought. Her house. Or at least what she had thought had been her house. What she now knew was not the case. Never could be. He wouldn't let it.

And neither would they.

She crouched down in front of Sam when they reached the top, took her by the shoulders, the hairs on her arms standing on end, every second feeling as if there were someone behind her. "Just grab a couple things that you want to keep, okay? I promise once we get our own place, I'll buy you whatever toys you want—it's just that right now we don't have enough arms to carry them all. We're only going to be here a couple minutes, and then we're going to go catch the boat."

"I have to get Louie some clothes," Sam said. "And a coat in case it's cold on the boat."

"You wouldn't want her to be cold." Diana listened for sounds downstairs, anything, but other than the wind outside, the house creaking, everything was silent. "I'll pack your clothes as soon as I finish in my room, okay?"

The girl nodded. "What if Daddy comes home?"

"If Daddy comes home, or if you hear anything—anything— just come and get me right away, okay? Right away."

Samantha nodded, looked around a bit, pensive. "Cassie's not here."

"No?"

"Uh-uh. I don't know where she went."

"Well, maybe you can say goodbye to her before we leave, or you can leave her a note."

Sam smiled. "I'll leave her a note. And I'll draw her a picture of a puppy. Or a wolf."

Diana kissed her on the cheek. "Well, we might have to mail that one. I'll get you in five minutes, okay?"

Sam nodded again, stepped into her room, hesitating a moment in the threshold as she flicked on the light. Diana slipped the mace from her purse into her pocket. She hurried to her own room, checked her watch, and pulled open the drawers of her dresser. Bras, socks, underwear, two sweaters. She went to the closet, and pulled down a few of her blouses. A skirt, two pairs of jeans. She hadn't bought any new clothes since they moved to the island, and that would be one of the first things she would do once she was working, had some money. Her own money. She would buy all new clothes for both her and Samantha. Not in the budget, Ford always said. If it was ever anything Diana wanted, it wasn't in the budget.

But it hadn't always been that way.

She remembered when they first met. The first birthday she spent with him. He had taken her to the South Shore Plaza in Braintree. "Buy whatever you want," he said. "As many outfits as you want. This is your day." But she hadn't bought as many as she wanted, she had only bought one outfit, and a pair of shoes. He was too nice, she remembered thinking, and she didn't want to take advantage of him. Her mother was wrong about him, she was sure of it. She remembered he bought her roses once a week for the first two months, had taken Samantha to the movies, to the park, out to Chuck E. Cheese's. "If she's going to be my daughter," he had said, "I've got to spend some bonding time with her." He had dropped to one knee when he had asked her to marry him. He had written a poem to propose to her with. It wasn't very good, even she knew that, but he had written it and that made it beautiful. Everything was going to be beautiful. She had never been more convinced of anything in her life.

Now she took a step back from the closet, and as she did, she felt a hand on her shoulder.

"Hi, honey," he said.

Diana pulled away, and spun around.

Ford put a finger to his lips. "Shh . . ." he said.

And then he slapped her.

Diana stumbled backward, losing her balance. She pulled out the mace, holding it out before her, but the spray stuck, and then he knocked it away, the can skidding across the floor.

"Are you kidding me?" he spat. "Pepper spray?"

She made to run, but he was on her immediately. He grabbed her arm, the bicep, to stop her from hitting the floor, pulled her forward and smacked her again. The smell of him assaulted her nostrils. Whiskey, cigarettes, and sweat. Diana swung out her own free hand, tight in a fist, hoping to connect with him, but he grabbed her by the wrist, and then pushed her against the wall, pressing his body tight against hers as she struggled. He bared his teeth, clenched.

"What the fuck do you think this is? I marry you, adopt your kid, and take you out here to straighten out your fucked-up life, and then you turn around and think you're going to hit me with some pepper spray and leave me? You? Leave me? After you go out and fuck half of goddamn Oak Bluffs? Is that what you think, you goddamn little cunt?" He let go of her arm for the briefest of moments, and slapped her again.

Diana winced from the pain of the slap, pins and needles, and she felt dizzy for a moment, her thoughts spinning, cloudy. Samantha, she had to get Samantha and get out, she never should have come back, nothing was that important, it was a mistake, all a mistake. How could she have been so stupid? Ford slapped her a third time, and this time she resisted after the hit, trying to push him away. She swung out herself, trying to connect with his jaw, but he quickly had hold of her, and he was much too strong.

"Uh-uh," he said, "not this time. You think you're going to slip out again, and play your little games? Trying to set me up with your nitwit little cousin calling me? You think I'm that stupid? That I'm going to fall for that? Really? No fucking way, Diana, no fucking way. You're not going anywhere. I'm angry this time, really angry. I give and I give and I give, and this is the thanks I get. It's no wonder that kid's father didn't want to marry you. You're a selfish little bitch who doesn't care about anyone but herself." He pressed his elbow against her chest, her sternum, and Diana could feel the tears flooding her eyes.

"And you're a piece of garbage," she stuttered. "Just like your father."

He slapped her again. "You know something? Maybe I am. Maybe I had the old man all wrong. Maybe he understood you fucking little bitches better than I ever could." He reached for the button of her jeans. "Won't let me fuck you, huh? Will let plenty of other people fuck you though, won't you? Well, I got news for you, Gladys, I'm going to fuck you tonight."

Diana pushed him, and Ford lost his balance for a moment, but then he grabbed her by the shoulders, and tossed her against the bed, jumping atop of her as he did. He straddled her, and slapped her, and then once again began pulling at her clothes, pushing down her jeans. Diana's face was throbbing, her head.

"Just leave us alone," she said. "Please, Ford. We'll go. You won't hear from us again. I promise." She looked up at him. His eyes. Automatic pilot. Nothing there. He was out of his mind, drunk beyond reason. Any trace of humanity was gone, lost in craziness and intoxication. She wasn't going to get away this time, wasn't going to reason with him. He was going to rape her and kill her, she was sure of it. But she had to get Samantha out, somehow. She inhaled deep and started to scream the girl's name, telling her to run. The door was open, the girl must be hearing her, she thought. Must have already heard most of everything—Ford coming up the stairs, sneaking, and then attacking her. Maybe she had already run. Please God, Diana thought, let her have run.

Ford pushed her jeans down to her knees, letting up for a second as he did, and Diana struggled beneath him, but he had his weight right on top of her again. She called out one more time to Samantha, and then the little girl was there, standing in the doorway. Wide-eyed and still. Frozen in time. She held Louie upside down by the foot, the doll's head brushing the floor. Diana looked at her and mouthed the word *run*, not wanting to alert Ford to the fact that the little girl was right there, but Samantha didn't move, and then Ford looked over.

"Sam, back in your room!" he shouted, and when she still didn't move, he jumped up quickly, and slammed the door, giving Diana the chance to jump from the bed. She tripped as soon as she hit the floor, trying to yank up her jeans as she went, and then Ford tackled her, landing on her back. Diana was flat on her stomach, pushing to get out from beneath him. He began to grind into her buttocks, and then he lifted her head by the hair, and knocked it against the floor. "A little cunt, Diana," he said, "Do you hear me? A fucking little cunt." He rapped her head a second time, this time harder, and Diana began to the feel the fight draining from her body, everything draining. Her head was spinning again and starting to go gray. She could feel Ford moving inside her from behind, and with one final push, she tried to move away. She felt something blunt and hard hit the back of her head, and then her cheek resting against the floor, she looked to her side and saw a man standing there. A tall man, with his hands behind his back. All dressed in black, slicked hair, and muttonchops. Watching them. And then she felt something again on the back of her head and everything went black.

46

She dreamed. A conversation in the kitchen. A man, shouting, and then his voice cracking as he started to cry. A woman's voice answered, slightly unsteady, and nearly impossible to hear. Asking him to stop. In the dream Diana was sitting in the kitchen, at the table by herself, and she could see Samantha in the front parlor. Standing completely still, her eyes looking far past Diana. "The child," the woman's voice said again, hushing the man. "She's just a little girl." But then something broke against the wall, and the man began to shout.

When she woke, she could feel an ache in her ribs, and the tenderness on the side of her head, swollen and pounding. Everything was sore. She couldn't see clearly, couldn't focus. A concussion, she thought, the bastard had given her a concussion. She wondered what time it was. Her watch was gone. Had she been unconscious a day? A few hours, or a few minutes?

She felt a cold dampness beneath her, and she looked around. The workbench, the bookshelves, her jeans and panties tossed in a pile beside her.

And then she jumped.

Ford was sitting on the cellar stairs, halfway down. Samantha on his lap. Her eyes wide with fear. Ford ran his hand down over the back of her head, staring at Diana.

Diana, jumped up quick, propping herself with her hands, unsure if she was still dreaming. Ford's eyelids were red, his eyes yellow. Drunken. Still. This time he wasn't going to stop. Wasn't going to sober up. Not before they were all dead.

Diana scrambled to her feet, and started toward them, but Ford placed a hand on either side of the little girl's head.

"Uh, uh, uh," he said. "I'd stop right there, violent lady. Mace lady. I saw this in a movie once, and I was surprised how easy it looked to do. It's all in the flick of the wrist, one quick twist, that's all it takes. Isn't that right, Sam?" He kissed her head. "And we don't need any more fighting. Tell Mummy, there's been way too much fighting, and not enough love. That's the problem. Not enough love. With other people, maybe, but not with Daddy." He kissed her again. "If we all just loved each other, like we should, we wouldn't have any problems at all. Just like the old days."

"Let her go, Ford." Diana's voice was trembling. She felt her spine stiffen, everything stiffen, her bones tightening inside of her.

"I'm going to let her go. Just not down here. Not in this cold cellar. Not anymore. She's been down here long enough." He ran a hand through her hair again. "I love my little girl, and she loves me. Don't you, Sam?"

The little girl hesitated, then slowly nodded.

"Sam and I have no problem with love," Ford said. "We know who we're supposed to love—and who we're not—and why, and we do that. We support each other in good times and bad like we're supposed to. The way people who love each other are supposed to, the way families are supposed to, the way we all used to. Don't we, Sam?"

The little girl didn't respond, and this time, his hand on the back of her head still, he nodded it for her. "Just like a puppet. My beautiful little brown-eyed puppet."

"Sam, honey?" Diana asked. "Are you okay?"

Samantha nodded.

"He didn't hurt you, did he?"

Samantha shook her head.

"Why would I hurt her? She's never hurt me. You've hurt me, Diana, you hurt me all the time, but Sam's never hurt me.

As a matter of fact, we were thinking about taking a little trip together, isn't that right, Sam? Maybe a long weekend up to Boston or somewhere like that. I told her we can go to the top of the Prudential Tower, have lunch at the Top of the Hub. Get all dressed up. She'd be my date," he said. "Then maybe we'll go to New York City."

"You're not taking her anywhere." Diana took a step forward again, and Ford once again placed a hand on either side of the girl's head.

"Just like that," he said. "Twist and shout. So easy to do. And with you trying to leave me the way you keep doing, sneaking off to meet with people you shouldn't be meeting with, what would it matter to me? Deserting me. I wouldn't have anything to live for anyway—my wife and child gone—so it isn't like I'd be taking a risk. I'd just be making sure I had the last up at bat. Take care of her, then myself, and if you want, Diana, you can always come with us."

"You're crazy."

"No, I'm not. I'm just trying to explain how it is. And how it could be—one way or the other—if we all care about each other, love each other, and cooperate, and how it could be if we don't. Loyalty, Diana. Do you remember that word? And love and honor and obey? You remember that? I think there was a priest there and everything. I guess you didn't pay much attention to him." He looked at the girl. "I think we have to go away for a few days, to give us all a chance to settle down and think about things. The way we've all been behaving. I don't think any of us have been behaving well—myself included—but you've taken it to a whole new level, Diana. You need to think about that, and what we can do so we can all be happy. Get things back to normal. The way they should be. And Sam and I have to think about things, too." He smiled, pressed his cheek against her head. "Things like hot fudge sundaes. And maybe going to Child World to get a new stuffed Elmo. Maybe a bicycle for the spring. And then maybe by the time we get back, we'll all be seeing things a little differently. A better way of looking at things. Understanding each other.

And appreciating each other more. And if we do that, there probably won't be any need to contact DSS at all. Nor the need to do anything silly—by you or me. Probably. Will there, Sam?"

"Don't you dare take her, Ford. You can't."

"I'm her father, remember? I can do what I want. We're all in this together, Diana. How's that old song go? *We're in this love together*," he sang. He laughed a little. I think that's what you've never been able to understand. You still act like you're a single parent, sometimes. But you're not. Sam belongs to both of us. Don't you, Sam?"

Sam remained completely still.

"Don't you, Sam?" he asked again, the edge creeping into his voice.

And then she nodded.

Diana's vision was beginning to blur again. Fury. And her head still aching. She almost wished Samantha would struggle a little bit, catch him off guard and squirm free. Enough time to get down the stairs and behind Diana. Then he could come at her all he wanted. She would kill him, tear his throat out with her teeth before he put his hands on her little girl again. She suddenly heard a dripping noise. Coming from the well. How could there be dripping in there, this time of year? There was no moisture anywhere in the basement. But everything suddenly seemed louder, the shifting of Ford's shoes on the dusty, wooden stairs, the bending of his knees as he went to stand, turn the brush of Samantha's clothes against his. Everything around her blurred just a little more, except for Ford and Samantha, clear and defined and heading up the stairs. Diana lunged, hit the bottom, and started up, but before she made the fourth step, Ford swung around, raised his foot, and kicked her square in the chest. Diana flew backward, her head hitting the floor, and Ford continued scrambling. Onto the landing and the door swinging shut behind him. Lock turning, and dead bolt sliding.

The back of Diana's head screeched with pain upon impact, and she could feel the immediate trickle of wetness, warm and sticky, moving down her neck, but she jumped to her feet, grabbing the rail for balance as she began to feel dizzy, and then once again charged up the stairs. She tried the knob, pushed. Nothing. She began to pound and to scream. Demanding he open the door, to give her back her baby.

Her baby. How could she have brought her back here? Taken the chance? With so much at risk. Her baby. She had been so stupid. How could she have been so stupid? And now he was running off with her. Diana's heart pounded, the blood from the wound on the back of her head, now moving over her shoulders. The whole thing was crazy. He was crazy. Nuts. How could he be doing this? Lunatic. No good, fucking lunatic.

She pounded some more. Shouting. But there was nothing from the other side of the door. After a moment, she began to plead. She would do anything, he wanted. Anything. They wouldn't leave, she said, they wouldn't go anywhere. He just had to give her Sam back, she sobbed. She would do anything. She would be his slave. He understood what she meant, she whispered between sobs, right? His slave. She would let him do anything. Anything.

She pressed her cheek against the door, her face wet with tears. "Please, Ford," she said. "Please."

47

She stayed at the top of the stairs, her ear against the door, listening. She still couldn't think clearly, every now and then seeing dark spots or flashes of light. And then she would begin to nod off. She couldn't nod off, kept telling herself that. Not again. Not if she had a concussion. She had to stay awake. She could hear movement on the other side of the door from time to time, no voices, but someone walking about, and she knew they couldn't have left yet. If they were leaving at all. Were they leaving? Would he really want to take Sam on his own, even for a few short days? Or was he just bluffing? Trying to get her to bend? Maybe, she thought, but she couldn't take the chance. She wanted to hear Sam, talking to her dolls, or talking to her animals. Cassie? And if she could get her close enough to the door, without alerting Ford, maybe she could talk her through finding the key. But then what? What if he caught her in the act? What would he do to her? Diana couldn't think about what he might do. If he had gone this far, he knew he had pushed it enough for her to press charges, serious charges, and he was capable of anything at this point. Capable of following through on the threats he had made. But she couldn't let herself think that way. The worst. If he did anything to Sam, she would kill him.

She would kill him first.

She still didn't know what time it was. Maybe he was working tonight, already asleep. That would be best. If he were working and she was sure of it, she could find a way out of here. She could get Samantha to come to the door, or with him gone, chances were he she would come on her own. But would he leave her alone and take that chance? Diana didn't think so. He might just take her to work instead. She listened again, but still there was nothing.

She went down the stairs, and arms folded, began to pace. Needed to move around to keep awake. Think. She had to think it through, but not overthink. Not second-guess him and think too much. That could just blow up in her face. But the anxiety, the sense of helplessness, was overpowering. She heard a noise in the corner. Scurrying. Mice? Rats. Rats could always come up through the well, she figured, travel through the underground stream. Small lights were still flashing across her field of vision. In the corners, the shadows. She thought of all the times she had escaped down here, hiding, reading. Once her sanctuary and now her cell. He still wouldn't come down here, not for more than a minute. Hadn't even earlier. Just grabbed Samantha and retreated to the stairs. Coward.

She looked at the stone walls, ran her hands over them. Completely solid. Impenetrable. Not even a window. She looked at the pipes overhead, gurgling as the oil moved through them, the cobwebs in the corners, and the laundry piled on top of the washing machine. Laundry left from the week before the complete chaos had begun. From when they still had a chance. She and Samantha. What happened to their chance? She cursed herself again for being foolish enough to come back, and she wondered if he really would kill them. A little rocking chair sat over by the well. A rocker Sam had used up until she was about four—a light shade of purple, now peeling, with a bunny painted on the cross board. A Beatrix Potter bunny carrying a basket of flowers. Diana remembered peeking into Sam's room and seeing her asleep in her chair, her head slumped to one side and a picture book open on her lap. So precious, so beautiful. Days gone past she could never have again.

She listened again for noise upstairs. Something. Anything. Wondered if he had locked Sam in her room on the second floor.

And what had he told her? Was he trying to turn her against Diana? Of course he would try, and Samantha wouldn't listen. Would never turn on her mother. Her protector. As small as she was, she knew him now. Knew what he was, what he was capable of. Diana remembered her eyes that night on the carousel, watching him in the control booth. Her eyes more terrified of him than they were of the specters surrounding them. The imprints.

They were all just imprints.

Diana sat on the floor, her back to the wall and head in her hands, and started to cry.

When she opened her eyes, the light was off. He must have opened the door and turned off the light, and yet the cellar wasn't completely pitch-black. The door was open at the top of the stairs. He had opened the door, and the room was lost in gray and shadows. But it must have been close to dark when she dozed off, she thought, so how could there be any light now? She couldn't have slept that long. Couldn't possibly have. She heard footsteps upstairs. And then more yelling. A man's voice, but not Ford's—this voice was deeper, hotter. Diana jumped to her feet, and then she saw movement on the other side of the cellar. A crouched form, a form that looked to be that of a woman, long dress, and loose long hair. Hiding in the corner, and the man upstairs was still yelling, now screaming down the stairs. Calling for the woman, or someone, to come out, calling her a whore. Calling her Salome. Jezebel. There was thumping on the stairs then, the man descending, and the shadow of the woman, crouched as if running beneath the blades of a helicopter, scurried across the room, looking to flee but with nowhere to go.

Diana pressed her back against the wall, terrified to move. The woman headed toward her, but didn't appear to see her, and then the man, towering in the darkness, was above her, grabbing her by the hair and pulling her backward, spinning her around until he caught her with the back of his hand. Twice. Three times. Each blow just a little bit harder. He let go of her hair with the fourth, and the woman landed back on the floor. Diana's instinct was to run to the woman, cover her and shelter her, but she couldn't move. It wasn't real, she had to tell herself; it couldn't be real. Maybe then, not now. It was all just images, pictures painted on the face of time. But then the man lifted a shovel from the corner, and raised it above the woman's head, and then the woman screamed.

Elizabeth.

Diana screamed herself, and as she did, she jumped up from the floor, her position against the wall, the light back on above her now. Despite the chill, she was sweating, her forehead damp. Everything in the room looked solid, bright, and real where the light reflected upon it. The light. Only leaving shadows in the corners now. Diana took two deep breaths. Dreaming. She had just been dreaming again. Of course. She stood up and began to pace again, her shoulders, her muscles beginning to relax. Dreams. The cellar was getting to her. Everything was getting to her. The house. Becoming impossible to tell what was real, what was not. She needed out. There had to be something down here that she could use to chip through the door. Wait till he was gone, for sure, and then start in. Or a crowbar. Maybe a crowbar. Something. Diana walked over by the shelves with the boxes of books. And then she heard a noise. Coming from the well.

Her hair stood up on the back of her neck. The noise was distant at first, but gradually getting louder. A scraping noise, and then something that sounded like breathing. Someone taking deep breaths themselves. Scrape, stop, breathe. Scrape, stop, breathe. Diana's heart began to race again. Dreaming. She must still be dreaming.

There were footsteps again above her now. Small, hurried steps. Running. And still more noise from the well. Diana still couldn't move, her mouth metallic with fear, and her stomach tightened as it moved up her throat. More noise upstairs. A voice. Ford's? She couldn't be sure. Her eyes were locked on the well. The breathing, the whispers. And then a small cry. And then as Diana heard the cellar door suddenly creak open above her—a slant of light following—she saw a hand reach over the stone edge of the well. A gray hand. Diana tried to scream. She ran toward the stairs, toward the light pouring down from above, and as she passed the well, the woman emerged over the top.

Diana stopped in her tracks. She wasn't dreaming now, she was awake. She was sure of it. The woman was dripping wet, her hair clinging to her face, and her eyes wide, blank. Her flesh blue. She wore a high-collared dress, a Victorian dress, the dress of the woman in the dream. The photo in the diary. The face. The woman opened her mouth as if to speak, but no words came through, and as she started to climb out of the well, straddling a leg over the side, Diana suddenly found her own legs and bolted up the stairs. She slammed the door shut behind her, secured the bolt. Catching her breath, she stared down at the lock. No key. How could the lock have opened without the key? Diana looked to the window. It was dark still in the house, but the day was breaking in blue gray. Later than she thought, earlier. Morning. Dawn.

Diana ran around the corner, through the front parlor and to the stairs. She had to get Sam.

None of it was real, she kept telling herself. None of it. Not here, not now. Even still, she was out of the cellar, and she had to get out of the house, had to get out before Ford got hold of her again. Ford. She suddenly heard screaming coming from below. The voices of the woman again, and the man.

When she reached the top of the stairs, she glanced into their room, and saw Ford sitting up on the bed, confused, disoriented, but waking. He jumped up when he saw her, began rushing her way, but Diana grabbed the knob and pulled the door shut, holding it tight.

She yelled out to Samantha, hoping she'd wake, praying she'd wake, told her to get her shoes, coat. Ford was at the door now, pulling from the other side. He was stronger. She wasn't going to be able to resist very long. The door opened an inch—he was still talking through, not yet yelling, talking through bared teeth, telling her she was being ridiculous—Diana pulled, both hands, and it clicked shut again. She called out again to Samantha. Diana was braced, back on her right heel, with the toes of her left foot tight against the door, keeping her leverage. Ford pulled again twice, but the door stayed fast. Diana clenched her teeth. She couldn't believe she was keeping it shut. How was she keeping it shut?

"Diana!" he said. "Enough! This is foolish!" He knocked again. Banged. Pulled on the knob. "I think I'm doing a pretty good job of keeping my temper, but don't push me, Diana. I've had enough." He rapped harder. She was losing her grip, her strength. "I'm supposed to be at work, Diana! I have to get back! Do you want me to lose my job? Is that what you want?! Who's going to pay for everything then? You?" The door opened a crack one more, time and again she pulled it shut, but this time as she did, she lost her balance stumbling backward.

She hit the floor, landing on her bottom, and bracing herself with her hands behind her, expecting Ford to fly out at any moment. She began to inch backward, in the direction of Samantha's room, mesmerized by the door. Ford was still banging, pulling on the knob—the knob was turning—but the door wasn't opening. How could the door not be opening? There wasn't even a lock on it. Not from the outside. Diana, wide-eyed, inched farther away, and Ford banged harder.

"Diana! Open this fucking door now! I'm not happy about this, Diana! Not happy! You need to let me out of here, Diana!" The door wasn't budging, not even a little, but then it rattled with a loud boom down toward the bottom. Twice. He was kicking it. The door wasn't that heavy, not that secure. If he was kicking it, it wouldn't last long. "Diana!" he shouted again. "I need to get back to work, Diana! You fucking little bitch!"

Diana jumped up. There was a bolt lock on the outside of Sam's door. New. Diana slid the bolt and rushed into Samantha's room, praying she would be in there, and felt a sudden wash of relief. Samantha was sitting up on her bed, Louie on her lap, and the stuffed wolf beside her. Her shoes and coat already on. She didn't say a thing, and she didn't move from the bed. She looked hesitantly to her left, and Diana followed her eyes. The woman from the picture was sitting in the rocker. The woman from the cellar, the well. Dripping wet.

Diana screamed.

She ran over and swooped Samantha up in her arms, Samantha reaching for Louie and the wolf as she did. Her purse was still on the floor in the hall, and she leaned over to grab it. Ford yelled louder. Diana ran out into the hallway, her bedroom door shaking with each of Ford's blows, and it was then that the man came out of the wall. He walked in long, quick strides, charging. His eyes on fire. Even in the shadows, she could see who he was. Slicked hair and muttonchops. And just a few feet away.

Diana leapt halfway down the stairs, losing her balance and tumbling against the wall. She could hear the noise above them. A cacophony of voices. The man's and the woman's. But mostly Ford's. He was demanding she come back. Demanding she open the door. When she stumbled to the landing, her eye caught the back parlor. The furniture had been rearranged. Looking just as it had when they first moved in. And inside the dining room, the table was set. As if for tea. The china dolls. All of them, sitting around the table. Diana froze, and then a woman came into the dining room from the foyer. An old woman, humped, red-rimmed eyes, and paper-thin skin. Balancing on a cane. A woman she had seen before. Pictures. Ford's. The aunt who had left him the home. Dorothy.

"This nonsense goes on all the time," she said. "I've just about had enough of it."

Diana ran past her and threw open the door and ran out into the night. She didn't want to turn, didn't want to see the house now, was sure the lights were all on now, everything illuminated. All watching her. Samantha hugged her tight and began to cry. Diana passed the cemetery, whispers suddenly coming from all around her, and started down the hill, Green Leaf Avenue, on the far side of Sunset Pond. Just through Trinity Park, she thought, across Circuit Avenue, Ocean Park, and then down to the ferry. It was almost sunrise, she thought, there had to be a ferry running soon.

She couldn't see the sun yet, but everything about her was bathed in gray. When she reached the foot of the hill, she put the little girl down, her arms exhausted. She looked about, catching her breath. The pond was covered in mist, cold meeting warm, the reeds all about it brown and dead, waiting for light, waiting for summer. Diana took Sam by the hand and hurried onto Pawtucket Avenue, into Cottage City, Trinity Park. The little girl was still crying, and Diana tried to hush her, console her. It was over, she said. All over. Just a little farther. They were just going to the boat, and once they were on the boat it would all be okay.

She looked to her left—a narrow white gingerbread with orange-and-green trim—and a man walked out onto the porch. Stopped and stared. He was round and bald, and he was smoking a pipe. There were people everywhere all about the park. Clustered in front of the gingerbread houses as if posing for pictures. Out on the porches and the cantilevered balconies above. Some fanning themselves, others sitting in chairs beneath the tall oaks—so many oaks—others holding the hands of small children, all dressed for summers, summers of a hundred years before, and all watching her. There was a man riding an old-fashioned bicycle like Diana had seen in the pictures, the pedals on the enormous front wheel, and an older lady in a hoop dress, all dressed in black, high hat with feathers, walking with a cane. Diana picked Samantha up again and started to run again, keeping to the circular road around the tabernacle, almost running into a small group of children holding hands. ring-around-the-rosy. Long dresses brushing the ground, tight at the waistline, and aprons. White aprons. The boys with them wore short pants baggy at the knees and straw hats and caps. They all stopped and stared. Everyone was staring. Diana covered Sam's eyes.

"Don't look," she said. "Please don't look."

Where was the cold? None of these people were dressed for early spring, none of them should have been here. Not this time of year. No one was here this time of year, not in Trinity Park.

It was always empty, always deserted. A voice called out, somewhere to her left. The voice of a woman, barely a whisper.

The girl who lives on the hill, she said, *she's the girl who lives on the hill.*

Diana kept running, but there was music now as she passed the tabernacle. A sea of voices. Singing.

We shall sleep, but not forever.

Diana didn't want to look, but she had to look. The tabernacle was full. Row upon row of benches, and in the back, folding chairs. Faces old and young, women in bonnets, and men with their bowlers perched on their laps, foreheads perspiring in the heat. The heat. The music continued, an organ, but the singing stopped, the people stopped all turning her way, suddenly frozen in time as if posing for an enormous group photo. A banner loomed above them—*May the Glory of the Lord Be in this Place.*

⤿

Ford slammed his fist into the door and the wood cracked beneath it. He screamed for Diana again, but now the house was suddenly silent. Either she was hiding or he was alone. He pulled at the knob and this time the door opened, swinging slowly inward. Ford took a step back, stared at the door, the floor and the threshold. For a moment, he was afraid to move. Terrified that someone was waiting for him in the hall. Something. He called out again to Diana. Nothing. The house was playing tricks on him again. That's all it was. Tricks. But then how the hell did she manage to lock him inside? He stepped slowly into the hallway, and listened. Nothing. The light on in Sam's room, but no one inside. Nothing. He hesitated, and then started down the stairs, trying to be quiet.

"Diana," he whispered.

Nothing. He whispered her name again. None of this was supposed to happen this way. None of it. He wasn't going to be his father. He *wasn't* his father. So Jesus Christ, why was she making him be his father? They could have had a nice life out here together. A nice quiet life. If only she had listened to him. If only she wasn't so goddamn high-strung. If only she didn't start fucking around on him. She couldn't see the stress he was under, what she put him through. Only thought of herself. Why for fuck's sake did she only think of herself? It didn't have to be like this.

Ford reached the first floor. All the lights were still on down-stairs. He looked right and then left. Listened. The cellar. He could hear sounds coming from the cellar. Sam's voice, barely audible, crying, and then Diana's quietly hushing her. They were back in the cellar. He couldn't believe they had gone back to the cellar. Must have just wanted him to think they had left, so he would leave himself, go after them. Tricking him. Again.

Ford opened the door as quietly as he could. No lights on down there. They were hiding in the dark. But how much could they hide? There was nowhere really to hide. Nowhere to run to. He flicked on the light, and waited, listened. Movement. Footsteps, but no more voices. "Diana," he said again.

⌒

They reached the edge of the circle, but a man sitting with a horse and buggy blocked the path to Circuit Avenue. A small girl with ribbons in her hair stood beside the horse, holding the reins. A light breeze whistled in the leaves of the oaks—everything suddenly looking, smelling alive—and rustled the ribbons in the little girl's hair. Samantha wiped an eye and waved to the little girl, but the girl just stared, not waving back, and Diana pulled Samantha closer.

"Don't look," she said. They circumvented the buggy, the man making no attempt to stop them, and reached the street, Trinity Park behind them now, the voices, the music, now somehow seeming much more distant. Echoes. Fading with the breeze. Gone.

As she stepped onto the street a car rushed past them. A car, swerving. A car. Thank God it was a car. Diana stopped for a moment, and caught her breath, her heart still racing. She looked up and down the street. Pavement, parking spaces, and desolate shops. Early April in Oak Bluffs just as it should be. 1995. The grocery market not yet open, the dim fluorescent nightlights on inside. Diana crossed the street, and took a right onto the pedestrian park on Healey Way. Open and deserted. The Nashua House Hotel and The Offshore Ale Pub ahead in the distance. Then the dead grass of Ocean Park now, the sea gray and cold beyond. They would just wait on the wharf for the next ferry. She didn't have a schedule but there would have to be one within the next hour.

"That little girl is getting too big to carry like that."

Diana turned quick to her right. A man stood on the porch of the Nashua House, one hand on the ornate rail, and one holding a cigar. A straw hat and bow tie. Three-day growth of grizzle. He puffed on the cigar.

"Much too big for a little thing like you."

⌣

Ford put a foot on the top step. He didn't want to go down there. He hesitated. Listened. More voices. Samantha, no longer crying, but whispering—"Is he gone?"—and Diana hushing her again. Ford took a slow breath, and the house creaked around him.

"Diana," he said, "if you just come on up, it will be easier for everybody. I don't want to have to lock you down here again. It will be better. We can talk this out. Nobody's wrong, nobody's right, we're just not seeing eye to eye right now. That's all. That happens in marriages, nobody's perfect. Marriage is a lot of work. Diana?" He waited. More footsteps. Puttering on the dusty dirt floor. They were moving to the far side of the room, scrambling like little rats. Little rats, that was all. They were little rats. Rats . . . "Diana. Don't make me come down there."

He listened again. "I want him to leave," someone said. Sam. Had to be Sam. "Make him leave." More rustling. Then another voice, indistinct, the words not clear. It had to be them. Or was his mind playing tricks on him still? The house playing tricks on him. Goddamn house. He was beginning to hate this fucking house. Hated it down here.

"I'm not leaving, Diana," Ford said. "This is my house. I pay the bills, I pay taxes. What do you pay? Besides nothing. I'm not going anywhere. It should never have come to any of this. If you had only listened to me for once. That's the problem with you—you're too obstinate, you never listen. Diana?" He took another step, his hands shaking now. He had started to sweat. He hated it down here—she knew he hated it down here, and that's why she was hiding. It didn't matter though. Things had gone too far. He was the man of the house, he had to straighten it out. He could get them, get back upstairs, and make things a little clearer. That's what this situation needed—a little clarity. One way or another, he was going to get through to her. Clearer. And if not . . . "Diana! Upstairs! Now! This is ridiculous!"

"Ridiculous," a voice repeated. Sam's. Definitely Sam's. But Sam wouldn't repeat him. Wouldn't dare. More movement. Footsteps going across the room again.

Ford breathed in deep, and ran down the stairs, stopping at the bottom, the sweat now dribbling down his temples, his sides. He looked about the room. They were nowhere in sight. Hiding behind something. Had to be. They had to be down here. And if they weren't?

"This is foolish, Diana. What are we? Little kids? Hide-and-seek? I know you're down here, so just come out now, and we can go talk it out. I won't lock you down here again. I promise. I need to see you. Diana. I . . . need . . . to . . . see . . . you." Ford took three steps forward, looking side to side. She had hit him before. Could try it again. Come up behind him. Let her try, he thought. She hits me, I'm going to get her good. Send her sailing into next fucking week. Sorry, judge, self-defense. He looked toward the well, the water heater gurgling in the corner, nothing. The little rocking chair in the corner, and boxes of books. The tool bench. The laundry machines. Nothing. "Diana, come out, now!"

He heard feet again. Tiny feet, scuffling. He moved to the center of the room, and now he did see a rat scurrying by the edge of the wall, casting a large shadow across the floor. It turned and looked at him, as if daring him to come after him. Rats. Rats made it worse. He hated rats.

"Diana," he said again. And then something from above. A creaking. The door. Ford swung his head around, and then leapt for the stairs, but before he reached the bottom step, the door slammed shut above. The key turning in the lock and the bolt sliding into place.

"Fucking bitch," he muttered, and he charged up the stairs.

⤙

Diana ran across Ocean Park toward the wharf. The park was empty, the boardwalk, too. Just the roar of the waves of beyond.

"Just a little further," she whispered to Sam. She turned once to make sure the man from the Nashua House hadn't decided to follow her. But he was nowhere in sight. There were eyes on her though; she could feel them. She looked up toward the covered roof deck of the Dr. Harrison Tucker Cottage, but there was no one there. Diana picked up the pace, passing the gazebo, and small blue cement pond. The water fountain off, the pond dry. She crossed to the boardwalk, and put Samantha down so she could catch her breath again. The waves broke on the shore, angry and loud, high tide, and the air was wet with the mist from the spray. Tinged in salt. Gulls crying. The wharf was empty, the sun now just beginning to break on the horizon, cracks of red spreading up into the dying blue night, and Diana heard the horn. The ferry was moving toward the shore.

⤙

Ford banged on the door, screaming Diana's name. Demanding she let him out. He didn't know how she tricked him—thrown her voice somehow, or somehow got back up the stairs when he had his back turned, quiet as a mouse—but she had. But how?

He would have heard her, seen her. But it was okay. It wasn't over. This, he told himself, is far from over. *He* would decide when it was over and how it would end. He banged again, but there was no answer on the other side. He needed something to break down the door with, had to be something below. He turned nervously, his heart racing even quicker, his nerves on end—God, he hated this fucking cellar—and looked down the stairs. No noise from down there anymore, nothing down there. Nothing. He had to remind himself of that—there was nothing down here.

∽

The gulls circled above them. One landing on the boardwalk just ahead, waddling like a drunk on the way to the bathroom. The bird stopped and stared. Diana and Samantha kept walking, but the bird didn't move. They sidestepped around him, and the bird pivoted, but didn't fly off. Still watching them as they went.

"He wants to come with us," Sam whispered.

"He can't come with us," Diana said. "No one can come with us."

The boat moved closer. A Steamship Authority vessel. Forty-five minutes, and they would be back at Woods Hole. The mainland. Off the island. Off the sea. Calling Freddie. Away from Noepe. Forty-five minutes, she told herself, hurrying along— they just had to get there. In the summer months there would be a long line of cars on Ocean Avenue, along the boardwalk, and even bigger crowds of people, but now there was nobody. Nobody there. But then suddenly there was. A young couple strolling toward them. Arm in arm. The woman with a colorful hat and a parasol umbrella. A beautiful woman, with high cheekbones and red lips. And the man, slim, a long mustache. Light gray suit, and gray felt hat. He pulled out a pocket watch. Looked at the watch, and then at Diana.

He smiled. "What was it Saint Augustine said? 'What, then, is time? If no one asks me, I know what it is. If I wish to explain it to him, who asks, I do not know.'"

"Please stay with us," the woman said. "It would be so pretty to have you with us."

The horn blew loud on the steamship again, and Diana held Samantha's hand tight, rushing forward. She wouldn't let them divert her, stop her. Wouldn't let them make her turn back. The couple turned to let her pass, eyes watching her curiously, but they faded before she reached them, and Diana picked Samantha up again, and once again began to run. They reached the Steamship Authority, and the birds cried out above them. Diana looked to her right, and the surf was crowded with bodies. All standing in shallow water, wading, all staring up at her. There were hundreds of them. The men dressed in striped one-piece swimming suits, and the women all in black, fully covered. Bathers. A schooner moved across the expanse behind them. There and then gone. They all were gone.

Diana opened the glass door, and the warmth from inside flooded out upon the cold spring morning. Only one man was inside, perusing a paper inside the booth. Small glasses, and sparse white hair. Bright white fluorescent lights above him. Rates on the wall behind. Paper notices taped to the glass. He stared at her a moment, over his glasses.

Diana looked at the clock on the wall. Six twelve a.m. The calendar in the booth. April 13th, 1995. 1995.

"Two for Woods Hole," Diana said.

The man hesitated. Took a breath. Pushed a few buttons on the keyboard in front of him, ran his fingers across it. Then he leaned over into the microphone. "Round trip?" he said.

Diana shook her head. "One way."

The man cleared his throat, sipped his coffee. Looked down at the ticket printing. "First boat of the day. Looks like the two of you should pretty much have it all to yourselves."

Diana looked out the window. The water now empty, as was the beach, and the boardwalk. No one. Just the breakers rising, white with sea foam, and the gulls, circling above. A white paper bag blowing down the beach. She pulled Sam closer, the little girl clinging to her hip.

"Let's hope so," she whispered.

‧

Ford reached the bottom of the stairs, moving slowly, carefully. It was hard to move, anxiety stifling his thoughts, his limbs. He felt like he was balancing on a high wire. One small step. He took two more deep breaths. Just a cellar. Nothing more than a cellar. He heard water dripping in the well. And then he heard someone whisper from behind him. He froze. Silence. The dripping slower, louder. Was there someone behind him? How could there be anyone behind him? Diana had fled upstairs. Locked the door. There was no one behind him. He had to remind himself of that no one. He had to look. He couldn't look. Couldn't turn. Instead, he took another step forward. He needed something. Something heavy. He would break the whole door down. He didn't care. Didn't care anymore. Didn't care.

More whispering. *He creates these problems all on his own.*

A hushing.

Then another. *Walks without the Lord. How in this day can he walk without the Lord?*

Ford felt his heart pound against the wall of his chest. Tricks. All just tricks. He shut his eyes a moment, too fearful to move any farther. Then the voice of his father.

If the little fucker had stayed out of the bedroom, minded his own business, we wouldn't have these problems.

His father wasn't here, he told himself. Couldn't be here. Fat bastard was in a coma, or some shit like that. Ford had taken care of that. Seen to it. He had been a man, for once. And he could see him now, bleeding on the floor, eyes gone empty. There, then gone.

No he wasn't there. Had never been there. Not here. It was all in his head—*the house?* He was just under too much stress, too much anxiety, the fucking little bitch was going to give him a nervous breakdown. Or worse, a stroke. Probably what she wanted. What she was hoping. He would count to three, take another deep breath, and open his eyes.

A rat squealed in the corner.

Never any good, a man's voice whispered. *Blasphemy. Perversions.*

Then his mother's voice, crying. Pleading for his father to stop. Ford could see her lying on the floor in their kitchen, half-in her nightgown, half-out, one loose breast sagging on the floor, and his father above, foot poised to kick her again. His mother had her arms up shielding her head. And a young Ford standing in the doorway.

It will go forever, said another, this one a woman. *Forever. We all are forever.*

Ford swallowed his breath. Why did Diana do this to him? She was doing this to him. She locked him down here. She knew he hated it down here. The little bitch. He just needed to get upstairs. A quick drink to calm his nerves. That was all he needed. All. He would leave for a few days, get his wits about himself.

The man fancies himself a wit, a man's voice whispered.

His thoughts. Inside his head. How the fuck were they getting inside his head? Twisting his thoughts.

No good, said someone, *never any good. Self-pitying, pathetic. Never the proper upbringing. Never on . . . the straight and narrow.*

If we leave him alone, one said, *how long can he last if we leave him alone?*

Well, obviously, said another, *forever.*

Someone laughed.

The patter of rat feet.

And then the sound of a blow, fist, bone, connecting with flesh, bone.

His mother crying.

His father shouting.

You little cocksucker.

Can't . . . mind . . . your . . . own . . . fucking . . . business.

And then the voices were coming from everywhere. All talking at once. Feeling as if they would never stop. Going on forever.

Talking so much that none were making sense. A cacophony of sounds, rising and smothering. Echoes. Racing toward him, and then swiftly past. Men,women, and children. Some he knew—siblings, teachers, neighbors, co-workers, Diana?—and some he did not. *Let him do it*, one said.

Well he has to do it, said another.

No choice.

He can't get out.

Will never get out.

The woman is gone.

And so is the girl . . .

"Stop it," Ford said.

But we're not going anywhere.

"Stop."

Not now.

"Please."

Ever.

Ford felt a rush of adrenaline shoot to his head. "Stop it!!"

Ford opened his eyes. The room was silent again. No rats. No voices. Just the sound of the water in the well. The dull yellow light in the center of the room, everything else hidden in the shadows. Everything. No windows. No air. Everyone gone. The town practically empty. No way for anyone outside to possibly hear him. No one had ever been able to hear him. That was the problem. No one ever listened. If people had just fucking listened. His hands were shaking. None of it was real. He had to tell himself that. None of it. He had to just get upstairs, and they would leave him alone. Out of this house.

Out.

He stared at the photo on the wall across the room. The old wedding photo. Barely visible now in the shadows. The dust.

He felt the hairs tingle on the back of his neck then. A shuffle on the floor. Too loud to be one of the rats. Footsteps. Slow, but moving closer. There was someone behind him. He could feel it. Beyond a doubt. Not his imagination, not the house. Someone. He didn't want to turn. If he turned he would see them, and that would make it real. If he saw them, it would all be real. His heart felt as if it had stopped, seized, his body, frozen in time. He didn't want it to be real. If it wasn't real, he could just leave the house, get on with his life. If he didn't turn . . . But he had to turn. If he was going to get back upstairs, he had to turn. Footsteps again. Dragging a little, moving slowly across the floor. Closer. Ford swallowed his breath.

When he turned his head she was standing less than three feet behind him. Young and beautiful and blue, her hair neatly pinned atop of her head and dripping wet from the well. A black dress and high collar. The faintest trace of a smile coursing her lips. In her hands she held a rope. And she was holding it out for Ford.

48

Diana and Sam ran up the gangplank, Diana holding her hand. The little girl's nose was running, and her cheeks were flushed, her eyes tired. She kept asking where they were going after Freddie's, if they were going back to live with Grandma, but Diana couldn't give her a straight answer—she wasn't sure where they were going. She would call Freddie like she planned, have him pick her up, and then she could figure something out. Staying with Phillip too long might be too close to home and Cybil? Even closer. And if and when Ford came looking, wouldn't that be the first place he checked after Freddie's? Diana stifled the sobs in her throat, still trying not to cry. But right now, none of it mattered. She just had to get away from here. Off the island. Get her head right. Sane.

She stopped and reached into the pocket of her coat, her fingers worrying a small piece of paper. The folded paper—the one Michael had given her. Call anytime, he said, and if you're ever in the area . . . need a place to stay. His apartment was big, two bedrooms.

They climbed the stairs to the upper deck. The horn sounded again, and not a soul in sight. She heard the voice of the captain crackle over the intercom, announcing the destination, and she could picture the crew below, pulling in the ropes as the ferry moved away from the dock. The island. Diana wasn't used to taking the ferry in the winter—just the warm weather—and the wind was biting, but biting right now was good; it just reaffirmed for her that they were still alive. They walked back to the stern of the ship—she wanted to see the island dwindle behind them as they moved away, make sure it dwindled, closure, safety—and she nearly stopped short in her tracks. Rows of long empty benches. Orange life preservers hanging against the iron stairs that led to the bridge. The painted white iron rails. And a man peering over the stern. Dark hair. Long blue wool coat, a peacoat, and his hands behind his back. No gloves, but the wool was good. Wool meant it was cold. Meant it was still April. 1995. And they weren't the only passengers aboard after all.

He turned nearly immediately taking them in, and he smiled. A tall man with dark eyes, beautiful eyes, and dark hair. Michael.

He laughed. "I was beginning to think I was the only one on board," he said. Laughter, she thought, joking, real. She wasn't hallucinating. He was real. Her muscles immediately relaxed, her heart.

"Just about," she said. She was still trying to catch her breath, her heart racing. "I haven't seen anyone else. I can't believe it's you."

She stepped close, carrying Samantha, but then her heart jumped again. The surf, down near the dock, was still cluttered with people from another time. Water lapping against them. All completely still, watching, and shrinking quickly as the boat moved away. The gorgeous elaborate mansions circling Ocean Park, the lampposts and gardens, the gazebo in the middle—band music, she could hear distant band music—and the board-walk. Away, she thought, thank God they were moving away. And Michael was with them. He followed her gaze, looking down upon the water.

"It's such a beautiful island, even in the winter. Isn't it?"

Diana laughed a little herself, nervous. She was losing her mind. That's what this whole thing was about. She was losing her mind. Now she was convinced. The people were there, and he was seeing nothing. She was losing her mind.

"It makes me never want to leave," he said.

Never. She looked at him again, her mouth dry. "Michael, what year is it?"

He furrowed his brow. Looked puzzled. "What?"

"The year?" she said.

"Nineteen ninety-five." He smiled again. "What year did you think it was?"

"Nineteen ninety-five?"

"Yes, of course, it is. Are you okay? You don't look very good."

"You don't see them, do you?" she said.

He looked perplexed. "See who?"

"The ghosts," she said. "Cluttering the water, down there by the shore, by the dock."

Michael looked back, but his face betrayed no response. "Well, the sea is always awash with spirits, isn't it? It's kind of what we talked about before. Time. Then. Now," he said. "I mean if anyplace were haunted, I would think it would be the sea." He smiled.

Diana took a deep breath and then took a seat on the bench. The island already so small. The ocean a rush of gray in their wake, loud, lapping, the hum of the engine of the ship. A buoy clanging somewhere. She felt like she was going to cry again, but she didn't want to cry, not in front of Michael, not in front of Sam. Not again. It was bad enough she was talking like a madwoman. And she now knew for sure that's what she was. Had become. Mad.

She pulled Sam up on her lap, and Michael looked at her scrutinizing.

"Is she okay? She doesn't look very good either." He approached them, and got down on one knee. His pupils, dark pools. Windows. "Hello there, princess," he said, running his fingers over her head. Lightly. "Are you feeling okay?" Sam didn't answer. Just stared. "You don't mind if I have a look at her, do you?" he said to Diana. "I'm a physician."

"What?" Diana asked.

"A doctor. I may have forgot to mention that. Along with being a painter and a teacher, I'm also a, uh, physician. I'm actually quite a few things." He smiled again. "I'm a lot older than I look."

Diana didn't know what to say, didn't know if she had the energy. She thought back on all their conversations. Searching. Hints or words. Sam had her head pressed against Diana's shoulder, still staring at Michael. He reached out and touched her forehead with the back of his hand.

"She's warm," he said. "I think she's running a fever." He asked her to open her mouth, and he peered inside. "Mouth looks okay, but you may want to call your doctor once we get to the shore. You can never be too careful. Especially these days."

"She might just be run-down. We've been through a lot these past few days. My husband is a lunatic," Diana said, and as soon as she did she still couldn't believe she had. A lunatic.

Michael betrayed no response. He was still looking at Sam, not Diana. "Well, we don't have to worry about him anymore, do we? You'll be safe now."

Diana drew back a little, pulled Sam closer. "What?"

A gull flew in from the gray of the sky. Landed on the deck behind Michael. The wind ruffling its feathers.

"I mean it looks like you're leaving the island," he said, "so I'm guessing that means you're leaving him, too. And from what you've told me, I can't blame you. It's for the best, Diana. Better for you. Better for her. Better for us." He patted Sam's head. "You're such a pretty little angel. You look just like your mother. I bet you'll be feeling better in no time. What's your name?"

"Samantha," she said.

"That's right. Samantha. Your mother told me that. Well, Samantha is a beautiful name. I had a cousin named Samantha, but she's not nearly as pretty as you."

Sam had her eyes locked tight upon him. "What's your name?"

"My name?" Michael smiled again. "My name is Dr. Randolph."

"Randolph?" Diana said. "No. Your name is Michael. Michael—"

Diana could suddenly see the portrait in her room at the bed-and-breakfast. The hair, the eyes. The eyes. And she looked again at the man crouched before her. Behind him, she could already see the shore, Woods Hole, growing in the distance. Michael was still looking at her, but now he was silent. She felt a tightening in her chest. She reached into her coat pocket and pulled out the piece of folded paper he had slipped in there the last time they met. She opened it with one hand, and her heart began to stutter. A quick scribble. *Dr. Pascal Beverley Randolph—325 Spring Street, Albany, New York.* No phone number.

She couldn't look at him. She hugged Samantha closer and shut her eyes. "I think I'm going to lose my mind."

After a moment she felt his breath. And then he leaned over and kissed her forehead. "No," he whispered, "I think you're going to be . . . just fine."

Epilogue

The realtor was waiting for them on the front porch. Smiling through a heavy black beard and mustache. His eyes were small and black tucked inside a thick bunch of weathered wrinkles. Red Sox cap, and trucker's vest, a button-down polo beneath. Wrinkled khakis. He didn't look much like a realtor.

"Only on weekends," he said to Brian, as he turned the key in the lock, giving the door a push with his shoulder. The door held. "My friend Carol owns the agency, and I just help her out. I work at the paper, the, uh, the *Gazette*, Monday through Friday. Carol used to work there with me before she went into real estate, so goes the connection. Though on this island, this time of year, most people are connected in one way or another, or at least know of each other. Relatively speaking, there are just too few of us. Makes it nice." He gave the door another shove, and this time it gave, opening with a creak, and the chimes clamoring off the stained glass. Flat little angels with trumpets and bows and arrows.

The man took a breath, and glanced up the stairs, almost as if he was listening. Lori was directly behind Brian, and the boys, eight and six, were already running about the late March lawn, patches of green, patches of brown, Max chasing Harry with a stick. Lori looked after them, a little hesitant.

"Don't worry," the man said. He had said his name was Jim. "They'll be fine out there. No one is going to bother them here."

"It's not them I'm worried about," said Brian. "It's whoever they come in contact with—little terrors."

Jim laughed. "Well, don't worry about that either. The homes up here are all winterized, but the majority of the residents are summer ones. A few weekends in the spring, a few weekends in the fall. And rentals of course. You can make a lot of money if you buy and decide to rent the place out during the summer."

The silence inside was loud and untouched. A dining room just off the foyer. Jim flicked on the light. A chandelier. The tables and chairs covered with dust. The chairs pulled back just a bit, an antique china doll sitting in each one as if awaiting a tea party. Jim stepped aside, allowing them to look at the room. He blushed when he saw the dolls.

"The people who lived here before had a little girl. Carol said she's been meaning to get in here, clean the place up a bit, but it's one thing after another, you know. She still has three kids at home, two of them teens—people say it's even more work once they become teens."

"Fireplace work?" Brian asked.

"It should." Jim stepped over and peered underneath. "Probably needs to be cleaned though."

Jim shut off the dining room light, and after moving through the bedrooms upstairs—nice size bedrooms for a house this old, the master bedroom even had a balcony, a pulpit, he said they called it—they started back downstairs, into the living room, moving toward the kitchen.

"Built in 1871," Jim said, "but as you can see, they've kept up with it. Kept it as original as possible whenever it's been renovated. Solid though, it's really a solid house. At one time it was the only one up this way."

"How long has it been empty?" Lori asked

"Just about five years, believe it or not," Jim said, "1995, I think. There were some legal holdups. The owner's wife had left him, apparently—they hadn't been here too long—and no one was able to track her down for a while after he died, no one had any idea where she went, so then the case had to go to probate."

Leaving. Left. Brian tensed up a little bit, looked away—out the back window at the enormous tree stump the boys had climbed upon—so his eyes wouldn't betray anything. The whole reason they were down here, moving, was because Lori had threatened to leave him. Kim Barnes, twenty-two years old, a substitute teacher doing an internship while in her senior year at Bridgewater State. Blonde and curved with full pouting lips. She started coming to his classroom—American History—every day after school, and before he knew it they were in the supply closet. Kim on her knees, leopard skin panties, or up against the wall, one leg wrapped around his hip as she dug her nails into his shoulders. And then it had moved from there to his house—couldn't go to hers, she still lived with her parents—and from there it was just a matter of time. Lori, after kicking him out for a week, had given him the ultimatum—either they leave together, or she and the boys were leaving without him. The town was too small, and the whore—as she called her—too close, the scandal too much. The school hadn't argued with his resignation, and the high school down here had offered him a job. Remote and safe, out in the sea.

Max jumped back upon the stump and pushed Harry off. Lori was moving about the kitchen, checking the stove, the faucets. The light switches. Jim looked at Brian staring out the window.

"The cemetery is nice for taking a morning stroll. A few historic graves out there. Whaling captains and such. The island is just full of history. Anyway," he continued, "the legal thing wasn't a huge issue because the house wasn't in both their names, just his, and he didn't will it to her, but you know, she was next of kin, so they had to give it the old college try. Then it just ended up going to his sister, and she and her husband both have good jobs up on the North Shore, so she just decided to sell it."

"And did they ever find the wife?" Brian asked.

Jim hesitated. "I believe so . . . after everything was said and done. I heard something to that effect anyway. Out in California or something. San Francisco. I guess she wasn't interested in contesting it at all though. The marriage obviously wasn't a good one, so I don't know, maybe she just wanted to leave it all behind her."

Lori was now checking the cabinets. The dishes all remained. Dusty. "What happened to him?" she asked.

"Him?" Jim asked.

She turned on her heels. "Yeah, him. The owner of the house."

Jim made a clucking sound with his tongue, then cleared his throat. "Well, he, uh, killed himself."

"Killed himself?" Lori asked.

"Yes," said Jim, "I guess it's better that you know about it upfront. Downstairs in the cellar. Sad thing. He had inherited the house from an elderly relative or something like that, and was pretty excited about moving here—I mean, obviously, it's a beautiful house. I guess his wife leaving him was too much for the poor guy."

"In the cellar?" Lori asked.

Jim nodded a little, looking uncomfortable again. "Yeah, early spring. I think he was down there a few days before anyone found him. Worked at the post office, but drank a little too much, so at first no one jumped on it. But then after he didn't show up for three or four days, well, you know. I guess they just sent somebody out here."

A few days, Brian thought. The kids wouldn't need to know about that.

Lori looked at him. Wanting him to read her eyes. Did this mean the house was out, or did this mean they had a bargaining chip? He wasn't sure. He shrugged a little.

"And what happens, if say, we bought the house, and the wife comes back?" Lori asked. "I mean, you know, declares the property should have been hers."

"Well, she can't," Jim said. "It's already been cleared through the courts, the deed belongs to his sister. I'm not even sure where she is."

"And you don't think she'll come back."

Jim hesitated. "No, I don't think she'll come back. It's all been taken care of. Through the courts."

Lori asked Jim if he could excuse them for a moment, and the man stepped back into the dining room, looking at the old photo on the wall. A sepia tinged wedding photo, looking to have been taken sometime much earlier in the century. Or probably even well before that. The nineteen hundreds. An old wedding photo. The man with slicked hair and muttonchops. The woman, young, beautiful, frightened.

Lori and Brian stepped out onto the porch. The boys were still chasing each other, now scrambling over the pipe-rail fence that separated the yard from the cemetery. You couldn't hear the waves—they were a little too far inland—but you could smell the sea. Brian bet that there were few, if any, places on the island where you couldn't smell the sea. It was all around you, something he loved about it already.

Lori huddled her arms about her.

"No wonder the price is so low," he said. "A little creepy, huh? Living next to a cemetery, and the guy killed himself inside."

Lori sighed. "Yeah, it is, but I think with any old house, you're going to have things like that. Maybe not suicide, but almost all of them are going to have histories, people dying inside, I mean. I love old houses." She looked through the doorway; Jim was still in the living room. "Who knows? Maybe it can help us knock the price down even further."

His antennae went up. "So you like it?"

"I love it," she whispered. "It is pretty much exactly how I would build it, modernizing it of course, I mean. And painting it. Are you kidding me? Out here?" She punched him lightly, affectionately, in the shoulder. "We can get them to drop the price twenty or thirty thousand, it will be a steal. It already is."

The boys darted about the headstones. There for a minute, then gone, just their voices, rising, passing on the breeze. Lori tilted her head up and he kissed her before pulling her close.

"It is chilly," she said.

"Yeah, but that will just be for another month or so," he said. "Just imagine the summers. The summers will be beautiful." And they would be. Beach during the day, blue skies and sun, and quiet evenings on the porch, the dusk quietly settling. And peace and solitude during the winter. Wonderful solitude. The island was beautiful. It would be good for them. It would be a good house.

About the Author

SEAN PADRAIC MCCARTHY'S short stories have appeared in *Glimmer Train*, *The Hopkins Review*, *Prole*, *Supernatural Tales*, *The Indianola Review*, *South Dakota Review*, *The Sewanee Review*, *2 Bridges Review*, *Water~Stone Review*, *Hayden's Ferry Review*, *Shadowgraph Magazine*, *Fifth Wednesday Journal*, and *South Dakota Review*. McCarthy's story "Better Man"—originally published in *december* magazine—was listed as a "Distinguished Story" in *The Best American Short Stories 2015*. He is a ten-time Top 25 Finalist in the *Glimmer Train* Fiction Open Award, and a 2016 recipient of the Massachusetts Cultural Council's Artist Fellowship in Fiction Award. He lives in Massachusetts.